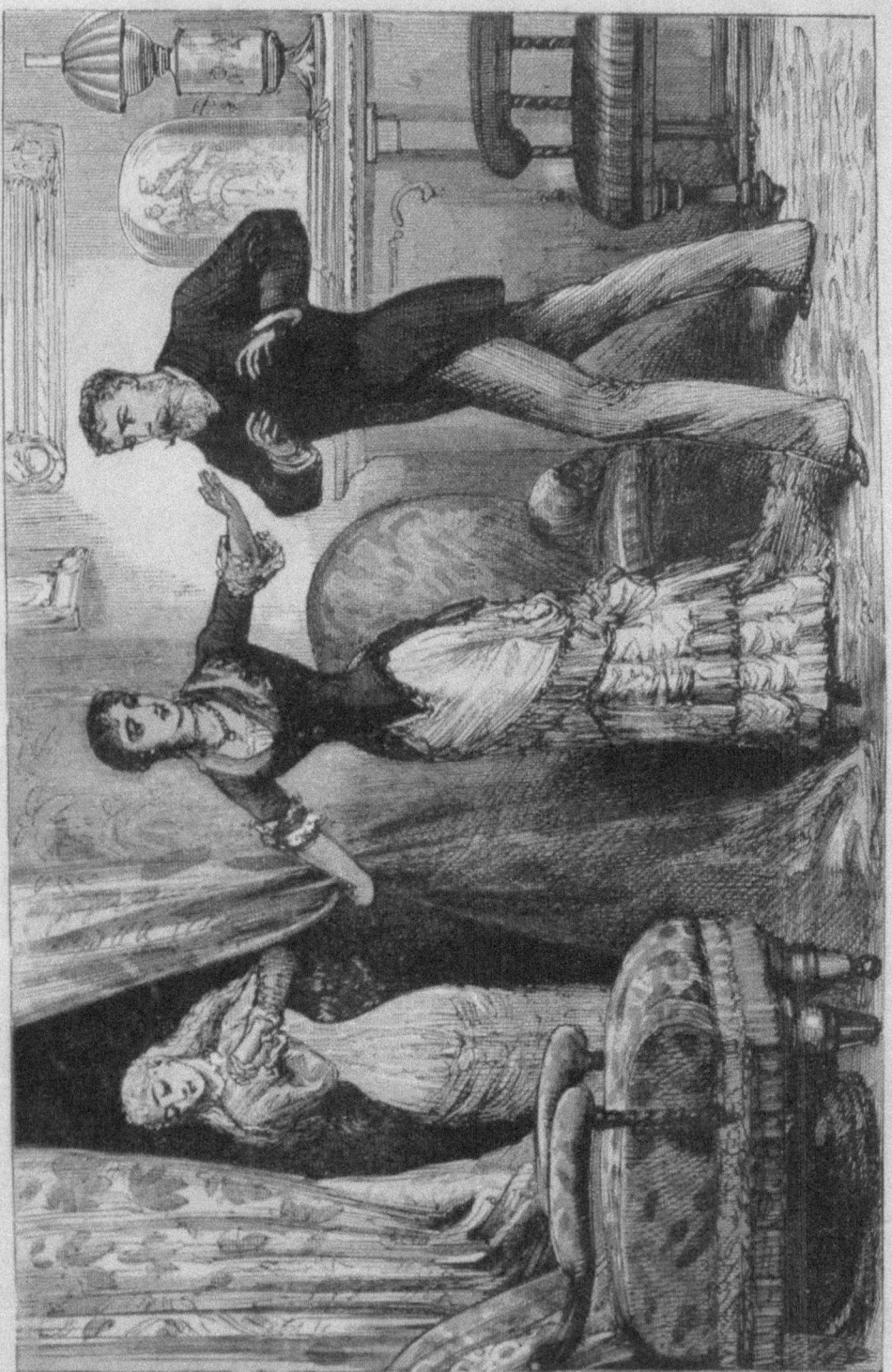

The portière was raised, and the woman, wan and pale, stood before them.

A FLAW

IN THE

MARRIAGE CHAIN.

'That was the first sound in the song of love!
Scarce more than silence is, and yet a sound.
Hands of invisible spirits touch the strings
Of that mysterious instrument, the soul,
And play the prelude of our fate.   We hear
The voice prophetic, and are not alone.''

LONGFELLOW.

ILLUSTRATED.

PUBLISHED BY

EDWIN J. BRETT.

—

OFFICE: 173, FLEET STREET, LONDON, E.C.

A FLAW IN
THE MARRIAGE CHAIN.

CHAPTER I.

MISPLACED LOVE.

T was warm, golden, glorious summer. The air was heavy with the perfume of roses, that, from the fairest maiden's blush to the deepest, richest, darkest crimson, as velvety as a maiden's cheek, hung their heads, as though drowsy from the luscious draughts of ether they inhaled.

There is a strange resemblance between roses and beautiful women; only women adore the one, men the other.

As Stephanie Hoyle paced the path in the rose-garden, she seemed twin-sister to the "Horace Vernet," the velvety leaves of which her skirts brushed as she passed.

Lithe, graceful, delicately moulded in figure, her countenance was exquisite. Her complexion was pure brunette; her lips of the pomegranate hue; her eyes brilliant, dark, capable to melt with tenderest love, to flash with fiercest fire, or shadow with a dusky shade more dangerous than declared, outspoken hate, even as the hood of the rattlesnake.

NOTICE.—With this Number is Given Away a Coloured Picture for binding with the Work.

Once more, for the hundredth time, she bent her eyes on the large, handsome Elizabethan house, to be seen through the beeches above the terrace gardens. Then, as she turned, twisting her long slender fingers nervously together, she murmured :

"Maurice is late to-day, or is my waiting vain ? Is he not coming ? Yet, for nearly a fortnight, he has never failed to visit the town at this hour and by this path."

She paused, then, a sigh heaving her bosom, continued :

"I wonder if he suspects the reason why I am always here ? Always, by apparent chance, meeting him ? He must. Can a woman who loves—loves with her entire being, her soul—help more than can man ; her eyes, her voice, her looks being traitors. He must know."

A rich crimson wave suffused neck and brow, a wave so hot it seemed to scorch her delicate skin.

Instinctively she pressed her hands over her face. In an instant she had plucked them away. Her dark eyes were dilated, her lips quivered.

"And what if he does know ? Why should a woman be a hypocrite in regard to her feelings more than the stronger sex ? Is not my love the joy, the food of my life, without which I must starve ? Do I not exist upon his glance ? Do I not even pine for but a touch of his hand, though the contact makes me dizzy and faint, as if my soul were issuing from my lips ? Is not everything that is his sacred to me ? Is not the hope to win his love sweeter than my hope of heaven ? Hope ——" and she halted abruptly, her small hands clenched, her breath coming quick through her tiny pearl-like teeth ; "if I fail—if—if I do—then heaven have mercy on him. I will have none."

She started.

The colour, only less deep, again rose to her cheeks ; she quickly placed her hand over her head.

A veil seemed to come over her eyes. She staggered ; she was as overcome by her passion as the roses by the heat.

"It is he—Maurice, at last," she murmured.

Her pleasure amounted to pain. She almost wished he had not come.

But she had heard his clear whistle among the beeches, and she knew well that in a few moments he would be in the rose-garden.

She was right.

Hardly had she taken from her pocket a small volume of poems, and pretended to be engrossed in their perusal, than the gate swung back, and Maurice Burgoyne, the only son and heir to Sir Jaffery Burgoyne, entered.

He was a tall, handsome, well-built young fellow of about eight-and-twenty. He walked with a free, erect, proud step; a silky red-brown beard fell over his chest, while eyelids white and blue veined, with long silky lashes, shaded a pair of large clear hazel eyes, honest, out-looking, and frank.

As those same eyes rested upon the slight undulating figure of Stephanie Royle, the brows above them contracted somewhat; then, giving an almost imperceptible shrug of his broad shoulders, he advanced with a quick step, a smile on his features.

"Well, queen rose of the rosebud garden of girls!" he exclaimed. "Do you walk here, coz, to make the flowers droop with envy?"

She turned, her cheek aglow, her eyes sparkling, yet with an assumption of surprise.

"Maurice!" she ejaculated. "How quietly you came. I never heard you."

"Rather, you were so engrossed in your book," he laughed. "I'll wager, coz, the subject was love."

"Well," she remarked, "I have heard it said that 'Love in a man is an episode; in a woman it is her life.' I believe it—with some."

He laughed pleasantly.

"You do right, coz, to add the 'some,'" he said. "In some, if love be a woman's life, it has a very short existence."

"That is not love ; it is its shadow—as delusive and heartless as the reflection of the sun in water."

He looked at her curiously.

Sometimes her sayings, her manner, startled him.

She was beautiful, he knew, but it was not that which won her Maurice Burgoyne's respect.

This small, graceful, dark-eyed girl—for she was no more, though in form so tiny by the side of his six feet of stalwart manhood, was his superior—far his superior—in intellect.

He confessed it frankly, and respected her opinion, while not infrequently he sought and was led by her advice.

"And what, coz, is your idea of true love ?" he smiled.

"That it is a passion much spoken of, rarely possessed. The woman who really loves recognises a total abnegation of self. To her the words 'lord and master' are not a *façon de parler*; it is a reality. She has but one will—his to whom she has given herself. It is sweet to her to yield to it—to humble herself, to feel herself his slave ; to throb and faint beneath his caress ; to live on his smile, to droop beneath his frown."

The words had issued from her soft red lips with a passionate fervour. Her dark eyes shone with singular brilliance, her slender fingers worked, her small frame vibrated.

Maurice Burgoyne felt a sensation of fear, even amazement, as he regarded her. He thought that to be so loved would be to him painful, terrible.

He reflected, too, that such a passion must be equally a misfortune to her who possessed it.

"Do any ever love like this, Stephanie ?" he said.

"Not many in these chill countries," she answered ; "but in the South, in the East, many."

"I think not," he rejoined. "I fancy where there is the greatest show there is the greater falsity."

"That is because you do not know," she retorted with a little laugh, nervously plucking the leaves of a rose she had gathered. Then her cheek went pale, her head drooped, as faintly the words came through her lips : " Maurice, I believe I could so love. If a woman do not so regard him who is dear to her, she does not love him."

She would have given much to have met his glance as she spoke, but she dared not.

" You honour our sex more than they deserve," he laughed ; " at least, speaking from my poor experience. Man believes it his right to adore and be the slave of woman. There," as they halted at the gate leading into the plantation, for they had been walking on, " do not destroy that rose as the last, coz ; it is perfect, and deserves a better fate. Give it me ; this one has already faded."

He plucked a blush rose from his button-hole, and, casting it on the gravel, added :

" Enhance the gift, Stephanie, by fastening it in yourself."

The colour on her cheek changing white and red, the girl complied.

Maurice did not perceive her emotion. He did not note how her fingers trembled.

Not for a second did he suspect that he was the object of the wild tempest of love in the heart beating so near his own.

Why, they had been children together. Besides, his mind was occupied by other things.

He thought, however, she looked amazingly beautiful, and stooping lightly kissed her forehead.

The contact made Stephanie Royle dizzy with joy.

" He does love me—he must," she thought.

" Now, au revoir for the present, coz," he said lightly. " If all the happiness attend your married life when it comes that I wish you, it will be happy indeed. Only modify your sentiments regarding affection. Imagine if your husband were to make you jealous."

" Did he," she answered, leaning over the gate, " I believe I should kill him." Then, breaking into a laugh, as if alarmed at her words being taken too seriously: "How easy it is to talk, isn't it? By the way, are you off to the town again?"

"Yes. Have you any commission?"

"No. I was thinking how frequently you go there."

"To pass the time, coz," he laughed, though a deeper colour came across the face he had averted. "To be always at Mereton Travers would be dull to say the least of it. I'll be back in time for a cup of your afternoon tea."

With a suspicion of desiring to stop the conversation, waving his hand he started down the path. Just at the bend, turning, with a bright smile he raised his hat.

Stephanie returned the salutation, and he disappeared.

For several moments the girl remained wrapped in pleasant reverie; then, attracted by the cool shadows of the plantation, unlatching the gate, she went through.

For a time she strolled lost in reflection. She held the blush rose he had rejected in her hand, often raising it to her lips.

A poor dependent now—so in her pride she called herself; one day she would be Mereton Travers' mistress.

Maurice loved her. She was sure of that. Such a passion as hers could not fail to get return. Nay, it had. Had she not felt it in the pressure of his lips, beneath which her forehead yet glowed?

She paused, having reached the spot where the path, diverging, led in two directions—one to the town, the other to a pretty wooded dell.

She would not take the former; it would seem like spying upon him. She turned into the latter.

The trees and bushes grew thicker; the grass on the wayside was gemmed with flowers.

Stooping, Stephanie Royle plucked a daisy, and pulling the white oblong leaves away one by one, murmured:

"He loves me, he loves me not."

She put no credence in the charm, but her pulses beat anxiously as she neared the end of the leaves.

"He loves me," and with the word the last leaf fell.

"Maurice, my Maurice," she whispered in ecstasy, the rich blood rushing to her neck and brow.

Her beautiful eyes dilated.

Her lips parted to give room to the quick fluttering breath.

He loved her, and she loved everyone !

She was so happy that she felt possessed by the goodness of the angels.

Suddenly low voices reached her ear.

One was a voice she knew.

Surprised, doubting, bending forward, and anxiously separating the branches, she looked into the dell.

There on the path beneath stood Maurice Burgoyne, clasping to his heart a young fair-haired girl.

Stephanie reeled back clutching the branches for support. An awful change had come over her face.

It was no longer an angel's.

It glowed with the dark passions of one in torment.

CHAPTER II.

STEPHANIE ROYLE'S RIVAL.

HEN Maurice Burgoyne had looked back at the bend of the path to wave the final salutation to his cousin, which had so pleased her, it had been to see whether she had stayed at the gate, and that he was not followed.

Assured of this, he increased his pace, with a light, quick step, hastening down the path until he reached where it divided.

"Cousin Stephanie startles me at times," he muttered. "She is a strange girl, I cannot make her out. She reads too much, I fancy. What an idea of love! Imagine being the recipient of such!" and he laughed softly. "It would frighten me for one. I should absolutely have to run for it, or go mad."

He turned into the path to the dell, and his thoughts continued :

"With what fervour the girl spoke. Can it be she loves already? but not hopelessly in that case. Her manner did not betray a disappointed affection. I wonder who it can be. I can scarcely call him happy. But there," and he threw up his handsome head with a laugh, "why should that concern me? If I have my secret, why should not Stephanie have hers? I may be certain that she would not give her heart unworthily, and my father will dower her richly."

As he ended, he halted almost on the very spot his cousin did later on, and parting the bushes looked into the dell.

What he saw affected him differently than had been his cousin.

On the green, flower-bespangled sward, in the soft shadow of a beech, rested a young girl, attired in a light simply-made muslin dress.

A cape of the same had slipped from her shoulders, while her straw hat had been removed, owing to the heat, leaving her small shapely head and lovely features plainly visible.

Lovely, truly, they were, and of the purest blonde.

Her complexion was clear white and pink, the features delicately cut, the expression sweet, gentle, feminine.

The eyes, however, made a striking contrast, being large, dark, and full of intelligence, while the brows that arched them were some shades darker than the masses of light, lustrous, golden hair that were braided closely round her head.

She appeared pensive, as lost in thought; her slender fingers were mechanically forming a bouquet of wild flowers.

Maurice Burgoyne for some moments feasted his eyes upon the charming picture.

Then, a smile on his countenance, as he re-called his cousin's idea of what a woman's love should be, too impatient to keep to the path, noiselessly he forced his way through the bushes, seized a bough of a tree, and lightly swung himself down into the lower path.

The girl sprang up with a startled cry.

Then a joyous light radiated her sweet face as she leaped forward.

"Dear Maurice!" she murmured.

"Catherine, my love," and with his strong arms he en-folded the slender girl, and pressed her to his broad chest

She rested there as if it were her proper place.

Her little white hands on his shoulders; her golden head pillowed on his bosom; her dark blue, fond, laughing eyes raised to his.

"What a fashion to come by, Maurice," she smiled.

"Did I frighten you, darling?" he asked gaily, admiringly gazing into her face.

"You startled me.   There was a path, you know."

"A path that would have kept me longer from you by three minutes.· No, it wasn't to be thought of."

And bending, again and again he pressed his lips to the girl's, that, vibrant with love and mirth, never turned from his kisses.

It was at this moment that Stephanie Royle, looking down, beheld the two.

For a space the shock overcame her.

Convulsed with indignation and jealousy, she tottered across the path, resting against the bushes.

Her hands were clenched, her face white to the lips ; but her eyes dark, fierce, full of threatening fire.

"Catherine Crawford.   She, she——" she hissed with angry scorn through her white teeth, while a dangerous light shone in her eyes. "He, Maurice, loves her. No, no ; I will not believe it.   Yet he holds her in his arms, he presses her lips, and she permits it. Hussy—base, fallen hussy ! As if he, Maurice, Sir Jaffery's heir, would ever wed such as she—the poor, wretchedly-paid companion of old Mrs. Winburg."

Panting as one who had run far, Stephanie leaned against the bushes.

At present her limbs trembled too much for her to move.

But her thoughts were active enough.

There was a *liaison* between Maurice Burgoyne and Catherine Crawford.

That she had discovered.

Jealous, enraged, she was ; but after a brief reflection she determined that at least on Maurice's part there was no seriousness in the matter.   He would not, he could not really have any intention to marry Catherine Crawford.   Marriage — absurd !   Sir Jaffery would never permit it.

She, Stephanie Royle, would not, and she had influence.   She knew she had, especially with the baronet.

Nevertheless, that Maurice should love anyone even for amusement was sufficient to arouse all his cousin's anger.

This fair girl, whom she had despised, whom now she despised and hated, had won that for which she had striven in vain.

"No," she muttered, rising erect, as her strength returned, "not in vain. What is the nature of the love he gives her ? That which he would blush, what he would not *dare* to offer me. Shame, disgrace ; and with a smile she accepts her lot. Oh, this pure, milk-and-water, white-and-pink piece of hypocrisy ! " and angrily she paced the path. " Still waters run deep, indeed. Maurice found Mereton Travers dull, so went to the town—the town. It was to this girl, to her arms, and she with a smile accepts her ruin. Ruin ! Yes, ruin it shall be," she hissed. " I'll denounce her publicly, I'll follow, I'll track her, I will discover everything. Every finger shall be pointed at her in scorn."

She stopped and pressed her hand over her forehead.

"But Maurice," she proceeded ; " in revenging myself on this base girl I must not win his hate. I must work carefully. Whatever she be to him *I* must be his wife. Let me remember that."

She paused in reflection.

Then with an effort she looked through the bushes.

Maurice and Catherine Crawford had moved down the path.

She saw them through the trees passing from sunshine into shade.

His arm was about her ; her head rested against his shoulder, his was inclined to hers.

Stephanie bit her lip, and pressed both hands over her heart to ease the sharp pain in it.

In doing so her glance rested on the faded button-flower her cousin had cast away.

A cruel bitter smile passed over her features.

"A blush rose, fair as Catherine Crawford," she reflected, "and he flung it away. Such is the fate of all of her class—a pleasure for a passing moment. Maurice threw this from him to accept the dark one *I* gave. I will take that as an omen of success. Catherine Crawford shall be flung aside, disgraced, unloved, overwhelmed by shame, while I reign queen of his heart, his lawful, loved wife."

Then cautiously continuing the path that ran parallel with that upon which Maurice and Catherine walked, she followed them.

A fascination drew her on, though the sight of her rival was cruellest torture.

"But," she murmured, "I must know all; I must have proof before I denounce and crush her."

When she came again upon them they had sat down.

Maurice, smoking a cigarette, lay on the grass, his head on the girl's lap, his eyes fixed on hers.

Catherine, her back supported against a tree, her hat tilted over her face, held a spray of honeysuckle merrily over his face.

The picture would have been a pretty one to any but Stephanie Royle.

In a jealous fury, indescribable, she beheld and watched, planning ruin to her rival. How she wished she could have heard what they said to each other.

That was impossible.

Only now and then their voices came to her as an indistinct murmur.

But she heard their laughter—they were happy.

"Oh, that I could annihilate her with my looks!" she thought.

How long would they remain?

She consulted her watch.

It wanted but half-an-hour to that of her afternoon tea.

Then she recollected that her cousin always returned for that, as he had promised to that day.

On raising her eyes, she found to her relief that the two had risen.

Her fierce glances saw the fond parting—saw how Maurice moved away, then strode back for another kiss.

"SILENCE," HE REPEATED WITH STERN AUTHORITY, ONE ARM EXTENDED AS IF A PROTECTING SHIELD OVER CATHERINE.

Finally he tore himself away, and, as he waved his hat even as he had to her, the watcher distinctly heard the words :

"To-night, darling, to-night !"

Catherine Crawford nodded a gay response, and soon disappeared among the trees. Maurice, lover-like, waited, looking after her, while a flutter of her dress could be seen.

This gave Stephanie Royle the opportunity she desired.

To reach Mereton Travers first.

Swift, light as a deer she fled along the plantation's winding path, through the rose-garden, under the beeches, up from terrace to terrace, until entering the open windows of the drawing-room, she sank breathless on a chair by her small afternoon tea-table.

"Safe !" she murmured—"safe. They meet again to-night—where ? That I will discover. There shall be three at the rendezvous instead of only two."

CHAPTER III.

THE MIDNIGHT RENDEZVOUS.

STEPHANIE ROYLE had hardly regained her breath and assumed her usual composure than the door opened, and Sir Jaffery Burgoyne entered.

In face and figure Maurice was his counterpart, but the baronet's tall form was stooped by age and failing health, his hair grey; nevertheless, in the eye, though dim, the wrinkled brow and shapely mouth, was an expression of haughty pride far surpassing the son's.

Rising in an instant, Stephanie was by his side, her arm extended to support.

"What, dear uncle, are you going to honour my afternoon tea-table to-day," she smiled gaily; "that is, indeed, kind."

"If you will let me," he rejoined, his eyes regarding her with a caressing glance, as she drew forward a chair and arranged a footstool.

"All the morning I have felt so much better, that my room grew dull. I'm taking a fresh lease of life, perhaps, and getting young again. I ought to," he smiled, fondly placing his hand on the head of Stephanie as she knelt by him, "having so sweet, attentive, and gentle a little nurse ever by me."

"If love did not make me so," responded the girl, pressing her lips to the baronet's thin, white hand, "gratitude at least would. To you, uncle, I owe everything. Do you think I ever forget it?"

"Tut—tut—tut," he broke in, patting her shoulder. "Has not the gain been equally mine? I was proud to have a son—a son to bear my name with honour to future generations, but I ever craved for a daughter until on my sister's death I took you; then I no longer felt the loss. Truly, child, I think I should miss you more than I should Maurice."

"Oh, uncle, what an idea!" she laughed, glancing up at him as his fingers smoothed her velvety cheek. "Indeed, you must be getting young again, for you are growing a sad flatterer. I shall soon be frightened of you."

The baronet laughed, well pleased at the compliment.

It was agreeable to one who in years gone by had been petted and flattered by charming women, to believe his attractions were not wholly dead.

Yet Stephanie Royle knew that his words were not flattery, but truth.

She had made herself a necessity to him, that by a little subtlety what she chose to desire he should. Her will should be his law, which he should carry out, believing it his own.

Then as his age increased, so would her power grow more powerful, more difficult for him to resist.

"I can twist him round my finger," she reflected, "so have a care, Cousin Maurice; my love is better than my hate."

"It's a true saying," proceeded the baronet. "A son is a son till he gets a wife, a daughter's a daughter all her life. Some day Maurice will be, I suppose, bringing home a new mistress for Mereton Travers, when you and I, Stephanie," laughing, "must make room for the reigning powers until you flit from me."

"Wherever you go I will go, uncle," she rejoined, as she bent over the tea-table to hide the angry spasm that contracted her small mouth at the mention of another mistress for Mereton Travers, another wife for Maurice than herself.

She wondered whether the baronet, in his pride of birth and race, would hold her, his sister's child, as no fit match for his heir.

What matter if he did. As she willed so must he.

"By the way, where is Maurice?" asked the baronet.

"About an hour ago," she answered readily, bringing him his tea, "he passed me in the rose-garden on his way to the town. He promised to be back to tea, and," as a firm, yet elastic step sounded on the terrace —"here he is."

"Yes, here I am," said Maurice gaily, as he entered; "ready, dear coz, for a cup of your excellent Assam. I hope it is not cold. You here, dear father! that is an unexpected pleasure."

Bending, he pressed the baronet's hand.

How frank, handsome, and happy he looked.

How sweetly, brightly, Stephanie Royle regarded him.

He would have believed anything than that within the last hour his secret was no longer one to her.

Despite the terrible effort it cost her, Stephanie maintained the same bearing throughout the evening.

She played and sang with Maurice. She gave him his revenge at bezique.

Maurice had rarely found an evening pass more rapidly.

Stephanie one more tediously.

When was he going?

At what hour could the rendezvous possibly be?

The time slipped on.

The baronet retired to his own apartments, yet Maurice made no sign of moving.

Stephanie decided that Catherine Crawford must steal out to her lover when old Mrs. Winburg and the other inmates of the cottage slept.

The girl's cheek flushed with indignation.

"Oh, the sweet piece of virgin purity," she thought sorrowfully. "Hypocrite!"

Ten, half-past ten, eleven.

Finally Stephanie herself rose, and said good night.

"You, of course, will smoke your usual cigar, Maurice," she remarked lightly.

"Yes, coz," he answered with indifference ; "I shall take it on the terrace, the night is so warm. Tell Greggs he need not sit up. I can fasten the conservatory door when I enter."

"Very well. Good night."

And she ascended to her room.

Here she rapidly changed her dress for a black one, removed every vestige of colour from about it, and enveloped her head and form in a lace shawl, then drawing aside the curtain, looked down upon the terrace. Yes, there was yet the glowing tip of Maurice's cigar.

Why did he linger ?

Could she be coming to him, the shameless girl ?

Putting out the lamp, Stephanie Royle quitted her room.

A gas jet, turned low, burned in the corridor ; beyond that, all was stillness and darkness.

Swiftly, noiselessly, she passed down the stairs, crossed the hall, entered a small ante-room, and cautiously opening the window, listened.

The night was dark, heavy, and oppressive. The singular silence over nature presaged a storm.

Maurice Burgoyne's tread on the terrace was distinctly heard.

As it sounded going from her, Stephanie Royle passed quickly out, drew to the glass door, and crossed to a projection of the balustrade where the shade, cast by a statue holding a basket of trailing natural flowers, effectually concealed her.

Through, however, the falling tendrils, she could see Maurice's position by the red tip of his cigar.

At that moment the clock in Mereton Travers tower struck a quarter to twelve.

Maurice halted, lighted a fresh cigar from the end of the one he had just finished, sprang quickly down the terrace steps, and took the path in the direction of the rose-garden.

At a safe distance Stephanie followed ; owing to the blackness of the night she was not distinguishable.

His tread, his cigar, acted as a guide to her through the garden, through the plantation into the dell.

When was he going to stop ?

Not here.

Still onward with a quick step.

Stephanie, like an evil shadow, followed, wondering, perplexed, but resolved.

Now in a lane that had but one termination, the cottage where Catherine Crawford lived.

Suddenly Stephanie missed Maurice ; the tread, which had gone cautiously, nay stealthily, down the lane, had ceased.

Was she to be baulked at last ?

No.

Swiftly she passed on, the pretty latticed-windowed, Gothic, rose-festooned cottage was before her.

At the instant a pale stream of moonshine fell from between the stormy clouds.

Stephanie Royle staggered back with a stifled cry of blended surprise and horror.

What, however, elicited it another chapter must reveal.

CHAPTER IV.

CAPTAIN MELTON RECEIVES A SHOCK.

NE—two, struck a clock with sharp metallic chime, and continued its beat in petulant haste, as if fearful other clocks would get a few seconds start of it, until it had numbered twelve, then it subsided into silence.

It was a bachelor suite of rooms in a medium-fashionable street westward. The furnishing also bespoke the bachelor.

The pictures, the books, the pipe-rack, and many other particulars all proved the absence of a woman's hand, a woman's taste.

A door led through into the sleeping apartment. At the present moment it was closed; but the clock had so well made itself heard through its panels as to arouse the bed's occupant.

"Noon, by Jove," he ejaculated, yawning and throwing out his arms; "and Linden said he'd be here by one. I don't feel as if I had had an hour's sleep. Well, I haven't had much more. It was a confoundedly late night. But," a smile passed over his features—"a profitable one."

The last recollection apparently had a more rousing effect than the yawn. He sprang up and began his toilet. Going to a glass he contemplated his reflection for a few seconds.

"Awfully seedy," he commented; "if it hadn't been for Linden, I wouldn't have got up until time for the club."

The speaker was a handsome, dark-featured man, with an erect figure; of that description, slight yet firm, which sets off clothes to an advantage.

His age was as difficult to come at as a pretty well-preserved woman's.

On first rising of a morning his complexion was sallow, his eyes heavy, the skin beneath them baggy, and the expression one of exhaustion.

At those periods, Captain Everitt Melton looked quite fifty.

When his toilet, a slow one, was completed, however, Captain Everitt Melton appeared no more than five-and-thirty.

Hence in fairness, and the likelihood to arrive at a correct estimate, it was as well to put Captain Everitt Melton's age between the two figures stated.

The door of communication between the sitting and sleeping-rooms might have possessed the same virtues as the fountain of youth, the difference in the captain was so great as he sauntered through it in velvet dressing-gown and slippers, to the breakfast already laid.

His skin was pliant and clear, his eyes animated, his hair lustrous and silky. Few men, indeed, at the age of five-and-thirty retained a more *distingué* air, nor a handsomer appearance.

A batch of letters was placed by his plate. Some large blue envelopes, others square, narrow, and white, with now and then a delicate Rimmellian aroma about them.

The former Captain Melton threw carelessly aside unopened.

The others he perused leisurely, sometimes with a smile as he partook of his chocolate, sardines, or anchovy toast.

"By Jove," he laughed, as he threw down one perfumed note, the writing of which as much demanded the intervention of the School Board as the spelling, "Miss Tottie is insatiable; like the horse-leech's daughter it is perpetually more, more. Her 'Ben,' as she terms it, comes off shortly, and she expects me to help her dispose of tickets."

Having brought his breakfast to a conclusion by a glass of Hockheimer, he took a pipe from the stand, and having lighted it resumed his seat, leaned comfortably back in it, and drawing out his pocket-book, began its inspection with an air of exceeding satisfaction.

The contents consisted of gold, notes, and acknowledgments of losses.

"By Jove, very far from a bad evening's work," he remarked, with a smile that was sufficiently controlled to prevent the betrayal of crow's-feet about the eyes.

Just then the clock again made itself heard.

"Half-past one," said Captain Melton, lifting his gaze to the horologe. "Linden's not punctual. Ah, here he is!"

There was a tread on the stair, followed by a quick tap with the head of a cane on the door-panel.

"Come in," called the captain, and a gentleman entered.

He was a young man with an easy aristocratic bearing, a fair well-looking face, and attired in a morning toilet of perfect taste.

"How are you, old fellow?" remarked the captain extending his white slender hand. "Late rather, eh? Overslept yourself, I suppose, as I did? Take some breakfast?"

"No, thanks," answered the Honourable Launce Linden, dropping languidly into a chair. "Been going in instead to B. and S. Overslept myself, egad! It's well for you to talk. You to whom the green cloth was, last night at least, a veritable Tom Tiddler's ground. How much did you pocket?"

"Oh, a few hundreds," responded the other carelessly.

"And I, egad! dropped over two. I tell you what, there will have to be another appeal to the governor."

"What, for a simple two, Linden?" and he smiled incredulously.

"Not for a simple two, my boy," responded the young fellow. "It's only an item added to a precious long list of them. You can't tell what an expense that certain little party at Brompton is."

"Talking of certain little parties," exclaimed the captain. "Here's a cool request from Tottie, of the Topical Theatre."

And he tossed the scented, ill-spelt, ill-written note over to his visitor.

"All alike, egad! perfect cormorants," remarked Launce Linden, with a shrug, on reading it.

"Such is life, and such is woman," laughed Captain Melton.

"Of that class," interpolated Launce Linden quickly.

"Ah, I forgot," and there was an imperceptible sneer in the captain's tones, "you are rather a champion of fair women. One of Maurice Burgoyne's school."

"A believer in the possibility of goodness and virtue as well as beauty in the sex. Yes."

"When ignorance is bliss, 'tis folly to be wise," smiled the captain.

"What a cynical fellow you are, Melton. Are you a woman-hater? Don't you believe in good women?"

"Oh, yes; but that the specimens are so rare that it is easier and wiser to fancy you never come across them, or ten to one you will make a mistake, and suffer for your trust. I would take Congreve's remark as a definition of all pretty women, at least. 'They are the reflection of heaven in a pond, and he that leaps at them is sunk.'"

"Is that the reason you never entered the bonds of matrimony, Melton?"

"Bonds, indeed," laughed the captain. "The term is well chosen, Linden. Let poets talk of rosy fetters; practically they possess a grim and hard grip stronger than iron. But there, to preach such a sermon to youth is as useless as lecturing cats to renounce cream, especially while earth holds a Lady Gertie Culverton."

Launce Linden laughed, a faint colour passed over his cheek.

"Yes," he said as he rose. "We will take her as one of the rare specimens. You spoke of Maurice Burgoyne just now," he proceeded, possibly to change the conversation; "have you seen him lately?"

"No; he hasn't been in town more than twice during the season, and then only for a brief period."

"Egad! there must be some singular attraction at Mereton Travers, eh?" smiled the guest meaningly.

"There is: a cousin, Miss Royle. I saw her last season, a wondrous girl, the loveliest brunette I ever saw."

"Another of the rare specimens—eh, old fellow?"

"No. If I'm not mistaken, very far from it. But where are you off to to-day?"

Launce Linden having given the information the talk flowed into subjects solely interesting to the speakers until the clock was on the point of striking three, when the visitor rising, departed to keep an appointment.

"Either, I suppose," smiled the captain cynically when alone, "with Lady Gertie Culverton or her rival, Lottie Delmont."

Changing his dressing-gown for an out-door coat, making a few other alterations in his toilet, seeing his hat was well brushed, and selecting a fresh pair of gloves, he approached the window in time to perceive the arrival of the saddle-horse he had ordered at three.

Descending he mounted, took the direction of Piccadilly, and was soon in the Row.

Captain Melton's acquaintance was large, for his gloved hand was frequently raised to his hat.

Hardly had he made the first canter, than he came upon the Honourable Launce in the company of a lovely equestrienne, with golden hair, an unchanging rose-bloom cheek, and handsome, witty, bold eyes, who rode splendidly. As, shortly after quitting the Row, he passed through the gates, he encountered the Honourable Launce again, riding by the side of an elegant barouche, in which reclined a handsome, elderly lady and a fair, innocent, lovely girl, whose bright blue eyes were raised smilingly to the cavalier.

MAURICE, BENDING, KISSED THE BEAUTIFUL CHEEK, AS HE WHISPERED: "MY BEST, DEAREST, TRUE, BRAVE SISTER."

"By Jove!" smiled the captain. " I was not far wrong, only Lottie Delmont has had the first innings."

Turning his horse's head, the officer proceeded in the direction of Brompton.

He had got beyond the parks into a less fashionable locality, when, lifting his eyes, for he had dropped into something of a reverie, he gave so violent a start, that the abruptly tightened rein caused his horse partly to rear. The captain's face, too, had gone pale, a dark shadow had fallen over his eyes, for those eyes had rested on a woman, plainly, neatly, yet poorly clad in sombre garments. A thin white hand held her shawl, her shoulders were a trifle stooped, not from years, but apparently for the same reason that the feet slipped over, rather than walked the pavement, the listlessness of a hopeless, miserable, spiritless existence.

Her face was rather inclined, her eyes bent on the pavement. The countenance was wan, haggard, and thin, as that of those who have been worsted in the battle of life—as that of those, too, who lack sufficiently healthful nourishment to well hold body and soul together.

Yet, despite these drawbacks, there was no doubting the refinement of the features, nor that they had once been handsome.

A curse not the less deep because it died upon his lip, being rather thought than expressed, rose to Captain Melton's tongue.

His first impulse, apparently, was to wheel round his horse and gallop off.

Checking this, he rode on for a few yards, then turning, followed the ill-clad sad-looking woman at a distance, gaining confidence as he perceived she never raised her eyes from the ground.

Without doubt she was traversing a well-known route.

If Captain Melton's memory carried him back some ten years, his heart, at the sight of that woman, must have smote him, or it would have done so, had he not possessed an organ of that hardest of adamant—self.

It was not pity, but anger that rested on his handsome features. ,

Off from the main street, down another, into another, each poorer than the last, the woman went, and the captain, ever at a distance, followed.

Finally, the woman turned into a poorer one yet, and, on reaching the top, the officer was in time to see her he tracked disappear into a house ten doors down. He marked it easily, owing to there being a lamp-post in front, and reckoning down the numbers found that it was fourteen. Assured of this he rode swiftly away, muttering between his teeth :

"Confound it, and confound her ! Fancy her being in London. It must be stopped."

That evening as the woman sat in her single apartment, so poor, so wretchedly destitute of comfort, busy at her sewing-machine completing the work she had been that morning to fetch, a letter was brought her.

She regarded it in surprise.

Then as she recognised the writing, her pale cheek flushed ; the next instant, however, an expression of vague alarm stole into her eyes.

For a brief space she leaned back as one faint. She evidently lacked the nerve to break the envelope.

Finally with an effort she did so.

As she pulled forth the enclosed letter, a five-pound note fell out. Seizing it, crumpling it almost fiercely in her hand she flung it from her.

"Again," she murmured indignantly.

Then she read the few lines the letter contained.

A bitter cry broke from her white lips.

"Oh, God ! " she wailed. "Oh, my God ! "

She threw her arms out among the work on the small deal table, and her face, with its fair hair tumbling about it, on them.

For over an hour no sound broke the stillness of the miserable room but the wild, passionate, stifled sobs of the woman.

CHAPTER V.

FORTUNE FAVOURS STEPHANIE.

MRS. WINBURG'S residence was one of those cottages charming in their irregularity of structure.

But a single storey high, save for the attic in the thick handsome roof of thatch that projected far beyond the walls, the windows were small and latticed, while here one abutted, there another.

On the ground-floor two of the windows were bay, opening on to the well-kept garden. The door had a porch, while masses of carefully-trained creeping plants covered the trellis fastened to the walls.

One of the bay windows stood at the corner of the house, having before it a smooth velvety lawn, on which grew an ancient beech, the strong branches of which brushed the grape-vine on the wall, and formed the resting-place of numerous feathered songsters that from early morn began to sing greetings to the occupant of the room on the other side the lattice window, which invariably would be thrown open, and a few crumbs scattered on the sill as a reward, by the fair hand of Mrs. Winburg's young companion, Catherine Crawford.

As Stephanie Royle came down the lane, she had a side view of the beech and the lattice.

Even as the moon had thrown its pale beam suddenly upon the earth, she had beheld a man steal from among the branches of the tree, place a foot cautiously on the top of the bay window, then disappear into the casement, the arms of a woman having been stretched forth to receive him.

She had as little doubt of the identity of the one as of the other.

The man was her cousin Maurice, the other Catherine Crawford.

For an instant Stephanie was too overwhelmed by surprise and indignation to move.

Could she believe her eyes?

Could she *disbelieve* them? That was the question; mutely she answered, "No."

So this was the place of midnight rendezvous.

Words strove to issue from her quivering lips that were well not uttered.

The moonbeams yet cast a silvery dim mist of light and showed how white Stephanie was.

Yet her eyes glowed so fiercely that they were as spots of fire in arctic snow.

The man she loved, whom she had done so much to win, was in yonder room with a base girl who had inveigled him—into what?

A low, bitter, fierce laugh broke from her, then she cowered quickly to the hedge. A step had sounded coming up the lane, and she feared discovery. Happily there was a gap in the hawthorns, and Stephanie, gliding swiftly through, crouched down.

In a moment a man passed, attired half gamekeeper, half poacher, and carrying a gun in the hollow of his arm.

"Blarm me," he remarked, with a short amused laugh; "but I reckon other chaps know how to poach as well as me. I be sure it were a man. At least it looked martal like it?"

Stephanie Royle watched the face intently.

"I shall know that face again," she reflected, "and if I need a witness I will find its owner."

Then, when the heavy tread was lost in the distance, she crept forth again, and, as if under a spell, or attracted by some powerful fascination, fixed her dark eyes on the casement behind which were the lovers.

Stephanie Royle had undergone many fierce moments of agony in her love, as is the fate of those possessing her nature. She was doomed to go through many more; but none, past or to come, equalled the suffering of that moment.

The man to whom she, clever, beautiful, had given her heart, whom she worshipped, adored, at whose feet she was ready to lie, for whose caresses she pined, was with Catherine Crawford, his arms about her, his lips to hers.

The reflection was maddening. Every nerve in her delicate body quivered with fierce agony in her effort to prevent the passionate angry cry that tore her bosom in its struggles to make itself heard.

Finally, raising her arms towards the cottage, her eyes fixed on it, she said through her small white teeth :

" You, Maurice Burgoyne, have a secret, and now it is mine. Beware ! I have yours too, Catherine Crawford. Enjoy your brief pleasure, for it is nearly over. The sun is past ; the clouds of scorn and disgrace are closing about your life, for I will ruin you. I will release Maurice from your subtle meshes. He will not, dare not love you when you are a being of contempt to the whole neighbourhood. Aye, though at the sacrifice of ever winning Maurice Burgoyne's love, I will crush you ! "

Then, as if unable to bear the contemplation of that casement longer, turning, she proceeded swiftly back to Mereton Travers.

Now and again as she went, a startled hare would spring up almost at her feet and dart noiselessly away, or a bird, aroused by her presence, rustled its feathers among the branches.

But Stephanie Royle was too engrossed by what she had learned that night to be able to experience fear, though the silent woods were round her, and a distant church clock struck one.

In safety, however, she reached the house, and stole on tiptoe up the staircase to her room. Locking the door, leaving her lamp unlighted, she drew a chair to the window, put the curtain slightly aside, and, her chin supported by her hand, her lips contracted, her eyes dry and hot, watched the path by which Maurice Burgoyne must return, while her active brain planned the best means to denounce and disgrace her rival.

Slowly the night wore on, yet Maurice did not appear, and every minute that slipped by, Stephanie Royle's rage against him and indignant scorn of Catherine Crawford augmented.

Still he came not.

Unconsciously, Stephanie at last dozed, weary with the fatigue of passion and the exertion of the night.

She awoke with a start. She had been asleep. Idiot ! How, with this tempest at her heart, could she have slumbered ?

Of course, Maurice must have returned before this.

Why, as her gaze wandered to the window, it must be almost dawn. Yes, there was its first faint violet streak in the east.

Then Stephanie's eyes dropped more earthward, even to the path she had so anxiously been watching.

Coming swiftly along it, almost at a run, was a man.

It was Maurice.

The girl's hands clenched, her breath came short and quick between her lips.

On he came until, reaching the shadow of the house, he disappeared.

A brief stillness, then she heard his steps cautiously ascending the stairs, so quietly that only the ear of jealousy could have heard.

Should she meet him ? Should she let him learn that she knew all ?

In her passion the impulse was strong upon her, but she resisted it.

"No," she reflected as she heard Maurice's door almost noiselessly close ; " it is not upon him, but upon her my vengeance must fall."

Stealing to her bed she laid awake yet planning.

Before she fell asleep she had devised a means. There was one thing she wished, that Maurice could be away at the time of the denouncement ; if that only could be, her success against her rival would be certain.

Fate, or fortune, was with Stephanie Royle, for at breakfast the next morning Maurice, stating that he had received a letter from the Honourable Launce Linden, announced his intention of starting next day to spend a week or two in town.

A smile of joy, faint and transient, passed over Stephanie's lovely features. For the first time she was pleased at the idea of his absence.

"I will wait," she thought. "Not until Maurice has gone shall the blow fall—fall when Catherine Crawford shall have no friend near to support, protect, or even to sympathise with her."

CHAPTER VI.

STEPHANIE VISITS DINGLE COTTAGE.

AURICE BURGOYNE'S absences from home had ever been looked forward to with sorrow by Stephanie Royle. On this occasion, however, the day preceding his departure appeared as if it would never pass. She was so anxious for him to be gone.

Yet by no look, no word, was she different than usual. Neither Sir Jaffery nor Maurice could have detected a change. At last the hour arrived.

From the drawing-room window she had watched the dog-cart, bearing her cousin to the station, whirl away down the avenue.

Consulting her watch, she remarked half aloud:

"He starts by the 11.30 train. He will hardly be in time to save it. That is, he'll have no time to spare. I'll wait until then."

She did so, not very patiently, pacing the drawing-room. But, at last, putting on her hat and mantle, she descended from terrace to terrace to the rose-garden.

As she passed through it she heard in the still summer air the whistle of the coming train. Then its faint thud, thud—then its cessation; then the thud, thud resumed until it died away.

"He is off," reflected Stephanie, smiling; "the position is mine, I am safe."

Reaching Dingle Cottage she knocked and requested to see Mrs. Winburg.

There was nothing singular in her visit. Mrs. Winburg was a pleasant old widow lady, who lived quietly, but who possessed an ample fortune, and most of the gentry made calls upon her.

"I don't think my mistress is very well this morning, miss," said the neat housemaid. "P'raps you'd see Miss Crawford."

Before Stephanie could make response, the girl had thrown wide the parlour-door, and the visitor found herself as it were in the companion's presence.

As Stephanie stood, seeing Catherine so pretty, gentle, and innocent, seated in her neat morning dress near the half-open glass doors at work, her first impulse was to retire, haughtily refusing intercourse with Miss Crawford.

Her next was to step into the apartment and return with a slight, proud inclination the young companion's bow, as she arose from her chair.

A new plan had occurred to her. Supposing she let this girl know she had discovered her secret? Supposing she could frighten her away—frighten her into hiding herself from all, especially from Maurice, the price of her doing so being Stephanie's silence?

The plan was better, for it would shield her more from her cousin's anger. Indeed, she might so manage it that Maurice should never divine the part she had played in the companion's disappearance ; might even so scheme as to make him believe Catherine Crawford had ceased to love him and fled with another lover.

At least she resolved to try. If she failed she could yet have recourse to her first plan of publicly denouncing her.

"You wished to see Mrs. Winburg?" said Catherine Crawford's soft musical voice, as she advanced, on the housemaid retiring. "I am very sorry, but Mrs. Winburg caught a slight cold yesterday, and intends keeping her room to-day."

"Perhaps," rejoined Stephanie coldly, taking the chair the servant had placed, "I may be able to dispense with the pain of seeing her—pain to her and myself. That, however, Miss Crawford, will depend upon you."

"Upon me, Miss Royle?" exclaimed the young companion, surprised, her eyes opening in amaze, as she gazed on the dark, handsome, cold face before her.

"Exactly. The subject that has brought me here, Miss Crawford," proceeded Stephanie, "has in truth more to do with you than your mistress. It is a subject of a nature I would have had another take upon themselves rather than I; but that is impossible."

"Indeed, you must excuse me, Miss Royle," remarked Catherine quietly, yet with an under-current of dignity; "but your words leave me as mystified as ever."

"Or," put in Stephanie, her red lips involuntarily curling, "you deem it wisest in your position to make it appear so."

"Miss Royle!" and there was indignation as well as dignity in the voice, as the companion, her slight figure drawn erect, regarded the visitor.

Stephanie waved her well-gloved hand.

"Miss Crawford, do not let us lose time," she remarked. "There is no occasion. In one sense, I may say I am here as your friend, though I confess it was not with that feeling I came intending to see Mrs. Winburg; but we are both young, and if you will be your own friend, I promise to aid you."

The companion's little foot had been beating the floor impatiently, her small pretty lips working with controlled irritation.

"Again, Miss Royle, I say I do not comprehend you."

"Absurd." And a short laugh issued from Stephanie Royle. "Of course your denial is but natural, but to me it is useless, Miss Crawford. I know all."

"All!"

"All. And hence, as a friend of Mrs. Winburg, feel it my duty to inform her of what it is evident she is in ignorance."

The companion's face had suddenly grown paler. Had the truth only now occurred to her?

Had the first surprise of Stephanie's visit prevented her guessing it before?

"Miss Royle, what is that of which Mrs. Winburg should be informed?" she said, but her voice was less steady.

"That you, Miss Crawford, her companion, have formed a *liaison* with a person in this neighbourhood," replied Stephanie, rising, her own accents less firm from joy that the moment for crushing her rival had arrived.

"Miss Royle!" but the cry was almost of entreaty, as the girl stepped back.

"Not only that, Miss Crawford, but also that at midnight, when all the house is at rest, you admit that person into your chamber."

"How—how do you know this? How prove it?" gasped Catherine, white, trembling, leaning on a chair for support.

"How?" was the scornful rejoinder; "surely you do not imagine I would make such an assertion, such a charge against you, if I could not prove it? Do you wish me, Miss Crawford, to produce my witnesses? I can do so if you desire."

"God help me!" came inaudibly from the young companion's lips as, sinking on the chair, she covered her face with her hands, and bowed them on the chair-back.

For a moment there was silence. Stephanie stood regarding her victim, a smile, a flush on her cheek that made her brunette beauty dazzling, brilliant; but it was the brilliance, the triumph of a splendid demon.

Yes; this was triumph, her triumph, she the virtuous, over her who had forfeited that title; her triumph over her rival to Maurice Burgoyne's love.

Suddenly the companion raised her head. Her face was very white, its expression that of fear and anguish.

"Oh, Miss Royle," she exclaimed piteously, "what would you do?"

"Do! Have I not stated what I consider it my duty to do, as Mrs. Winburg's friend?" was the cold response.

"You would not tell her," cried Catherine in alarm. "Oh, you would not?"

"I most certainly should, Miss Crawford. I most certainly shall. Do you imagine," haughtily, "I would make myself a party to the shameful disgrace you have brought on this roof?"

"Miss Royle, you are wrong. Believe me, you are doing me injustice," pleaded Catherine wildly; "I may have acted imprudently, but, before Heaven, I am innocent of wrong."

"Do you then mean to say, Miss Crawford, that at midnight you have not admitted your lover to your room, where he has remained till dawn?" exclaimed Stephanie with proud contempt.

The companion wrung her hands in her distress.

"Miss Royle," she cried, "you do not understand, and, Heaven help me, I may not tell you. Would that I dared. But, as you are a woman, and young, show me mercy. Be merciful."

"So far, I will," answered Stephanie; "I came here to declare all I have heard to Mrs. Winburg. I will however, give you a chance of hiding your disgrace, of retrieving your name."

The companion made only a distracted motion of her hands.

"Quit this neighbourhood instantly, acquainting no one with your intent, nor with your future residence. Swear by that which you hold most sacred to do this, to be silent to every one, to keep your whereabouts a secret, and I, too, promise to be mute respecting what I know."

Catherine Crawford paced the room in agitation; the tears were on her cheek.

"Miss Royle!" she exclaimed, abruptly halting, "you, who know so much, know also the name of him whom ——"

"Pardon me—yes, I do know it; but 'tis best it should not be mentioned between us," replied Stephanie coldly.

"And the oath you would exact from me is that I should leave this place, and keep my future home a secret from—him?"

"Exactly."

"That is impossible." The words came forth low but firm. "I will leave this place if you desire, but I will make no such promise, for I should break it. Wherever I go, whatever I do, he must know."

Stephanie's countenance went pale with fury.

Did this girl dare to brave her.

With difficulty could she control her fury as she rejoined :

"Then my course is clear. I must see Mrs. Winburg."

"No, no," cried the companion, her terror re-awakened. "Give me time, time—but a week to decide. Oh, how have I ever injured you, Miss Royle, that you can be so hard ? "

"You must decide at once," was the answer. Then with mocking scorn : "You injure me ? Your arrogance is great, Miss Crawford ; how could a person like you injure me ? "

"Easily," retorted Catherine, the words coming rapidly, but low and distinct between her lips. "Miss Royle, why should you take this disclosure on yourself ? Why should you show no pity ? Why are your words as hard as the glance of your eyes vindictive ? There can be but one reason."

"And that, pray ? " demanded Stephanie haughtily.

"You love Maurice Burgoyne."

The words came forth abruptly, impulsively. The worm had turned. But the words were unwisely spoken. Was not the speaker in her hearer's power ?

Stephanie Royle's face went red, then whitened with fury. Her dark eyes flashed, her small hands clenched, her pale lips quivered, her voice was broken with passion. In her rage she was terrible.

"How dare you ? " she hissed. "How dare you speak thus to me ? Love Maurice ; and did I, do you imagine you, whom he makes his toy, his pleasure for an idle hour, would part us ? Do you, miserable woman, think the love with which he would honour me, is the same as that with which he has blighted you ? "

Catherine made an effort to speak, but terror at the other's aspect held her mute. A faintness seized her, she caught a chair for support.

"You have pronounced your own doom," continued Stephanie; "this very day, this very hour, all Valeshire shall know what you are. You shall be flung forth with scorn and loathing from this house. The very servants shall turn from you as from some reptile in their path; every finger shall be directed at you in contempt; every glance averted that is not an insult."

"Mercy, mercy," cried Catherine, sinking on her knees overwhelmed.

"In all this world none will grant it you—lost—degraded," proceeded Stephanie passionately. "Mothers shall pluck their innocent children towards them as you pass. Men will look upon you with rude joke and laughter. Then seek the arms of him you love and test him. The glamour you have cast over him will be gone. He will rid himself of you—he will turn from you like the rest. He will pay you for your love and leave you to—your fate."

She had advanced slightly as she had given utterance to the above. Her arm was extended, her dark, beautiful eyes literally in a glow; her face was terrible but splendid.

Catherine Crawford, overcome by fear, cowered from her.

Was this woman before her sane? She could not be.

"Mercy," she again pleaded. "Help."

"Help," laughed Stephanie, "from whom would you seek it. Would you summon the household? It is I who will summon it. Is is I who will say: Look at yonder girl, who to you has appeared all purity and innocence. Would you know what she is? Would you know how her time is employed? I will tell you——"

"Silence!"

The word rang through the apartment, as the glass doors were flung open, and a man, his face flushed, his eyes kindling with rage, strode in.

"Maurice!" cried Catherine with an exclamation of joy, as she clung to his knees. "Oh, save me from this fearful woman."

"Maurice," gasped Stephanie, "you here. Still, what matter——"

"Silence!" he repeated with stern authority, one arm extended as if a protecting shield over Catherine. "Not another syllable, you who thus disgrace your sex. This lady is my wife."

CHAPTER VII.

STEPHANIE PUTS ON THE MASK.

EADER, have you ever beheld the change of colour, the expression of a tiger's eyes and jaws, when irritated by the keeper, and the brute feels at the same time so conscious of his power, yet, behind those bars; so conscious of his impotency? If so, you may form a conception of Stephanie Royle's expression as Maurice Burgoyne's words reached her ear.

Her graceful form seemed to shrink, the colour of her eyes and lips changed. It was a mobile face, adapting itself wondrously to every varied feeling, and in each possessing a singular power of attracting admiration by its great beauty.

"Your wife!" she ejaculated, low but distinct, while her lips scarcely seemed to move. "*That* girl your wife, Maurice? It is not true. You—you dared not."

"It is true, as Heaven is my witness," he answered quietly, raising Catherine, and with one arm holding her fondly to him.

"Oh, Maurice, Maurice," sobbed the young wife, her face hidden on his bosom. "What have I done? Can you forgive me?"

"Forgive you, darling," he rejoined. "It is I who should ask that of you. I was a coward, unworthy of your love, to have desired secrecy. I am glad it is over. In any case, how could I have expected you to have remained silent under the fearful, unwomanly, the disgraceful charges, the threats," and his eyes rested, full of scorn, upon his cousin, "that were hurled at you. Trust me, dear, they shamed the speaker more than you."

That expression of Stephanie Royle's had been but transient.

At any rate it died quickly from the surface, merely, however, to augment the fierce hidden tempest of rage convulsing her bosom.

Every nerve of the delicate frame quivered from the tension put upon it. What use was passion now, since she was really Maurice's wife? No law in England could pluck them asunder.

No law—at present.

The words came as if whispered in her ear. Could Maurice be really long happy with one so much beneath him?

No.

The small thread of red and white constituting a woman's beauty holds but for a time, let it only begin to change, and so will men. Sometimes even its very familiarity would estrange the heart that had once been held captive.

Stephanie in those brief moments told herself that she knew Maurice better than he knew himself. That she might yet at least have revenge on her rival, by making her life wretched, by—who could tell—estranging these two.

To do that, her quick, clear, perceptive brain warned her, she must appear to be no enemy to either, but, on the contrary, rather seem their friend.

Enemy. Could she ever be that, save in madness, to Maurice, whose looks of scorn, whose bitter words, lashed her like whips of steel?

Years ago she had loved him, she must to the end. If she plunged metaphorically a dagger in his heart, it would be doubtful whether she would not suffer the most keenly. Revenge and love are two of the world's riddles.

These reflections had flitted through her brain in the brief space occupied by her cousin and Catherine's interchange of sentences.

As the former spoke of her charges and threats being unwomanly, she raised her eyes to his sadly, reproachfully, and said in accents of singular sweetness :

"Not if what was believed had been true, Maurice. Why did you not confide in me ?"

"Confide in you ?" he repeated, surprised by her sudden change of manner.

"Confide in me. Do not you imagine your joy, as your sorrow, would alike have been shared in ? In all the world, I have but you and Sir Jaffery for relations, friends. Maurice, you might have trusted me. Your mistrust cuts me to the heart. But there," with an expression of humble resignation, "it is over. I feel that, save for Uncle Burgoyne, I am alone in the world."

With lowered head she moved to the door, when Maurice's voice broke in :

"Stephanie, stay. I am sorry, deeply sorry to have pained you. I might have told you. I am sure you would have respected my confidence, only——"

"Only," and she regarded him with a sad smile, "you mistrusted me ? Do not deny it, Maurice ; you dreaded did I know your secret I would divulge it. Mark me, Maurice," and her beautiful eyes kindled, "I am disappointed in you in more than this. It was not noble, manly, to keep your marriage concealed. It was not just to her you have made your wife, to let her be exposed to the suspicions that must, that *did* arise. It was cowardly. Had you loved Miss Crawford——"

"Had I ?" he exclaimed.

"Well, loving Miss Crawford more bravely, would you not have proved that affection by confessing that love to all the world ?"

"You are right, Stephanie, I feel you are," he responded almost contritely, "but the error shall be righted now."

"Love," she proceeded. "Maurice, do you really know what it is ? When true, unswerving sacrifice of everything—of wealth, position, the world's opinion even—to the being loved. You sacrificed nothing. Do men ever? No, they expect that at the woman's hands."

"Would to heaven I had trusted you, Stephanie," he remarked; "you are braver, cleverer than I. You could have given me the courage I needed. You have even now. There shall be no secrecy any longer."

All this while, the young wife, her head on her husband's breast, never moved her eyes from Stephanie's face.

"I would have given you courage, Maurice, as I would have given you everything," proceeded Stephanie Royle in tones so sweet, so gently melancholy, that they thrilled the hearer. "Yes, Mrs. Burgoyne, you divined the secret your husband failed to. Why should I not confess it? I loved you, Maurice."

"Stephanie!" he cried, the blood rushing to his brow.

"Yes," she continued calmly; "with that love you cannot comprehend. The love that is ready to sacrifice everything, even its own happiness, to the being loved. Do you recollect my definition of the passion in the rose-garden? Those words came from my soul; that is how I could, nay, how I did love. To touch your hand was joy, to receive a smile made me happy all day. Your wishes it was my pleasure to gratify if I could."

"Stephanie," he broke in, distressed and much moved, "peace, I pray you; think of what you say."

"That, Maurice, for which I feel no need to blush. I said I loved you—that to minister to your comfort was gladness to me. But my dream is over. Had you pretended to care for me and deceived me, I would have killed you. You did not do this, you merely loved another. My heart will not break," she smiled; "far from it. I can even hold my hand to her you love, and say: 'The words I spoke just now were uttered under misconception. I am sorry for them. I apologise, Mrs. Burgoyne. Can you forgive me?'"

While speaking she had advanced and now held her pretty gloved hand to Catherine, who felt a cold, icy shiver run through her.

The husband was touched to strong emotion.

"Heaven bless you, Stephanie," he said tremulously. "You make me trebly feel I have been unjust to you. Catherine, dearest, speak. There was a cruel commencement to this interview, but the end promises happiness far beyond our conception."

"Forgive," answered Catherine, slightly rising, but not quitting her husband's side; "how could I do otherwise, Miss Royle? Are you not my husband's cousin, nay, in his eyes, sister?"

She took the hand held to her, thankful that a glove was between the two palms.

"The pardon is not a very warm one," smiled Stephanie. "And I am to owe it to being Maurice's cousin. Well, perhaps even that is more than I deserve. I was enraged, and my tongue uttered hard words for a woman to forgive. I will be patient, in time you may regard me differently. But whether yes or no, make but Maurice happy, be to him a fond, faithful wife, and, Catherine Burgoyne, you shall ever possess a friend in me."

Then abruptly turning.

"Maurice, are we friends?"

"Friends, Stephanie," he exclaimed fervently. "Better ones than we ever have been, for now, for the first time, do I know the depth, the sincerity of your noble, generous nature. God bless you."

Taking her hand he pressed his lips to it.

"Thank you," she murmured sweetly, then, averting her face, as if unwilling to show her emotion, bade both hurriedly farewell, and passed through the open window into the garden.

From thence she hastened to Mereton Travers. There was a smile on her handsome face. A frown could not have been harder, colder.

"It was a difficult part to play, but I have played it well, I think," she reflected. "He trusts me, she does not as yet, but she shall, and the victory shall be mine in the end. I'll be revenged on her, and win him back."

No sooner had Stephanie Royle retired than Catherine Burgoyne threw her arms round her husband's neck, and exclaimed entreatingly :

"Oh, Maurice, dear Maurice, do not trust her, do not. She is false, she is our enemy !"

"Catherine," he ejaculated, a touch of anger in his voice. , "That is unjust, unkind, unlike yourself. She had cause for anger, yet see how nobly she forgave. Recollect, Stephanie has been as a sister to me——"

"With the desire, Maurice, of being more."

"Can love be controlled, Catherine ? Could I have helped loving you, though you had given me no return ?" he rejoined. "Poor Stephanie, she rather deserves our tenderest pity than blame. How frank, how noble of her to own her passion, the passion she could not conquer."

"How unfeminine," commented the young wife mentally.

"When, Catherine, you know her better, as you must, you will recognise her excellent qualities, and love her for her own sake as for mine."

"For yours, Maurice ?" said the wife, suppressing a shiver.

"For mine," he repeated. "Catherine, not only is she my cousin, but I love her as a sister. I should be sorry if our marriage caused an estrangement between us."

"Maurice !" exclaimed Catherine quickly, "it shall never do that—never."

"That's right," he laughed, kissing her. "You must not judge Stephanie from to-day, darling. Few women ever judge any of their own sex fairly. My cousin is an angel."

"She is a demon," thought Catherine Burgoyne decisively. "And I feel will be a dark, dark shadow across our path, even to the ruin of our happiness.

CHAPTER VIII.

STEPPING INTO THE WEB.

OT only had Maurice, urged by Stephanie's cunningly-chosen words, resolved to confess his union with Catherine, but on reflection he recognised that, for his wife's sake, it was now compulsory.

The scene which had transpired in the sitting-room of Dingle Cottage could not have failed to rouse the suspicion of the servants, ever argus-eyed in all matters that did not concern them. Had he contemplated yet to keep his marriage secret, relying on Stephanie's aid and silence, which he told himself he might do safely, it would be at the expense of placing Catherine, the future Lady Burgoyne, in a most equivocal position.

No, there could be no further concealment, and he was almost pleased that his having missed the London train by two minutes had forced him to take the step.

"Maurice," remarked Catherine, when they spoke of it together, "your cousin said that true love meant self-sacrifice. That the happiness of the loving can only exist in that of the beloved. She is right. If this confession, that you have looked upon and wedded one so lowly as I, will harm you with your father, it will make me wretched. Rather, I would prefer you to keep our marriage still secret. What, Maurice, do I care for what the world says or what it thinks, as long as my conscience does not condemn me, and I have your love."

The young husband drew her fondly to him and gazed with emotion on the earnest innocent face, before he pressed his lips to hers.

"You women, Stephanie and you Cathie," he exclaimed, while the wife shuddered involuntarily at the coupling of the names, "shame me by your courage—the unselfishness of your natures. No, I have done you wrong, darling, and will not let the day pass before I have made reparation. . I will return immediately to Mereton Travers and acquaint my father. If he, in his anger, banish me from his roof, rest assured, love, it will only be until his passion subsides, and we can live very comfortably on the income my mother left me."

Embracing her, bidding her take courage, Maurice Burgoyne left Dingle Cottage.

Catherine nervously watched him depart, yet there was a little throb of pleasure in her pulse, so natural to a woman at the idea of having her title of wife confessed, and possessing a home that Maurice might enter in the broad light of day.

Meanwhile, it must be owned that Maurice's courage somewhat like that of Bob Acres, oozed out the nearer he approached the all-important moment.

He and his father had ever been the best of friends, but he well knew what his rage would be on learning his only son and heir, the sole representative of his branch of Burgoynes, had made, as he would term it, a *mésalliance* —that Maurice, in whose union he had contemplated, even planned, increase of social position, if not wealth, had wedded the poor penniless companion of old Mrs. Winburg, a girl but a step removed from a domestic, without family, without antecedents.

"What a storm it will be!" reflected Maurice. "When the pater's tongue gets into full swing it utters words difficult to bear. He'll say things of Catherine—I can guess what he well say—that I, as her husband, and loving her, should not hear. I wonder if it would be better to write the news?"

Thus communing, he passed the gate into the rose-garden, and came abruptly upon Stephanie Royle.

There was not a trace of that past emotion on her features.

She met him with a free, unconstrained smile.

The portière was raised, and the woman, wan and pale, stood before them.

"MRS. BURGOYNE, YOUR VOICE IS EXQUISITE."

NOTICE.—With this Number is Given Away a Coloured Picture for binding with the Work.

"So soon back?" she said lightly. "By-the-way, Maurice, I forgot to ask how it is you are not on your way to London."

"I missed the train, Stephanie," he replied, walking by her side.

"But there was another an hour later," she remarked, arranging her rose bouquet.

"Yes, dear Stephanie, but I am not going. As you can understand," he went on, his eyes bent gloomily on the path, "more important matters keep me here. I am determined to follow your brave advice, and own my marriage to my father. There will be a terrible row."

The girl's dark eyes glanced furtively at him.

How quietly he spoke to her of his marriage! Had he forgotten her confession, absorbed by his own troubles, or was it her own manner that made him apparently so indifferent?

Men were selfish. Perhaps that made women love them.

At any rate, though Stephanie's red lips tightened, she was glad that, as usual, he brought his troubles, his confidences, to her.

"You are right," she smiled; "and having been a bad, bad boy, Maurice, I own you merit some punishment."

"Mine will be disinheritance."

"Nonsense! Sir Jaffery might threaten, but you are his only child."

"And, as he will say, have disgraced him."

"Well, certainly, you have not augmented the family honour," she rejoined. "The world, Maurice, will be of his mind. Still, the matter is beyond alteration; therefore, all had better make the best of it. Uncle will justly be angry, and as you are in the wrong, you must keep your temper, whatever he says."

"That's it. However I may make up my mind to be cool, a fellow loses his self-control before he is aware of it."

"That would make matters worse, indeed. Don't destroy my roses, please," she smiled.

"Never mind the rose, Steph," he remarked. "I thought of writing to Sir Jaffery."

"I don't think that the best plan."

"Well, the fact is, though I wish him to know the truth, I dread the telling him. I own it. I am a coward."

There was a pause; then the girl spoke gently:

"Maurice, shall I tell him?"

"You!" he exclaimed, halting, and regarding her in half doubt, half joy. "You do not mean that? You would not!"

"Why would I not?" she replied, quietly. "Maurice, I would do this, and more, for you. You ought to know that. I may not do much good, but I should be better than a letter, for I could seek to soften Sir Jaffery's anger, and plead your cause."

"You, dear Stephanie, would do that?" he exclaimed, his eyes fondly bent on her, while the idea swept through his mind that, had he never seen Catherine, he must have loved this good, beautiful cousin. "If—if my father would hear anyone, he would hear you. But how can I ask you to do this? And still, if you would——"

"You do not ask," she interrupted, smiling. "I offer and you accept."

"Stephanie," he cried enthusiastically, clasping her hand, "you are an angel. I told Catherine you were."

"And she did not believe it," said his cousin, with a clear, musical laugh, with more concealed venom in it than the forked tongue of the snake.

"She does not know you as I do, Stephanie. I bade her wait until I had proved your worth. It was but a matter of time."

"That is all," she smiled. "The proof of a friend is in what that friend can do. Sir Jaffery is now in the library. I'll go at once, and plead Catherine's cause and yours."

"Heaven bless you, dear," he said gratefully. "Every word you utter makes me the more regret I did not confide in you from the first. I shall learn wisdom from the past, and in all things trust you in the future."

"Remember that promise, for I shall," she laughed.

"I will, do not fear."

He yet held her hand, and now raised it to his lips.

Stephanie gave a peculiar smile, then, plucking away her fingers, hurried from him.

She was a skilful actress, but he was an easy victim.

He stood watching her as she went from terrace to terrace, and reflected.

"She is a dear girl. I never knew her good, noble qualities thoroughly until now. If I ever forget what I owe her to-day, may Heaven forget me!"

CHAPTER IX.

BANISHED.

"MAURICE married?—married in secret!—married without telling me!"

And weak as he was, Sir Jaffery started erect from his chair, his eyes dilated, his tall figure quivering, his face flushed by so violent a passion that it even for a moment awed Stephanie Royle, who had created the storm.

"Dear uncle, pray be calm," she pleaded, assuming an air half-timid, half-contrite. "It is not I who have offended you. The thought of doing so is far from me. The task I have taken upon myself is an unthankful one; still, I fancied, if you heard the truth from my lips, it would be better for you—better for Maurice."

"Maurice! If you are not jesting with me, Stephanie, if what you say be true, never again shall he enter this house, never will I hear his name mentioned in my presence."

"Oh, dear uncle, how could I jest upon a subject that I know must occasion you such pain?" she replied, with meek reproach. "Has anything ever shown itself in my conduct that would make you believe I would rejoice in your suffering?"

"Stephanie, you have been as a daughter to me," proceeded the irate Sir Jaffery. "Better, probably, than would have been my own, had I had one, judging from Maurice. I am furious. I cannot contain my anger. But, child, it's not with you; it's against this—this fellow! Married! I'll not believe it."

"Would, uncle, I could say, Do not. Would from my heart I could declare, for Maurice's sake and yours," said

Stephanie earnestly, "that I had been deceived—there was no foundation for what I have told you."

"No foundation when you tell me, child, you had it from Maurice's own lips."

"From no other, uncle. When I learned it I upbraided him, I confess, for deceiving you. I declared, my anger too was roused, that he had done wrong, and was adding to that wrong by playing the hypocrite to so kind, so indulgent a father."

"Kind and indulgent no longer," broke in the baronet; "but hard, unforgiving as granite."

"Urged by my words, he decided to tell you everything—to entreat your forgiveness."

"Never."

"Then his courage failed him. Conscious how he deserved your anger—your reproaches—he feared to meet them; and I, rather than this secret should yet be one to you, uncle, offered myself to be your informant. Maurice gratefully accepted my proposition. 'I want my father to know the truth, but I dread to tell him,' he remarked. I could guess the reason, though he will never own it; though he will prove manly enough even to deny it, to without a murmur suffer for his folly, his mad infatuation. I am assured that, secretly, he is keenly sensible of the cruel disgrace he, your heir, has brought upon his family."

The words, spoken with the innocent air of one only anxious to bring about reconciliation, were calculated really to increase the storm; to Sir Jaffery, who regarded them under the first head, they were as oil on fire.

"Disgrace—cruel disgrace—my family!" he cried, clutching the arms of the chair into which he had fallen back. "What do you mean, Stephanie? Who has the fellow married? I command you to hide nothing from me. What low-bred, inveigling woman does he expect me to call daughter-in-law?"

"Dear uncle," she replied, "only be calm. Think of your health, how precious it is to me, and I will tell you everything. It is Maurice's own desire. But while you are so excited I tremble at the effect my replies may have. The knowledge of whom he has wedded I fear will hardly allay your fury. Yet whether this trouble is all owing to her, we have no right to say. Maurice may love her so as to hold small in comparison the offending those who love him," proceeded Stephanie, crafty in word and look. "Nevertheless, did she inveigle and lure him on, dazzled by his high position, and the prospect—a great temptation to those lowly born—of one day being Lady Burgoyne, Maurice—and I applaud him—will never be so dishonourable as to confess it."

"Lady Burgoyne! She? Never!" cried the baronet furiously—"or rather, if that must come to her, not a shilling of mine shall go with it. Lowly born! Stephanie, who is she? One of the housemaids?—your own woman? or——"

"No, uncle, not quite so low as that," with pained reproof. "It is you now who wrong Maurice."

"And what matter since he has so wronged himself and disgraced me? Who is this woman? You know I read that in your face."

"Yes, uncle."

"Who is she?"

"The young girl whom old Mrs. Winburg engaged nine months ago for a companion."

Stephanie uttered the words hesitatingly and low as if herself conscious of the enormity of her cousin's transgression in selecting such a person for a wife.

Sir Jaffery knew nothing much of Catherine, but he judged from his niece's manner that she must be a totally unfit match for his son, even setting aside social position. He regarded Stephanie in the light of Maurice's defender; her tone, her behaviour, led the baronet to imagine she was pleading for her cousin; hence the belief that she was ashamed to own who he had married made him imagine the disgrace trebly bad.

"A companion! A miserable, mean-spirited girl, who, for a few paltry pounds, hires herself to bear the whims and ill-tempers of a cross old woman!" he cried. "Never shall she enter Mereton Travers; neither shall my unnatural son, never. To think how proud I was of him. Heaven, what have I done that disgrace should come upon me at my age, and by the hand of one I most loved? Maurice, Maurice!"

For a space his emotion overcame him. He buried his face in his hands.

A shadow fell over Stephanie's features.

She need have had no fears. Sir Jaffery's pride dominated his affection. Raising his head he continued:

"Not another hour shall he remain beneath this roof. He has a fortune from his mother. He shall not have a shilling from me. Go, Stephanie, send him here. He shall learn my opinion, then we part for ever."

"No, no, uncle," and the girl knelt by his side, "do not, pray do not see him while you are in this spirit. I think words are said in anger that never can be recalled. Reflect, why should you futher expose yourself to excitement. Already you will suffer from this."

"Suffer! I shall never recover it. But what would you have me to do, Stephanie? Go, he shall. I'll never see him."

"For his sake as well as yours, uncle, do not see him," she responded quickly. "I dread it. Poor Maurice, he might in his anger say what he might never be able to pardon himself for afterwards."

"Poor Maurice!" ejaculated the baronet angrily, "you pity him, Stephanie?"

"Uncle!" the words came as a whisper, while her head bent low, "I would do much for Maurice. I love him."

"Love him!"

"As a sister," she added quickly.

"Sister! Why not have loved him? I would rather see you Lady Burgoyne a hundred times than that—that girl."

Stephanie bit her lips.

"He shall go," working anew into rage.

"Do not see him, uncle. Write," suggested Stephanie. "It will show you are calmer and therefore more determined. That yours is no hasty decision uttered at the moment of passion."

"You are right, Stephanie, you are right; not even will I look upon his face again."

He drew the writing materials towards him, paused a moment to reflect, then wrote:

"My niece, with a delicacy and kindness you do not merit, has informed me of the disgrace you have brought on our house. Words are useless on a matter that is irremediable. I refuse to see you—now or ever, and demand your instant departure from beneath this roof, where the veriest stranger would be more welcome to me.   "JAFFERY BURGOYNE."

"It is hard, uncle,' remarked Stephanie.

"Hard! it is just. Take it to him as my answer. I have no other—none."

The girl took the envelope with assumed sadness and retired. She was content with the interview. She had desired that they should not meet, and they had not.

"I guessed it would be thus," said Maurice gloomily, when Stephanie had brought him the letter in the rose-garden; "yet I fancied he would have seen me—once."

"I did all that I could, Maurice." There were tears in her eyes, her voice.

"Do you think I doubt that, dear Stephanie?" he exclaimed, his face kindling, as he took her hands in his. "If such an advocate as you failed, I could have had no hope."

"Thank you," she rejoined gratefully; "but, Maurice, I do not want to deceive you in any way I hardly persuaded uncle against not seeing you; indeed, I deemed it best. Had you met, he might have said—you might have said—that which might have never been forgiven by either. Besides, uncle is already much excited; further excitement would have proved dangerous, I fear. Wait, only wait until he is calmer; then, remember, I shall ever be by his side to plead your cause."

"And that you will do so, Stephanie, I am assured. I shall never be able to thank you for what you have done; but a time will come when both I and Catherine will find a means to express our gratitude. I shall go back to the house; my valet can pack and bring my belongings."

"That would be best, wisest," put in Stephanie. "But, Maurice, you will keep me informed of your doings?"

"Every step I take, dear Stephanie."

"And I, on my side, will let you know of my success," she remarked, with a faint smile. "Do not, dear Maurice, expect too much, too soon. Uncle is naturally irritated against me for my taking your part, rather than his; but that will speedily pass, so be patient, only patient, and trust me. It may be weeks, months, even years; but"—decisively—"I will succeed; you shall come back to Mereton Travers."

"I will be patient; I will trust you, Stephanie. God bless you, my more than sister."

"Yes," she smiled; "henceforth brother and sister."

She lifted her pretty face so witchingly, yet so innocently, that Maurice, bending, kissed the beautiful cheek, as he whispered:

"My best, dearest, true, brave sister. Now good-bye, I must see Catherine at once."

"Of course. Go, Maurice, by all means, go!"

A moment after he was hurrying along the woodland path.

Stephanie, leaning over the gate, with a bitter smile, recalled that other time when she had done so—hope, love in her heart.

At the bend, Maurice, glancing back, as then, waved his hat.

Stephanie made a response.

As, however, she did so, she murmured, half aloud:

"Yes, I will succeed. You, Maurice, shall return to Mereton Travers; but never Catherine Burgoyne, never—never!"

CHAPTER X.

COMMENCING HOUSEKEEPING.

SUMMER was on the wane. Already the tints of autumn were beginning to glow among the rich foliage of the fine old trees in Kensington Gardens.

The plants were either losing their floral beauty, or in some cases running wild, needing the pruning knife.

In the pretty gardens, however, surrounding a certain charming, trellised, verandahed house in Kensington, shut from the road by a moderately high wall, summer yet seemed to linger. The lawns were fresh and smooth, the beds filled with flowers, the gravel paths clean and firm, while blooming creepers climbed up the trellis and peeped through the bedroom windows, curtained by delicate white muslin.

As the sun had stolen its arched way across the heavens, shifting the shadows of the trees upon the lawn, a graceful figure—a woman, of course—attired in light summer toilette, might now and then have been seen flitting past the open French windows. Sometimes the notes of a clear, full, sweet voice would float out into the garden. Sometimes the notes of a piano, struck by a firm, crisp touch.

The hour was near four, the voice and the piano had for somewhile been silent, when a gentleman on horseback halted before the house, dismounted, threw the reins to a groom who had been waiting some few minutes, opened the gate with a private key, and entered the garden.

First he approached the windows, stepped under the verandah, and looked in. No one was there. The graceful owner of the voice and crisp touch had gone.

Coming away, the gentleman proceeded round the house to the back.

Here the pretty garden was larger, more shady, more peaceful.

"I thought I should find her in the old place," thought the gentleman with a smile. "How charming she looks. Quite a picture."

On a rustic seat beneath the branches of a wide-spreading tree, the boughs of which swept down low, as if eager to caress her lovely golden head, was the owner of the sweet voice.

Her straw garden-hat was laid aside, for the sun only fell in tiny flecks like kisses, while the lady's face was turned towards a book resting on her knee.

Crossing the lawn, coming within the shadow, the gentleman exclaimed, laughing:

"Well, madam bookworm, what intricate plot are you seeking to unravel now?"

The lovely head was raised quickly, a sunny smile rose to the red lips, as the lady sprang up, crying:

"Maurice! Is it you? Why, I didn't expect you for an hour."

"And are sorry I've come, no doubt," he laughed, embracing her. "I've been unfortunate enough to interrupt the novel in a most interesting part. Well, I'll go away again."

"You'll do no such thing, you silly boy," retorted the young wife, linking her arm in his. "I don't believe any novel going possesses the interest of real life."

"Not certainly wedded life, eh? Why, Cathie, we are getting quite old married people."

"Very," she remarked with comic gravity, "if we reckon from when we commenced housekeeping."

"Not quite a month ago, is it?" he said, breaking into a merry laugh. "But this, darling, you know, we must reckon as our honeymoon. We never had one worthy of that name before."

"Nor could anyone have had a happier, Maurice—except—except for one thing."

"Yes, I know, my father's resentment. Still, Catherine, the time is early yet."

"Early or late, Maurice"—and the shadow of a sadness fell across her face—"I shall never forgive myself, until he, Sir Jaffery, has forgiven you. Only when that time arrives shall I cease to feel that in yielding to my own great, but selfish love, I have done you a severe injury."

"Catherine," he exclaimed; "never, my darling, let me hear such words from your lips. Do you imagine anything could have compensated me for your loss? But why frighten ourselves with troubles that may prove brief. I repeat the time is early yet, only one little month, darling—not much for a man to recover the shock occasioned by the failure of his proud and dearest projects."

Catherine lifted her eyes quickly to her husband's face, questioning, anxious somewhat.

"Besides," he went on; "why should we despair of ultimate forgiveness, when we have so earnest and kindly an advocate as my cousin Stephanie by my father's side? If anyone be able to win us pardon from him it is she. Does she not tell us that already he betrays signs of softening; even that she has dared the experiment of naming me in his presence, without being rebuked. Heaven bless her, she is proving our friend indeed. You, yourself, must acknowledge that, Cathie. Your opinion has changed since you knew her first."

"She has been very kind," responded the young wife, as they slowly paced the lawn, passing from sunshine into shade, she leaning on his arm, her fair head resting against his shoulder.

"And, Cathie, you confess you were awfully wrong in your first reading of her, eh? Come," he said gaily, "be generous enough to confess."

"There is little generosity in those who refuse confession when in error," she smiled; and he did not mark the evasiveness of the reply. "I never thought she would have been so kind."

"Because, love, you did not know her. I assured you how it would be. Well, that being settled, now for the reason why I am home earlier. I have asked two friends to dinner, and thought you would like to give the cook notice."

"Therefore," she laughed, "lose nearly half-an-hour after you are here before you tell me. One thing, Grimshaw is almost a *cordon bleu*, so no doubt will be equal to the occasion."

"And another thing," laughed Maurice, glancing with fond pride at his wife, "in the contemplation of so sweet, so fair a hostess, neither Everitt Melton nor Launce Linden will have much time to criticise the dinner she gives them."

"In case, however," remarked Catherine, dropping him a curtsy for the compliment, "they should have so little discernment as not to look with Maurice Burgoyne's eyes, I had better at once give Grimshaw notice."

"Do so, while I smoke a cigar, pet."

As Maurice lighted one, his eyes followed his wife until she disappeared into the house.

"What a deucedly lucky fellow I am to have won her," he muttered, recommencing to pace the lawn. "Well, there is one step in my life at least I shall never repent, even though Sir Jaffery carry out his threat of leaving me only the proverbial shilling. What is wealth compared to a fond, faithful woman's affection? With Catherine as my life companion, the small fortune my poor mother left me will more than suffice. Still, I hope, I trust my father, whatever will he makes, may consent at least to see me to our being friends."

"A letter for you, Maurice."

"A letter!" he swung round on his heel, and perceived Catherine returning, the letter in her hand.

"It is from your cousin, Miss Royle."

He hurriedly ran his eyes over the contents, then exclaimed in delight :

"Why, they are coming to town! They'll be in London to-morrow!"

"Coming to town to-morrow!" ejaculated Catherine, and there was scarcely the same ring of pleasure in her voice as his.

"Yes, listen to what she says:

"My DEAR MAURICE,—I have a surprise for you, but for want of time I must deliver it in telegraphic sentences. We are coming to London; indeed, I hope we shall arrive there sometime to-morrow. I told uncle I needed a change, and he consented to the suggestion. Dearest love to Catherine.—Your affectionate cousin "STEPHANIE."

Concluding, Maurice Burgoyne, ejaculating a delighted "Bravo," crushed the letter in his hand.

Crushed it, destroyed it, for there was a postcript to this effect :

"Sir Jaffery still shows faint signs of yielding towards you, but not towards Catherine ; any word even that suggests her existence fills him with rage—a rage most dangerous in his state of health. Keep this from poor Catherine ; keep it from her."

CHAPTER XI.

THE DETERMINATION OF DESPAIR.

HE same bright sun that had shone so brightly on the lawn when paced by the young husband and wife sent its rays into the small garret of the haggard, ill-clad woman whose appearance had created that angry alarm in Captain Everitt Melton.

But somehow the beams here were dull, sickly, and yellow, as if, chameleon fashion, they partook of the objects they rested upon.

For half-an-hour the monotonous whirr of the sewing-machine had been the only sound to break the stillness.

The woman bent over it, only her foot and long thin white fingers, as she guided the work, moving.

But now the whirr abruptly ceased ; the last stitch was done.

"The last, the very last," murmured the worker, as she sank back on the rickety chair. "It is hard to die, but how much harder at times to live."

A moment she sat helplessly regarding the fine linen on her lap. The despair that in its depth becomes dull, stunned resignation was on her features.

Her eyes, of a pretty violet-blue, were bright, hard, dilated. Tears in them would have been even a relief to the beholder, but so many had been shed, years ago, that the fount seemed dry.

"After this," proceeded the woman, half aloud, "they said they could give me no more, that times were bad, they had not even enough for their regular indoor hands. With the work it was starvation, without it it must be."

She paused, her lips trembled with some violent emotion.

A vision of a pretty village-town in Devon rose before her, of vast stretches of golden gorse and bronzed bracken, of purple heather-clad hills, of fond sweet faces and happy laughter.

She saw herself in a fresh chintz-curtained room, with rose-festooned window; a pretty, soft-cheeked, bright-eyed happy girl, with a future full of pleasurable hope, standing before a glass, coquettishly fastening a rose in her hair, because—because she was to see him that afternoon. The only man she had ever seen to whom she could give her maiden, innocent heart.

Indeed, it had gone from her into his keeping whether she would or no.

What a charming picture that appeared in the woman's remembrance now, yet how she cowered from it, how bitterly it wrung her heart.

"Oh," and abruptly she threw forth her arms, "to think of then and now; to recall that life and this"—she glanced round the wretched garret—"I wonder the contrast does not kill me at a blow. Oh, that it would. If it only would. To think how I loved him. So much, so truly, trustfully; ah, with all my soul. Oh, Everitt—Everitt!"

That recollection even failed to bring tears, only passionate sobs that seemed to rend the thin weak figure, as the woman bowed her face on her hands.

Almost instantly, however, she rose up, a resolute expression on her features, and began to fold the work and place it in brown paper.

Then putting on her worn bonnet and threadbare shawl, taking the parcel in her arms, she descended the creaking stairs.

In the passage she encountered a stout elderly woman, whose hands and general appearance bespoke hard work, as plainly as the plump countenance an honest kindly heart.

"Going out, Mrs. Harriot?" she said, cheerily, peering into the wan face. "Well, it's a fine arternoon, that it is It'll do you no end of good."

"Yes, it is very beautiful. The sun has almost been too much in my room," responded the woman, edging to the door.

"That's 'cause your eyes is weak from working, I 'spect. Will you be long?"

"No, not very. I am only going to take this work home."

"Then when you return you come in and take a cupper tea along with me and my good man. It'll be ready by then."

"You are very good, thank you very much," and opening the door the woman hurried into the street.

"Only take the work home," muttered the landlady on the door closing. "Little enough, but, poor thing, you ain't got even the strength for that. Tell you what it is, Joe," entering the parlour where her good man was seated making picture-frames from gold beading, "if hever there was a lady born it's that Mrs. Harriot, and if hever a woman's starvin' and walkin' straight into her grave, it's her. I've ast her to come in to tea when she come back, and I shall git somethin' nice."

Meanwhile, her work delivered, and the few shillings received in payment, the woman slowly retraced her steps.

She felt, however, very weak, as the stream of people in the Knightsbridge-road jostled her, while the vehicles rolling by dazed her brain, so crossing she went through Albert-gate into the Park. Here the green was a relief to her weary eyes, the throng less, for she kept away under the trees.

She was drawing near Hyde-park-corner when glancing up she staggered as from a blow, and caught at a tree that she was fortunately near for support.

Within ten yards of her were two gentlemen walking arm-in-arm in the same direction as she was going. One was Captain Everitt Melton, and it was upon him Mrs. Harriot's eyes were fixed.

"It is he!" she gasped; "Everitt."

A moment she stood, her breath coming quick and short, her thin fingers shaking with emotion.

Then, as the officer passed farther on, apparently moved by some sudden impulse she summoned her strength and followed, tracking him as he had tracked her.

It was not so difficult at this hour, for many persons thronged the way, and the two she had to keep in view walked slowly, often stopping to exchange a remark with some acquaintance.

Quitting the park, they proceeded down Piccadilly.

Here the two halted before a palatial building—a club.

Were they going in ?

One was, not the other.

Captain Melton, raising his hat, passed on more quickly now. But the fever of excitement gave the woman strength, and she kept him in view.

Down one, two, three streets she went, growing at times reckless, it appeared, about concealment.

Finally Captain Melton, stopping before a house, opened the door with a key and entered.

The woman hurried on. She must ascertain the number.

As she reached the door it opened, and a servant came out.

"I beg your pardon," began Mrs. Harriot nervously ; "have you not a gentleman residing here—a Mr. Everitt!"

"Not Mr. Everitt," interrupted the girl, with a due sense of the importance the title gave to the establishment, "Capting Everitt Melton. Yes, he's our fust-floor lodger. He's jest come in. You'd better ring if you have anythink to leave for him, and give it to the man-servant."

So saying, she hurried off on her errand.

But the woman had nothing to leave. On the contrary, she walked rapidly away, repeating the name and address frequently as she went, apparently to impress it on her memory.

She now proceeded rapidly homeward, only stopping twice to make one or two purchases. One was writing materials.

"Well, here you are at last," exclaimed the stout land-lady, appearing in the passage as her lodger opened the street-door; "you're a bit late, ain't you?"

"I was detained unexpectedly."

"Work before pleasure, that's the motter of us bread-winners, Joe says, and he's right, ain't he? But come in, I've kept the tea on the 'ob."

Mrs. Harriot gladly would have refused, but her heart was a sensitively susceptible one, unfortunately for her, and she could not pain the good-natured landlady by refusing her hospitality.

She entered and took her seat at the table and gratefully drank the cup of tea that was offered.

When the meal was over and she arose to return to her room, she took the landlady's hand as she thanked her for her kindness, then bending, kissed her.

"How strange and low she is to-night," reflected the landlady; "never seen her so low afore, Joe—and she's crying, too; for if there ain't a tear on my cheek. P'raps she's got no work. In that case why doesn't she sit here, instead of frettin' solitary like up there. I wonder what she's got to do so 'ticerler, as she said."

What the woman had got to do so particular was the writing a letter. Not a long one, yet apparently of much difficulty and pain.

Frequently she paused in reflection. Sometimes to give vent to brief, passionate, outbursts of weeping.

Finally, however, it was completed, enveloped, and addressed.

Then, going to a drawer, she took from it a small roll of tissue paper.

They were bank-notes.

Carefully she counted them, made them into a packet, placed them in a separate envelope, addressed, and stamped it.

After that she wrote another letter. It was to her landlady.

In it she placed her few remaining shillings for her rent. Then she leaned her face on her hands, murmuring:

"Now I am without a penny in the world."

The moments slipped by, yet she never moved.

Was she asleep?

Sometimes an occasional sound rose from the street: the shout or shrill whistle of an errand boy, who, though familiar with work, was as yet to care a stranger.

Still the woman never altered her position.

The hours passed, and Big Ben, with deep voice, marked them as they sped.

Half-past ten.

The woman rose. Her face was pale, haggard, her eyes hard and set, her lips compressed. Her every move had that quiet decision that shows a set resolve.

Once more she put on her bonnet and thin shawl, took up one letter and the packet, leaving that addressed to the landlady where it was; gave one lingering glance round the room, blew out the meagre light, quitted the room, and softly descended the stairs.

The voices of her landlady and her "good man" sounded in the parlour.

The woman paused a second, then crept stealthily past, let herself out of the street-door, closed it noiselessly after her, and hurried away never to return.

Having posted the letter and packet she held her shawl more tightly around her, and, with quicker tread, proceeded in the direction of—her destiny.

CHAPTER XII.

TWO WOMEN.

AURICE BURGOYNE had no need to tell his beautiful wife to look her best. Catherine fully intended to, but the intention did not result from the smallest atom of vanity.

Fond and true, she cared not what others thought of her, so long as she pleased her husband's eyes; or rather, would not have cared but for that husband's sake.

The world declared Maurice had ruined himself by marrying beneath him. His friends, one and all, regarded the union as a *mésalliance*.

Hence, devoted to her husband, Catherine eagerly sought to make herself appear worthy of the sacrifice he had made.

It must be owned she had small difficulty. Her tall figure, rounding into the dignity of womanhood, her well-cut, delicate features, the sweet expression, the sunny smile that concealed the firmness of the small lips and rounded chin, the wealth of thick golden tresses, plaited around the head, adorned by one natural flower, presented a picture with which few would not have been struck.

Maurice Burgoyne's eyes sparkled with fond admiration as she advanced to receive and be introduced to his friends.

Yet not more full of admiration were his than his guests'—certainly not than Captain Everitt Melton's.

"By Jove!" he reflected, as he bowed low before her, "what a splendid woman! What sweetness, yet what a presence! And," as his dark eyes dwelt on her, "she even yet has not reached perfection. At thirty she will be handsomer than at twenty; at forty she will be irresistible, for she will rule as well as fascinate."

The opinion hastily formed by this man of the world was confirmed during the half-hour's chat before dinner, which, with that quiet assurance the captain possessed, he devoted exclusively to his young hostess, leaving the Hon. Launce Linden to be entertained by Maurice.

The latter was rather delighted than otherwise.

"Melton is struck," he thought. "To-morrow he will make all Clubland sound with praise of my darling. Men will envy me instead of blame. Never has Cathie looked better."

And never before had the young wife sought so much to appear so.

Flattered by Captain Melton's attention, eager to make an impression on her husband's friends, she talked her best, displaying all the lively brilliancy of her nature, in total ignorance of the fire she was awakening in the dark unprincipled heart of her companion, that the smile in his dark eyes hid a light dangerous to a woman's happiness.

"Good heavens!" he thought, contemplating her animated face as she conversed, "what might I not have done, what been, had such a woman loved me!"

Seated on the couch, bending slightly forward, Catherine's dress close to him, her bright, pure, innocent eyes upon him, was it wonderful he should forget or never dream of contrasting with his present surroundings that pale, haggard, once pretty woman, whose appearance had startled him in the Knightsbridge-road, who now sat alone, motionless, thinking, in her wretched garret!

"Had we met," he proceeded mentally, "why should she not have loved? Why should she not love me even now?"

If Captain Everitt Melton's character has not been fully shown previously this last sentence will declare it plainly.

Under his friend's roof, about to sit at his friend's board, he could calmly contemplate making the attempt of winning the affection of his friend's wife.

How ignorant was Catherine, as leaning on his arm he led her to the dining-room, of the evil thoughts in the heart of this handsome, pleasant, amusing man.

Could she but have divined half the truth, with what horror would she have shrunk from him—how she would have fled for protection to her husband.

Few, however, there are in this world who do not wear a mask over some secret, and Captain Melton had worn so many that they had become as his nature. Hence, unsophisticated in this new sphere in which she moved, it is not matter for surprise that Catherine failed to detect the snake beneath the friend.

If no personal cause for dislike exist, do we not always care for those who, lively, pleasant, make our dinners and evenings pass off with success instead of failure?

The little dinner of this *partie carrée* was a veritable success. Everybody was in the best spirits, even Launce Linden, now the conversation was general, and Melton did not entirely usurp pretty Mrs. Burgoyne.

In conversation Captain Melton carried off the laurels. Full of anecdote and *on dit* he never let a moment flag.

How, was it possible Mrs. Burgoyne had never heard the *prima* of all *prima donnas*, Nilsson? How fortunate, he had a box for the opera for next week. Would she accept it? And thus—and thus, until Catherine rose and with glowing cheek and bright eyes, went to the drawing-room to await the gentlemen at coffee.

"They do not despise me," she exclaimed exultantly, as she contemplated herself in a large pier-glass. "They will not go away and laugh at Maurice's wife. I have done my best and succeeded. I am sure Maurice, dear Maurice, will be pleased. Done my best," and she broke into a silvery laugh. "There has not been much effort about it. It seems so easy to talk, to amuse and be amused. Words like smiles rise as it were unbidden."

STEPHANIE, HER HEAD BENT, APPARENTLY LISTENING TO MAURICE, NEVER LOST SIGHT OF THOSE OTHER TWO.

No. 4.

Moving to the piano in the fulness of her excitement and great happiness, she began to sing. Never had she sang better.

As the last note died away, a voice said by her side:

"I do not wonder Mr. Burgoyne so rarely visits the opera, when he has so sweet a nightingale at home. Mrs. Burgoyne your voice is exquisite. Nilsson herself——"

"Oh, pray hush in time, Captain Melton," laughed Catherine, rising, "or instead of believing half your flattery I shall discredit all."

She crossed to where the coffee had been placed, laughingly accepting a compliment from Launce Linden on the way, and sitting down filled the delicate Dresden cups.

How the time passed so quickly none could have told, but it had sped amazingly. The hour was near eleven when the guests departed.

"Well," asked Maurice, "how do you like them, Cathie?"

"Very, very much—especially Captain Melton; he knows such a great deal, and is so entertaining," she replied. Then, her hands on his shoulders, her face turned smilingly to his: "And what, Maurice, do you fancy they thought of me?"

"My darling, my queen, my wife," he answered, clasping her to his breast, "you need no reply to that question. To-morrow I shall be one of the most envied men in town. All London will be on the *qui vive* to see the lovely Mrs. Burgoyne."

Naturally, Catherine was the subject of conversation between Launce Linden and Captain Melton as they turned their steps from Kensington. The former's praise far surpassed the latter's. The officer appeared only to agree in his companion's laudatory remarks.

"I don't wonder at Burgoyne risking disinheritance for such a woman, eh, Melton?"

"For such a woman," said the captain, "a man might risk his chance of heaven. There is no woman I have seen to equal her."

"No, egad! She's one you'd like to walk down Regent Street with," put in the honourable, "and be seen at her side in the Row, or in her box at the opera."

Captain Melton smiled. He fully intended that honour and pleasure should be his at least.

An unscrupulous man feels safe in relying upon his resources.

His mind was full of Catherine. Her beauty, her intellect, had affected him like good wine. He felt excited, restless; even the confinement of the hansom they had taken was unbearable. He needed action, exercise, so proposed, on reaching the neighbourhood of St. James's, to continue the way on foot as the night was fine.

"Are you for the club?" asked Melton.

"Not particularly—not at present, at any rate; too early yet for many to be there."

"True. Let us stroll down to the House; Disraeli speaks to-night. Stangrove may admit us to the gallery."

"All right. He's in the Opposition now, but he's bound for the Premiership, you see if he is not."

On reaching the House, however, they found the Leader of the Opposition's speech was not likely to come on until late, so they didn't enter. As they came away two policemen passed carrying a closed stretcher.

"What's up?" remarked Launce Linden, adding; "Let us go and see; anything for excitement."

Captain Melton had no objection, so they followed the policemen.

Soon, down by the bridge, on the bank of the dark rolling river, they perceived a group of figures bending over something in their midst.

Drawing nearer, they saw other policemen were among the group, and that the yellow glimmer of light rising from the centre was from their lanterns.

Was it owing to contrast with that light or some other cause, that the night suddenly seemed to grow darker, darker with a sullen gloom, while the river rolled on with a turbid whispering moan ?

"What's the matter, policeman ?" asked Launce Linden, making his way to the centre, the crowd having made an opening for the officers carrying the stretcher.

"Only a woman drowned, sir !" rejoined the police-man.

As his gaze fell upon the saturated garments, decently arranged by some kind hand, clinging to the figure, awfully displaying its thinness ; on the worn, pale features, now at rest, and around which the long black hair laid heavy and dank, he exclaimed, half-indig-nantly :

"Only ? Is a woman's life of such small moment ? Poor thing ! "

What was that ?

A sound of a low startled cry, an ejaculation close at his elbow.

He turned. It was Captain Melton who stood there. He was bending forward looking at the poor drowned thing at his feet, so that Launce Linden could not see his face.

"It's enough to touch any man," thought the young fellow. "It may strike home to Melton, whose life has been of the gayest."

He little guessed how much it struck home.

Again, within the few weeks, the officer gazed upon the woman he had seen in and tracked from the Knights-bridge-road.

"Is she dead, officer ? " he asked, in a tone strange to himself, though no other had observed it.

"Oh yes, sir, dead enough," was the response. "I 'spect starvation's druved her to it. She's thin enough ; while you see," and he took up the white wet hand, "she's got a weddin' ring on. Now, Joe, let's lift her."

"Come away, Linden," whispered the captain hurriedly, grasping his friend's arm.

"Willingly. It's no pleasant sight. It's so likely to haunt a fellow.

> " One more unfortunate
> Weary of breath,
> Rashly importunate
> Gone to her death.

They're not rightly quoted, I know; but I reckon it about describes the case. Good heavens!" as they passed beneath a gas lamp, "how pale you are, Melton."

"I daresay I am. I own it's given me a turn. It—it is not pleasant—such sights as those. Hullo, here's a hansom, let's take it to the club."

Dead—dead. There was no mistake about it. Dead. Dead by drowning, by—suicide.

Meanwhile the police had raised the unhappy woman on the stretcher, and were about to lift it to their shoulders, when another gentleman appeared on the scene, with the same query. Seeing for himself the facts of the case even before the men replied, he asked :

" Is she dead, poor thing ? "

"Oh yes ; there's little doubt of that."

But the gentleman had bent over the woman, touching her wrist, her heart, her forehead rapidly with his hand, even lifting the white eyelid with its wet fringe of lash. And now he answered :

" There's every doubt about it, my good fellow. There is life in the poor thing. It is probably but a flicker, yet if you hasten, hot water quickly applied, and warm blankets, may bring the flicker to a flame. Make haste—at the first public-house I'll give her some brandy. I am a doctor."

Captain Melton accompanied the Honourable Launce. to the club, but did not remain long there.

Two women had disturbed his usual equanimity that evening. They occupied his mind, and when that was the case the captain never ventured his luck on the green cloth. He went home to bed.

He rose late, and though he looked older, more worn, when he began his toilette, his appearance was younger when he completed it.

Preparing to take his breakfast, he found among the letters on the table one addressed in a caligraphy that brought a scared expression to his features.

He tore off the envelope and read—read a sad, reproachful, womanly epistle. Blame expressed with a gentleness that pierced more keenly than passion. It even touched slightly the man to whom it was addressed. Then followed a sad farewell :

"For ever, Everitt. You and I shall never cross each other's path again. You crossed mine once, and shadowed it for life. It will not last much longer. I am weary of existence, even if I had the means to support it, which I have not. My last pence I expended for the materials to write you this farewell, for by to-morrow I shall no longer exist, and you—the only man I ever loved ; and my love was true—will be free."

Captain Melton put down the letter, lifted up the packet, opened it, and took out the bank-notes it contained.

Slowly he examined them.

"Every single note," he muttered. "She's kept her word. She has not used one, though starving—in penury."

He again took up the letter ; he looked gravely, thoughtfully upon it. Then with a slow laugh, he tore it into fragments, and flung it in the fire.

"Bah ! your news, Harriot, comes late," he remarked, as he drew the toast towards him. "I knew I was free yesterday. Free ! Ah, if only Mrs. Burgoyne were free also ! "

CHAPTER XIII.

STEPHANIE'S FIRST VICTIM.

THE shock that Sir Jaffery had sustained from the knowledge how his son had married had been far severer than Stephanie chose to own to Maurice.

Had he been aware, there was a possibility of his forcing his way into the baronet's presence and pleading for pardon. Were this so his cousin trembled even for her own influence, being certain that after that first violent outburst of passion, Sir Jaffery's heart in secret craved for the son of whom he had been so fond and proud.

It was bitter for the father to look upon the terraces, the woods, the gardens of Mereton Travers, and to reflect that his son, their rightful heir, was disinherited, was to be an outcast from the roof that had sheltered his ancestors.

The blow had fallen with double effect owing to the already delicate state of the baronet's health.

A stronger man, possessing the same feelings, would have taken the matter in his own hands, would have written, though a letter of blame, yet one calculated to bring an answer—it might be an angry one—nevertheless which, by opening a correspondence, would set the seeds of future reconciliation.

But the baronet's weak frame had been prostrated by the shock. Physical and mental energy alike were feeble He shrank from exertion either of brain or body. His ideas, his wishes, he desired those around him to divine and carry out as their own.

He loved his son—he hated his son's wife; but there is little doubt the former would have dominated the latter if Stephanie had really pleaded for her cousin as she made Maurice believe. But with a skilful craftiness, wonderful in one so young, while apparently the son's friend, she widened the breach between him and his father. While her will, her ideas, seemed subservient to Sir Jaffery's, she wound the enfeebled old man round her finger as easily as a skein of silk.

Each day her power augmented.

Each day he relied more on her, he felt her a greater necessity to himself.

Each day his love for her increased, and each day, after the first fortnight, his brain and body became weaker, and his craving after Maurice less.

That his desire had not been understood, that no step had been taken by others towards an attempt at reconciliation, irritated him. He felt he was not only injured but insulted; that nobody but one, "his sweet, self-sacrificing little nurse, Stephanie," cared for him.

The heart that at first had been inclined to soften towards Maurice began to harden under the girl's crafty influence, while his dislike to Catherine grew to fierce hate, abhorrence.

He held her accountable for all the trouble that had swept down on Mereton Travers, and could almost have pitied his son for having been the victim of so designing, selfish, unprincipled a Circe.

Those midnight and most imprudent visits of Maurice to Dingle Cottage had of course reached Sir Jaffery's ears.

They had "slipped out quite innocently from her lips before she was aware," so the girl pleaded with a distressed, half scared, and tearful face.

"She ought not to have spoken of it. What would Maurice think of her?"

"Maurice think of you!" ejaculated Sir Jaffery, much incensed. "Do you then regard him more dearly than me?"

"No, no, uncle," she cried, hastily. "Oh, you know I do not; I hold no one in the world, dear uncle, as I do you—my almost father. Have I not told you all ? Is it not my happiness ever to be with you ? " She slipped her hand in his, he pressed it fondly. " I regretted saying what I did, because—because it was Maurice's secret and the knowledge could do no good ; indeed, I feared it might rather anger you the more against him to think how he could have permitted himself to do such an act, and against her for running the risk of having evil charges levelled at her good name—evil unfounded charges, uncle," with virtuous defence of the young wife, " because he was her husband, and no law in the land could make him other."

" Would to heaven it could," ejaculated the baronet, grasping the arms of the chair passionately with his weak hands. " I'd mortgage Mereton Travers to the last farthing if money might free the idiot from that Circe."

" Maurice is so generous, so honourable."

" So idiotic, rather, to fall a victim to the first designing schemer who lays her nets for him."

" And," put in Stephanie, with an innocent little laugh, " for his money and this fine old estate. Also for the pleasure of one day being Lady Burgoyne. I wonder whether the spirits of the past Lady Burgoynes, all high dames and honourable, will feel very indignant when the portrait of Lady Maurice Burgoyne, *née* Catherine Craw- ford, takes its place amongst theirs in the picture- gallery ? "

" Takes its place ! A likeness of that woman ! " said the baronet, a flush on his pale, aristocratic face. " Do you think I am so lost to the respect I owe my ancestors that I would permit their memory to be so disgraced ? Never—never. If Maurice ever returns here it must be —alone. His wife shall never enter these walls."

Stephanie's own words. She smiled as she heard them.

A feeling of prophetic triumph seemed to irradiate her form.

Sir Jaffery, like herself, could forgive Maurice, not Catherine.

While she had influence over him that determination should never alter. No, the wrong she had endured was too great to be forgiven.

She raised her head quickly, startled by her companion's strange breathing.

The baronet, exhausted by the excitement of his anger, was lying back in his chair very pale, and drawing his breath with difficulty.

In a second Stephanie was by his side, leaning tenderly over him administering restoratives.

After a few minutes Sir Jaffery recovered. A smile spread over his features as, taking his niece's pretty head between his white delicate hands, he drew it down and kissed the soft cheek.

"My gentle little nurse—my sweet angel of consolation, I could have forgiven Maurice had he given me such a daughter-in-law as you, Stephanie. What a happy united home ours would then have been? Had the boy no eyes? Could he not recognise gentleness and sterling worth when he saw it so near him?"

The girl's cheeks were crimson, her breast heaved at her triumph.

Sir Jaffery, gazing at the countenance he imprisoned so close to his own, was struck by its peculiar loveliness. Stephanie's long dark lashes modestly veiled her eyes as she said half mirthfully, half sadly:

"No, uncle, you would have termed that a *mésalliance* too; and you would have been right. Maurice—dear Maurice is worthy a wife so much better in rank and position."

"So I thought—so I intended, child; but in my sorrow —in his disgraceful sacrifice of his name's honour—I have learned your true worth, and I could have wished—— But—there, what is the use of talking. It is too late— too late."

Too late? No, not if she could help it.

Such was the daring, wild thought of Stephanie, as with a pathos beyond words she kissed the old man's hand.

As yet so small foundation had she to go upon—indeed, no foundation at all, save her wild imaginings, that she could not even plan with any certainty. Nevertheless, as she paced the rose-garden that evening she repeated the words :

"It is not too late ; it shall not be. I will part them. I will win his love from her."

Now slightly alarmed by the weakness of Sir Jaffery, she arranged the cushions of his chair, and advised him to rest. With a smile he obeyed his gentle nurse, and before a quarter of an hour, had fallen into a doze.

Seating herself on a low stool, where she could see and not be well seen, Stephanie, her chin on her hand, gazed fixedly at him.

Many were the varying thoughts that flitted through her brain.

How pale, how weak he looked. Supposing he should die. No, that would not do. That—that other will was made, disinheriting Maurice, she knew ; also that without doubt it provided handsomely for her. But that was not what she desired. She wished Maurice might yet be master of Mereton Travers. Before such a thing could be, much had to be done. Sir Jaffery must live. As yet she had taken no step, but she must soon, very soon.

Time had better be no more lost. She need not fear her influence over the baronet weakening now. The more his health declined the stronger it would be.

The shadows of night began to steal about the grounds and into the room, darkening it in the corners to impenetrability, yet the girl sat watching the white aristocratic face that alone was visible, and thinking.

So absorbed was she that she could not resist uttering a startled cry when the baronet suddenly spoke, breaking the stillness.

"Stephanie, in your uncomplaining devotion you render me selfish," said Sir Jaffery. " This life is not natural for you. You are young and beautiful; you need amusement and congenial society. For the last ten minutes I have been watching you."

Stephanie started, a fear at her heart. If she had only chanced to utter some of those thoughts that had been racking her brain aloud?

"And your solitary appearance touched me. Why should your existence be shadowed because Maurice has ruined his? No, Stephanie, from this moment I regard you not only as a daughter in love, but in position. You shall dress, visit, receive, and act as though indeed you were my child. And to commence, 'we will go to London. You shall be introduced to its gaieties."

"Uncle, dear uncle." Stephanie had risen, and now threw her arms round his neck.

She was glad of the darkness more than ever, for she felt she could not have concealed the triumphant expression on her features. Her cheeks were flushed, her eyes bright and sparkling.

It was the very thing she had been longing to do, to go to London. Night after night had she lain awake, seeking to find some plan by which it could be brought about. She was helpless, she could do nothing at Mereton Travers.

But what might she not do when in town, when visiting as a sister that pretty, happy home in Kensington.

"What," said the baronet, patting her cheek, "you are delighted?"

"I cannot tell you how much; I was longing for us to go—not, dear uncle, for the gaieties of London, but to avail ourselves of its talent."

"Talent, Stephanie!"

"Yes, dear uncle, that you might place your health once more in the skilled hands of Sir Adam Clarkson. You are not well; you are not so strong. What, uncle, should I feel were you to be ill?"

"Bless you, Stephanie. Yes, I believe I have your love at any rate. Well, we will kill two birds with one stone; you shall enjoy the gaieties, I the physician. We can start, I suppose, the day after to-morrow."

"Certainly, dear uncle. Now I'll ring for the lights."

That evening she wrote her letter to Maurice, and that evening, pacing the moon-lighted rose-garden, she had exclaimed:

"All goes well—all, all. It is not too late; it shall not be."

The day after the morrow, Sir Jaffery and Stephanie started for London.

CHAPTER XIV.

WEARING A MASK.

"AND so you are very happy, and seeing all the gaieties of town?" said Stephanie Royle in her soft, low, musical tones.

She was seated in the rustic garden-chair on the lawn of the Kensington villa, beneath the branching tree.

By her side was Catherine Burgoyne.

Not the same Catherine that Stephanie had last seen As beautiful—nay, more beautiful; but with a dignity, a self-possession, a consciousness of her own influence upon those around her.

Stephanie Royle, a quick observer of character, saw this, and with satisfaction. This was no longer the humble companion, but a woman, gentle, amiable, feminine enough, yet with a proper self-consciousness and pride. A woman with intellect and spirit.

"She is a woman men will admire, flatter, love," she reflected. "So much the better for me. So much the better, too, that her knowledge of this new society, in which she moves, is as yet but indifferent. If I work with my usual skill, my influence over her shall be as great as it is over my uncle and Maurice. Only for that we must be friends. Her mistrust in me must be removed."

For this end Stephanie had cleverly laid her plans since her arrival in town, which had now been for over a week, and with marked success.

She was a frequent visitor at the villa, and a welcome one, as, for Maurice's sake, Catherine tried to overcome her repugnance to her cousin.

This was the thin end of the wedge.

Stephanie's well-acted amiability and desire to be friends drove it gradually home ; and almost as sisters they sat, on this afternoon, under the shady branches of the tree.

"Happy!" laughed Catherine lightly. "Could I be otherwise? Yes ; and I am seeing London gaieties,—a new experience to me."

"And, Catherine, I perceive a pleasant one," smiled the other.

"Indeed, a very pleasant one," was the response. "I have never known, I fancy, what life was, until Maurice brought me here, Miss Royle."

Whenever Stephanie heard her name uttered by the young wife, a terrible agony pierced her heart, as if a knife, keen and sharp, had been plunged into it.

An agony so great that it seemed to contract all her nerves like a shock of electricity.

The colour of her eyes changed, her lips compressed.

The emotion was so transient as to be unobservable and almost instantaneously she rejoined with well affected gaiety :

"Miss Royle, when am I to be Stephanie, pray, Cousin Catherine?" Then, with a sudden sadness in her beautiful eyes, a touching pathos and pain in her accents, placing her hand on her companion's, she said : "Is it possible that you have not yet forgiven me?"

Catherine impulsively clasped both hands over the other's, and bending, kissed her.

"Forgiven you, Stephanie? How could I do otherwise. Do not I also need some pardon, cousin?"

"'Stephanie,' 'cousin,'" said the girl joyously. "At last. Now I feel indeed I am pardoned, that all is forgotten, which being so, let neither of us refer again to the subject. We may easily find pleasanter—the people whom you have met, for instance, those you like, and those you do not. Perhaps some of Maurice's friends may be mine."

Catherine was easily beguiled into the topic, and with ready eloquence, marked by both wit and gaiety, she described those whom she had met, adding her own opinions, likes, and dislikes of them.

"The Honourable Launce Linden," remarked Stephanie; "yes, I have seen him.   But I do not think I have even heard of Captain Melton.   What kind of man is he?"

"One of the pleasantest, best informed, and agreeable friends of Maurice's I have yet seen," rejoined Catherine earnestly; "I gave him the preference over Mr. Linden the first time we met."

"And I would lay a wager of a box of gloves that Captain Melton returned the good opinion he had created, by admiring his lovely hostess."

"Captain Melton can flatter like most men," smiled Catherine with a pretty shrug of her shoulders.   "But he can do more, he can entertain and amuse.   Altogether he is very good and kind; the very first opera I ever saw I owe to him."

"I must make his acquaintance," smiled Stephanie; "not difficult, I daresay, as no doubt he is a very frequent guest here!"

"Very, three or four times a week," proceeded Catherine, innocently oblivious how her companion was urging her to talk upon the subject of Captain Melton, and how as she drank in every word was piecing all together, and reflecting how, or whether, they would be useful to her scheme.

So the time slipped by, Catherine chatting in the best spirits, Stephanie storing up every word, when they were interrupted by the sound of footsteps on the hard firm gravel.

As they lifted their eyes in the direction, two gentlemen came round the corner of the house.

Catherine burst into a merry, musical laugh.   "Speak of—no—speak of angels and you'll see their wings," she whispered; "you will soon make the acquaintance of Captain Melton, for this is he with Maurice."

She rose as she spoke; Stephanie did the same, falling a step or two behind as the gentlemen advanced.

"She might have made the first quotation," she reflected, her eyes, shadowed by her lashes, intently fixed on the officer; "*that* man has very little of the angel about him," then she gave a sudden start.

One rapid glance shot from her eyes before they were lowered for a brief space.

Only for a brief space.

Speedily they were raised again, and in all the time that followed, under cover of the long, dark lashes, she watched Captain Melton—watched, and evidently with satisfaction, for her spirits rose into gaiety.

The introduction over, the four for awhile stood chatting on the lawn, then, somehow—was it Stephanie's doing? It might have been, yet so done none observed it—they paired off, the cousins together, Captain Melton with Catherine, pacing different paths.

Stephanie, her head bent, apparently listening, all interested, to Maurice, never lost sight of those other two.

She smiled when Catherine's musical laugh rang, as it did very frequently, on the air.

"How happy Catherine is!" she remarked on one of these occasions.

"Is she not?" answered Maurice, enthusiastically, his eyes fondly regarding his beautiful wife on the other path. "And Melton is such a capital fellow—full of anecdote, never letting talk flag."

"He is most fascinating, I can see that," said Stephanie, quietly. "I should think exceedingly so to our sex, who, despite what our enemies say, have brain enough to appreciate it in you gentlemen."

"Brain enough!" laughed Maurice. "My dear Stephe, if you were to be taken as the standard of women, our sex, in the matter of intellect, would fly up to the beam."

So they talked until once again they joined company, and went in to Catherine's afternoon tea.

During the slight refreshment, Stephanie was the most silent, consequently the most observant.

After the tea, Captain Melton took his leave. To Catherine he smilingly said "*Au revoir*" as he lightly kissed her hand, for, with her permission, he would look in at her box at the theatre that night.

Almost immediately after he had taken his departure, Stephanie's fly was announced.

She rose at once, excusing herself from staying to dinner under the plea that Sir Jaffery was not so well that day.

"That is," she smiled, as Maurice handed her into the vehicle, "he is actually as well as ever, only a little irritable, and does not like to be too long alone, fancying himself neglected."

Then she waved her tiny gloved hand, and, as the fly drove off, sank back on the cushions with a strange expression on her features, which soon betrayed deep, earnest thought.

Sir Jaffery had placed a carriage at his niece's special service, but she naturally did not use it when she made her visits to Maurice.

She had no desire for the baronet to learn of them, and feared the chatter of servants.

That the intelligence might reach him through another channel was not in any way probable, for Sir Jaffery never left his own suite of apartments and saw few friends.

Reaching Regent Circus, she dismissed the fly and proceeded some little way on foot.

Twilight was descending; the shops were being lighted.

Stephanie stopped before one—a chemist's. Looking in, she perceived there was no one there but the assistant behind the counter. She drew her veil more about her face and entered.

"Would you," she said, taking a paper from her purse, and handing it over the counter, "if you please, let me have this?"

The man took it and read the writing.

It was but one ingredient, but a doctor's signature was to it.

He bowed an affirmative and retired to the end of the shop, where the girl, watching with a slight curl of her red lips, saw him refer to a book.

She knew it was a medical directory. Evidently satisfied, he returned, took out a small bottle from a drawer, then he reached a large labelled bottle from one of the shelves.

As he poured from one into the other, he said :

"I suppose, madam, you know the properties of this drug ? It is a dangerous one in ignorant or unskilled hands."

"Perfectly," she replied quietly. "It is to soothe irritability arising from excitement or latent mania."

"Yes," as he corked the bottle, labelled it, placed it in paper, and sealed the ends by aid of the tiny gas jet. "Great care is required in measuring the drops. A drop-glass is very useful. Perhaps you have one ?"

"I have not ; but they for whom this is needed have. Thank you," as she paid. "Good evening," and she passed from the shop.

At the next stand she took a cab to the end of Portland Place, alighted, and proceeded to Sir Jaffery Bugroyne's town residence.

On being admitted, she did not go to her uncle, but straight to her room.

Locking the door, she took out the phial, removed the paper wrapping, carefully rubbed off the label, destroying both by burning.

Opening her desk, she put the phial in a secret drawer and locked it.

This to her was apparently a relief, for she drew a deep breath as one freed suddenly from anxiety, as she sat down on the chair placed ready before the handsomely-appointed toilet-table, with its gold-mounted dressing-case, mother-of-pearl backed brushes and hand-mirrors.

For a space the girl was singularly thoughtful.

Then lifting her eyes, beholding her reflection, she broke into a low, rippling laugh.

" Really," she murmured, " it seems as if matters form to my hand. Catherine Burgoyne likes Captain Melton very much. He is amusing, entertaining, good, kind, and places her under small obligations. On Captain Melton's part, he is deeply in love with Maurice's wife, and Captain Melton is a bad, bold man. How do I know that? I suppose by intuition."

Again she laughed, and rang for her maid to dress her for dinner.

CHAPTER XV.

THE IMPLIED APPOINTMENT.

HE renowned, world-known physician had seen Sir Jaffery, and had had a private interview with Stephanie Royle, whose tender solicitude and clear intellect in grasping his remarks quite charmed him.

The baronet's indisposition was nothing serious. That is, there was no danger, at present, of its shortening life. The shock he had received and the violent anger following thereupon, had assuredly been the cause of his present physical and mental prostration.

The system, as it were, was taking rest, enforcing it. All that could be done was to keep it from any further shock or irritation.

There was a certain amount of cerebral nervousness, as of the whole nervous system, which must be overcome by degrees, with cheerful society, and keeping all cause of irritability from the patient.

"Be assured, sir, that shall be my care," said Stephanie.

"I am assured of it, my dear young lady," responded the physician, pressing her hand with quite a fatherly pressure. "Do not be down-hearted yourself," for tears had glittered in the girl's eyes. "It may take time, but your uncle will recover."

Gratefully, Stephanie thanked the speaker, received his prescription, another kindly pressure of the soft, white hand, then saw the door close upon him.

As it did so, a smile flitted across the girl's lips.

"He is a very great physician," she murmured. "There is no doubting that. Yet——" She paused abruptly. The smile again crossed her face, then was gone.

"He is in no danger," she reflected as she ascended to her uncle's apartments. "I am glad of that."

Stephanie did not maintain her influence over Sir Jaffery without much sacrifice of her own personal comfort. She devoted to him hours which she would much have liked to have spent more agreeably, for the baronet was not a very lively companion.

Possessed by a strange lassitude, devoid of even the desire to rouse himself, annoyed by any society save hers and his valet's, he would sit for hours content in doing nothing, for thought itself apparently was in abeyance.

The only matter he urged with any persistency was, that his "attentive little nurse" should go about and be amused. Yet she knew and he confessed that he was strangely nervous when she was absent.

"But why, dear uncle?" she asked one day. "All that I can do, Sidford can, and I am sure would."

"Yes, yes; Sidford is a good servant, my dear, good and attentive. I've not forgotten him in my will," answered the baronet, speaking in low, quick sentences, and his eyes moving restlessly as was now habitual with him when at all excited. "But—he is only a servant."

"Why should he be other, uncle?"

"I don't want him other, but—but if *he* came here, how could Sidford, only a servant, keep him from this room—keep him from me?"

"Keep who, uncle?"

"Maurice," with fretful fear. "He is in London?"

"Yes."

"Supposing he were to try to force his way to see me. Sidford could not prevent him, but you might, and I couldn't see him, I couldn't, I'm not strong enough for the interview. Stephanie, it would kill me."

"Have no fear, uncle; Maurice will not attempt to come," she said decisively.

"No, no," with quick revulsion of feeling, "what am I longer to him? What does he care if I am ill—wretchedly ill!"

"A great deal, I should hope, uncle, and do believe. But remember there is a greater influence than ours exerted over him now. An influence to which in comparison ours is very weak."

"Yes, yes, yes, I know; that woman's—the one he calls his wife. Some Scotch, over-the-border marriage, I suspect. Still, I wish he was not in London, I wish he was not."

A sudden light as of the lifting of a veil had come over Stephanie's face.

How and where had that secret marriage been performed?

She had never thought of that.

It had taken place while Catherine had been old Mrs. Winburg's companion; consequently, as Stephanie knew, she had never been a whole day absent.

It could not, therefore, have been an "over-the-border" marriage.

Again, the ceremony could not have been performed at any church, or by any clergyman resident near Mereton Travers, for Maurice and his name were known for miles round.

How, where, then had it? Had she at last found a key that would be of immense value in the scheme she was laying?

She must find out.

With unusual tenderness she kissed Sir Jaffery that day when she left him to his doze.

His words had been like a revelation. They seemed to have opened to her the doors of success.

On Stephanie leaving, she summoned Sidford, her uncle's valet, one who had grown iron-grey in his master's service.

"Sir Jaffery appears rather excited this afternoon," she remarked in the pleasant tones she generally adopted when speaking to inferiors, "but I have given him his medicine, Sidford, and now he feels inclined to doze."

"Yes, Miss Royle," replied the valet respectfully. "Have you any directions to leave, miss?"

"None," smiled Stephanie. "To ask you to give Sir Jaffery every attention, would be ungrateful to one who has shown the devotion you have, Sidford."

"Thank you, miss. Sir Jaffery's a good master, and I've tried to be a good servant."

"With success, Sidford. You will not find either my uncle or those who love him unappreciative of your goodness."

The valet again bowed respectfully; then, as she passed him, going into the corridor, he closed the door of the ante-room, and crossed slowly to that of the apartment where Sir Jaffery was sleeping.

"It's strange," he muttered reflectively, passing his hand over his chin, "but I don't like her. What's more, I mistrust her. I daren't say so, or all the household, who are her devoted slaves, and think she only lacks wings to be an angel, would be about my ears; while, despite my long services, I believe Sir Jaffery would dismiss me on the spot. I hate, or rather I've no confidence in people who always address you with a smile, and in the same tone of voice."

He ceased as he entered the other apartment. Softly closing the door, he approached the sleeper. Sir Jaffery's head leaned back against the chair, and slightly inclined to the shoulder.

His face was very wan.

The muscles were relaxed slightly; the expression on the features, the pose of the whole figure, especially that of the long, slender, white hands, were eloquent of intense physical exhaustion.

"Well, such a big physician as he is ought to know best, I suppose," reflected the valet dubiously, continuing the same train of thought, "but it's strange to me, very."

Moving to a side-table, mechanically he took up the medicine-glass with an air of hardly being conscious of what he did.

"AND SWORN ALLIES," HE ADDED, ONCE MORE KISSING THE SMALL HAND SHE EXTENDED.

No 5.

"I wonder why Miss Royle always gives Sir Jaffery his medicine in the morning. She never misses. Nonsense," and he placed the glass quickly on the table, "what an old idiot I am. Just because, beautiful as she is, I don't like her. What advantage would her uncle's death be to her? Rather the contrary, for if he disinherits Mr. Maurice, and makes his nephew his heir, Miss Royle would have to go packing from Mereton Travers. Poor Mr. Maurice, I wish I could help him back to his own."

With a sigh the valet took a seat at a side-table, and began a perusal of the morning papers.

Meanwhile, Stephanie, hastily dressing, started for the Kensington villa. She was impatiently anxious to solve the mystery of the how and the when her cousin had married.

"If I can find Catherine alone," she reflected as she crossed the park. "She is so guileless and unsophisticated that I can get everything out of her, that is, if there be anything to get."

On coming up the road she was annoyed to see a saddle-horse, in charge of a groom, outside the green door.

"Can it be Maurice's? If so, he is going out. Yet will he do so if I go in?" she reflected. "For once I want him absent. Still, why should I not obtain what I desire as well from either or both of them?"

"No," she proceeded as she still advanced, "that is not Maurice's horse; I remember his is a far lighter bay. It is a visitor, an early one; no doubt it is some friend of Maurice's. I may be able yet to have my *tete-a-tete* with Catherine."

From the neat housemaid she learned that Mrs. Burgoyne was at home, but not alone; Captain Melton having just called.

"Captain Melton," thought Stephanie with a quick heart-beat, then she added, "and Mr. Burgoyne?"

"Mr. Burgoyne went out early, miss," replied the servant, moving towards the morning-room.

Maurice absent and Captain Melton making a *tete-a-tete* visit to Catherine! Matters were working well, truly.

Stephanie hesitated a second. Should she let the housemaid announce her? Should she prevent her doing so?

She quickly decided the former. To retreat might cause Catherine surprise; possibly open her eyes, if they were now unopen, that it was hardly *comme il faut* for a young and pretty wife to receive early visits from gentlemen, or for gentlemen to stay long if so received.

"Miss Royle," announced the parlour-maid, opening the door.

And Stephanie, bright, smiling, amiable, passed in, her eyes, with a strange delight, noting the two persons already present.

Catherine Burgoyne was seated at the piano, her hands resting on, yet not pressing, the keys; her head was slightly turned over her shoulder as she addressed her companion, who bent forward with a most flattering attention.

"Excellent!" reflected Stephanie. "If Maurice could but have a glimpse of so charming a picture."

"Stephanie! most welcome, dear!" exclaimed Catherine, rising from the piano and advancing, her voice and manner totally free of constraint and full of sincerity.

The officer had stepped back with a contraction of the brow and bite of the lip, which though transient did not escape the visitor.

"Is it not kind of Captain Melton?" proceeded the young wife. "The other evening I was speaking of a song I much desired to possess, my mother having sung it. Maurice has tried many places and failed. They said it was out of print, but Captain Melton——"

"Was so fortunate," put in the officer, bowing, "to come across a copy, with which he had the pleasure of hastening to Mrs. Burgoyne."

"An equal pleasure to both, I am sure," smiled Stephanie. "You like music, Captain Melton, and Mrs.

Burgoyne sings divinely. There was music in Eden as well as flowers, and both have descended to earth to serve our purpose."

The officer's dark eyes darted a keen glance at the speaker. Her voice was in tone, as her face in expression, innocent enough, yet surely there had been a deep, a subtle meaning in her words.

Had she discovered the captain's secret?

"Confound her!" muttered the officer beneath his breath. "What can surpass a woman's quickness in perceiving a man's love for another. Question," he proceeded, *sotto voce:* "am I to regard her as friend or foe? If friend, well. If foe, which I doubt, why then," and a smile flitted over his features, "I have her secret too, and it must be seen which of us is the stronger."

At that moment Stephanie, raising her eyes, encountered the glittering ones of the officer. They seemed to possess the fascination, the danger, of the serpent.

The girl started, an instant her colour faded; but in a second she recovered herself.

"Catherine," she said, "will you not let me hear the song that you are so glad to have?"

"Certainly," was the ready response.

As the young wife took her place again at the piano, Captain Melton moved towards Stephanie and with a peculiar light on his face, said in a whisper:

"When you entered, Miss Royle, Mrs. Burgoyne and I were speaking of a young man who had killed himself owing to an unrequited love."

Stephanie felt there was a hidden significance in these words.

A moment her heart fluttered, but quickly, with a slight shrug of her shoulders, she said in well acted carelessness:

"Are people still so romantic as that, Captain Melton?"

"So it appears with some."

"And what would be your advice in such a case?" she enquired, meeting his glance steadily.

"To live—and make oneself—either man or woman, beloved by those they desire," he answered, looking into her eyes. "To kill oneself is the act of a savage, an idiot; an act that astonishes the crowd, and makes wise people only feel contempt. In love as in war, Miss Royle, one should think of victory, not death."

Stephanie grew interested.

"And the means of obtaining victory, Captain Melton?"

"That," he smiled, "is my secret."

A new sensation possessed Stephanie. She saw power in this man.

She knew his secret. Had he divined hers? If so, why should there not be a compact between them?

If they had the same end in view, why not work together?

"I should like much to know it," she rejoined quietly; "is it not possible?"

For a space of silence they looked at each other.

Then, as Catherine's full voice was dying softly away on the last notes of her song, the officer said with intention:

"It will be a fine afternoon, and the Row, at about five o'clock, will be pretty full." As he concluded he moved quickly to Catherine's chair.

"I understand," reflected Stephanie resolutely; "rain, storm, or whirlwind, I will be in the Row at five."

Then she also moved to the piano to add her praise to the officer's. Two merciless fates spinning the destiny of their victim, the poor unsuspecting, happy young wife.

CHAPTER XVI.

STEPHANIE OBTAINS VALUABLE INFORMATION.

"CAPTAIN Melton is really very agreeable," remarked Stephanie, when the officer, abandoning all hope of a further *tete-a-tete* with Catherine, had taken his leave.

"Is he not? I know no one more so save one, and he, of course, I need not specify!" laughed the wife, taking up some crewel-work.

She sat at one end of the softly-cushioned couch, Stephanie at the other.

"At least, not to me," smiled Stephanie. "Maurice, of course, has no equal; that is, I suppose, what every wife imagines. Each husband is a *rara avis*, or the woman is wise enough to pretend so."

"Ah, yes, there are wives and wives; but there is no pretence on my part, Stephanie. Maurice is the best, the kindest of men."

"Had you not been of that opinion, my dear, you would hardly have sacrificed so much for him."

"Sacrifice!" ejaculated the wife raising her eyes in surprise. "I! The sacrifice was all on Maurice's part."

"So far as money went, probably, but is money everything in this world? Believe me, Catherine," and Stephanie laughed softly, "I am too vain, or too appreciative of the rights of my sex to imagine a man commits a sacrifice by forfeiting that most degrading of earthly possessions, to obtain the woman he loves, always providing that the woman be worthy."

"Always providing that," remarked Catherine gaily.

"As, my love, in your case," continued Stephanie, nodding her head playfully. "How circumstances make, or I should rather say, crush people. You, as old Mrs. Winburg's companion, are totally different to you now as Maurice's wife."

"I am," smiled Catherine; "that old past existence was slightly depressing. I felt like one living in a well, conscious of power, strength, and the world beyond, but not able to push off the lid and be free."

"Maurice did that for you; and the poor companion blossoms forth into a brilliant member of society at whose feet gentlemen not as fortunate as Maurice humbly lay their devotion."

Catherine burst into a silvery amused laugh.

"Stephanie, what a flatterer you are."

"Truth is not flattery," remarked the other with amusing sententiousness. "Catherine mark my words: you are born to shine, to be a star in society. Maurice will be known as that beautiful, clever Mrs. Burgoyne's husband; hence he has made no sacrifice."

"No," and mirth sparkled in the wife's eyes; "that was all on my side."

"Exactly," was the grave response.

"In mercy, how so?"

"In consenting to a secret union. In allowing yourself to be married in the dark as it were," proceeded Stephanie, her pulses beginning to flutter with nervous anxiety as she neared the goal to which she had been so skilfully approaching. "You sacrificed a woman's greatest right, her greatest pride—to be led to the altar by him to whom from that moment she devotes herself, in the light of day, in the face of all the world."

"You are right, Stephanie. That is a just pride in a woman, but I would have sacrificed that and more for Maurice. As to being married in the dark," a whimsical expression in her eyes, "it was not *quite* in the dark, but very nearly."

Stephanie Royle raised her brows interrogatively.

"However do you mean, dear?" she said innocently.

"'Nearly in the dark.' I have often wondered how you

managed it, considering the close attendance you had to show old Mrs. Winburg. Do you mind telling me?" with naive interest. "You know every woman likes to hear about weddings, especially of the secret or runaway description."

"Certainly," was the ready response.

Catherine dropped her work on her lap, and Stephanie, assuming the most innocent of interested expressions, leaned slightly forward, really eagerly curious.

"When Maurice wished that we should be married," began the wife, "I urged delay. Why I asked him, could he not be patient and wait?"

"For what?" asked Stephanie simply. "For Sir Jaffery's death, when, as his own master, Maurice could act as he pleased?"

"Oh no," exclaimed Catherine with almost horror in her features. "Wait for Sir Jaffery's death! We never thought of such a thing. We were far, far too happy to desire others to suffer. No, Mrs. Winburg had more than once spoken of going for a change, either to Edinburgh or Liverpool, in both of which places she had relations; when she did that she had promised me a holiday for a few days. I wanted Maurice to wait until then, but he would not listen, especially when Mrs. Winburg put off her going from the coming spring to autumn, then from autumn to spring.

"'She will never go,' said Maurice. 'She is like a limpet; once taken firm hold of a place, it will want no end of force to remove her. Besides, what a heap of other circumstances may happen. Catherine, you say you love me, that my happiness is dear to you; then, as I can never be happy until I know you are my wife, that no power in this world can part us, will you not yield to my prayer?'

"What could I say?" pleaded Catherine.

"Nothing but yes," answered Stephanie in a low tone, for she found it difficult to conceal her emotion and the mad and jealous passion this recital aroused within her breast.

She pictured to herself those two together. The woman's head on the man's breast, his arm around her. She saw her face raised to his, the cheek reddened perhaps from the kisses with which he had strengthened his argument. She saw his eyes—the eyes whose glance had thrilled her to the soul, making her dizzy and faint with the hope of a great happiness—fixed with all the fervent glow of love upon the woman before her—the woman she hated.

Her face paled, then burned. Her throat seemed to swell as she listened. Her small hands tightened convulsively from her effort to maintain the calm interest she had assumed.

"It was 'yes' I said," proceeded Catherine. I had not the strength to be firm, and yet, for his sake, I often blamed myself for yielding.

"'But Maurice,' I asked when it was decided, 'how is it possible for us to be married secretly in Valeshire, where you are so well known? And Mrs. Winburg would never spare me long enough to go any distance.'"

"'I have thought of all that,' he laughed. 'No, Catherine, I have not left you a loophole to creep out of. I have had but one confidant in my love: Robert Ford, my old college chum. He is coming on a brief visit to Mereton, and he shall unite us.'"

Stephanie started. Her dark eyes seemed to dilate, quickly she bent them on her lap.

"'But,' I asked, 'is he a clergyman?'"

"'Of course he is. In a brief space he is to have a church of his own, and preach to the edification of his congregation. One day, I have promised him he shall have the living of Mereton Travers. That is, when it is mine to give.'

"So," proceeded Catherine, "Mr. Ford came, and one night, very late, with the moon for our light, in one of the glades of the Mereton Travers Woods, Maurice and I were made man and wife."

The speaker's voice had grown low and soft as she ended, and there was a thrill of emotion in it as she recalled this scene, when, the shadow of the trees on the grass flecked with pale moonlight, she, trembling and nervous, stood with Maurice Burgoyne before Robert Ford, whose almost whispered reading of the words apparently yet rang in her ears.

It had been an impressive scene; it was an impressive remembrance.

A sudden silence had fallen on the two. Catherine broke it.

Bursting into a musical laugh she exclaimed:

"It was very romantic, was it not?"

"Very," responded Stephanie, making a supreme effort to smile; then she added: "Hark! is not that Maurice's voice?"

"Indeed, yes. It is he," cried the young wife, springing up.

She advanced quickly to the window, which stood partly open; then stepping out, went to meet her husband.

No sooner was Stephanie Royle alone than she rose from the sofa, her slight form quivering, her eyes sparkling, her face flushed with triumph, with a cruel exultation.

"She is not married; she is not, I am sure of it," she cried mentally.

"I am certain that when Robert Ford came to Mereton Travers he was not even ordained. Has Maurice purposely deceived her, or is he himself ignorant? But I must not be too sure; I must get wiser opinion upon the matter. But if I am right—if I be only right"—and she raised her arms in ecstasy—"what a fall for you, proud, happy Mrs. Maurice Burgoyne! Burgoyne? No; *Miss* Catherine Crawford. Oh, I must find out—I *must* find out! If Maurice has done this intentionally or no—providing that I am right, and there be a flaw in the marriage chain—how easy will it make my work! *She* Maurice's wife? No, no—never!"

She dropped back on the couch laughing a laugh terrible to hear, so lacked it generous mirth; rather in its hysteria did it verge on tears.

Was her surmise correct? Had the doubt ever crossed Maurice's mind?

Stephanie hastily recovered her habitual expression, for she heard her cousin approaching.

"Stephanie here!" she heard Maurice exclaim, the evident pleasure betrayed in his voice sending a thrill through her. "That is good. We can tell her the news at once."

News. What news?

Stephanie Royle moved hastily to the window. At the moment it was pushed wider open and Maurice entered.

There was a bright shine in his eyes as they met hers. His hand pressed hers lingeringly.

In those happy bygone days he had trusted in her, had found support in her, as men will in a woman's intellect when it is stronger than their own, and Stephanie felt he trusted in her now—nay, probably more so than in the past.

"How is my father?" he asked.

"Better," she responded cheerfully. "The improvement is slow, but it is improvement. The doctor yet, however, forbids the least excitement. No subject that might create it must be touched upon, or he will not answer for the consequences."

Maurice dropped her hand and turned away with a sigh.

"But your news," questioned Stephanie, gaily, to change the conversation. "I heard you when you were in the garden say you had some."

"Ah!" he exclaimed, facing round again, the cloud gone, the smile returned. "You see, Stephanie, Catherine and I never had a honeymoon. I don't understand any reason why we should be done out of it, so I am proposing that we should take it now."

"Take it now!" That, of course, meant Maurice intended leaving London.

The cloud that had quitted his face appeared to have settled upon hers.

Was Catherine to escape her when all things apparently were going so well?

"Really?" she managed to articulate quietly; "and where do you think of going, Maurice?"

"To the American's Paradise," he laughed.

"Paris," broke in Catherine, who was leaning on his arm. "Oh, is it not delightful?"

"For you," responded Stephanie, with a forced smile; "but for me, I am left in London desolate."

"What a pity, Stephanie, you cannot come also," remarked Maurice. "You could not, of course, leave my father."

"Leave Sir Jaffery? I would not for fifty Parises, Maurice," she answered quickly.

Moved by an impulse of gratitude, he took her hand, saying, as he touched it with his lips:

"May heaven reward you, my darling, for your kind devotion to him."

When Stephanie, soon after, thinking of that tacitly arranged rendezvous in the park, took her departure, husband and wife alike spoke in praise of her.

"By the way," smiled Catherine, as seated side by side she playfully twisted the end of Maurice's long moustache into a stiff point, "I told her to-day about our romantic marriage, dear; she was much entertained."

"You told her! Why?" he asked, for him almost sharply, while the expression of his face grew grave.

"Because she asked, Maurice," with sudden eagerness, her hands on his shoulder. "Why do you cease to smile? Are you angry with me, dearest?"

"Angry with you, my love?" and he bent his face fondly to hers. "No. How could I be. Still, there's no need to talk about our hide-and-seek wedding—and—and —well, I don't know why—I wish you had not told Stephanie."

"Do you know, Maurice," laughed the young wife, " I fancy if Stephanie had asked you instead of me—despite your looking so grave—you would have told her quite as readily, so do not blame me."

"I might," he smiled, as he looked down on the pretty face nestling on his bosom.

Yet he did not believe he should. Nevertheless, how could he blame this fair being, whose heart gave every throb-beat in unison with his own, who was dearer to him than all the world beside.

Meanwhile, with moody brow, Stephanie Royle pondered, during her way homeward, upon Maurice's news.

They were going away for a month, perhaps months.

If she could only have gone too.

Why should not she ?

The means flashed into her brain like an inspiration.

Sir Jaffery was nervous of being in London because Maurice was there.

The physician had said travelling might do the baronet far more good than harm in giving matter to occupy his mind.

Supposing she persuaded him to go to Paris ?

He need never know Maurice and his wife were there.

If he discovered it later and charged her with deceit, she could plead how it was for his and Maurice's sake— she being hopeful to bring about a reconciliation.

She knew then he would easily pardon the deception.

"I will try," she reflected. "At present I must keep my thoughts clear for the meeting with Captain Melton. It's a bold step I'm taking, but I will not flinch ; and that settled, I will arrange this other matter."

CHAPTER XVII.

AN EVIL COMPACT.

HE afternoon had not proved so fine as the morning. A cold wind bringing a mist with it had arisen, and when Stephanie Royle entered the Row, attended merely by her groom it was thinning considerably.

It was not quite *en regle* for a girl of her age and position to appear in so public a place so poorly escorted. But as yet Stephanie knew very few people in London, while the veil she wore was of a thick texture.

As she cantered over the tan, her dark eyes scanned every equestrian in search of Captain Everitt Melton. Surely he would come.

Come? Of course.

She had not been there many minutes before she beheld him, handsome, elegant, aristocratic.

Almost at the same time he perceived her, and rode forward against the stream to meet her, raising his hat in greeting.

"Miss Royle!" he exclaimed, simulating surprise. "Really, I am——"

"Pray, Captain Melton," she interrupted, with quiet decision, "spare yourself the trouble of pretending an astonishment you do not feel. You knew I was coming here, and at this hour."

"As you please, Miss Royle," he smiled, amused at her honesty.

"Yes," she added, "you are aware I have come to continue the conversation commenced this morning."

The officer was struck by her open confession. So bold, so daring.

He gazed upon her in admiration, and at the moment, with the brilliant light in her eyes, the deep rose flush on her cheeks, she was wondrously beautiful.

Captain Melton thought he had never seen any girl more so, though she was not his style. Yet his pulses beat, under the passion throb at his unprincipled heart, as he confessed it would be by no means disagreeable to be the confidant, to hold the secret, of so splendid a being, and to have this young girl herself in his power.

He moved the animal he rode a trifle closer. The expression of his eyes grew ardent, as well as admiring.

A woman readily understands such signs.

Stephanie took no further heed than to draw her horse slightly away.

At present, she knew no fear. She held herself her companion's equal. It was secret for secret.

"Captain Melton," she said, "before we proceed to other matters, it is best we should comprehend each other. The fact of my meeting you here, you who to me are almost a stranger, is open to a false construction. I admit it; but you perfectly are aware why I have come."

"Perfectly," he smiled lightly, bending over his horse's neck. "From the conversation that took place this morning at Mr. Burgoyne's you desire——"

"Your friendship," and she extended her small gloved hand towards him.

They had quitted the Row by, it appeared, mutual understanding, and were under the trees.

The Captain gallantly pressed his lips to the girl's slender fingers.

"Decidedly," he rejoined, "let us be friends. Why not?"

"I see no reason," she remarked, looking steadily into his eyes, "why we should not be the best."

"You shall find me a devoted one," he answered.

"I have long needed such," continued the girl, fearlessly bringing her horse closer, "and the first moment

I met you, Captain Melton, I knew I had found what I sought—a fascinating and an unscrupulous man."

"You are flattering, Miss Royle," he laughed, but it was constrainedly. "I thank you for so good a character."

"I need none. Were you not what I say I should not be here," was the calm response. "You love Catherine Burgoyne."

"You say so," he remarked, raising his shoulders.

"And know. Do not seek to deceive me, Captain Melton. It is useless. I do not say you have no right to love her—my cousin's wife. On the contrary, such a friend as you is what I require—one who knows the human heart, one who allows no scruples to interfere with his will, his desire; one who knows how to conquer."

The officer was silent awhile, lost in profound wonder and admiration of his beautiful companion. He knew her—read her like a book. She was in his eyes magnificent.

"Speak frankly," he said; "you have a confidence to make."

"Yes. For that purpose I have come," she rejoined in a low, constrained voice.

Her cheeks had grown pale, and convulsively she twisted her riding-whip in her hand.

"Need I tell you my history? No, you are aware of it already. The history of a woman with an unrequited affection. I love "—and a tear of rage fell on her cheek —"my cousin, Catherine Burgoyne's husband."

"I know it," he responded calmly.

"Yes, I am aware my secret was in your keeping," proceeded Stephanie, with low, rapid, feverish utterance, "or do you think I would have confessed it? But from a child I have loved him with a love that has grown with my growth—a love I had every hope of being returned until she came across his path."

"And he married her? Love is a fatality. I speak, Miss Royle, from experience."

"True.   But I will use your own words : In love as in war we should think of victory, not death.   That "—and she leaned nearer him from her saddle—" we should make ourselves beloved."

"That opinion I still hold to," replied the officer quietly.

" And to carry out that plan is my desire."

"Can one so beautiful fail ?" he rejoined. "Impossible !"

"Impossible !" she cried almost fiercely. "Am I more beautiful now than I have ever been ? And has not Maurice Burgoyne set me aside for her ?"

" He has.   What would you do ?"

" Have revenge."

" On whom ?"

" My rival, and her you love."

"Really !   And you would have me aid you in this, Miss Royle "—he smiled coldly—"against Catherine Burgoyne, whom you affirm I love ?"

She gave an impatient exclamation.

"Why wear a mask before me, Captain Melton ?" she ejaculated irritably. "Have I treated you thus ? Be honest.   Have we not vowed to be friends, to aid each other ?"

"Miss Royle, of course I must be honoured if in any way I can serve you," he remarked, "but I hardly see——"

"How ?" she interrupted rapidly. "I will tell you. It will be to your advantage, as mine, to sever these two. I would—I will part them.   As they are fond and loving now, I will pluck them asunder.   As they live now in a security that is false, I will weave my plans about them —plans that shall succeed.   Help me, Captain Melton, and I declare to you this loving pair shall become as nothing to each other."

As she poured forth the words, slow, rapid, vehement, he regarded her with amazed and increasing interest.

For a moment the slight girl, not yet twenty, dominated the man, who knew every turn in life.

"But how?" he asked.

"That is my secret," she laughed shortly, repeating his reply of the morning; "only I intend to be generous and confide it to you. Listen." Side by side for nearly half-an-hour they paced under the trees talking in low voices.

Captain Melton no longer smiled nor sneered. He recognised the power of this lovely girl, her capability to act without scruple, without fear, in the cause of her love, so great as to be terrible. The countenances of both were earnest.

Little did Maurice and Catherine, seated on the rustic chair beneath the tree, chatting in their great happiness of their journey, hand clasped in hand, and gaze fondly meeting gaze, imagine the destiny those two under the twilight shadows of the park trees were weaving for them.

At last Stephanie checked her horse. It was time to return.

"Shall I accompany you, Miss Royle?" asked the Captain.

"No, I thank you, my groom is sufficient. You have then decided?"

"Yes, I too shall go to Paris," he rejoined.

"And," she smiled, "we shall meet there. Still, when there——"

"The means to make Maurice Burgoyne believe in the infidelity of his wife shall be found," he put in. "Leave that to me."

"I do. And you?"

"Will play the part of Mrs. Burgoyne's sworn friend and champion. If need be," he smiled, "I will challenge him, and so prove his lady's worth by trial of battle; only, I will not kill him for your sake."

"Were you to," she laughed, "I should kill you. But see how it darkens. Farewell. We are friends?"

"And sworn allies," he added, once more kissing the small hand she extended.

Then, making almost a gay salute with her riding-whip, Stephanie Royle turned her horse's head and galloped away.

Captain Everitt Melton sat motionless, following her with his eyes.

"Who but a woman, and a jealous and revengeful one —who but one like yonder fair rider—would have thought and made out such a plan, could have conceived such a scheme?

"She is a genius; but she is terrible. Ah, love can make fiends as well as angels! Tut! Have I turned moralist? I, Everitt Melton? What is this girl to me? I love Catherine Burgoyne. I have vowed to win her affection. If this Stephanie Royle can aid me, so much the better."

Thus thinking, he rode slowly from the park to his club, where he hoped he might during the evening meet Maurice Burgoyne, and learn when he started for Paris.

CHAPTER XVIII.

IN THE GAY CITY OF PARIS.

"WHOM do you think I have just met in the Champs Elysées?" inquired Maurice Burgoyne, entering his suite of rooms in the Hotel de Maubert, where Catherine sat with Stephanie, who had just called in.

It was one of those dull misty days to which during the last few years the gay city of Paris has been no stranger. Maurice had gone out alone, Catherine being slightly indisposed.

"Pray do not tax a woman's curiosity," laughed his wife. "How could we guess? I only hope, love, it was no one disagreeable."

"On the contrary; at least, you will say so," responded Maurice gaily, "for he is so special a favourite with you, Cathie, that 'pon my word I think at times I ought to be jealous."

"Then I have guessed who it is," cried Catherine, mirthfully clapping her hands. "You mean Captain Melton, Maurice."

"There, what do you think of that, Stephanie?" exclaimed her cousin whimsically, unconscious of how he was playing into the hands of her whom he addressed. "Have I not cause for jealousy? I say only 'a special favourite,' and so she guesses to whom I refer at once."

"Which should be a great consolation to you, Maurice," laughed his wife, "for it shows I have not two favourites. Am I not right, Stephanie. Pray be on my side."

"I fear I cannot," smiled Stephanie Royle, slowly shaking her head. "I possess one of the most jealous dispositions conceivable, and I own the Captain is excessively fascinating."

"Confessed," proceeded Catherine in the same lively strain, "that may be an attraction to us ; but the question now is, what is the attraction to him ?   Recollect, Maurice we were not the only ones who came to Paris ; a certain Miss Royle arrived too."

Stephanie slightly raised her shoulders.

"No, I cannot plead guilty," she remarked.   "With me Captain Melton is not a special favourite, for he had the want of gallantry to confess to me that he preferred blondes to brunettes. 'Consequently, as a brunette, I immediately placed him low in my estimation."

"I suppose, *ma cousine*, a man may have a choice," said Maurice, "even as have ladies."

"True, but gentlemen are generally complimentary enough to hide the fact from all those they do not admire."

"Well, if my suggestion is doomed to fall through," continued Catherine, "why has Captain Melton come to Paris ?   He made no mention of such a likelihood while we were in town."

"He says business—an indefinite reason ; still, if there be any other, perhaps, as he is an especial favourite, he may inform you, my love.   You will soon be able to put him to the test, as I have asked him to dinner.   You will stop, Stephanie, will you not, and make our little party complete ? "

Stephanie had heard of the Captain's arrival with secret pleasure.   Of course she was aware he was coming, and she would gladly have accepted the invitation, being anxious to see Everitt Melton ; but it needed three hours to the Burgoyne's dinner-time, and she imagined the officer on his side might have a desire to communicate with her.

She was not wrong, for—having stated a previous engagement as an excuse for her refusal—she returned to the hotel where Sir Jaffery was staying, and found a note awaiting her that had been left by a *commissionaire* half-an-hour previously.

Though it had neither beginning nor ending, according to the usual fashion of letters, she had no doubt from whom it came.

"I am in Paris," it said; "when can I see you? I have found a means most unexpectedly, that I imagine you will not only approve but admire. I shall be by the Madeleine at nine this evening, and will wait half-an-hour for your reply."

There it ended; no name, no address.

"He has found a means, so soon," reflected Stephanie, a delicate flush of pleasure on her cheek, as leaning back in her chair she gazed at the lines. "Truly," with a light laugh,

"When to mischief mortals bend their will,
How soon they find fit instruments of ill.

I wonder what it is? How impatient shall I be until I have learned. How is that possible? I cannot go myself to the Madeleine. I dare trust no messenger. I have it. A woman's chief privilege is to change her mind; I will accept Maurice's invitation to dinner. Captain Melton will be there, and together we will contrive a *tete-a-tete*, if I indeed be the woman, and he the man I take him for."

Hastily she penned the following:

DEAREST CATHERINE,—Attribute it to the attractions of your own society, or the "fascination" of a person who shall be nameless, but I have managed to put off the previous engagement which compelled me to refuse Maurice's invitation of this morning; hence, if the fourth place of your little *partie carree* has not been filled, I shall be delighted to occupy it.—Yours affectionately,   STEPHANIE.

She despatched it by one of the servants, who brought back the reply in due course.

Stephanie Royle arrived punctual to the minute, and was already seated in the Burgoyne's sitting-room when Captain Melton was announced.

She was standing by the open window that opened on to a balcony as he entered, and for a second he was not aware of her presence. On perceiving it he could not command the transient delight which shone in his eyes.

Catherine, too, had noted it, and smiled as the officer moved quickly across the room to the girl.

"How extremely fortunate I must consider myself," he remarked in a low tone. "This is a pleasure I dared hardly have hoped for, and it is important that I should speak to you."

"We must manage to find an opportunity," responded Stephanie, in a rapid low tone, yet with the most conventional of expressions. "Here is my cousin Maurice."

She walked across to Catherine's side, and the captain turned to greet his host. Almost at the same moment dinner was announced.

As soon as dinner was over, Catherine rose from the table, Stephanie did the same, and Captain Melton hastened to open the door.

"I will follow you shortly," he managed to whisper to Stephanie as she passed.

"Do so, and if possible come without my cousin; he says he has a letter to write," replied Stephanie in the same tone.

Directly they reached the drawing-room, Stephanie urged Catherine, who had been complaining of headache, to lie down.

"There is a couch in the recess yonder," she remarked, pointing to an alcove draped with curtains; "the brief rest and subdued light will do you a world of good before the gentlemen come in for coffee."

"Really, Stephanie, I think I will take your advice. But it seems so inhospitable to you."

"If that deters you I shall ring for my bonnet and go. There, lose no time, but hear reason for once."

Laughing, Catherine obeyed. Stephanie, steeping her handkerchief in eau-de-cologne went and laid it over her temples.

"How good you are," said the young wife, gratefully, as slightly rising she kissed the other's cheek, and when she sank back she thought, with compunction, that she had most cruelly misread and unjustly maligned her cousin-in-law in the past.

"I'll seek to make amends in the future," she reflected as her eyes closed, relieved from the light of the tapers.

To modify them yet further, Stephanie dropped the curtains, carefully arranging them, promising to give Catherine warning when she heard the gentlemen approach.

Then she drew a chair in such a position that anyone who entered might instantly perceive her. Here she waited anxiously for Captain Melton's coming.

Her patience was not severely tested, in less than five minutes the door was opened and the officer appeared.

"WHAT DO YOU MEAN, ROSE?" DEMANDED HER MISTRESS SOMEWHAT SHARPLY.

No. 6.

CHAPTER XIX.

THE MYSTERIOUS TWO.

RESPONSIVE to the quick cautionary sign of Stephanie Royle, Captain Melton closed the door noiselessly, and advanced towards where she sat.

As he did so, rising, she stepped into the balcony. He followed, and they stood there, side by side.

The night was as yet moonless, but the mists had dispersed, and a myriad of stars hung like single gems in the ear of beauty from the sky.

The hum of Paris, light-hearted and gay, rose about them; the lamps of the boulevards stretched out before their view.

The scene was pretty, animated; the night still.

That persons should be attracted to the balcony was no wonder. But to these outward attractions both Stephanie and her companion were indifferent.

"You cannot tell how delighted I was to see you when I entered, Miss Royle," remarked the Captain, speaking low.

"I had refused to dine here to-day," she answered, in the same tone, "but changed my mind after the receipt of your communication. I could not otherwise have met you, and I was impatient to learn what you had to tell."

"And I, too, was anxious," he responded. "Where is Mrs. Burgoyne?"

"I persuaded her to lie down on the couch in yonder recess," and Stephanie motioned slightly with her hand. "There is no danger of observation or eavesdropping. I have lowered the curtains. She cannot see us from there. And my cousin?"

"I have persuaded to write his letter, and for that space leave me to your and Mrs. Burgoyne's care."

"That is well. Then we are safe. But we must lose no time. Proceed, Captain Melton, at once."

Leaning on the balcony, partly concealed by the trellis and the plants growing over it, Stephanie listened, at first with disappointment, then with doubt, finally with increasing interest, to the officer's whispered communication.

"Well," he interrogated, on concluding, "what is your idea?"

"That the plan would be excellent, if——"

"If what, Miss Royle?"

"You could really be sure of what you say. To me it seems so improbable. If you were deceived, is it likely he could be?"

"All I can speak upon is my own conviction. All I can say is, see for yourself and judge."

"Can I?"

"Assuredly. Name your own time and place to-morrow. Only discretion is necessary. You will remember that, of course?"

"As if I could forget it!" she laughed softly. "Is not my stake, as yours, too highly prized? But I am a stranger in Paris. Can you name no suitable place?"

"Certainly. If you will not object to come to this address," writing it on a leaf of his pocket-book, "I will meet you there, and you shall be convinced. You shall run no danger, Miss Royle."

"What danger could I run, Captain Melton?" said the girl, with a toss of the head and proud flash of her beautiful eyes. "I fear nothing. Surely what you know of me already must have shown you I am no coward. I will be there at noon if that will suit."

"Perfectly," he said, bowing. "Of all women, Miss Royle, I know none so brave. Pallas and Venus in one."

"Then to Pallas give the laurels of victory," laughed Stephanie, as she moved towards the window. "To-morrow at noon, Captain Melton, I'll put this strange statement of yours to the test."

"One instant, Miss Royle," detaining her by a light touch on her arm. "Have I your permission to act upon my belief, should opportunity offer, at once?"

"If you do not risk the whole by it, Captain Melton."

"Be assured I shall not. No risk can be run."

"Then I leave it to your judgment."

"Thanks." He raised her hand to his lips. Then they stepped back into the drawing-room at the same moment that Catherine appeared from the alcove and Maurice came in, followed by the coffee.

That evening, the night being so clear and fine, Maurice Burgoyne walked home from the Théâtre Française, to which he had gone alone, Catherine feeling too unwell to accompany him. Altogether the piece had not pleased him, and he had come away before the fall of the curtain.

The rue in which his hotel was situate was one of those handsome ones for which Baron Haussmann may be thanked. Straight, broad, and long, a pedestrian had a full view of almost the entire street on entering it.

Now the moon had risen, and sent a stream of silver light upon it.

Maurice, casting his eyes as one is apt to do at his own particular residence, saw the lights still bright in the drawing-room. Looking closer, he perceived two figures standing in the balcony.

Were they two figures? Surely. Who could they be? Had Stephanie returned? She had expressed much sympathy with Catherine's loneliness, being so indisposed. Certainly one figure he was sure was a woman's.

He was walking down the opposite side of the way in the full moonlight. They would see and recognise him if they chanced to look in his direction.

Ah, they moved. He, curious to guess, slackened unconsciously his pace. The female figure altering her position, came in the pale rays of the light issuing from the open window. Why, it was Catherine herself! He could not mistake her face. But who was her companion? Ah, she was looking towards him; she must see him.

Taking off his hat, he waved it. The lady made no response, but stepped quickly into the room, dropping the curtain behind her. Yet not so rapidly but that Maurice saw the other follow.

Other one—man or woman? Ah, it must be Stephanie.

No one else would visit her at that late hour. Besides, Catherine had said she should refuse herself to all visitors.

"There is one consolation," he reflected, as he now hurried on, "Catherine must be much better."

Springing upstairs he opened the sitting-room door, entered, and stood perplexed.

The gas was turned down; the apartment was empty! where had the two fled? Where, if the visitor had gone, was Catherine?

Maurice looked into the recess beyond the alcove, then into the balcony, imagining they might have returned there.

No; no one was there.

"It's strange," he muttered, "very."

Quitting the room he proceeded to his wife's sleeping apartment.

The lamp was shaded, yet he could see the outline of Catherine's form, still in her evening dress, lying on the bed.

"Well," he exclaimed, advancing, "you soon got rid of your guest."

There was no reply. Drawing aside the curtain he beheld his wife's sweet face calm in slumber.

Slumber?—nonsense! She could not be asleep so soon. What did it mean?

And he gazed upon the beautiful face with a look of bewilderment.

"Catherine!" exclaimed the husband, and his voice was somewhat sharp.

She sprang up at once, a startled expression in her eyes, as one aroused from unconsciousness.

"Maurice!" she exclaimed, astonished; "are you not early, or have I slept so long?"

"Why you must have been feigning Cathie," he remarked, with an effort at a smile. "What made you quit the balcony so suddenly? I am sure you must have seen me. And where is your friend?"

For an instant Catherine could not comprehend her husband's inquiry, but the next moment she exclaimed in accents of surprise:

"My friend? I, on the balcony? What do you mean, Maurice? Is it I who am dreaming or you, dear? I have never quitted this room since you left."

"Then, on my life, I believe you must have walked in your sleep. I distinctly saw you as I came up the street standing in the balcony with someone. You looked in my direction, I waved my hat, when you and your companion quickly, without making the slightest response, entered the apartment, dropping the curtain behind you."

"Maurice," said Catherine, regarding him fixedly, "I see you are not mad, but I cannot comprehend you."

"Do you mean, Catherine, you were not on the balcony?" he inquired, looking straight at her.

"Most certainly, Maurice. I repeat I have never left this room. If persons were on our balcony I was not there; and, indeed, know nothing of it. Surely, dear, you believe me? Why should I deceive you?"

He still gazed at her perplexed, then, stooping, kissed her cheek.

"Of course I believe you," he said. "But there were persons there, and that must be seen to. I made a mistake, I suppose, in taking the lady for you."

"Don't say 'suppose,' Maurice," remarked his wife gently, with reproach. "It seems as if you still mistrust me."

"Nonsense, Cathie. I am quite certain I was mistaken. But let us go and look at the room again. What right had any but ourselves to use it? It is like their impertinence."

They went, she hanging on his arm.

"Maurice," she remarked abruptly, "do you not fancy you have made two mistakes? Don't you think you must have taken the rooms adjoining for our own? I learned to-day from my maid that they had been taken by a lady."

"Indeed. Humph! That might have been possible. Yet, no; I could have declared they were our windows. In fact, I am certain."

"Don't say 'certain,'" proceeded Catherine laughingly, continuing her argument—how Maurice recalled it at a later date. "Night is so deceptive."

"But there are lights in our room, Catherine," he exclaimed, "while those of the next are dark."

"The lights here are too low to have reflected through the curtains dropped as they are," said his wife, pointing to the lowered lamps, "especially with such a bright moon outside. As to the next apartment, the lamp may have been extinguished since. Trust me, my love, this is the explanation. What other could there be? Why should people stand on our balcony? Had I indeed been there looking for your return, why should I deny it?"

"You convince me, Cathie, I must have made a mistake in the windows, yet never was I so sure of anything as I was that the lady was yourself. But there, enough of it, my dear. Let us have supper, and I will tell you about the piece."

"Did you like it, Maurice?"

"Not much; I cannot stand the plots which the French dramatists select. Still, you shall hear."

So Maurice chatted of the piece throughout the supper, the little event of his mistake passing from his mind.

The clock was near upon midnight when Catherine retired to her bed-chamber, and Maurice strolled out into the balcony to smoke a cigar before he followed.

The moon had sailed round now, and its full light fell on the side of the rue on which was the hotel.

Maurice lapsed into thought, and, when his cigar was half-consumed, began to pace the balcony.

What was that, close up by the light open ironwork that divided the space allotted to the two suites of rooms ?

Maurice lifted it.

It was a man's glove.

How had it come there ?

It was of a peculiar colour. No one, as he could remember, had worn such who had called upon him that day.

Then how had it come there ?

It must have fallen through the ironwork, dropped by someone in the next balcony. No doubt it had belonged to the second figure he had seen, which as he had suspected, must have been of the male gender.

Catherine's explanation was correct. He had evidently been mistaken in the balconies.

Assured of this, Maurice Burgoyne tossed away the end of his cigar, and re-entered the sitting-room without a thought, carrying the glove in his hand.

CHAPTER XX.

MADEMOISELLE JOSEPHINE HERAULT.

TEPHANIE ROYLE quitted her hotel the next morning, and having walked some little distance took a *fiacre* to the address Captain Melton had given her the previous evening.

It was in anything but a fashionable quarter.

The streets were narrow, the inhabitants mixed, and, like the houses, not altogether of the cleanest.

Grisettes not quite as picturesque as those frequently represented on paper, and blue-bloused men as if, so like were they, they had stepped out of Gavarni's immortal pictures.

At the entrance to the street mentioned on the slip of paper she held, according to her direction the *fiacre* stopped, and Stephanie alighted.

At the same instant Captain Melton stepped forward.

He was attired in a foreign-looking furred cloak and soft-felt hat that to any casual observer would have quite destroyed the identity of the fashionable well-bred English officer, especially when added thereto were a pair of blue-side spectacles.

Stephanie smiled as she took his arm.

"I perceive," she said, "you have taken precautions."

"As yourself, Miss Royle," he rejoined, with a glance at her plain dark dress, neat bonnet, and thick veil. "It is wisest. Neither, I expect, care for recognition in such a *locale* as this."

"True. Is it far down, this house?"

"It is close by. It is, in fact, here. Now, Miss Royle, you shall judge."

As he spoke he entered one of the houses, the door of which stood already open. Ascending the stairs he halted, pushed wide a door that stood ajar, and led his companion in.

Stephanie beheld before her a small apartment furnished in French style. Bright common prints were on the walls. A faded, worn velvet flounce, its colour indefinite, hung round the mantel-piece, on which were a few china ornaments.

But her gaze wandered rapidly over these to rest on the occupant of the room—a woman, standing before the mantel-piece, her elbow on it, her eyes fixed on a novel of Pigault Lebrun's that was supported against the wall. What was it that made Stephanie halt abruptly, and her eyes open in surprise?

Captain Melton, watching her, smiled evidently with satisfaction.

"Allow me," he said, "to introduce to you, when she can draw herself from that entrancing page, Mademoiselle Josephine Herault."

The woman turned. Stephanie started back with a cry of surprise she could not suppress, for in countenance, height, figure, and style of hair, as that and colour of dress, stood in front of her the fac-simile of Catherine Burgoyne.

"Good heavens!" she ejaculated. "Can it be possible?"

A sudden fear possessed her at first that it was Catherine herself; that it was a trick, that she had been deceived. The second glance negatived that belief. The likeness was great, but there was a difference.

The face wanted the repose, the refined expression of Catherine Burgoyne. Though the features themselves in form were even more delicate, the eyes were less innocently mirthful, the hair of a richer gold. Yet it was only in such close proximity as Stephanie's to Mademoiselle Josephine Herault, and in the strong light of day, that this difference was perceptible.

At any distance, her figure, her carriage, her every movement which had evidently been already tutored and practised, was Catherine's.

"It is wonderful!" proceeded Stephanie. "I could not have believed it. How—how can it be?"

With a stately smile, and a slightly proud erection of the head, Mademoiselle Josephine sat down as one who had no concern in the question. Let those answer it who cared to. It was nothing to her.

"How, it is impossible to say," responded Captain Melton. "Enough for us is the fact, I think, and that," raising his voice and now using the French tongue, "Mademoiselle Josephine, who already has apartments in the Hotel de Maubert, is kind enough to lend us her services."

"The kindness extends thus far," remarked mademoiselle, with a little disdainful smile; "I will do what monsieur desires on the terms monsieur has mentioned."

"But," inquired Stephanie of the officer, "you say Mademoiselle Josephine has apartments in the same hotel. How is that? I do not understand. Being so exceedingly alike——"

"There is no danger, no risk," laughed the Captain in English, a language the other did not understand. "Mademoiselle is an adept in disguises. You, I perceive, no longer mistrust my plan."

"I compliment you, I congratulate you," replied Stephanie. "Is there necessity for me to remain longer?"

"None in the least. Mademoiselle," he continued, changing back into French, and with an air of mock gallantry, "this lady desired to see you to put my assertion to the test. She is convinced of your beauty and ability. Hence we will no longer detain you from those fascinating pages after which I perceive you are craving. *Bon jour*, mademoiselle, until this evening."

"*Bon jour*, monsieur, and *au revoir*," rejoined the handsome Mademoiselle Josephine, with a coquettish yet half disdainful movement of the head. "I own Pigault

Lebrun is more entertaining, mademoiselle," casting a curious glance at Stephanie's veil, but unable to penetrate it as she made a farewell salutation in return to the other's *bon jour*. "I wonder who she really is?" she added, returning to her reading.

"I see," remarked Stephanie, as they descended the stairs, "you have concealed our names from this person."

"Most assuredly," smiled the captain. "I believe mademoiselle will take no interest in this affair further than carrying out our desires; but at the same time it is policy not, my dear Miss Royle, to put ourselves in her power. Trust me, I shall take care of that."

"Thank you;" and never had Stephanie spoken more sincerely.

Like many, she feared her own sex more than the opposite.

"But this strange, this unaccountable likeness," she proceeded; "I feel yet dazed by it. It seems more than chance, more than a coincidence. Nature could not play such a freak. Still one is English, one French. She is French?" she questioned, looking quickly at her companion. "That hair, however, is purely of the Saxon hue, while the peculiarity of the darker eyes and brows—— What are this woman's antecedents?"

"I really cannot inform you, Miss Royle," he answered; "I wish I could. I doubt if mademoiselle knows much about them herself. Indeed, as to who were her parents, I know she is ignorant, for she informed me as much. Her first recollections were of almost an infant crawling and playing with several others on a red-brick floor; a door mostly open, and a field beyond; also of she and her companions being guarded by a wrinkled old woman, with saboted feet, in a blue serge dress, a red hand-kerchief twisted round her grey locks, and long gold ear-rings in her ears. She does not remember it as a pleasant life, and was infinitely relieved when, a child of seven, she was brought to Paris by a man and woman, the keepers of a cabaret. Here she grew up, becoming waitress to them. This is her own story, and from that point, Miss Royle, I think we have no need of pursuing it further. Whatever were her antecedents, what she has been, what she is, is no concern of ours. Enough she is the very person we need, and she is willing to be used."

"And she shall not go unrewarded," remarked Stephanie, as they drew near the *fiacre*.

"Nor, I trust," smiled Captain Melton, opening the door and handing her in, "shall we."

"I believe we shall not, if we succeed," began Stephanie in a low earnest tone, "in shaking his faith; then——"

"Then," concluded the officer, "the flaw in the marriage chain shall easily cause a disuniting of the whole."

As the *fiacre* drove off, Captain Melton, proceeding in the same direction, followed it with his eyes.

"She is a courageous girl. Fear and she, I should fancy, were never companions," he soliloquised. "I admire her immensely. If I had not seen Catherine—— Ah," he interrupted himself, "but I have seen Catherine, and all other women, the loveliest, lose by comparison. Yet it is not altogether her beauty wherein lies her charm, or I might place myself at the feet of Mademoiselle Josephine. It is in the subtle influence of her sweet nature; so pure, so innocent, so single-minded, and governed by an intelligence of the extent of which she herself is, I believe, ignorant. She is lost in her present sphere, in this colourless, cooing, dovecot life she leads with Burgoyne. I wonder if he is aware that the validity of his marriage might be questioned? His cousin doubts it. But if he be, his jealousy, his suspicions will bring it to light. If I have read Catherine Burgoyne correctly, her pure, proud spirit will revolt against the slightest slur cast upon her fidelity. If he wish a separation she will grant it. Then—may not I win her?"

Stephanie Royle's thoughts ran somewhat in the same groove as she was driven homeward. She felt she had

never acted more wisely than when she had taken Captain
Melton into her confidence, for she recognised success
now assured, even though Sir Jaffery should become
reconciled to Maurice.

By the way, were the latter taken back into his father's
favour, did he find himself reinstated once more as heir
to Merton Travers, might that not make him more
nervously tenacious of his wife's honour?

She, Stephanie, must think of that.

Ascending the hotel staircase, in the corridor she met
the valet, Sidford.

"How is Sir Jaffery?" she inquired.

"He appears better, miss?   But the restlessness of this
morning increases," replied the valet.   "He desires to go
out."

"I see no reason why he should not, Sidford.   Do
you?" asked Stephanie, with an appearance of deference
to the servant's opinion.

"None whatever, only I thought——"

"That this morning I seemed against the idea," put in
Stephanie.   "Yes, but the fact is, I am so nervous.
Sir Jaffery being so much better since we have been in
Paris, I fear any excitement that might occasion a relapse.
Still, as my guardian wishes it, it may do yet more harm
to thwart him."

"I think that possible, miss," replied the valet
quietly.

"Your opinion convinces me, Sidford.   Let the carriage
be ordered after luncheon.   I will but remove my bonnet
and come to Sir Jaffery."

It may be well to mention that Stephanie's bonnet and
her general attire had undergone a slight metamorphosis
during the transit in the cab.

A cluster of delicate-hued flowers had appeared in the
neat bonnet, a handsome collarette of Vandyke lace en-
circled the girl's throat, and lace to match fell over her
perfectly well gloved hands.   The veil had disappeared
and a handsome gem brooch secured the mantle.

Before Stephanie left her room she wrote a hurried letter to the following effect :

DEAR MAURICE,—This morning Sir Jaffery is marvellously better. So much so that from one until about two he is going to take a drive in the Bois. Pray do not be there, do not let him see you. I am so, so hopeful for the future, that I dread a shock, against which the physician so gravely warned us, should undo what with such care we have accomplished. I know you will perceive the seriousness of this. Maurice, accept me for a Cassandra, and believe that before another year has passed you will be back at Mereton Travers.—Yours sincerely,

STEPHANIE.

Despatching this by a messenger, she repaired to the baronet's apartments.

Maurice read the letter with emotion and exceeding gladness. He really loved his father passionately. He rejoiced that he was better, and was quite ready to take Stephanie for a prophetess, "heaven bless and reward her."

Yet he did not carry out the request in her letter. He did go to the Bois, but took up a position where he could see and not be seen.

In due course the carriage appeared containing his father and Stephanie.

The baronet was pale and aged, yet a smile was on his face, an amused light in his eyes as he turned them in every direction, watching the gay crowd. Only it was the smile, the amusement of a child, not of a man with a man's intelligence.

Maurice buried his face in his hands with a bitter moan.

"Oh, my poor, poor father !" he murmured. "How changed. If he would but see me, my love should win his forgiveness. It could not fail. But I dare not risk it. I dare not. That is, not yet. I must wait the proper time when he is stronger. I must trust all in the hands of dear Stephanie. What should I have done without her ? What would he ? How shall either of us be able to make return for her unselfish goodness ? "

And with a sad heart he retraced his steps to his hotel.

CHAPTER XXI.

SEEDS OF SUSPICION.

"I CAN'T make it out. It's—it's most singular."

The speech was Maurice Burgoyne's.

A *fiacre* had just whirled past him, from the window of which he could have sworn his wife had looked.

It had been but a flash. She appeared to have leaned forward, then perceiving him, to have drawn quickly back with a rapid movement, seeking to bring the folds of her veil together over her face ; while as she vanished he distinctly noted that she had a companion, and that one of the male gender.

"It's all nonsense," he proceeded, his eyes following the *fiacre*, his brows slightly drawn. "It cannot be her. What could Catherine have to do in this quarter of Paris ? Besides, she said she only intended to do a little shopping this morning. Of course it's another mistake, but—but confound it all, it was her very bonnet. Am I in a dream ? Certainly for the last few days I have felt in a vague state of bewilderment. Ever since those two figures on the balcony. To make a second mistake. Yet I have, for if Catherine chose to hire a cab she would scarcely permit a cavalier to accompany her—she, my wife."

Altogether, to say the least of it, it was a very perplexing circumstance. If ever Maurice had looked upon Catherine's face, he could have declared he had just done so. Still, he was in error, for had it been his wife why should she so evidently have tried to avoid him. She had no secrets to conceal.

Totally unsettled by the occurrence, Maurice Burgoyne changed his mind as to the direction he was taking, and returned to his hotel.

He had been nearly three hours absent. Catherine would surely have come back by this time.

Entering his apartments he found them empty.

Why did he feel annoyed, almost angry? Angry with Catherine for the first time.

"If she was so capable of going out," he reflected, his forehead clouded, as he rang the bell sharply, "why could not she have accompanied me? Where is Mrs. Burgoyne?" he enquired of the French maid he had engaged for his wife, who answered his summons.

"Madame is out, monsieur."

"When did she go out?" asked Maurice, with difficulty maintaining indifference.

"About an hour after monsieur," remarked the maid; "madame said she would return for certain in an hour."

"And two have passed," involuntarily broke from Maurice's lips.

"Probably madame has been delayed, monsieur. Madame went shopping, and time passes so quickly."

"That will do," said Maurice, dismissing the girl, nervously growing aware that his curiosity in respect to his wife's movements might be regarded as peculiar, and be commented upon by the soubrette.

A jealous husband is ever a subject of mirth and contempt to the French soubrette, and Mademoiselle Rose, retiring to her room to complete the ornamenting of a dress of Catherine's, began with much relish to concoct quite a romance out of this little event.

To her it was quite natural that madame should have a *cavalier servant*, and equally natural that the *cavalier servant* should be the handsome English *capitaine* who was so liberal to Mademoiselle Rose, with both compliments, francs—and kisses.

Meanwhile Maurice paced the sitting-room angry with himself for the state of mind he was getting into.

What more natural than that Catherine should go out? What more natural that she should be delayed? In Kensington he would have thought nothing of it. No, nor in Paris either, but for that face.

Ah! at last. That was her voice in the corridor. To whom was she speaking? To any of the hotel people? No; she had returned, but not alone.

"Confound him," muttered Maurice, ignorant why or wherefore, as he recognised the accents of his wife's companion. "He seems ever here."

Then the door opened, and Catherine, bright and animated, her soft complexion brilliant from her walk, entered with Captain Melton.

"What, have you returned, Maurice?" she exclaimed gaily, advancing into the room.

"Yes," he remarked, with a lingering irritability in his tone, "to my surprise to find the cage empty."

"Whose fault is that, dear?" she laughed; "yours for returning earlier than you said, or mine for being later?"

"I was not certain whether I did specify the time of my return; but your maid said you would be back in an hour."

"So I did," proceeded Catherine, taking off her bonnet and smoothing her hair at a glass; "but the Paris shops are so dreadfully seductive. Time slips away you know not how."

"I do not doubt it, my love," still with that under-current of cynicism the visitor perceived, though the wife did not; "especially when to the fascination of the *modiste* is added the escort of so agreeable a companion."

"There, Captain Melton," laughed Catherine, glancing over her shoulder, "that is a compliment for you. Indeed, Maurice, I have cause to be very grateful to Captain Melton," she added, "for with my adventurous exploring spirit I tried to make a short cut back to this hotel, and the consequences were that I speedily lost myself in a labyrinth of small unknown streets. I believe I should be wandering there now, had not Captain Melton, like a good Samaritan, come across my path and extricated me."

"By hailing a *fiacre* as the best method," put in Maurice, "and bringing you here."

"A *fiacre!* Oh, indeed no," she laughed; "such a luxury would have been difficult to find in that locality, I think. We walked. What made you imagine we took a *fiacre?*"

"I merely thought that the most easy method under such a difficulty."

"It certainly would have been the quickest," responded Catherine reflectively, "but I did not think of it, though really, if I had, there was no vehicle to be got. Was there, Captain Melton?"

"Most assuredly not, my dear Mrs. Burgoyne," exclaimed the officer, laughing carelessly; "and even if there had been, you know, old fellow, there exists a Mrs. Grundy in Paris as in London, and what would she say to have seen me dashing about this gay capital in company with *la belle dame Anglaise,* of whom all Paris is talking?"

The words were spoken lightly, in apparent good-humoured jest, but they hit so exactly in with that event of the morning, that Maurice, his face darkening, turned his glance sharply first on the speaker, then on his wife.

There was no sign of a hidden meaning in the officer's countenance, but a colour had risen to Catherine's cheek, and there was the shadow of a frown in her beautiful eyes.

"Captain Melton," she remarked quietly, "I cannot see there would have been anything for Mrs. Grundy, French or English, to talk about; harm exists only where harm is meant."

"And harm can never emanate from, nor be felt towards, Mrs. Burgoyne," responded the captain, bowing low, "who outrivals the sun, for, as astronomers tell us, even that is not spotless. I am only content in having been able to render you so slight a service."

"Slight! Indeed, I hold it a great one," responded Catherine once again in her merry vein. "My dear Maurice, you would have had to send the crier out to cry me, 'lost, stolen, or strayed,' but for Captain Melton, yet you have not thanked him."

"Melton, I am sure, is quite certain of my gratitude, Catherine. Between such old friends things are understood better when not spoken. But I must request you will be more careful in the future; also to avoid short cuts, and take your maid with you. You may not always be so fortunate as to come across Captain Melton. Have you been to Galignani's this morning?" he added, addressing the officer and moving towards the balcony.

Captain Melton followed. Catherine looked after her husband with a vague sense that something was wrong, then taking her bonnet she quitted the room.

"What can it be?" she reflected. "I never saw Maurice like this before."

Reaching her bed-chamber, and summoning her maid, her surprise was further augmented by the behaviour of Mademoiselle Rose. With a superfluity of action with her hands and eyes, she exclaimed:

"Ah, madame has returned. Monsieur's mind will now be at ease."

"What do you mean, Rose?" demanded her mistress somewhat sharply.

"*Tiens*, madame. Only when monsieur rang a while ago to ask where you were, he seemed quite distracted at madame's absence. Monsieur is so jealous——"

"Jealous!" ejaculated Catherine, flashing indignantly round at the speaker.

But Mademoiselle Rose proceeded simply, without apparently noting word or look.

"Of madame's safety and comfort."

Catherine, turning to the glass, mentioned the dress she intended to wear that afternoon. She could not enter into a discussion with her maid. Maurice was, she knew, nervously careful of her, though "jealous" was a strange word to use.

For the first time Catherine felt annoyed. She thought Maurice was foolish, wrong to have made any remark concerning her absence to her maid. Besides, after all, she had been only an hour beyond her time.

It was absurd, very, so treating her like a child. She must really speak to him.

Catherine's eyes falling on her reflection in the glass, perceived the irritable, annoyed crumple in her white forehead. But even as she looked it was gone, a sunny smile had taken its place.

"And should I complain," she thought, leaning back in her chair; "is it not his very affection for me that makes him so? Is it for me to call it foolish? No. Let me reflect what would be my suffering if he grew callous respecting my actions. If—if—ever I were to lose his love. Dear, dear Maurice."

An exquisite sigh escaped her lips, an expression almost beatific rested on her features as she sank into a transient pleasant reverie.

Mademoiselle Rose had noted the frown, the smile, the sigh, and the rapt expression, and Mademoiselle Rose read them her own way, one reading being that the frown was for Maurice.

The result of Catherine's meditations was that instead of annoyance, she felt proud of her husband's anxiety on her account, and loved him, if possible, still more dearly for it. Then, her toilette completed, she returned to the sitting-room.

Captain Melton had gone. Maurice stood just within the lace window-curtains, his back to her, his arms folded, his eyes bent on the street beneath.

He was thinking how he could bring up the subject of that face he had seen so like hers to Catherine. He felt an awkwardness about it which he would not have experienced, though that did not occur to him, if Catherine had not been out that morning. Yet he did not suspect her of deceiving him. No, not for a second. At least he told himself so.

He repeated that self-assurance as a soft arm was slipped fondly round his neck, a lovely head was nestled on his shoulder, and a sweet face looked into his, as its owner said :

"Why so grave, dear husband ? Am I not yet forgiven ? Really I did not think my offence so heinous, or I would have controlled my exploring proclivities. I would rather not go out at all than see that shadow on your brow— that is, if I am its cause. Am I ? "

Was she ?

Maurice caught his wife to his heart, and fondly pressed his lips to hers. How pure, how innocent, how lovely she looked. How could he even hint he suspected her ? But he did not. No, of course. Yet, after his late tone, his suggestions about a *fiacre*, his gravity, if he told her of that face that he had found it so difficult to convince himself was not hers—the sight of which had brought him home so much earlier than he had intended, might she not, quick and sensitive, imagine he had suspected her, despite all his protestations ?

He would not risk it. That is, not at present. After dinner, perhaps, apropos of nothing, when, as was their wont, they sat together side by side, her head on his shoulder in the shadow of the curtains, while he smoked his cigar.

Yes ; that was how it should be.

And the next day ? Well, the next day he would try to find out who was this singular double of his wife—her double even to the dress she wore. Yes, that was the most peculiar circumstance of all.

That recollection had gleamed into Maurice Burgoyne's brain as he sat finishing his glass of burgundy before following his wife to the sitting-room.

At the same moment the waiter brought in a letter, which had been just left by a commissionaire. Maurice glanced at it as he rose from the table, intending to carry it with him to the other apartment.

The writing was strange, while on the envelope was written "Private."

Who could write to him in that fashion? Another mystery.

Mechanically he resumed his seat as he tore off the envelope. The first thing he sought for was the signature.

There was none—the letter was anonymous.

With more curiosity than surprise at first Maurice Burgoyne began the perusal of the unknown writer's communication :—

Anonymous letters are, I am aware, regarded little above the dagger of the hired assassin, which stabs in the dark. Nevertheless, even as police spies, whom we hold in contempt, they are at times necessities, as in my case. I am your friend —a warmly sincere one; hence I hold it as a sacred duty .to reveal to you what has come to my knowledge; but were I openly to do this, your anger might throw discredit on my words, and all I should have gained would be your enmity for my reward. No, I cannot risk that; neither can I the leaving unwritten what I have to write; hence I must do so anonymously. Between two evils, I choose the least. If you will, proceed no further—destroy the letter. Then the future will rest with you; you alone will be answerable, not I. I have done all I was able to keep a name, until now honourable and unsullied, yet so.

Destroy the letter !

Few men would have possessed the moral courage to have done so after such a commencement. Certainly, Maurice Burgoyne had not.

Maurice Burgoyne, you are being deceived by one near and dear to you.

"Who could that be but Catherine?" interpolated Maurice, mentally.

And your honour is at stake. Possibly your doubts may already be excited; possibly already you have guessed my meaning. What, then, will you do?

Like an honourable man, proceed at once and let her know your doubts, the subject of this letter, bidding her deny it? Yes, like an honourable man, but a fool.

One who is capable of deceiving is capable of denying. The touch of a pair of white arms, the glance of bright eyes swimming in tears, half of reproach, half sorrow, the words parting the red lips murmuring, "And you whom I so love can mistrust me," and man becomes helpless. He is the victim, the jest of the fair Circe, who finding the one veil she wore penetrated, with a smile wears a thicker, until the victim awakes one morning to find himself duped—his name dishonoured.

This will not be your case. Pray heaven no! Yet be warned—watch! Keep your secret for her sake and your own. Watch! Then you may save. Let not your suspicions be known before you have proof. Indignation of the innocently maligned will be your reward. She will hate, she will fear you, and you, as she, are lost.

I repeat—be warned! In silence watch, and in less than a week the fallacy of your doubts or their justice shall be proved. Only—make the housebreaker aware you are guarding the door. Then he will enter by the window. To the guilty as to the wronged forewarned is forearmed.

ONE WHO WATCHES OVER YOU AND HER.

"It—it is all false—a confounded, base plot of some enemy to ruin Catherine's happiness and mine," cried Maurice Burgoyne, crushing the letter in his hand and leaping to his feet, trembling with rage.

"STEPHANIE," HE SAID, IN A LOW TONE, "I AM IN TROUBLE, BITTER TROUBLE."

CHAPTER XXII.

THE YELLOW GLOVE.

THOUGH no names but his own had been mentioned, Maurice knew well enough to whom the innuendoes pointed.

It was Catherine, his wife, who was deceiving him, who was false to him!

Truly, anonymous letters were even worse than the concealed assassin's dagger. But the cruel intention this time should be foiled. No foe should triumph over wrecking their felicity. Catherine should know at once, and together they would trace out the hand that penned this cowardly attack.

Swiftly he moved towards the door. His grasp was already on the handle, when he reeled and rested against the wall, sick and giddy, his hand pressed to his forehead.

Why, at that very moment, breaking through his anger, his belief in Catherine, like a storm-cloud, though too golden with sunshine, had come that recollection of the mysterious two in the balcony—the glove he had found there.

Catherine had denied knowledge of those two. How?

By the touch of soft white arms, the glance of eyes suffused by tears, and whispered words: "Maurice, do you mistrust me? Why should I, who so love you, deceive?"

Great Heaven! She had denied almost in the words of the letter. How, too, had she argued as to the impossibility of persons being on their balcony. And yet how sure he had been that those two had been on theirs and no other. Again, the occurrence of that morning. Her losing her way. The face he had seen in the *fiacre*.

All this came rushing like an overwhelming flood upon the wretched husband. He staggered from the door, flung himself on a chair, and dropped his head on his arms crossed on the table.

"Oh, my God!" he gasped in agony, "preserve my reason, my brain is turning. I am going mad."

But what was to be done?

That was the question that haunted him. His desire would have been to have told all to Catherine, but a power over which he appeared to have no control seemed to withhold him. Was it fear? Was it doubt?

He would not have confessed it. Nevertheless, those two circumstances, so mysterious, which had so perplexed him, would not be banished. Over and over again he prepared to tear the anonymous letter into fragments; over and over again his hands paused.

Over and over again he crossed towards the door, purposing to seek his wife. Over and over again those two recollections arose, and he returned into the room tortured by doubt, indecision, madness.

What was he to do? How to act?

Until now he had considered the case in the way the letter had put it. Suddenly he began to think of it chiefly in reference to Catherine's feelings.

Of course, whatever might be the appearances she was innocent. Then what would be her suffering when she learned the cruel suspicion cast upon her?

Only such sensitive natures as hers could understand how crushing the blow would be. Fatal, perhaps—at least fatal to her peace of mind, to her belief in his trust in her.

"No," he reflected, pacing the room, "I cannot do it. I could not. What words could I frame the announcement in? Would not my very mention of this vile letter be as an accusation? Better, better do as men who are wise should—treat the communication as though it had never been made. At least," and he pressed his hand to his aching temples, "I cannot do other to-night,

I am in no state of mind to decide. Only I'll never believe but that Catherine is the best, truest of wives, and no word of mine shall raise a barrier between us."

Was it the barrier he feared? Or had that crafty, subtle epistle crept into him, poisoning his healthful blood, and, unaware to himself, Maurice Burgoyne was leaning towards the advice and warning therein given!

The confused state of his brain made him dread an interview at present with his wife. She would be sure to notice his agitation, the change that had come over him. Imagine passing a whole evening *tête-à-tête* with her, having that base letter in his pocket!

Still, it must be. Already she must be surprised at his delay. Headache—sudden indisposition must be the excuse.

Taking a final glass of Burgundy, assuming as composed a demeanour as was in his power, he proceeded to the sitting-room.

As he opened the door to quit the dining-room, Catherine's musical laugh fell on his ear.

Always happy, always gay. Could that be so if evil were in her breast—if she were deceiving him?

A bitter smile crossed his features. He was a man of the world and knew how to answer the mental interrogation. A woman who could deceive a husband's trust was capable of anything.

"What!" he reflected in angry self-reproach. "Am I regarding her as guilty? My wife, into whose hands I have placed my honour? Would I not trust in hers as my own?"

Nevertheless, looking in the direction from whence had proceeded Catherine's laugh, he was glad to perceive her in company with Stephanie.

The latter had on her walking-dress, which, as the two were evidently going to his wife's dressing-room, she intended to remove.

In that case she would stay the evening and he would be saved a *tête-à-tête* with Catherine.

Maurice Burgoyne drew a long breath of relief. Then a troubled feeling fell on him.

When before had he been glad of escaping from his wife's society?

And all because of that vile, slanderous letter.

If things were to go on like this they would send him distracted.

No, he was determined. He would wait until Stephanie had gone, then inform Catherine of everything.

Taking a book from the table, he threw himself on a couch, in hopes to distract his thoughts from that grim subject that tortured him before his wife and cousin's return.

The volume chanced to be Webster's "Duchess of Malfi," and the first words his eyes rested upon were:

> Foolish men
> That e'er will trust their honour in a bark
> Made of so slight, weak bulrush as is woman,
> Apt every minute to sink it.

The colour rushed to Maurice's face. Springing up, he flung the volume from him.

"Is everything in league against my happiness?" he muttered, angrily. "Am I never to escape from that thought?"

He strode towards the table whereon stood his wife's work-basket.

Mechanically, yet with the action of an angry man, he began to toss the articles about in it—the delicate embroidery he had admired, the crewel-work he had laughed at, yet had loved to watch her slender fingers so busy upon.

Suddenly he started, for he had disclosed, beneath, as if thrust there hastily for concealment, a glove—a man's glove, of the same peculiar hue as that he had found on the balcony.

Stay! Was it not the same, and by chance had got into its present place?

Maurice Burgoyne put his hand into the pocket of his coat. The latter was the same he had worn on that night.

In a second he had produced—the fellow glove !

How had it come into Catherine's possession ?

With a countenance black, stormy as thunder, Maurice Burgoyne stood gazing at the two, oblivious of all else, even of his wife and cousin's return, though their voices sounded in the corridor.

CHAPTER XXIII.

MAURICE CONFIDES IN HIS ENEMY.

ATHERINE'S hand was upon the door before Maurice Burgoyne recovered from the stupor caused by blended pain, surprise, and indignation.

Thrusting both gloves into his pocket, he turned to greet his cousin, assuming as unconstrained a demeanour as was possible, for this was no time for an explanation.

"I fear, Maurice," laughed Stephanie, who looked exquisitely charming and peculiarly happy this evening, "that you will begin to consider me a nuisance, for I am always here, though politeness will, of course, prevent your confessing to it."

"I can assure you, my dear Stephanie, you cannot come too often to please me," he rejoined, earnestly, for in this trouble that seemed like a cloud enveloping him, and thickening every hour, his old reliance in his cousin was coming back.

"Yes," she laughed, gaily, "that's what I meant. Politeness necessitates such a reply; but the fact is, I find the evenings so dull at our hotel. Sir Jaffery, though very much better, dines still in his own room, and etiquette will not permit me to visit or receive guests alone," she sighed. "If you and Catherine were but restored to favour, then I should make her chaperon me, though," laughing, "you hardly look matronly enough, I must confess. I fear the cavaliers would be so dividing their attentions that I, who have yet to be established, should be jealous."

"My dear Stephanie," put in Maurice, gravely, "against that, age is not a wife's safeguard, but her own pure feelings and the ring she wears."

"The ring which some people," with a merry, roguish toss of her handsome head, "term a fetter. Ah, and I verily believe some wives too, though for that class of wife I have small compassion."

"If the ring is wrought into a fetter," put in Catherine, with a sweet, quiet smile, "is not the husband sometimes to blame equally as the wife?"

"My dear," with a pretty shrug, "upon that point we may not argue on fair ground, as I can speak only from supposition, while you, no doubt, do so from experience."

"No experience of that description," smiled the young wife, turning a bright glance on her husband.

Her face instantly clouded, and she added with concern:

"Are you not well, love? You do not look so, but as though you had a headache."

"Yes," remarked Stephanie, "I observed it when I entered, and was about to mention it."

Her handsome eyes had indeed noted it, also the tumbled contents of the work-basket, into which she had so deftly slipped the glove.

She needed no other assurance to be aware her plan had succeeded.

"It is a headache," replied Maurice, glad of the excuse offered. "It came on suddenly. French cookery, I fancy, does not suit me. If you will excuse me, Stephanie, I'll smoke my cigar on the balcony. The night air may remove my indisposition."

Catherine had crossed to him, fond concern in her face, proffering advice, entreating to be let seek restoratives.

Almost coldly he bade her not make a fuss about such a trifle, it annoyed him.

She drew quickly back, startled, pained by a tone so unusual. Maurice took no notice; indeed, he had not perceived it, as lighting his cigar he passed out on to the balcony.

Catherine said no more; she reached her work and began a new subject. She had not yet arrived at that stage of familiarity to make Stephanie her confidante.

Meanwhile, Maurice Burgoyne, a prey to an agony he had never before experienced, leaned over the balcony, his eyes fixed on the street beneath, but not seeing anything. The old words were ringing in his ears.

What was he to think? What was he to do? Could he still believe the hints in the anonymous letter were without foundation? Who was the owner of those gloves, and how had one come into his wife's work-basket?

Could he believe Catherine guilty of light conduct—that is, of conduct unbefitting his wife? No. Nevertheless, he would be a fool, a madman, to blindly trust, and not sift this strange matter to the bottom.

Still, how was he to commence? Should he tell Catherine; or should he not?

How his brain whirled. Calm reasoning was impossible. What he decided to-night he might regret to-morrow, when too late. If he had anyone whom he could consult? But in whom dared he confide?

As the thought passed through his mind a hand was placed lightly on his arm. Looking round, his eyes encountered the handsome face of Stephanie, raised wistfully to his.

"Maurice, dear cousin Maurice!" she murmured in low anxious tones; "what is the matter? Something, I am sure. You are in trouble."

"No, no, no," he rejoined, with an effort, throwing his hair from his forehead. "Why," laughing, "what a commotion women make about a headache."

"Nonsense!" with pretty sympathetic irritability. "Maurice, do not treat me as a child. Possibly your words may deceive and satisfy Catherine; they cannot me. I have been too accustomed to read your features not to believe in my skill there rather than in your speech. Something has happened to annoy you; you are in trouble."

"Even if I were, Stephanie—even if you were right," he answered, gloomily, resuming the position she had found him in, "there are some matters that cannot be shared."

"That is true. Do not think I would force myself into your confidence," she replied, gently, almost humbly. "Forgive me, but I saw your trouble, and the old longing came upon me to try, to hope to help you. There was a time, you know," with a little laugh, "that you used always to bring your troubles to me, seeking my advice—mine, ha, ha! Now it is Catherine you consult, of course; only—only, Maurice, take my advice in this at least; if you are in trouble, do confide in the most proper person to confide in—your wife."

Had she meant what she said, had the words come from her heart, instead of all being purest, cruellest acting, her voice could not have been sweeter, more earnest.

Maurice Burgoyne was moved. His lip trembled. He felt grateful, and, strengthened by the interest shown in his affairs, the old craving after his cousin's advice, the availing himself of her superior intellect, was creeping back more and more.

"Stephanie," he said, in a low tone, "I *am* in trouble, bitter trouble, but it is of a nature I cannot confide to Catherine."

"Nor me?" she remarked, half interrogatively.

He did not at once answer. His eyes were fixed on the street. Stephanie watched him earnestly.

Abruptly, her hand again resting on his arm, she said, softly:

"Maurice, do you recollect that evening in the rose-garden, at Mereton Travers, when you told me you would never more have a secret from me—that you would in any difficulty seek my advice? Cousin, I would not for any consideration force myself upon you, but—but—if I can help you, please let me. You know how gladly I would."

"Stephanie," he replied, pressing the little hand fondly, "God bless you; you are a dear, good girl, and I value your intellect and advice too much to slight it. I *will* confide in you, for I sadly need some one in a case where a woman's advice surely would be the best. Hush!" as glancing back through the curtains, he perceived Catherine return to the apartment, "I cannot speak now—but leave early, and I will see you home; then you shall hear. Go to my wife now, dear."

Stephanie returned the warm pressure of his hand, and with a heart elated with secret triumph, and sparkling eyes, rejoined the fond, innocent wife—the sincere friend she was working so successfully to ruin—yes, ruin; for the hidden threads were tightening, the meshes growing very small, leaving no chance of escape.

*　　*　　*　　*　　*

Stephanie listened to the story Maurice had to tell with the profoundest interest. At first he had hesitated over the recital, but assured of her attention and sympathy, he spoke freely, recounting everything.

"Maurice," said his cousin, in her sweetest tones, "I will not believe it. Catherine's love I am sure is wholly yours. She would not—oh, she *could* not," with a shiver, "be guilty of such deceit!"

"So I feel, so too am I certain," exclaimed her companion, his heart already lighter from the confidence he had made, and Stephanie's belief in his wife's fidelity; "yet how explain that face? How that detestable letter?"

"As to the letter," with a scornful move of the head, "treat it, Maurice, with the contempt it deserves. Yet stay; from what you say, it must surely be a friend who penned it. A friend who has been deceived, as you have, by this double of Catherine's, who is in Paris, therefore they have given you this warning with a kindly intent. May I see the communication? Do you mind?"

"Certainly not. Here it is!" and he produced it.

"The light is not strong enough for me to read it now," continued Stephanie, looking at it as though she did not know every line already.

"Take it home with you, dear. Let me have it to-morrow with your advice."

"You have told me enough already, Maurice, for me to give you that," she answered. "This resemblance of someone to Catherine is very, very singular, considering that it deceives you, her husband, and I think, for Catherine's sake, as your own, you should try to solve the mystery."

"Just my opinion," exclaimed her cousin. "I shall tell Catherine."

"There you are wrong," interposed Stephanie, quietly.

"How?"

"For many reasons. One, why should you pain her by letting her know the cruel suspicions that have been levelled at her? You are aware of her sensitive, and I might say, proud nature. The more innocent she is, the more keenly she will feel it. If I can read character I would not answer for the result."

"How do you mean?" asked Maurice. "What result?"

"The effect upon her mind. It might sadden, cloud it for ever, especially if she fancied that for one moment you had doubted her fidelity. Believe me, Maurice, when mistrust once creeps into the brain, it is no easy matter, try as we will, to eradicate it. Events, chance words, meaningless, innocent enough, are ever recalling the doubt to us. She may ever be suspecting that you suspect her. She will shrink from any man addressing her for fear you will be jealous. Her life will be wretched."

"You are right. I'm sure you read Catherine correctly. And I should go mad to pain her, to give her unnecessary suffering; unnecessary, for I'd swear it's a base calumny. But then, what would you advise, Stephanie? Remember those two on the balcony, and—and the gloves?"

"Both mysteries coming in connection with that letter," proceeded Stephanie—"mysteries that must be explained; but for Catherine's sake I would not seek it yet, Maurice. Nay, on reflection, I would follow the advice of the anonymous letter. I would keep silence, and watch ; not quite for the purpose it specifies, but that you may discover who this concealed friend is, and who is Catherine's double. When you have unravelled this, and the plot which you say you half suspect it is, it will be a proud moment for you to tell Catherine ; and, too, a proud moment for her, the learning the firm trust you placed, despite appearances, in her wifely honour. Maurice, had she never loved you before, she must with all her being, with all her soul, then."

The sentences so calmly, so sagely spoken, had, as the speaker was aware they would, a great effect on their hearer.

His cheek flushed, his eyes brightened, his heart swelled with a sense of relief almost amounting to delight. A terrible weight seemed lifted off him.

"Stephanie, you are like my guardian angel. The clear sensible way you put the case gives quite a new face to it. I will gladly accept your advice, for I feel it is the best."

"No, no," she laughed, lightly. "Do not be too impetuous. Think calmly over it to-night, and decide to-morrow."

"I have decided, and no reflection will change me, Stephanie, to follow the course you advise. And it is your advice ? "

"It is, Maurice. Keep silent. Behave as usual to Catherine ; let her, poor thing, suspect nothing of this cruelty—and watch."

They stood in the deep shadow of the hotel wherein Sir Jaffery resided. As Stephanie spoke she extended her little hand and clasped Maurice's with an encouraging pressure.

Returning it, he stooped and touched her uplifted face with his lips.

A thrill like an electric fire ran through the girl's every never at this kiss from the man she loved. She felt dizzy; her pulses beat almost to be heard; she feared longer to remain, lest she should betray her agitation.

"My good, kind Stephanie," he had whispered; "my sister, indeed."

In rejoinder she murmured hastily:

"Good night, dear Maurice. To-morrow I will see you."

Then leaving him she hurried into the hotel.

Swiftly she ascended to her own room and threw herself on the bed.

She yet seemed to thrill and throb beneath Maurice's kiss, the touch of his lips yet felt on her brow. Her breath came in short, quick gasps.

"Oh!" she cried, half aloud and passionately, "how easily I could have won him but for her, how easily have made his love mine. And that shall be yet," she added, after a pause, starting up; "that shall be. They cannot help themselves. Blindly they walk into our trap. We must succeed. Let her one day be Mrs. Everitt Melton, let her be happy then if she please; what care I, if I am Maurice's wife?"

After that she crossed to her escritoire, took the anonymous letter from her pocket, and locked it carefully away in a secret drawer.

CHAPTER XXIV.

DRAWING THE NET CLOSER.

OR a time matters went on pleasantly at the Hotel Maubert; that is, at least upon the surface, for it would have been against reason to have imagined that Maurice Burgoyne could forget those events which had cast so cruel and torturing a doubt upon his wife's fidelity.

He had strictly followed Stephanie's advice, and had allowed no difference to appear in his manner to Catherine. Indeed, if anything, he was kinder; but those bitter memories haunted him.

At the very moment when she would be fondest—her lips pressing his, her eyes gazing into his face, or her head nestling on his breast, the remembrance would come vividly into his brain.

Eagerly, as if his life depended on it—certainly his happiness did—he would read every line of the delicate exquisite face, and ask himself if falsehood, sin, could wear so innocent a mask. With passionate impulse he would press his wife's soft slight figure to his bosom, seeking to learn the truth in her heart, beating so near his own.

"No, no," he would cry, mentally; "all is a false fabrication, a wicked plot, a strange succession of coincidences. Anything but that my darling is untrue."

He would rain kisses on her face that amazed Catherine, and made her faint with the sweet, great sense of how he loved her. Her soul would hang on her lips with very joy.

Then abruptly he would release her and move away, amazing her again by this changeful humour.

The fond young wife believed she understood the cause, however. Her woman's instinct had already told her that Maurice was labouring under some trouble that he was keeping from her. A trouble, she told herself, she must not ask to share. The estrangement from his father, Sir Jaffery.

She could only sympathise with him, keeping her own grief at being the cause secret, and trying to make amends by greater affection.

What would have been her horror had she known Maurice's real thoughts at those moments. How, carried away by his belief in her, confession of everything would hover on his lips, when a glance of hers, a gentler pressure of the fair arms about his neck, recalled the warning of the anonymous letter, the words: "She who can deceive a husband is capable of anything"; and he would break away with a mental cry:

"Lamia, Lamia! How fair and true was she in Lycius's eyes; yet oh, how foul and false."

No plotters could have plotted with more subtlety. From constantly brooding over his secret, from getting almost unconsciously into the habit of watching his wife, the doubt of her infidelity grew from being ever present in his mind, familiarised to him, and not to be so impossible. His brain became irritated. He was nervous, restless; supremely wretched, he began to feel injured. Catherine's gaiety seemed callousness—a wrong done to himself.

Oh, if some beneficent angel had stepped in to bring about that confession, what misery and despair might have been prevented.

But it was not to be. The blow was to fall.

Maurice, urged by Stephanie's advice, remained mute, while Catherine, believing she knew her husband's sorrow, sorrowed too in silence.

"I am the cause—the sole cause," she reflected. "For his love for me he sacrificed everything—and I nothing. If I have brought him happiness, I have brought also trouble. Better for him had I never said 'Yes.' Oh, God," she added, with a frantic prayerful entreaty, "never let him think so. For the words uttered cannot be unsaid—I am his wife. The law cannot be broken— his wife I must remain. Let him not repent he made me his, for I cannot free him, and to feel I was distasteful to him, that I was his curse, would kill me."

Catherine, however, was much cheered by the reports Stephanie brought respecting Sir Jaffery, and wondered Maurice was not more so.

The baronet was daily getting stronger, growing indeed almost like his old self, and more than once had of his own accord mentioned Maurice.

At least so said Stephanie.

"He seemed curious as to where you were, and how you were getting on, which is a good sign," she remarked one day when alone with her cousin. "I think were it not for one circumstance his forgiveness would soon be won."

"And that circumstance ?" queried Maurice.

"Your visits at midnight to Catherine at Dingle Cottage. True, she was your wife. But Sir Jaffery speaks of it in terms I do not care to repeat, for by some means the information reached him. To say the least, he declares it shows a capability of deceit on Catherine's part towards Mrs. Winburg, using his own words. But there," interrupting herself with well-acted confusion, "you and I are aware how wrong he is, and how in ignorance he maligns our poor Catherine."

"But, Stephanie, I should like to hear what he said," put in Maurice.

"Why ? People when they are angry or believe them- selves unjustly used say anything."

"Still I should like to hear. If not I may imagine his words worse than they were."

"They were spoken in anger, Maurice, and—and" reluctantly—"I'd rather not tell you just at this time."

"But you must, Stephanie. I will know."

"Then," she said, "if you will know, Maurice—and, by the way, it was given as a message: 'Tell Maurice from me, if you ever see him, that one who could so easily deceive others may one day deceive him.' Then he quoted Shakespeare. He ever quotes Shakespeare, you know, only adapting it to the occasion:

> Let him look to it; have a quick eye to see,
> She has deceived——

She stopped, seeing the shadow like thunder on her cousin's face, and quickly added:

"I told him, Maurice, that Desdemona was innocent, and the purest of women."

"Thank you, Stephanie; that was like you," he remarked warmly, pressing her hand. "I said I trusted all to you, and I do, dear. Even this one trouble will soon come right, I feel. But," and his eyes dwelt with even fondness upon her, "what should I have done without you?"

It was a few days after that Catherine, breaking a brief silence as she and Maurice sat at dinner, asked:

"My dear, what kind of amusement is the *Bal de l'Opera?*"

"The *Bal de l'Opera!*" exclaimed her husband, looking up rather surprised. "Whatever, my love, made you think of that?"

"Why because it comes off next week, and everybody is speaking of it—that is—Captain Melton was speaking of it to Madame Franton this afternoon. They say it is quite a brilliant scene, and very gay."

"Oh, it's gay enough."

"You have been there, Maurice?"

"Yes, three years ago."

"Do ladies go?"

"Ladies—well, yes. French ladies, I believe. They go in masks and dominoes, of course, and with friends. They take a box generally to see it, and—well, leave before the what they call 'fun' begins."

"Do they all wear dominoes who go there?"

"No; many go in costume, Pierrots, Vivandières, and the like; many gentlemen simply in evening dress;" and Maurice entered into greater explanation of the aspect and gaieties of the Opera Ball.

Catherine listened with innocent delight and amusement. The description charmed her. To her it was so new, so original.

"Oh, Maurice, dear!" she ejaculated, clasping her hands, and her eyes sparkling with mirth, "it must be fun to watch. How I should like to sit an hour or so in one of those boxes and see it."

"You, Catherine?" he remarked.

"Yes, dear. Only as a spectator. Is it wrong?" she asked, a little surprised, for only that afternoon Captain Melton had hinted it was the most natural, the most customary thing for ladies, visitors to the gay capital, to do. "Is there any harm?"

"Harm? Well, no; nor wrong, of course, as some Parisian ladies go. Still," added Maurice, hesitatingly, "it is not a place where I should like my wife to be seen, nor to which I should like to take her; and you could scarcely go with anyone else."

"My dear, I would not think of going with any other," put in Catherine, laughing. "There, not another word, my love. Since I have learned your opinion—and I know you are right—I shall think no more of it."

"Then you have thought of it?" queried her husband.

"Only in this way," she replied, unconstrainedly. "Madame Franton spoke of it to-day, and said we ought to go once just to see it, as it would amuse us."

"Very thoughtful of Madame Franton," said Maurice, with a knitting of the brows. "Very much obliged to her. I cannot say I thank Melton for the introduction. I do not like her."

"Neither do I, dear; yet one must be civil. But she can do no harm, as I am not likely to take her opinion instead of yours."

"I should hope not, Catherine," remarked her husband, gravely.

"Why, how seriously spoken," she laughed. "As if it were at all probable, you silly, silly fellow."

Leaving her chair, she came to him. Her arms were round his neck, her soft cheek pressing his.

He kissed her fondly, caressing the golden head, and it was a happy evening that followed, though the husband and wife passed it alone.

Before the sun again arose Maurice Burgoyne, haggard, distracted, mad, was to regard himself as disgraced, dishonoured, duped.

CHAPTER XXV.

THE OPERA BALL.

Hotel du Louvre.

EAR MAURICE,—Can you come here this evening at ten? I shall be alone, and have news for you—good, very good news, I hope. You will understand to what my news refers. You trusted in me, *mon cher* cousin, and I shall prove myself worthy of the trust. Do me one favour in return. Say nothing, hint nothing of this to Catherine. I am rather given to *coups de théâtre*, and if my hopes be only realised, I should like to give her so sweet a surprise myself. I should wish to see her face when I exclaim, "Catherine, Maurice is forgiven; Sir Jaffery pardons!" It is all the reward I ask. Do not deprive me of it. You can make any excuse for your absence.—Yours in sincerity,   STEPHANIE.

This letter had been delivered to Maurice when alone. "Private" was written outside, and he had hastened to open and peruse the contents before he was interrupted.

How great was his joy as he followed the lines. Stephanie had succeeded, or was succeeding. He and the father he loved would soon be reconciled. Were that not nearly certain never would his cousin bid him come beneath the roof that covered Sir Jaffery. She dared not.

It had been long waiting, but the waiting had been crowned with success. Soon all of them might quit Paris, of which, lately, Maurice had grown rather weary, and together return to Mereton Travers — dear old Mereton.

"And it's all her doing—brave, good Stephanie's," he ejaculated, rapturously, pressing the letter to his lips. "God bless her."

Then he crushed the missive into his pocket, and rapidly wrote his reply before Catherine's return.

He would gladly have told his wife of this golden promise in their lives, but he could not refuse Stephanie this trifle she asked—so slight a favour, yet one that proved how unselfish and affectionate was her disposition.

It was, though, no easy task for him to keep his secret during the ensuing hours, especially when Catherine, laughing, rallied him on his exceedingly high spirits.

He found an excuse for his absence that evening as Stephanie had suggested. It was not difficult, for Catherine put faith in all he said, only jestingly she remarked, as before going he embraced her with more than usual tenderness :

"Do you recollect, Maurice, that this is the night of the *bal de l'opera?* Take care you do not pay it a visit before your return."

"I patronise that wild orgie!" he laughed. "Not I ; I am bent on far different business. Good night, love. Do not be dull."

Another embrace ; then he ran down the stairs, sprang into the *fiacre* waiting, and was driven to the Hotel du Louvre.

When was he to embrace his wife again ? Ah !—perhaps never !

Stephanie received Maurice with effusion.

"Oh, Maurice !" she exclaimed, "how have I prayed for this time, however I knew it must come, to see you once more, as I may say, beneath your father's roof. Ah," she smiled, detecting the glance he had thrown around, "you are too sanguine. Surely you did not expect Sir Jaffery to be here."

"I am so full of delight at the contents of your letter, dear Stephanie, that I know not what to expect," he rejoined, yet retaining her hand, as they sat down together on a couch. "I have called you my good angel so often and ever with such cause, that the title seems hackneyed, I need a better."

"Sufficient for me now, Maurice," she replied with a momentary droop of her dark lashes, "is to be your sister and friend."

The simple word "now" brought back to Maurice Burgoyne the remembrance that Stephanie had once confessed her love for him, her hope to have won him ; and a greater pity, a greater tenderness, a greater admiration stole over him as his eyes rested upon her.

How meekly she had after that first passion taken her disappointment ; how she had proved the depth of her affection by her behaviour to him since, devoting her thoughts, her time, her actions to his good.

"God bless you, Stephanie," he said gratefully, in a low tone, pressing the hand he yet retained.

The girl released her fingers with a little laugh.

"And now to prove my friendship, Maurice," she remarked. "Sir Jaffery's health has so much improved that, after consulting Sidford—that good Sidford, who is so much your friend too—I have resolved to bring about a meeting between you and the baronet, if you consent."

"If I consent, Stephanie ? As if I could do other," he rejoined eagerly. "My only hesitation will arise from thoughts of him. I have done him harm enough already, Heaven pardon me. Did I do more, I could never pardon myself. And did you not tell me that the physician warned you against a shock, which might be dangerous ? "

"Yes ; but there must be none, Maurice. Sir Jaffery must be aware of your coming ; he must give his consent to your doing so."

"Ah, will he ? "

"From my soul I believe yes," replied Stephanie confidently. "The fact is, though I have not informed you—not wishing to give rise to hopes that might be disappointed—for some little time Sidford and I have been cautiously feeling our way, mentioning your name as by accident, bringing up events of the past, which must have brought you and your affection as a son to his memory. At first he frowned, then he appeared to take no heed, then he listened, then he grew thoughtful after any of these occasions, and finally to-day he asked of his own accord where you were. I told him in Paris. 'What, here?' he exclaimed. 'In this city?' Then, Maurice, I ventured on an untruth. I told him you had followed us here. I said that you could never feel real happiness estranged from him; that, though you would never dream of forcing yourself into his presence unbidden, you lived in the hope that one day his anger would soften towards you, and he of his own desire would summon you to his presence."

"That, dear Stephanie, at least is no untruth," remarked Maurice. "And how did he take it?"

"In silence at first, showing an irritation I believed assumed to conceal emotion. At any rate I acted on that belief to plead your cause, your affection for him. 'Dearest guardian,' I ended, 'consent to see Maurice once. Let him himself entreat you. Remember, you have never given him the opportunity to speak; you have judged him unheard.' Still he was silent; then he said: 'Well, well, I will see. Partly you are right, Stephanie. There will be no harm in an interview; though not yet, not yet; I am not strong enough for it. In a few days, perhaps; only he must come alone.' I call this much gained, Maurice; before the week is out it shall be more."

"Much gained!" he exclaimed enthusiastically. "It is everything, Stephanie; and all is owing to you! Let me but see my father, and I feel I can not only win his pardon for myself, but also for Catherine."

A sensation like an iron hand grasping her heart, almost stilling its pulsation, came to Stephanie at the mention of her rival's name.

But smiling sweetly she replied:

"Ah, Catherine; we must not forget her, A quarter to eleven. Five minutes more, Maurice, then you shall go."

But as they sat talking the five grew into ten—fifteen, and finally it was Stephanie herself who, her eyes having frequently wandered to the clock, dismissed him.

No. 8.

SWIFTLY HE SWUNG ROUND, FOR THE EXCLAMATION HAD COME FROM BEHIND HIM.

As Stephanie dismissed Maurice, she said :

" I have altered my mind while we have been chatting, Maurice, about keeping our news from Catherine. It is not fair to her, who will rejoice at it as much as ourselves. Besides, it will sound sweeter in her ears coming from her husband's lips."

Never had Maurice loved his cousin so much as at that moment. He regarded her almost as so angelic a being that this world was unworthy of her. With reverence he kissed her white forehead, the brain behind which was even then beating with anxiety respecting the cruel plot that was being levelled against his happiness.

" Yes," she murmured with a laugh, low and trium-phant, as the door closed on her cousin ; " tell her, your good angel gives you full permission ; tell her when you see her—— Surely," consulting the clock once more, "by this time Captain Melton must have succeeded. I hope I have not let him go too soon."

Meanwhile Maurice hastened quickly back to the Hotel Maubert.

The permission Stephanie had given him to inform Catherine of everything had added considerably to his pleasure.

Eager to have her participate in his happiness arising from a probable speedy reconciliation with his father, he sprang up the stairs and entered the sitting-room.

He fully expected to find her there, for glancing up from the street he had seen that the lights were burning brightly, not turned down as they generally were if his wife had retired to her own apartment.

But no one was there. She, no doubt, then, was coming back.

Maurice, however, was too impatient to wait ; he hastened to her dressing-room.

The door was slightly ajar, and within he caught a glimpse of Mademoiselle Rose seated in a fauteuil reading a novel, as he had seen her before when waiting for her mistress's return from the theatre.

Surprised, pushing the door wide, he said :

" Where is Madame Burgoyne ? "

" Madame ? " exclaimed the soubrette, instantly springing to her feet. " Oh, monsieur, madame is out."

" Out ? " cried Maurice in amaze he could not control.

" Yes, monsieur. About half an hour after you had gone a letter came and a *fiacre* for madame. Madame said the letter was from you. She dressed at once—ah, in all haste, and drove off in the *fiacre*."

Stunned by this startling intelligence that Catherine should leave the hotel at such an hour, alone, and under pretence of having received a letter from himself, all his old doubts rushing back, Maurice turned to quit the room, having no desire to betray his agitation to Mdlle. Rose, whose keen black eyes were regarding him fixedly.

" Ah, monsieur, I forgot," exclaimed the soubrette. " A quarter of an hour or so ago, a letter came for monsieur. It is on the table of the *salon*."

A letter ! That possibly would explain what now to him was inexplicable—Catherine's absence.

As he departed, Mdlle. Rose gave a malicious little laugh, and hummed with much point a *vaudeville* song.

The words were far too low to reach Maurice Burgoyne, who strode back to the dining-room.

There, on the table he perceived the note which had previously, in his excitement, escaped his attention.

Seizing it, he reeled, and placed his hand to his forehead, for he recognised the same writing as that of the anonymous letter.

A moment—only a moment—he hesitated whether he should open it, then he tore the envelope to fragments in his cruel impatience to get at the contents.

You followed the warning, and displayed your wisdom. You have watched. Now you are able to pluck away the veil and save yourself from dishonour, from being the most humiliated being in men's eyes, a wife's dupe. Mrs. Burgoyne, in a mask and blue domino, with a knot of scarlet ribbons on the left shoulder, is now at the *bal de l'opera*, and *not* alone. If you doubt, use your own eyes, and prove the correctness of my statement. You may easily. *La belle Anglaise* is known.

"At the *bal de l'opera*," ejaculated Maurice, staggering back, pale, haggard. "She—Catherine—my wife!"

Only a space did he remain inactive. He gave himself no time to reason whether the anonymous communication might be false. He only thought if it were true—only thought that he must test the assertion, must at any risk prove it."

Seizing his hat, he ran downstairs like a madman, hailed a passing *fiacre*, and called as he sprang in:

"To the *bal de l'opera*."

CHAPTER XXVI.

WHAT HAPPENED AT THE BAL DE L'OPERA.

T was mignight, but the theatre was already beginning to swarm with maskers in all disguises, dominoes, and in evening dress. Through the two doors they poured in an endless stream—through the passages into the *salle*. Speedily it became a difficult matter to retain your footing in the Nosse-aux-Lions, for the surging crowd of revellers, among which were to be seen all styles of costume from the days of antiquity to the present, elbowed by the more grotesque and fanciful, such as savages, *pierrots*, monks, nuns, field-marshals, and *debardeurs*.

It was one moving mass of colour and animation. Quips and jests were given and received without offence ; laughter rose into the air, blended with voices and the shrill accents of women.

Each instant the shouts, the mirth, the hubbub increased, until the *foyer* somewhat resembled pandemonium broke loose, while above it and adding to it came the crash of the music of the orchestra.

From the boxes leaned other maskers, either enjoying the scene safely from a distance, or waiting until inclination made them join the wild throng.

It was with its wreathing, moving colours, its music, its brilliant lights, its laughter, a spectacle once seen never to be forgotten. Each one apparently had resolved to get as much amusement out of the passing hour as was possible.

Everywhere were signs of gaiety. For the time care seemed to have been flung aside—banished—for surely in that merry excited throng it had no resting-place.

Yet stay, there was one face, set, white, and stony, where it alone held sway. The face was Maurice Burgoyne's.

Standing, his lips pressed firmly together beneath his moustache, his hand tightly gripping his crush-hat, his eyes sought in every direction for the blue domino with the knot of scarlet ribbons on the left shoulder—his wife's disguise.

He was heedless of everything but that search. He hardly heard—he never noticed—the jests that were flung at him at times from small lips budding red beneath the mask through which eyes as bright as diamonds sparkled.

"What, hasn't she kept her appointment?" laughed a *debardeur*, halting in front of him. "*Mon Dieu!* what wonder monsieur has a face like acid wine."

"Shall I find her?" broke in a *pierrot* flapping his long sleeves. "Ah, I know, in a pink domino. Yes, I saw her. She was drinking champagne with a monk whose nose showed him no sugar-and-water drinker."

"Go home to bed, *niais*. Your face is like snow in August. It freezes one."

So went on the jests. Maurice brushed them away as the irritating touch of the fly, while his gaze wandered again and again over the throng—unsuccessfully. He drew a deep breath of relief. Had he indeed been fooled —duped?

What matter as long as it had not been by Catherine. As long as she was innocent.

"Good heaven!" and he shivered from head to heel. "My wife in such a wild, boisterous scene as this, even as a spectator. She would not."

Relieved, he nevertheless made his way through the shouting, laughing crowd.

Dominoes of all hues passed him—pink, mauve, blue of every shade, but none with the scarlet knot of ribbons.

"It is all false. I thought it, I knew it," he muttered, as he made one more tour of the *salle*. "Yet what could have taken her out at such an hour?"

It was singular, but he felt he could forgive any reason but her presence there, which would have been rendered yet worse from her knowlege of his disapproval of the place.

Abruptly, with a quick catch of the breath, he halted; his gaze, straying round the triple row of boxes now filled with maskers, had been arrested by a knot of scarlet ribbons on the shoulder of a mask in a blue domino.

The person's arm was resting on the cushion of the box, but her face was turned in to the interior where a male masker was just visible.

For a space Maurice Burgoyne stood white, stunned, his eyes rivetted on that knot of ribbons. There was a rapid beat at his heart, a surging in the brain.

The maskers swayed him as they jostled by, but he paid no heed. The only sense left him seemed sight, and that was fixed on the blue domino.

Was it a coincidence? Strange but merely that? Great heaven! no.

The domino had turned, and, leaning forward with amused interest, looked down at the gay grotesque crowd. Her mask was removed, her fair hair fell softly on her shoulders.

It was Catherine; it was his wife!

His teeth clenched, a hard, terrible expression in his eyes, Maurice began resolutely to force his way through the motley throng towards the staircase. He had counted the number of the box in the row. He would proceed thither, and confront his guilty wife.

Again his gaze travelled to the *loge*. Even as his white face turned in the direction the male masker bent forward, and with familiar audacity, as if aware there would be no reproof, kissed the pretty golden head.

The blue domino started, looked with laughing mock indignation over her shoulder, then resuming her mask, arose.

A demon of fury was in Maurice Burgoyne's soul. This was the woman he had loved, had held so pure.

Pure! and with a smile had accepted a man's kiss publicly in such a place as that.

Dishonoured, duped, deceived!

What had Sir Jaffery said? What the anonymous letter?

Both were right; he saw it now. Saw it! Was it not there before his eyes?

Oh, heaven! this was her for whom he had sacrificed so much.

At the foot of the stairs he was for a moment unable to proceed, owing to a crowd of maskers descending. For a space he could not move; he was hemmed in.

Maurice Burgoyne's face was flushed now. His pulses beat as if the fire of fever were in his veins. His brain was maddened.

The crowd had somewhat thinned, he sprang up the stairs, forcing his way.

The quip paused on the masker's lip at the expression of his countenance.

Reaching the corridor, he hastened to the *loge*.

The door stood slightly open.

He thrust it wide, and beheld the only occupant, a Mephistopheles, who was leaning over the box regarding the prismatic throng beneath.

Maurice had reason enough left to command his agitation as the mask turned.

"Monsieur," he said, "your pardon, but this moment there were two persons here: a lady in a blue domino and scarlet knot of ribbons, and——"

"A Hamlet, Prince of Denmark," laughed the mask. "Yes, monsieur is correct; as they left, I came in."

"A thousand thanks."

And bowing, Maurice retired.

She had escaped him then!

Only for a space. He would not leave until he had found her.

Along the corridors, from a *loge* eagerly examining the throng beneath; among the throng itself, scanning the boxes, went Maurice Burgoyne, calm through the very intensity of madness.

Nowhere could he catch a glimpse of the blue domino and her sable-clad companion.

Had she seen him and fled?

Should he find her at home, peaceful, and full of innocence; startled, half indignant, half fondly reproachful at the charge cast upon her virtue? Of course, denying everything; some wild excuse, hastily concocted, advanced for her absence.

Maurice laughed bitterly as the ideas floated through his fevered brain.

He felt disposed to put it to the test; but he found it impossible to tear himself from the ball.

"Maurice—my husband!"

The words, in accents of alarmed surprise, fell suddenly on his ear.

Catherine! Again he had found her.

Swiftly he swung round, for the exclamation had come from behind him.

So there was the blue domino and scarlet shoulder-knot. There was the male masker, Hamlet, Prince of Denmark, within three feet of him.

With a muttered cry of wrath, he sprang forward.

The two had already made a retrograde movement, leaving a momentary space which a swarm of dancing *pierrots* and *débardeurs* as rapidly filled, for a *bal de l'opera* abhors a vacuum, and Maurice was separated from those he would have reached.

He yet, however, kept them in view and pursued.

Soon some of the maskers took in an idea of the affair, and with laughter and jest threw themselves in his way; but the countenance he turned on them, so fierce, so full of scorn and loathing, made many fall back.

Eagerly he pressed on, for he saw by the direction the two were taking that it was possible they purposed to quit the theatre.

Once outside, once in a *fiacre*, they would be lost.

This he would prevent.

He would unmask his wretched wife.   He would leave no ground for excuses, for denials.   He would see her crushed, humiliated, convicted ; then quit her for ever.

Again and again, as he followed, he asked himself :

"Who was her companion ? "

He had first sprung to the conclusion that it was Captain Melton ; but now he fancied him taller, slimmer ; while, too, the hair of the mask was fair.

Yes, they were evidently making for the large door of exit.

All now depended on a few minutes.

He darted on.   He was within three yards of them.

They evidently knew he was following, for they quickened their pace.

They were at the doors, but they could not escape.

So he believed, so it seemed, when some half-dozen of partially intoxicated revellers, forming a circle, barred his passage.

With a curse, Maurice struck at them.   One toppled head over heels.

To spring over his prostrate, sprawling body was the work of an instant.   The next he had dashed through the door into the street.

The two had disappeared.

Panting, eager, furious, he looked down the line of vehicles.

There was one just moving away.

Maurice ran to another.

"Who is in that cab ? " he exclaimed.   "A lady——"

"In a blue domino," said the man, noting something was wrong.

"And a gentleman ? "

"Yes, monsieur."

"Follow them," cried Maurice, pulling open the door. " Keep them in sight, and I'll give you a napoleon above your fare.   Quick !   Off !   Lose not a moment ! "

The driver needed no other urging. Seizing the reins, his vehicle was soon rumbling and jolting after the other.

From the window Maurice Burgoyne watched the *fiacre* in front, between which and his own the distance did not increase, though it did not much decrease.

From street to street they went. Oh, the agony the miserable husband suffered!

How his love for Catherine had clasped about his heart, as the roots of the stately oak clasp the earth that affords it life-nourishment; and to have it, with all its trust and fondness, plucked away thus!

Suddenly, with a start, he recognised the *quartier* they had entered—one not of the most respectable class.

A few moments after the *fiacre* drew up.

"What is it?" demanded Maurice, looking forth eagerly.

"It has stopped, monsieur," replied the driver. "The lady in the blue domino and the gentleman have alighed."

Maurice leaped out.

"Where have they gone?" he demanded. "In which direction?"

"They have gone into that house, La Pomme de Paradis," he answered, pointing to the one the *fiacre* was just leaving.

"La Pomme de Paradis!" gasped Maurice, leaping out of the vehicle.

A few seconds later he had entered.

"*Eh bien, monsieur!* What do you desire?" asked the *garçon*. "Supper?"

"A lady and gentleman just now entered," answered Maurice, commanding his voice, and the *ruse* flashing into his brain. "They have ordered supper. I am to join them."

"This way, monsieur," and the *garçon* led him up-stairs.

Maurice Burgoyne's pulse beat hot and fiercely. In a few seconds he would be in the presence of his miserable wife, denouncing her.

How would he bear to look upon her face, once in his eyes so lovely, now that of a Lamia revealed.

The *garçon*, suddenly stopping, looked back.

"*Tiens!* Nothing was said about monsieur's coming," he suggested.

"That is because they forgot to mention it," replied Maurice, slipping a napoleon in the waiter's palm.

"Ah, I understand. It is here, monsieur."

He placed his hand on the door knob, then remarked in a tone of surprise :

"*Tiens!* It is locked."

He knew well it would be so. He was acting his part as were others.

Maurice knew none of this. Enraged at the barrier, he seized the handle, and shook the door violently.

"Open!" he cried hoarsely ; "I command you, or the law shall compel you. Open!"

There was a stifled cry within the room, then silence.

Maurice drew back a step, then with a terrible impetus sent his shoulder in full force against the door.

The lock gave, the door burst wide, revealing darkness beyond.

"Lights!" shouted Maurice.

There was a hurrying of feet on the stairs—the loud voice of the landlord.

Maurice, remembering the waiter held a light, seized it, and rushed in.

Guarding the door that none should escape, he held the light above his head and looked round.

No one—not a soul.

Supper was there, but none to partake of it.

Cautiously he moved more into the room, his eyes glancing into every corner.

No one!

Then his eyes detected another door.

In a second he was at it, shaking it, for it too was locked.

The landlord loudly expostulated.

"Man," he cried fiercely, " would you have me call the *gens d'arme* to my aid ? "

Then he dashed forward—once, twice—and the door fell back.

An ante-room, but once more empty.

Empty ! but the window was open.

Maurice sprang to it.

Beneath was a low outhouse in a yard. In the latter was a short ladder, while the yard-door leading into a side street was open.

It spoke for itself.

They had eluded him ; they had escaped. Maurice drew back sick and giddy.

At that moment the *garçon* lifted up some white object from the floor, and held it, half-doubtfully, half-questioningly, to the husband.   It was a woman's handkerchief.

Maurice, seizing it, moved the delicate cambric between his shaking fingers, seeking the initials of the owner.

Here they were, a monogram he himself had made—C. B.

"Great heaven ! " he groaned inaudibly, as reeling he leaned against the wall for support.   "What further proof do I want ?   It is my wife's."

Then rousing himself, conscious of the curious eyes resting on him, he flung down gold more than sufficient to defray all the damage he had done, rushed down the stairs, sprang into the *fiacre*, and drove back to the Hotel Maubert.   Ascending the stairs, proceeding along the corridor abruptly, near his apartments he came upon Mdlle. Rose with her finger on her lip.

Hush, monsieur ; madame has returned," she said in a whisper.   "Madame is not well.   She has gone to bed and sleeps."

Maurice stood staring vaguely, dully, at the maid, then with a low suppressed laugh passed her, saying she might go to bed, she would no longer be needed, and proceeded to his wife's room.

CHAPTER XXVII.

THE ACCUSATION.

AURICE BURGOYNE, entering his wife's apartment, closed the door behind him. Its aspect recalled to him that time when he had come there with only doubts in his mind; or rather, not even doubts, but surprise at those two he had seen on the balcony. Now what were his feelings? Doubts no longer, but certainties.

Catherine laid on a couch, still in her evening dress, asleep.

He advanced and looked down upon her.

Her face was pale, very pale; on it were traces of fatigue, exhaustion; her bosom heaved as that of one breathless from running or in terror; her slender fingers moved restlessly, while, even as he stood, a sigh as of suffering escaped her lips.

In the husband's eyes these were but signs of the excitement she had undergone after detection, and knowledge of the part she had to play to deceive him.

He felt scorn, not compassion, as he touched her shoulder, exclaiming in deep, hoarse utterance:

"Catherine!"

At the sound of his voice she sprang up and pressed her hands to her temples with that scared, wandering expression seen in the eyes of those roused from stupor. Then as she beheld who it was by her side, uttering a cry of joy, she threw her arms round him, saying:

"Oh, Maurice, Maurice, at last! Thank heaven you have come."

Quickly catching her wrists, he removed them from his neck, and holding them away, answered sternly:

"Yes, I have come at last. Come for an explanation of your conduct this evening. What explanation have you to give?"

"Ah, Maurice, no wonder you are angry; but you will not be when you hear. You will be enraged, as I am," proceeded Catherine excitedly, a flush rising to her previously pale cheek. "Rose told me of your return, of your finding me absent. Ah, what could you have thought? Oh, Maurice, Maurice, what can it mean? Maurice, I have been cheated, cruelly deceived!"

A curiosity came upon him to hear what excuse she would give. All was over between them; he should regret it less, he felt, the more he knew how base she was. He watched her agitation, her excitement, and deemed it excellent acting. Thus he merely said:

"Yes, I found you absent. You had left hurriedly in a *fiacre* that had been sent for you."

"A *fiacre*, and with it, Maurice, a note purporting to come from you," she proceeded, attributing his coldness to causes she believed she was about to remove. "Now I know it did not; and it is you, Maurice, my husband, who must seek the writer, who must redress the wrong done me."

"The wrong done *me*. As your husband," he remarked, "trust me, I shall find a means. Pray what did the note say?"

"Only these words: 'Come to me at once, dear Catherine. I have sent a *fiacre*, the driver knows the directions. Do not lose a second. In great haste,—MAURICE.'"

"Where is the note?"

"I cannot find it. I placed it in my pocket, and either I have drawn it forth with my handkerchief, or it has been taken from there by someone."

A bitter smile faintly appeared on his lips.

"Maurice, husband," she exclaimed, "why do you look like that? Good heaven, Maurice, you do not doubt me?"

"Doubt, why? What cause could I have to, Catherine?"

"What cause, indeed?" she proceeded gravely. "None. But you have cause, great cause to search into this cruel mystery of which I have been a prey, and expose it."

"What mystery?" he exclaimed irritably, for his own wrongs were eager for utterance. "Why do you not say?"

"I cannot, while you look thus," she answered tremulously. "I cannot understand you. You seem to express neither surprise nor interest. You rather appear to scorn my words. What is the matter?"

"Matter? Surely, Catherine, has not your own speech given me matter enough? There," and releasing her he began pacing the room, "you can speak better thus and I hear. Proceed. Cannot you perceive how you are maddening me? You state you had this note—which you have lost. You went in the *fiacre*—well?"

She regarded him with sad, wondering, humid eyes, then, passing her hand over her forehead as if a weight were there, continued in a low voice:

"Yes, astonished at the summons, but fully believing it was from you, I went. As you are aware, I am ignorant of Paris. Where we went I know not. I only thought you had sent for me, that you had given the driver directions, and my mind was free from suspicion.

"Finally the cab stopped before a house in a quiet street. Hardly had it done so than the door was opened by an elderly man, something like a butler, who ushered me into a back drawing-room, nicely furnished, where was an old lady.

"Greeting me politely, she said that you had been compelled to go out, but would return in half an hour, and had left word for me to wait."

Maurice Burgoyne stifled an impatient exclamation. Was ever a lamer, more improbable story concocted? It shamed him almost to listen it.

"My surprise increasing, I ventured to try to learn who the speaker was, and if she knew at all why you had summoned me.

" She seemed to catch my desire and said :

" 'I am a friend of Sir Jaffery Burgoyne's, madame, and I believe Mr. Maurice's desire for you to come arises from something in reference to the baronet.'

" This allayed my wonder ; it seemed so probable, at least to me. The woman, for lady I may no longer call her, placed some books and magazines on the table for my amusement, then withdrew.

" Half an hour, nearly an hour passed, you did not return. The woman reappeared, and asked if I would not take a glass of wine—the decanters stood on a side table—as I must need some refreshment. I refused, but asked for a glass of water ; the room was so close and warm I felt faint.

" She answered it was not water I saw, but lemonade, and filled me a glass. I drank it eagerly, and she left me.

" I returned to the magazines, wondering at your prolonged absence, and feeling drowsy, which I attributed to the atmosphere of the apartment. From that moment I remembered nothing until I became conscious of the woman leaning over me bathing my face with water.

" I staggered to my feet.

" 'Where is Mr. Maurice Burgoyne, my husband,' I cried.

" 'Mr. Maurice Burgoyne ;' she exclaimed with assumed surprise. 'Goodness me, madame ! how should I know who never even heard of him ?'

" 'Never heard of him ?' I cried. 'And you said you were a friend of Sir Jaffery's. You know he had appointed to meet me here ?'

" 'I know nothing of the kind,' she retorted. 'I knew you came here to meet someone who hasn't come. I know a quarter of an hour ago I found you in a faint, and that is all.'

" I stared at her bewildered, indignant.

" 'I tell you what it is,' she proceeded. 'It's my opinion you'd better get home, I can't be kept up any longer. It's near three o'clock.'

"I looked at my watch, and with a cry of horror saw she was right.

"Terrified, I ran to the door, dashed it open, flew to the outer one, and sprang into the street. A *fiacre* chanced to be passing. I called it.

"'Hotel Maubert,' I cried, as getting in I nearly again fainted on the cushions.

"Reaching here, I heard of your return from Rose. My suspicions were confirmed. You, Maurice, had not sent that letter. But who had? Why, for what purpose, had I been deceived? The mystery was beyond my unravelling, but it must not be beyond yours, Maurice. As my husband, it is you who must do it."

There was a thrill of pain, of reproach in her voice, for his manner chilled her to the heart.

His face was set and stern, but showed no trace of that indignation natural to a husband whose wife had been so treated.

As she ceased he turned upon her. Stern, but yet with scorn, contempt in his eyes.

"And do you imagine that I am to be thus deceived?" Then with a voice of concentrated rage and irony, Maurice exclaimed: "Woman—base, crafty as you are, despite the mask of innocence with which nature has cruelly cursed you—do you conceive to trick me by a story so ridiculous, so absurd?"

"Maurice!" she articulated in astonishment, stepping back, her eyes dilated with amaze as they rested upon him.

But the flood-gates of his wrath were open and he heeded no interruption.

"Mystery? For what purpose could they treat you thus? Ah! what, indeed! Therein truely would be the mystery," laughing bitterly.

"Maurice," she grasped, pale and alarmed, "what has come to you? Are you mad?"

"Were I, where would be the wonder?" And now, though his accents never rose high, they were rapid, passionate, and terrible. "Great heaven! what more is fitted to overthrow the sanity of man than to find the wife he has deemed pure as the angels, false, base as the commonest clay of earth?"

"Maurice!" she again grasped, grasping the couch for support, as his cruel words rained on her.

"Cover not yourself with greater infamy by excuses as false as they are badly constructed."

"Maurice, I swear what I have said is true."

"True? Silence! I know everything. Did not I, but an hour ago, see you revelling in that wild scene."

"Maurice, I do not, cannot comprehend you."

"Stay then. You told your story; I'll tell mine," he continued, making a supreme effort at control. "On returning to this hotel, I not only found that you had quitted it at a most strange hour, ostensibly through a note from myself, but also a letter, just left by hand. Hoping it might give some explanation of your singular absence, I tore it open. My surmise was correct. It told me, did I wish to find my wife, I should do so at the *bal de l'opera*."

"I! At the *bal de l'opera!*" cried Catherine, amazed. "Preposterous, Maurice! Surely you never put belief in a statement that bore such falsehood on its face? Oh, heaven, you knew me better than even for a second to sully your love for me by a suspicion!"

"You were absent. The reason given I know to be untrue," he answered with a shrug of scorn. "The letter——"

"Which must have been from the same base hand that penned mine," she broke in, more calmly.

Not quite. The letter bade me test the truth of its assertion that I should find my wife at the ball, in a blue domino, having a knot of scarlet ribbons on the shoulder; also that I should not find her alone."

"Oh, this is absurd—too absurd for serious treatment," said Catherine.

She was rapidly gaining composure.

"I need not ask you if you went, I perceive, Maurice, you were capable of putting that insult upon me. Shame upon you."

"Yes," he responded in a low, hard voice, "I went. I proved the statement correct. I found you."

"Found me—I—at the ball?"

Then she broke into a laugh, her lip curled, and sitting down, she beat her foot impatiently on the floor.

"This surpasses even absurdity." Then: "Maurice, tell me, are you suffering under delusion? Have you, too, been deceived, or have you ceased to love me, and this is some plot to rob me of honour? If you can suspect me, who never wronged you by any unwifely thought even, surely I have a right to suspect on my side?"

"You act your part marvellously well," he rejoined; "so much so that, had not my own eyes been my informers, I might have believed you. Now I may not. Can you, dare you deny, Catherine, that you were there, and not alone; that from a *loge* on the second tier you watched, unmasked, the throng beneath; that you permitted your companion to touch his lips to your hair unreproved; that, after, you mingled with the throng, and coming unexpectedly upon me, uttered my name; that you fled; that in a *fiacre* you, with your companion, proceeded to a house in the Rue Poutain to supper; that my arrival—for I was in pursuit—scared you, and, oh heaven! you escaped by the window."

Catherine's face, which at first had expressed bewilderment and perplexity, as though she could not credit her ears, had now grown calm, and full of a noble dignity.

"Maurice, from the manner in which you speak, I could be convinced that you believe what you say; if so, there is some terrible mystery here that, at present, you nor I can read."

"Is this your reply, your refutation, Catherine?" he asked in the same tone.

"Refutation ! Excuse !" she answered proudly. "I stoop to make none to charges of which, Maurice, you, who know me, should hold as innocent as I know I am. Oh, Maurice," and her features, her voice softened into tenderness, "will you not believe me ? What I have said, I swear by my honour—and yours, which, if possible, I hold yet dearer—is true. Husband, trust me, and together let us seek to unravel this cruel riddle plotted by some enemy."

He was silent. He was moved. His very love, and that was not shaken, pleaded for her.

He gazed with eager scrutiny at the pale lovely countenance, the eyes of which, so pure to their very depths, so fearlessly met his. He marked in them the affection, the gentle pleading. He saw the graceful figure inclined, the fair arms partly extended towards him, and he asked himself :

Can I have been made a dupe ? Is this the face of one who could have laughed and mingled in that gay scene ? Could such a face cover so base and sinful a heart as must have beaten in the breast of the wearer of the blue domino whom I pursued.

No !

While doubt and perplexity racked his brain, a voice within him cried—No !

Catherine detected the change with a thrill of delight. On her knees she fell before him, clasping his with her arms.

"Maurice, dear Maurice !" she exclaimed, "you will believe—you will trust me. You are the victim of some fearful plot, as I am. Why and wherefore, who can tell ; not either yet. But only tell me you no longer doubt a love that, before heaven, I vow has never swerved from you, even in thought, and it shall be discovered—the plotters unmasked. Husband, your face looks kinder. Speak to me once—ah, but a word in your old sweet fond voice ! False to you, dear ! Oh, Maurice, how could I lightly forfeit that which constitutes my life—your love ?

Take that from me, and it would be kinder to deal death in return. Maurice, dear Maurice, husband—your affection is so precious to me, that though innocent and cruelly wounded, I kneel to plead."

She leaned her cheek against his knee, her face gazing up at him.

"Maurice! husband! as true as ever was wife am I to you! Darling, take me to your arms!"

One moment, then he bent over her.

"Catherine!" he exclaimed, "you swear this—you swear——"

He stopped, started, the red blood rushed to his cheek as she rejoined:

"I do—I swear!"

He swiftly stooped and plucked from the ground, among the folds of her dress, where it may have fallen from her bosom or pocket, a scarlet knot of ribbons.

"Perjuress!" he cried in scorn, as he dashed it in her face, "behold the proof of your guilt! We part, never from this moment to meet again!"

Tearing himself away from her astonished grasp, he hastened from the room, as Catherine, uttering a stifled scream, dropped insensible on the floor.

CHAPTER XXVIII.

FAREWELL FOR EVER.

HEN Catherine recovered from the swoon into which she had fallen and recalled what had passed, her feelings would have been difficult of description even to herself.

But for what she had experienced, she could almost have imagined the whole had been a nightmare dream. All appeared so unreal, so terrible, so inexplicable.

That such charges should be made against her—so conscious of her innocence—was fearful; but that Maurice—her husband—should believe them was worst of all.

And he did believe them. Catherine knew *him* well enough to be certain that he never would have addressed her as he had, had he not. Also that when he declared he had seen her at the *bal de l'opera*, he spoke from conviction.

What could it all mean?

What enemies had they to whom their estrangement and unhappiness would be sweet?

For that some foul plot was being concocted against her and Maurice she felt assured.

As the night passed on, Catherine paced the room in too great an agony for rest.

Surely—oh, surely—Maurice could not have meant those last words—that they were to be parted for ever? They had been uttered in the moment of bitter passion. He would, he must listen to her when he was calmer.

But how had that knot of ribbons got into her possession?

She saw only one way; it had been placed in her pocket when she had been insensible at that strange house.

Another molecule of this mist of mystery.

Once during this dreadful thinking and surmising the idea forced itself into her brain that possibly Maurice, finding Sir Jaffery unforgiving, had repented their marriage, and would be rid of her.

She instantly banished the thought as unworthy him and her.

"Nevertheless, I *will* discover the truth of this. If my husband will not put faith in my innocence, I will work alone until I unmask and denounce the perpetrators of this plot."

Bitter paroxysms of grief, of despair at her impotency to remove her husband's doubts, had interrupted these reflections, but she was calmer and more composed when, dawn having long made itself apparent on the window-blinds, she threw herself on the bed, and, exhausted in mind and body, dropped into a restless slumber.

When she arose, not only was she still composed, but a sense of what was due to her dignity as a virtuous wife was upon her.

She had sued, had pleaded at her husband's feet. Had she been guilty she could have done no more.

Thus must she not act, argue, reason fondly, gently— yes, and if that fail to make him believe, then, as a right, must she demand for him, as her husband, to free her name from this undeserved and foul stain?

Ringing for Mademoiselle Rose, Catherine dressed with more than her usual care, and proceeded to breakfast, her face pale, but wearing its usual expression.

Would Maurice be there? Had he, as she, passed the remainder of the night in reflection, and now would be eager to repent his accusations, or seek an explanation?

She wished this might be so; but no, the sitting-room was empty. She was to breakfast alone.

Catherine bit her lip to check its trembling, and rang the bell for the chocolate. The people, of course, would know that they had quarrelled; they should not, if she could help it, divine worse.

"PERJURESS!" HE CRIED IN SCORN, AS HE DASHED IT IN HER FACE, "BEHOLD THE PROOF OF YOUR GUILT!"

Taking her seat at the table, she perceived a letter by her plate.

It was from Maurice.

Quickly she seized it, then paused. Better wait until the waiter had brought the chocolate, and there was no chance of interruption.

How dilatory the man was. How he lingered adjusting this dish and that. Would he never go?

At last the door closed, and Catherine's trembling fingers tore off the envelope.

At first the lines written within swam before her eyes. She could not decipher a word. Speedily the sensation passed, and she read:

CATHERINE,—After the occurrences of last night, another interview would be but useless pain to both. Neither could it serve any purpose, no excuses having power to overcome the fact that at the very moment you were denying my charges, you bore the evidence of your guilt about you. Unhappy, false wife, neither are these the only charges I can bring. Listen. Do you recollect that night when I saw two persons on our balcony —you, as I stated, and another? Do you recollect how you persuaded me I had been mistaken, that they must have been in the neighbouring balcony? You convinced me, for you are beautiful; heaven has given you a mask of innocence, and I loved much. Yes, convinced me, though that same evening I found a man's glove in our balcony. I thought of what you said, and decided it had fallen over from the next apartment. But I retained the glove, and a few evenings after, found its fellow hidden, thrust deep down in your workbasket.

"Great heaven, am I awake!" gasped Catherine in amazed bewilderment, then forcing herself to be calm, she read on:

Do you remember the story you told me one afternoon of your having lost your way in Paris? That very morning I had seen you in a cab with someone in a distant *quartier*, you were leaning forward, your face turned to the window. Do you imagine, Catherine, I could have been mistaken in a countenance I had so loved? If so, I could not have been deceived in your dress. Seeing me you drew quickly back, and I, stunned, willing to disbelieve my senses, hastened home to question you. You were absent; you returned with Captain Melton with the account of having lost your way.

Again, fool, idiot, I believed you, I put aside the similarity of dress, and thought Paris must contain your double. Nevertheless, I determined to acquaint you with what I had seen, that together we might try to discover who this woman was. Fortunately or unfortunately I delayed my relation until after dinner.

When you left the room, and I was preparing to follow you for coffee, a letter was brought to me. It was anonymous. Such communications should have small credit placed in them, but in this case it was different, for it confirmed what my own doubts had surmised, my eyes had seen. It bade me watch to save my name from dishonour, for with that was it threatened. I need not enter in detail upon what is stated. It did but warn me, no more.

As heaven hears me, after my first agony I refused to put credence even in this. I determined to find out the slanderer, the writer of the letter. I refrained from acquainting you with it, to save you from the pain an innocent woman must suffer from such an accusation—though false. Besides, I fancied were I to have shown you, despite my assertion, you might in secret imagine I mistrusted you. How thoughtful I was of you! How you must laugh!

I did not show it you, I confided in your fidelity; and what has been the result?

Enough of so sad and melancholy a subject. Words are useless now. What your feelings are I cannot tell; what mine are you may imagine, for no woman ever had my love save you.

But I cannot, I may not write more. I quit Paris to-day. In my desk you will find a hundred pounds; that will be sufficient for present needs, and later you shall hear what arrangements I can make for your future maintenance from my lawyer, through whom all further communications must pass. Farewell for ever.   MAURICE BURGOYNE.

The young wife's countenance had undergone many changes during the perusal of this—to an innocent woman —fearful letter ; but towards the conclusion the features became set and resolute. The fair brow knit, not with perplexity, pain, but hardly, firmly.

The accusation so suddenly and startlingly made was too great, too terrible, to waste time in useless tears— despair !

No ; it needed more than that now—action, quick and prompt.

Rising, she walked the apartment to and fro, her eyes bent on the carpet, her hand yet grasping the letter.

"This is too horrible, too serious," she thought; "I must see Maurice, I must, and he must hear me. I no longer blame him. How could he help but believe under such apparent proof? Not with tears, or with entreaties must I meet him, but with the calm dignity of an outraged wife, and demand that this matter be sifted—sifted to the bottom. Yet how to see him? Where to find him? He leaves Paris, he says, to-day."

A great change had come over Catherine Burgoyne. From the gentle, clinging, fond woman, allowing her individuality to be absorbed in another, she had become the firm, self-contained, self-reliant, determined one.

For a quarter of an hour she continued pacing—pacing slowly.

Then hurriedly she partook of some breakfast. She felt she might have much to go through that day, and would need all her strength. Then she retired to her own room and rang for Mademoiselle Rose.

"I am at home to no one this morning," she said quietly.

"Yes, madame. Does madame go out?" enquired the maid meekly, but her glance full of eager curiosity.

"Yes, but not at present. I will ring for you when I wish to dress. I have letters to write."

Once alone, however, she never opened her writing-desk, but sat buried in reflection.

When the clock struck eleven she rose up and rang the bell for the lady's-maid.

She had come to a decision.

The only way to ascertain news of Maurice was to seek it from Stephanie.

She would take the risk of going to the hotel and asking for her. She might not be able to receive her there, but no doubt she would come back with her.

Then calmly she would to recount what had occurred, and beg her, for Maurice's sake, to intercede with him, to implore him to hear, to believe her.

"*Le Capitaine* Melton has called, madame," remarked Mademoiselle Rose.

"And you refused me?"

"As madame desired, yes."

"That is right. Now my cashmere dress. I shall wear that."

She spoke on several trivial matters while under her servant's hands, then started for the Hotel de Louvre.

What reception was awaiting her there?

CHAPTER XXIX.

THE FLAW IN THE MARRIAGE CHAIN.

CATHERINE had her doubts whether Stephanie could see her in Sir Jaffrey's apartments. If she could, she felt certain she would.

The other had acted affection so well that Catherine must have possessed a nature equally deceptive as her own to have mistrusted her.

She knew perfectly that Stephanie would side with Maurice. Nevertheless, she believed there would be sufficient friendship for herself for her to listen to her version of this singular mystery.

Feeling it would not do to send up her card, she had written these words ;

DEAR STEPHANIE,—I must see you for a few minutes. I implore you to let me, either here or at the Hotel Maubert. Maurice has often called you his good angel. I believe his happiness, as mine, rests upon you now.—Yours in much trouble, CATHERINE.

This she had secured in an envelope, which, on reaching the hotel, she sent up to Stephanie Royle.

Would she see her ?

It was just possible, for Catherine was aware the baronet never quitted his room until late in the afternoon.

She waited impatiently the waiter's return. To her it seemed he would never come, and she wondered whether the space of time was a good or bad augury.

At last he appeared, and bade madame follow him upstairs. Mademoiselle Royle would see madame.

Pleased, Catherine obeyed.

" Ah," she reflected, " if Stephanie will be my friend, all yet must come right."

The suite of apartments engaged by Sir Jaffrey was elegantly furnished, especially the sitting-room into which the visitor was ushered.

Stephanie was already there, seated at a small work-table, in a most ravishing and becoming toilette.

But her countenance was pale, save for the two vivid flushes on the cheek. Her eyes were hard, her small mouth set and cold.

Catherine saw not the expression at first.

Throwing back her veil, she hastened forward, her hands extended as she exclaimed :

" A thousand thanks, dear Stephanie, for this interview ! I am in sad, sad trouble, dear, unjustly in trouble, and I come to you for aid."

" To me ? " was the chilling response, as Stephanie rose, her eyes full of scorn and disdain, her lip curled indignantly. " How dare you, woman, appeal for aid to me ? "

" Stephanie ! "

And paralysed by amazement, Catherine recoiled a step.

" Do you think, woman, I would help you back to enjoy the name, the honour you have disgraced ? "

" Stephanie ! "

" I have seen Maurice, I know everything. I perfectly agree in the step he has taken, which being so, madame, this interview need not be prolonged."

And she moved her small hand imperiously in the direction of the door.

" Stephanie ! "

" Miss Royle, madam."

" Miss Royle, then, for heaven's sake, listen to me. You are speaking under misapprehension," proceeded Catherine earnestly, excitedly. " You have heard what Maurice said ; but he has been most grossly deceived, for all that he believes is false—false. I am as pure and faithful as any wife ; but he has left me, his confidence shaken. Miss Royle I want but an interview with him I want to learn where he is. I came, hoping you would assist me, for his sake ; for if he will hear me, now he is calmer, I am certain I will show him he has done me wrong—innocently—cruel wrong."

"Possibly. I am aware of your suasive, fascinating power over him," was the cold rejoinder. "But supposing"—with covert scorn—"after the lesson he has received, he should not so readily yield to your charms and blandishments. What then ?"

"What then ?" And Catherine drew her beautiful figure erect with queenly pride. "Then I would demand, as a right, that this mystery should be unmasked. I would demand, as his wife, that my name, my honour, should be cleared, and cleared by him, from the foul slander cast upon it."

"And if he refused ?"

"If he be coward base enough to refuse though he hardly could, considering my honour is as his, then, Miss Royle, I myself, outraged woman, outraged wife, will work day and night—aye, devote each hour of my life to bring the slanderers to punishment. And I will, Miss Royle ; trust me, I will. Neither Maurice nor you know me yet. I have, I own, never known myself until this trouble has come upon me."

Stephanie, proud, rejoicing in her triumph as she did, yet shrunk before the calm dignity of her visitor. A fear of her—a belief in her power came suddenly upon her. But only for a moment.

"You will do rightly," she said with quiet contempt. "Of course, what you say is natural, or rather it is natural for you to say it. As for Maurice not knowing you, I fancy from what I can judge, that what he does know will quite suffice him."

"Then you refuse to tell me where I may see or write to him, Miss Royle ?"

"I should refuse, certainly, were I aware. I am not. He leaves Paris to-day—perhaps has already gone."

"And this is how it is to end !" exclaimed Catherine, with an involuntary burst of pain. "To be innocent, yet to be condemned unheard, as I may say. The criminal has that granted him which I am refused. But I will seek Maurice. I will find him. He shall hear me. If he refuse, then I will appeal to my country for justice."

"You dare not."

"Dare not! Are you aware, madam, of what a virtuous loving woman is capable when her honour is slandered?" was the haughty response. "Tell Maurice this: that I am true to him, that my heart is more agonisingly rent by the knowledge that he mistrusts me, than by the false charges made upon me. Tell him that as I have held his name I will hold it—pure, unsullied. Never shall real shame rest upon his wife."

"His wife!" Stephanie had turned quickly upon Catherine, her face was brilliant, her eyes glowed and glittered like the jewelled eyes of a snake. "*His* wife! Ah, ah! you are *not* his wife. Was never, are not now!"

"Miss Royle!" Then Catherine smiled scornfully. "A new mystery, a fresh plot, as lacking foundation as the other."

"No mystery. It's clear enough. If some are so anxious to wed that they will do so secretly at strange hours, in strange places, and in strange fashion, they should not be surprised if at times there is a flaw in the marriage chain, which renders them no wife."

Catherine's countenance had gone white.

"What do you mean?" she gasped.

"Simply this, and probably it will show how mad it would be to apply to the law. The man who wedded you to Maurice had not been at the time properly ordained to perform such a ceremony—knew it was legally none."

"It—it is false!" cried Catherine.

Stephanie shrugged her shoulders.

"Believe so if you please," she said; only should you find Maurice, ask him."

"Do you dare say that during all these months, no tie —no tie made sacred by law and man bound us two?"

"I do; I swear it is so."

"And—and Maurice knew this?" asked Catherine hoarsely; "knew that that I was not—that is, if what you say be true—not his wife; that I was——Oh, my God! I will not believe it. Woman, I begin to see through these terrible mists. The past is returning to me. Maurice has gone, I cannot find him, and this base falsehood is of your concocting. Were Maurice here——"

"He is here," interrupted Stephanie, in a quick, cold whisper; "ask him."

Catherine turned swiftly, and beheld her husband.

He had entered, and on perceiving his wife's presence had quickly shut to the door, standing pale and stern, his hand yet grasping the handle.

"You here!" he murmured with suppressed agony.

"Maurice, thank heaven you have come!" exclaimed Catherine excitedly, eagerly. "No better time could you have arrived. Tell me, is what Miss Royle says true?"

"True—what?" he demanded huskily.

"Maurice Burgoyne," she proceeded, steadily regarding him, "I will make a request that shall answer you. Can you look me in the face," and a tremor came into her voice, "and say I am not your wife?"

He started, the blood rushed to his brow. He did not meet her glance, but turned towards Stephanie.

"What," he said half reproachfully, half angrily, "have you told her? Why did you do this?"

"Why not, Maurice? This morning when you told me how you had been disgraced, I told you, as you knew, that your name was unsullied, for you were a free man. Why should she not at once be made aware?"

"No," he put in as an angry negative.

Catherine stood silent, her eyes bent scrutinisingly on one, then the other; her bosom heaved in quick short heaves.

"Then," she suddenly exclaimed, "you did know this, Maurice. Oh, God, you while you professed love, were plotting against——"

"No," he ejaculated, striding forward, "by heaven I swear I did not know; never knew until—until I was told."

"By your cousin, Miss Royle," she put in with quiet contempt.

He went on as though he had not heard:

"I believed, before God and in the eyes of man, we two were wedded as firmly as any man and wife. I swear it, Catherine," as he met her eyes cold, scornful, terrible to bear. "Even now," he proceeded earnestly, excitedly, "it is not so bad as it appears. There was a flaw, but one that might be regarded as none, without either party desired. A flaw that was none did both consent to accept the union—acceptance ratifying it."

"And I refuse to consent to its acceptance," broke in Catherine, haughty, cold, with imperial dignity; "I accept the flaw. I hold Maurice Burgoyne to the flaw, for I would sooner live under disgrace than as the wife of such a man. I loved you—for I did not know you; but the veil is lifted, I see all clearly now, and, Maurice Burgoyne, I despise you."

There can be no description of the ineffable scorn that was in the words.

Pale, haggard, he cowered before it.

Catherine turned from him to Stephanie.

"Yes, I see all plainly. You have played your game with success. You love this man and you have won him. I envy neither."

She did not see the fierce, vindictive, fiendish flash in Stephanie's eyes; she had turned, and before they had recovered from the effects she had caused, she had gone.

Maurice Burgoyne suddenly reeled as if struck by a blow.

"Oh, Catherine, Catherine," he cried, "do we part like this?"

In a second Stepanie was by his side. Her face was radiant with triumph. She had succeeded.

"Maurice, dear cousin," she exclaimed, "do not give way; the blow is bitter, but think what you have escaped; why heed the words of one who, possessing such a love as yours, could so abuse it?"

"I know, I know," he broke in, "what is done has been necessity, but, Stephanie, nevertheless my heart is breaking. I loved her so fondly, and—oh, heaven!—I love her still."

Dropping into a chair he bowed his head on his arms flung out upon the table, and sobbed like a woman.

Stephanie watched him with set lips, a pallid face, and fierce angry eyes.

"Fool," she thought, "weak, weak fool."

Meanwhile Catherine hastened back to the Hotel Maubert.

The news of the flaw in the marriage chain had stunned her. The knowledge that she was no wife paralysed her brain. Of only two things did she seem conscious—that Maurice had not knowingly wronged her, an idea that gave her some comfort, and that all had taken place was the work of Stephanie Royle.

Before she reached the hotel she had decided on the course she should take, but she had undergone too much for immediate action; more than once she had feared her strength would fail her on her way home. She managed to reach it, however, and ascend to the sitting-room.

There she sank upon a couch in a dead faint. Scarcely had she done so than the lace window-curtains were parted, and Captain Melton stepped from the balcony into the room. He had called again, and finding neither husband nor wife at home, had informed Mademoiselle Rose, with a compliment and a couple of francs, that he would wait.

CHAPTER XXX.

BAULKED OF HIS PREY.

OVING forward Captain Melton looked upon the woman he loved, and to win whom he had committed such baseness, with a heart beating so loud it might have been heard.

The blow had fallen, he knew that. Their plot had succeeded—the husband and wife were separated.

Well, what was to be the result?

Would she, so cast-off, be glad to accept the refuge his arms would give her, to accept the title of his wife?

"Aware of her innocence, however much she may have loved the fellow, she must hate him now," he reflected. "He was never worthy of her. She was lost with him. Yet women are strange riddles; the sentiment of an old love, though abused, will cling to them like perfume to a faded rose. Still, I have not done so much, and succeeded so far, to be baulked at last. As she has been caught in one net, so may she in another, nay, so shall she, but it must be a wary and a skilful one."

Bending over Catherine he seemed about committing the audacity of touching her forehead with his lips. But whether it was the purity of her lovely face, or a remnant of honour yet lurking in his breast, he drew back, merely detaching a ribbon from her dress, and placing it in his pocket.

What was he to do?

Standing, his chin in his hand, he fell into a reverie. He felt whatever he did he must do it cautiously.

Finally resolving, he fetched some perfume from a side table, poured some in his hand and sprinkled it on Catherine's face.

At the sharp contact she sighed wearily, and after a second application opened her eyes. They rested on him vaguely a moment as though he had been the continuation of a dream. But then she sprang to her feet, exclaiming haughtily :

"Captain Melton, by what right are you here ?"

The officer had drawn back, and was standing deferential, reverentially both in face and mien.

"I crave of you a thousand pardons, Mrs. Burgoyne," he began, when she interrupted.

"I can dispense with them, sir. I would be alone. I, as you see, am not well, and do not desire visitors. Mr. Burgoyne——"

"I never wish to see him again," he exclaimed, "without it be as an antagonist with twenty paces measured between the barrels of our pistols."

She regarded him in silent wonder. He seized the opportunity, speaking rapidly, earnestly :

"Mrs. Burgoyne, you asked me by what right I am here ? I have none save that of a friend. I came half an hour ago. You were absent, but so urgent did I feel the necessity for seeing you that I requested permission to wait. I did so, and was in the balcony when you entered. Before I could make my presence known you had fainted. I would have rung the bell for aid, but paused. I felt you would rather I did not, that you had no desire for the curious, unsympathetic people of this hotel—even of your lady's-maid—to witness your distress."

Still Catherine gazed at him with a soul-searching glance that almost cowed him.

For an instant Captain Melton felt irresolute. His heart quailed before the purity of soul that shone in the beautiful eyes before him.

But shaking off the slight sentiment of honour that endeavoured to assert itself, he continued :

"For pity's sake do not deny, dear Mrs. Burgoyne. Not, at least, to me, whose only wish is to be your

friend," he added, almost entreatingly. "I can conceive
how a nature so pure, so true, revolts at the gross slander
flung upon it, and by him who should have been the last
to believe. I can understand how with a woman's pride,
a woman's modesty, you would hide this unjustly
inflicted wound from the cold eyes of the world, but in
this world, at this moment, you need a friend. I entreat
you let me be one to you, Mrs. Burgoyne. That which
has occurred is no secret to me," he added in a lower,
more sympathising tone, "though I swear I will make
that confession to none but you."

"What !" ejaculated Catherine with scorn of Maurice,
not of her companion, as she rested one white hand on a
chair ; "has he told you ? Has he proclaimed his shame
and mine from the housetops ? "

"He told me," answered the officer with half-averted
eyes, as if reluctant to give her pain, yet felt it necessary,
"because you are not the sole one he accuses. I, too, am
the innocent object of his accusation."

"You ? " she exclaimed.

"No less. This morning he charged me with being
your companion at the *bal de l'opera*."

"You ? Great heavens ! And your reply, sir, to
this ? "

"That he lied," retorted the officer with sudden
fervour. "Not only could I," I said, "prove, did I
please to stoop to exonerate myself from so vile a charge,
that I was last night not even in the vicinity of the *bal
de l'opera*, but that I would stake my honour, my life,
that he as basely maligned you as me. However, I will
not pain you, dear madam, by a recital of his words or
mine, suffice that I dashed my glove in his face and left
him. Then I thought of you. I recalled the happy
hours you had afforded me, how you had seemed from
the first to honour me with some regard, and an impulse
I could not resist brought me here to crave most humbly
to be your friend in this bitter moment of trial."

His voice spoke more eloquently than his words.

Catherine, suffering under her keen sense of wrong, of loneliness, of desertion, aware that in the whole wide world she had no friend, was touched.

She had always liked Captain Melton. By word or glance he had never allowed her to suspect his true feelings towards her.

"Indeed, I have been most cruelly maligned, the victim of a plot laid by some enemy that I cannot guess," she said more kindly. "I am, too, indeed in trouble, but though, Captain Melton, I sincerely thank you for your sympathy, it is a trouble in which no one can help."

"Do not say that, I beg. Left suddenly friendless in a strange city—a woman——"

"And," she put in, drawing her head proudly erect, "an unwifed wife. Yes," with a return of bitterness, " I perceive, Captain Melton, Mr. Burgoyne has taken the pains of informing you of the whole matter, as no doubt he will the whole world if it care to listen. I go again into that world the victim of a flaw in my marriage ceremony that makes it none. The victim, yet none the less a woman to be shunned—avoided. A woman from whom virtue will shrink with averted eye and gathered skirts. Sooner than appeal, sooner than seek to make myself Maurice Burgoyne's wife, I accept my position. Thus, you perceive, though I thank you for the intention, no one can aid me."

How beautiful she looked. How calm, queenly, and grand. How scorn and contempt sat upon her small exquisitely-shaped lips and gleamed in her clear eyes.

Her loveliness set Captain Melton's very soul on fire. Before he was quite aware of what he did, he was at her feet, addressing her in passionate accents.

"You are wrong. Oh, believe me, you are. If Maurice Burgoyne can so treat the pure angel that heaven sent him, not so would others, only too humbly grateful for a smile from her lips. Maurice Burgoyne has slandered you, or believed all too readily in slander cast. Yet are you tamely to bear this? Have you a right? No,

Catherine, for I will not sully my lips nor your ears by an utterance of his name—you are free. Yet not as a discarded wife shall you meet the world's glances, but as the bearer of an honourable name—as the wife of a husband who worships the very ground you tread. I love you, Catherine. Myself, all I possess, I lay at your feet, only too proud if you will take them up."

He ended, breathless with his own ardour, with the fervour of his hope, agitated by his passion, which her beauty had enhanced.

Catherine's cheek had flushed with indignation. Her eyes flashed. It seemed an insult to be thus addressed in her great trouble. But as the words " as the wife " fell on her ear, she felt that, however ill-timed was the speech, it meant no insult.

" Rise, Captain Melton," she said quietly. " Though I thank you for the confidence you thus place in my honour, which Maurice so easily mistrusted, what you ask is impossible. I cannot carry my affection so readily from one to the other. Love and I are parted for ever."

" That I will never believe. It would be too cruel," he broke in passionately. " I have been too premature, perhaps, but that you will forgive. And oh, Catherine, my love shall be such that you shall forget this painful past. Catherine, from the moment I saw you, I loved— loved as I never imagined myself capable. Yet think, have I not kept it in control ? Have I ever insulted you by word or glance ? Pity me, then, when you are free to be again won—give me hope."

He caught her dress in his hands, pressing it madly to his lips. He prostrated himself on the ground before her. His ardour, amounting almost to frenzy, frightened her. She dropped upon a chair. She dared not call anyone. She had not strength to break away and quit the room. She had undergone so much that morning. Her head began to swim.

" Leave me, Captain Melton, I entreat you," she implored. " I am ill, suffering."

"Oh, Catherine, do I not know it? Can I not read as a book every expression of a face so fair, so pure, saints might envy? Catherine, the thought of it drives me mad, that you should have to front the world with so cruel a stain upon you! It shall not be—it is too terrible!"

"Heaven help me!" she exclaimed, bowing her face on her hands; "it is terrible, indeed!"

"But it is a terror you need not undergo. Catherine, you shall reign a queen in society, and shame the man who once called you wife. Yes, the humiliation shall fall on him, not you. Only be mine—mine!"

"I cannot answer you. Go, I pray! Oh, pray leave me!" she moaned, for her senses were deserting her. Her countenance had turned deathly pale. She dropped in her chair.

"Heaven! and this is Maurice's work!" cried the officer. "Catherine, I cannot leave you—I will not, to suffer alone, my darling!"

"Leave me," Catherine again imploringly said.

Captain Melton started to his feet, and in tones of deep respect said:

"Henceforth what you wish it will be my pleasure to fulfil; only you will not banish me entirely? I may see you again? Remember you are alone. You may need advice. Pray let me help you. Perhaps you will quit Paris?"

"Yes," she answered quickly; "it would be too fearfully painful to remain."

"Then you will need some assistance," he persisted. "As you believe in my affection, accept mine."

She clasped her small hands impatiently. Would he never go? Anything to get quiet, solitude for a little, little while.

"You are very kind," she replied. "Come here at six this evening. I shall have arranged my future plans by then, and if I need help and advice, will accept yours."

Captain Melton's heart gave a bound of delight. If she acquainted him with her plans, his success was assured.

Already he had determined to proceed to London, if not with her exactly, at least by the same train, in the same boat; so, in fact, to lay a system of snares that, if he could not win by other means, to compromise her and force her to accept his love. Concealing this under a mask of the greatest, almost reverential, respect, he kissed her hand after expressing his thanks, and took his leave.

Directly he had gone Catherine rose up. A moment she stood battling with her weakness; then calm, apparently composed, cold, and impassive, quitted the apartment, murmuring:

"Now, at last, I am free."

When Captain Melton called at the Hotel Maubert at six that evening, to his rage and indignation he learned that Monsieur and Madame Burgoyne's apartments were now to let, and that madame had taken a *fiacre* four hours ago, and gone, quite unattended, to the railway-station.

"Has she left no letter?"

"No, not any."

"She has escaped," muttered the captain through his teeth, "but only for a time."

Then, hailing a cab, he drove to the railway-station.

That night Maurice received a letter from Catherine, sent under cover to Stephanie. It simply contained these words:

"Necessity has compelled me to retain my jewels. They were your gifts when I believed in you. But I accept nothing more from you—no, never; not a shilling even if I were starving!"

"This must not be—it shall not, mad, foolish girl!" cried Maurice, who at once instituted a search for Catherine even as had the captain, but with like result— failure. Catherine had totally disappeared. Not a trace could either find.

Stephanie smiled in secret. Her rival had gone; Maurice was free. He had been reconciled to Sir Jaffery, whose recovery was now singularly rapid. Together they were to return to Mereton Travers.

She had triumphed!

CHAPTER XXXI.

NOT EASY TO FORGET.

BACK at Mereton Travers.

The greater the pleasure upon which we build in expectancy, the more disappointed are we when it is ours.

Stephanie Royle had succeeded quicker and better than she could have hoped in separating the man she so loved from her rival.

As she schemed and plotted, they were back at Mereton Travers.

Once more Maurice was her own, his comforts her care. Morning, noon, and night they met. As in the old, old times they wandered amid the heavy languid perfume of the rose-garden, that made the girl faint with love.

Even better than in those old times. Maurice no longer made these diurnal "visits to the town for recreation."

Nevertheless there was one drawback, "a rift within the lute" that modified Stephanie's happiness. Maurice himself was not as of old. He was changed.

No longer was he the bright, happy man she had waited for and seen, passing from the terrace into the rose-garden, on that afternoon when she had discovered his love for and assignation with Catherine.

The once clear, careless brow was shadowed, the mirthful eyes veiled by a sadness ever present ; the buoyant step heavier, sedate. He was no longer the man who, happy with the vitality of health, looked hopefully into the future, but one who found life a burden to be borne.

Stephanie had never guessed how sincere and deep had been his love for Catherine. It maddened her.

She saw that if she succeeded in winning him, he would never give her the affection he had bestowed on her she hated. That she would embrace the shadow; not, as her rival, the substance.

Maurice, thoroughly assured of his wife's guilt, had torn himself from her. But so bitter had been the wrench to his heartstrings, that, torn, lacerated, bruised, never again could their health be restored.

Stephanie, however, had one consolation. Changed, sad, shunning society, he seemed to rest more and more upon her, even as had Sir Jaffery. She was indeed really mistress of Mereton Travers.

The two men bowed to her will. Yet she was not content.

Content! Did she not love?

All the power and luxury she possessed she would have surrendered without hesitation for the right to draw Maurice's weary head to her bosom, to kiss the brow with her warm lips until the old sunny look came back to it, and his eyes smiled on her as of old.

She would have given ten years of her life for him to have taken her to his breast and gaze upon her as she had seen him gaze on Catherine.

"And shall it not be?" she reflected, pacing her favourite resort, the rose-garden. "Must not such a love as mine win return? Only let me be patient, and I will make myself grow such a necessity to him, he will not be able to live without me. Have I not owned that my love is his? Must not that confession come back to him when he sees my eyes falter, my colour pale or redden, and my lips smile beneath his glance; when my hand trembles at contact with his; when he cannot move or desire aught but I am ready to do him service? Abused, as he believes, by Catherine, such devotion as mine must the more deeply move him. Only I must be patient— patient. True, a year has passed. It is long. Then the blow he received was great."

The click of the gate checked her soliloquy. She turned with a quick flutter of the pulses, hoping it was Maurice.

It was instead Sir Jaffery, pale, delicate in appearance still, but, if anything, perhaps owing to that long and strange—strange, that is, to all but Stephanie—torpor, better than previously to his illness. He carried a stick, upon which he occasionally leaned as he came along the garden-path, Stephanie hastened to meet him.

"I saw you alone, my love," remarked the baronet, taking her arm, "so joined you, having something to say."

"Anything of importance, guardie?" she smiled.

"I think so; you, too, think so, I fancy—Maurice."

She started, her eyes fell slightly as she asked:

"What about him, guardie?"

"A great deal, Stephanie. I am much concerned about the poor fellow," proceeded the baronet with feeling. "The influence that wretched woman, who has been the ruin of his life, must have been powerful, his passion for her intense, by the effect the discovery of her true character has had upon him."

"Yes, guardie," Stephanie merely rejoined half interrogatively.

"Week after week, month after month, I have been watching to see him rouse himself from the despondency the finding his faith abused occasioned, but in vain. If anything it increases. He lives here a dull, monotonous, unnatural life. He should be roused, or he will become seriously ill."

Again Stephanie said:

"Yes, guardie."

But now her active brain was busy. Did the baronet mean to urge Maurice to quit Mereton Travers for a time? To find distraction in London? She bit her lip and waited.

"If he will not rouse himself," proceeded Sir Jaffery, "he must be roused by his friends."

"Yes, guardie."

"And I want you, Stephanie, to aid me in the work."

"Indeed, guardie, gladly would I if I could. Maurice's state fills me with concern."

"I know it—I know it, dear child. As to if you could, why, Stephanie, on you will rest everything. Still," and he smiled, "I do not fancy it will fail because of that."

Doubtful as to his meaning she discreetly kept silent.

"There is a saying, that the best way to drive one nail out is to drive another in. I have been thinking over the matter seriously, and I see but one cure for our Maurice."

He paused, but she merely waited interested.

"There is but one way to crush this passion of his for an unworthy object. To drive it out by another for one worthy his affection and his name."

Stephanie's heart beat wildly. A cold sensation crept upward to her brain. What was the baronet going to propose? Rapidly her thoughts summoned to her mind all the eligible young ladies near Mereton Travers.

"Do you understand, Stephanie?"

"I imagine so. You want Maurice to love someone else. Someone worthy of him."

Sir Jaffery smiled as he looked at her. He guessed her meaning.

"Yes," he rejoined, exactly. And, Stephanie, I have selected the one. One who will give him such a loving devotion that it must eradicate that other. One, the only one, I believe our Maurice will ever be got to wed. He may do so out of gratitude, but her affection for the young fellow is so great, that I believe she will overlook that, for his sake. Silly child," he said fondly, taking her hands in his, "do you think I am blind, if Maurice is? No, I am not as he, engrossed in myself. Stephanie, you love our Maurice, and you shall wed him."

The girl uttered a low, quick cry. She could not suppress it. Then, plucking away her hands, she covered her face, over which the crimson blood rushed in waves.

Had she not but a quarter of an hour ago said it would come, and lo! it was here. Sir Jaffery's own lips had proposed it.

The baronet laughed, amused at what he deemed the maiden modesty of his pretty ward.

"There, there," he remarked, patting her shoulder, "you need not blush, my dear, at an old man like me divining your secret. Why, I have read it in your eyes, in your every move. And so might Maurice, and so shall Maurice, for if he has not strength to open his own eyes, I must for him."

"Oh, guardie!" she murmured.

"Nay, nay, don't misunderstand me, child. I shall let him know how my wish is set upon seeing you his wife—a wife who will make his happiness hers. I tell you, dear, it is Maurice's only chance. And I have not been mistaken—you do love him?"

She looked up; her eyes were brilliant with joy, her cheeks covered with delicate blushes.

"Oh, guardie!" she murmured, "he is dearer to me than life. If—if I could but aid him!"

Then she fell forward on the old man's bosom, weaping tears of joy.

Maurice was hers—hers!

After that she hastened to her own room, while Sir Jaffery also returned to the house to seek for Maurice, determined at once to carry out his purpose. As he reached the broad terrace fronting the house, his son rode quickly up the avenue, sprang from his horse, threw the reins to the groom waiting, and wearily mounted the steps. He was indeed changed—thinner, aged, spiritless.

"Maurice," said the baronet, advancing, "these rides do you more harm than good. You always look tired-out, exhausted, after them."

"Like the foot-racer," smiled the young man, "that undertakes a contest beyond his powers. I race with memory—the prize, forgetfulness; and memory ever conquers."

"Tut, tut! That you, Maurice, so placed that a bright future may be yours, should ruin yourself for a worthless woman——"

THEN, AS WITH A MOAN, HE DROPPED BACK AMONG THE FERNS, SHE FLED TO THE HOUSE.

"Hush, sir," was the quick interruption. "We are parted; to me she is now as dead; for what I know, she may be; nevertheless, I cannot hear her spoken against, however she may merit it."

He turned away as he ended, but Sir Jaffery put his hand on his arm.

"Stay an instant, Maurice. I will obey you; I will respect your desire; but tell me, this life you have now led for twelve months surely you will not continue? Is it manly? Life was given to us for better uses than despair. Besides, the time cannot be years distant when you will be master here. As a duty to the name you bear, the family you represent, Mereton Travers must have a mistress."

Maurice started and shuddered.

"You see this, Maurice?"

There was a pause. Then low and sadly he answered: "Yes."

"Then, my boy, I would have you look around you. I would have you select this time where you will not be deceived, where there is so strong a proof of love."

"Not now, sir; for heaven's love, not now," broke in the young man, trembling with agitation.

"Why not now, Maurice? The longer you live like this, the more difficult will it be to rouse yourself; and you must——"

"I will, I will, sir. I was only thinking of it to-day,' he broke in hurriedly. "I will take a run up to town."

"That is good, very good," exclaimed the baronet. "Yet you will consider, Maurice, of what I have said as a duty."

"I will, father; still, there is no haste."

"There should be no great delay. And tell me, Maurice, have you any idea where your love would be placed?"

"I have no love to give, sir. I have already given all."

"Then the choice of a wife will be indifferent to you?"

"Almost," with a slight rise of the shoulders.

"Then knowing, my dear boy, how your happiness lies next my heart, let me select for you. It shall be one to whom you are everything, whose affection has been proved——"

"You mean Stephanie," interrupted Maurice Burgoyne, in a low tone, with averted eyes and a little shiver.

"I do. Maurice, she loves you!"

"She did, sir; she pities me, I believe. But she must know better than all others I have no love to give."

"Loving you, thinking fondly of you, grieving at the change in you as I do," persisted Sir Jaffery, "she will, I feel, let that be no obstacle. Maurice, I should like to see her your wife."

His son paced the terrace awhile, and Stephanie, from the shadow of her curtain, watched. Why had Maurice given that shiver at the mention of his cousin's love?

There was one barrier to the girl's success—a slight one, yet a barrier. The young man could never forget that—though for his sake—it was Stephanie who had been chiefly instrumental in the discovery of that flaw in the marriage chain which Catherine had so quickly taken advantage of to free herself from him.

"Don't speak to me now, father, about this. At least, say no more at present," he exclaimed huskily, coming back. "You have taken me rather by surprise. But I'll promise to think over what you have said, and if Stephanie can be satisfied with the affection I can give her, why I care for no woman so well, only—only I'll neither bind myself nor her at present. To-morrow I'll go for a while to London. When I come back matters may be arranged."

"I am content, Maurice," replied Sir Jaffery, warmly pressing his hand.

Then he went into the house, as his son, descending the steps, walked quickly towards that part of the grounds called, for its cultivated wildness, the Wilderness.

Here he flung himself on the grass, his face prone among the ferns, and cried in his agony :

"Oh, Catherine, Catherine ! can I ever forget you ? will it be possible for me ever to call another wife ?   If you had been but true ? "

In his suffering he writhed where he lay, crushing the delicate wild flowers beneath his weight.

Meanwhile, full of joy, Stephanie Royle sat in her chamber. She had divined the subject of conversation on the terrace. She had marked the struggle in Maurice, the hearty grasp of Sir Jaffery's hand, the light on his face as he had left his son, and she told herself Maurice had consented.

Long she sat at her window in a sweet love-dream.

Would Maurice speak when they met ? Should she see her guardian first ? No ; she would like best to hear it from her cousin's own lips.

She had seen the direction he had taken, and an hour later, when the shadows were creeping from the west across the land, she threw a light shawl over her head, descended to the garden, and walked towards the Wilderness.

All was still. She heard no sound. Yes ; suddenly a sigh, and there, almost at her feet, lay her cousin, his face buried in his folded arms.

"Maurice ! " she exclaimed.

He made no response. He was asleep. What madness, for the dews were falling, and here among the long grasses they were ever thickest, for the twilight was already about the trees.

Kneeling, placing her hand on his shoulder, she called :

"Maurice, dear Maurice, you must get up."

He turned his head with dreamy eyes and looked at her. Then his countenance brightened, as, rising more erect, he drew her, half-resisting, half-faint with joy, to his breast.

"What, is it you, darling ? How good of you to come," he whispered fondly. "I was wishing for you—

dreaming of you, and lo! you are here. My heart has been well-nigh breaking, but you, my darling, can heal it—you alone."

"Oh, Maurice, Maurice," murmured Stephanie, as she laid on his bosom. Ah! he did love her then, he did.

"Come, come, do not be so coy," he laughed, as gently he raised her face. "Am I to have no reward. Ah, my sweet!"

And Stephanie felt his lips raining ardent, impassioned kisses on her brow, her cheeks, her lips. She rested on his arm as in a trance. He loved her. Loved her even as he had Catherine!

Maurice, drawing back, looked fondly on her face, smoothed the braids of her hair, again and again kissed the eyelids, that, unable to bear his passionate gaze, had dropped. Ah, there was to be happiness at Mereton Travers at last!

"My darling, my sweet," proceeded Maurice, "how your heart beats, or is it my own? No, you, too, have suffered. But it was your own fault, silly child. You should never have gone away. Tell me, you will never leave me again to hunger for your love, will you, Catherine, dear wife?"

Stephanie sprang up with a cry. Tearing herself away from his grasp, she gazed eagerly, affrighted, in his face. His eyes met hers vaguely, almost with a scowl.

She guessed the truth before Maurice exclaimed:

"Where has she gone, my Catherine? She was in my arms, but now—— You are not her. You are Stephanie Royle, who Catherine said plotted to part us."

"Oh, heaven!" gasped the girl, pale, sick with terror and humiliation. "He did not know me. He is mad!"

Then, as with a moan he dropped back among the ferns, she fled to the house.

It was true. The strong man had finally succumbed to over a year's futile search after oblivion.

That night Maurice Burgoyne was in the clutches of brain fever.

CHAPTER XXXII.

MAURICE PROPOSES TO STEPHANIE.

OR five weeks Maurice Burgoyne lay ill, during which Stephanie nursed him with unremitting attention. Yet it was no pleasant task, for the sick man's mind in delirium went back to the days when he loved and believed in Catherine.

Stephanie had to listen to the tenderest terms addressed to her rival; sometimes had to receive them, being mistaken for her.

Worse still, once that scene at Dingle Cottage came back to Maurice's memory and he heaped on Stephanie words of scorn and dislike.

She sat motionless, her face white, her lips compressed, but never swerving from her purpose. Firm, resolute, still; all this, she told herself, was said in the madness of fever—that she had conquered, that he was hers. Had not Sir Jaffery as good as told her so?

And when Maurice was unconscious she could steal to his bedside, press cool kisses on his fevered forehead, and watch the pale wan face and restlessly moving head with the fond pride of possession. Sometimes she would gently pillow it on her bosom, when the weary, weary restlessness would subside, a strange peace would seem to come to the sufferer; but invariably she would be angered and driven away by his lips softly whispering her rival's name:

"Catherine."

Yet she came again and again to him to be filled with joy, and to suffer.

One evening, just as the setting sun was filling the room with a soft red glow, Stephanie Royle had pillowed

Maurice's head on her arm, and leaning over him was watching his countenance wrapped in deep slumber.

That day he had been pronounced out of danger, on the road to recovery.

Her breast was full of ecstasy. He would live! He whose wife she was to be.

"Maurice, my darling," she whispered, half aloud, "dearer to me than all men; oh, my love!"

Stooping, she kissed his forehead—his lips. Then she sprang back, red and confused. His eyes were open, regarding her.

"Stephanie," he whispered feebly, "dear Stephanie."

Then with a smile he sank again into sleep.

Had he heard her?

What matter if he had? Was she ashamed of her love? Why should she not confess it; crave for it, if need be, as the starving beggar for bread?

Ah, had he not called her Stephanie? No longer by that hateful name of Catherine. He had recognised her.

And the girl, giving loose to her passion, kneeling by the couch, wept and laughed, and covered Maurice's thin wasted hand with tears and kisses.

The sick man's recovery was rapid, too rapid for Stephanie, to whom it was supreme happiness to sit by the sofa on which he lay, reading, talking to him, or playing and singing to him as he desired, to wait upon him, eager to forestall his wants.

Had Maurice responded to her love at first it is a question whether he might not have found her imperious, exacting; as it was, the very difficulties that had lain in her way to win his affection, had exalted him in her ungovernable, passionate nature into a deity, and as a slave she would have served him on her knees, rather than not have served him at all.

One thing troubled her: Maurice never spoke of, never hinted at his regarding her as more than a cousin.

He would clasp her hand tenderly in his, express how much he owed her, declare to show his gratitude would be impossible. But he never asked her to be his wife. Yet daily he gained strength, and when strong enough he intended to carry out his projected trip to London.

Would he speak before?

No.

The day arrived for his departure, but not a syllable she could grasp had passed his lips. On the morning he was to leave, Stephanie sat sick with disappointment in the morning-room when Maurice entered.

"Well, dear, I am off," he smiled advancing.

The colour dropped from her face as she rose to meet him. How handsome he looked—the handsomer for the delicacy of illness.

Stephanie remembered those blissful moments when she had rested his head on her breast and kissed that pale forehead. She almost wished he were ill again. It was happier than to live here without him.

"Yes, off, she responded, forcing a smile; "and leaving Mereton Travers to dulness and despair. How selfish men are!"

"I trust I am not. I trust I shall prove not," he answered, his eyes resting on her almost caressingly, making her brain giddy, her pulses throb. "Stephanie," he added, taking her hand, "I feel this journey a necessity; yet I undertake it with no pleasure. Pleasure, at least for a while, is impossible to me. Still, if you will aid me, take compassion on me, I am resolved not to despair. I will not say more now, dear, not until my return. Farewell, dear Stephanie—my good angel, my gentle untiring nurse. If happiness be in store for me in that future I fear to contemplate, it must come to me from you, darling. Farewell."

He had put his arm around her, and drawn her to him. Now stooping he kissed her cheek.

Stephanie's eyes closed, she trembled violently, she seemed about to faint. Then abruptly she threw herself on his bosom, weeping passionately.

"Oh, Maurice, Maurice!" she sobbed; "how can I bear this place and you away? to have brought you back from death as it were to lose you, Maurice!"

She clung to him. He felt how wildly her heart was beating. He was weak yet; he was moved, touched. He held her closer—closer. His voice was tremulous, agitated, as he bent over her and whispered:

"Stephanie, dearest Stephanie, why should I delay for my return that which can as well be spoken now? You know my history; you are also aware that a sincere love such as was mine once can never be repeated. Stephanie, I love you but not with the love worthy one so pure, so good. I feel it an insult to offer you so poor a gift, yet no other can I give, my darling. Do you understand me?"

Only too well. Even as she triumphed in her success the girl was mad with fury. He loved her with a love not worthy the name. A second love—a shadow of that he had given Catherine. Surely her passion was worthier a warmer return. Never mind. Might she not win it?

These thoughts passed swiftly through her brain as he spoke. When he ended, raising her face half with assumed timidity, half with impulsive fervour, she rejoined in low accents:

"Maurice, have you not yet discovered that you are dearer to me than all the world?"

"Dear Stephanie, I am not worthy. You are kind," he rejoined. "Will you—will you, when I shall feel capable of being a little worthier of you, dear, be my wife?"

The word was spoken at last, and Stephanie was happy.

But there was still bitterness blended with Stephanie's joy. Even in her cousin's proposal to her, his words, his voice, sang a requiem over that dead but never-to-be-forgotten love.

"Ah, Maurice!" she however murmured, burying her head on his shoulder, "Heaven has made me too happy. My king, my—husband."

Again he held her to him and kissed her. Then he drew back, for Sir Jaffery was heard calling.

"Good-bye, Stephanie," he said, "good-bye. I will return soon."

One pressure of the hand, one glance, one smile, and he was gone.

As the door closed the fond light in her face died out. Her eyes lit with fury.

"His second love—his second love!" she exclaimed. "He gives me no more than that, having given that woman his best. Oh, would I could see her dead at my feet! How different are the kisses he gives to me, cold, with hardly life in them; not as those of fond wild passion he pressed on my cheek, my lips, when he took me for her. But they shall yet be. I have triumphed so far, I will triumph to the end!"

She stopped, quelling her excitement, for the door had opened, and Sir Jaffery had entered.

"So it is settled," he said, smiling, as he advanced. "Maurice has wisely spoken. I am glad."

"Yes, dear guardie," she answered softly, "Maurice has asked me to be his wife—in time."

"And you, Stephanie?"

"Ah, guardie," as she leaned her head on his shoulder, "can you doubt my reply?"

Despite the drawbacks, the stings to her self-love, that was a proud day to the girl. A new spirit animated her as she walked through the handsome rooms of Mereton Travers, as she traversed its splendid grounds, for she felt they were hers—that she was indeed their mistress.

"They are mine—mine—all mine, all mine," she thought, "and also Maurice, he is mine too."

Meanwhile Maurice was speeding towards London, slightly confused, bewildered by the unexpected event of the morning.

He was engaged to Stephanie.

He had asked her to be his wife.

He was neither glad nor sorry. His feeling was rather a stunned passivity.

He had intended it before his illness ; he had intended it certainly after when he had experienced her devoted attention.

Yet he had delayed, and had intended to defer it until after his visit to the metropolis. Why, he would have found it difficult to say, except that the old love still clung like the remains of a subtle perfume about his heart.

But it was done now. What matter ? It was but a few weeks earlier than he had purposed. Only now he must think no more of Catherine.

Did he think of her ?

Often, wondering what had been her fate. Yet not wondering ; he believed he guessed it too well. Still all his efforts to gain news of her had failed.

Reaching town, he repaired to his lodgings in St. James's. The pretty house in Kensington had long been let to others. Maurice could never look upon it again— at least, so he thought, but in that he was soon to be tested.

Having taken rest and refreshment after his journey, he ordered his horse, conceiving the best way to make his presence known in town would be to visit the park, the hour being that when it is most crowded.

Hardly had he ridden through the gates in Piccadilly than he encountered the Honourable Launce Linden.

"Hullo, Burgoyne! in town ?" exclaimed the latter, reining in his horse. "Why, what's the matter ? You look awfully pallid."

"A man generally does when he comes out of brain fever," smiled Maurice, as they rode on together.

The time was far too long ago for Launce Lindon to guess that Catherine could in any way have had to do with his friend's recent illness.

That passage in Maurice Burgoyne's life had been but a nine days' wonder among his friends.

Question, answer, surprise had been rife, blended with the usual amount of "I told you so's" and "I thought as much," the universal opinion being that there never had been a marriage, and that Catherine, preferring someone else, had run away from Maurice ; or Maurice, finding Sir Jaffery obdurate, had given up "the connection."

The "which" being indefinite, the subject was one avoided in Maurice Burgoyne's hearing ; hence society had already forgotten it, and Launce Linden never thought of the woman he had known and admired as Maurice's wife when he said :

"Brain fever, by Jove! How did you get into that?"

"From overheating in riding. When convalescent, the doctor recommended me change of air, so I came up to town. I'm fortunate in meeting you, for no man can better put me *au fait* as to how affairs are going."

Slowly the two rode on, Launce Linden talking, Maurice half listening, half lost in musing, when, as they had to halt a space, owing to a momentary stoppage of the stream of vehicles, looking up, he beheld the eyes of a lady seated in an elegant pony-carriage fixed upon him.

It was one of the loveliest, most beautiful faces, he thought, he had ever seen, save one. Then it was the reverse of that one which he held unsurpassable.

The complexion was a clear, rich olive, the face superbly oval, the brows as dark as night, arched, the lips *vermeil*, mobile, delicate of mould, while from the clear forehead rich masses of dark silky hair were braided back, looped into heavy plaits and coils behind.

A strange sensation passed through Maurice Burgoyne as he gazed upon the occupant of the pony-carriage, in which she reclined with the graceful ease yet dignity of a Juno. Then, becoming aware that he might be deemed impertinent, he lowered his eyes, at the same time whispering in Launce Linden's ear :

"Who is that splendid woman driving the two chesnut ponies?"

The other, turning in the direction, instantly raised his hat, whereupon the lady, smiling, acknowledged the salutation.

"You know her?" said Maurice.

"Yes; she is the last importation from America—the great actress."

"Actress?" ejaculated Maurice. "She looks rather a duchess."

"Why not?" laughed the other. "I can assure you she looks a great deal more the thing than many who wear by right the ducal coronet. But surely you have heard of her—Genevieve Marinja, the American star?"

"Of course, yes. Mereton Travers is not so far out of the world. Can it be her? But she is foreign."

"Her father, I believe, was a Mexican, and a hidalgo, as a natural sequence—*cela va sans dire*," laughed Launce Linden.

"Is she married?"

"No. At present she lays no claim to any title but miss, though half the masculine portion of the upper ten is at her feet. A secret this, in confidence, Burgoyne, but it is more than rumoured that the Duke of Oxford made honourable proposals to her, and she declined with thanks. Let me introduce you, and become yourself the envy of I know not how many who would give twenty years of their life for the honour."

"A thousand thanks, I will accept gladly," replied Maurice, then rapidly checking the other as he was about to make up to the carriage. "Stay, not now—another time."

For another gentleman had taken his place by the lovely Mexican, and, leaning from his saddle, was laughing and talking gaily.

It was Captain Everitt Melton.

Maurice no longer suspected him. He had already exonerated him from having any part in that suffering of his past life. But at present he could not overcome a certain repugnance, which even his name occasioned.

"Very well, old fellow," rejoined Launce Linden with marked readiness. "That fellow Melton gets in everywhere, and by Jove!" he muttered, "seems rather in favour. What can the woman see in him? Suppose, Burgoyne, you go to-night and see her act, and if we can get to her dressing-room after, I'll introduce you then."

"A thousand thanks. I shall not fail."

He did not. From when the curtain rose, to when it fell, Maurice Burgoyne sat in a box entranced. Then he went round and was introduced. It was a brief affair, for the successful actress was surrounded by admirers as a queen by courtiers.

But Genevieve Marinja, who apparently was all graciousness and amiability, bestowed on her new admirer one of her sweetest smiles, and a soft touch of her slender fingers, as she swept on to the brougham waiting.

Maurice drew back, a feeling of vertigo upon him. Then with his friend passed out into the open air.

"She is a magnificent actress," remarked Launce Linden.

"She is a magnificent woman," responded Maurice.

"She is. And you should see her at home—the actress, but the perfect lady, too."

"I should like to," said Maurice.

"Well, I think I could get you an invitation to her ' at homes.' I will try."

"I should indeed be indebted to you."

"By the way, she is living in your old house at Kensington," proceeded Launce.

"My old house!" ejaculated Maurice, starting.

"Yes, the people who had it have had to go abroad for a time, and Marinja has taken it while they are absent. Are you going to the club?"

"Not to-night," answered Maurice. "The day has been a fatiguing one, and, you know, I am yet not quite convalescent."

So they parted. Maurice Burgoyne walked slowly home, thinking of the beautiful Mexican, Genevieve Marinja. Her face, her acting, had entranced, enthralled him.

"If I could ever really love again," he reflected, "it would be this lovely being."

And only that morning he had asked Stephanie Royle to be his wife.

Was she already replaced in his heart? Had she for a second time a dangerous rival?

CHAPTER XXXIII.

GENEVIEVE MARINJA AT HOME.

N Catherine's pretty boudoir, of which the young wife had been so happily proud, sat the actress, the rage of town, Genevieve Marinja. The sun stealing in through the half-closed jalousies showed that neither the style nor the arrangement of the apartment had been altered. Only here and there had been added some costly vase, piece of china, or picture, while on a side-table was a casket, that, when opened, sent out myriads of hues from gems set as bracelets, necklets, rings, brooches, and the like.

The actress reclined in a low chair reading, her cheek lightly resting on her hand, while at a little distance her lady's-maid, as also dresser, was engaged in making some slight alteration in a rich purple velvet robe, banded with satin, and glistening with jet.

"What is the hour, Brandon?" asked the actress, breaking the silence, and throwing the book from her, raising her beautiful rounded arms wearily above her head.

"On the stroke of half-past three, madame. Do you drive to-day?"

"No; I expect a visitor. Hark, that was the gate-bell; perhaps it is he."

The lady's-maid quitted the apartment, and speedily returning, announced that the visitor was Captain Everitt Melton.

The look that passed over the actress's face showed that it was not the one she had expected. Nevertheless she said at once:

"I will see him. You can take the dress into the ante-room, Brandon. Are you not well?" she required with concern. "You look pale, troubled."

"It is nothing of consequence, madame," was the reply, "merely a headache."

"Then give the dress to Margaret to finish, and lie down, or take a turn in the garden."

"Thank you. I would rather finish the dress myself, madame. But should you require anything, with your permission, I will send Margaret."

"Very well, do so," answered Genevieve Marinja, but her eyes followed her maid curiously, as, gathering her work together, she passed under a silken *portière* into the ante-room. Then, her beautiful face lighting with a sunny smile of welcome, she turned to greet her guest, Captain Melton.

At that period the captain was the envy of many, for he was evidently a favourite with the beautiful actress, from whom men were craving a smile, for whose love men would have ruined themselves.

For months the officer, borne on by his passion for Catherine, increased to fever heat by baulked desire and failure at the very moment of apparent success, had sought for his and Stephanie's victim in vain.

Not the faintest clue could he discover. Instead of quitting Paris, she might have quitted life, she had so disappeared from all who had known her.

Irritated, maddened, he might yet have dreamed of her, though renouncing the fruitless search, had not Genevieve Marinja appeared; when, struck by her beauty, her talent, he, as half male society, became her admirer, a devoted attendant in the crowd in which owners of high and time-honoured titles mingled.

Is there anything more perverse, more difficult to read or understand than a woman's fancy?

Out of all her wealth and noble suitors, the actress chose to show most favour to Everitt Melton, handsome and entertaining enough, but whose means of living were a mystery to even his most intimate acquaintances.

Some averred that it was more than favour the actress gave him—it was love. And there were moments that Captain Melton almost believed so himself.

"I come to compliment you on your success last night," he said, taking a chair near her, after kissing the white slender hand she had extended.

"Well, yes," smiled the actress, with a pretty movement of the shoulders; "if one may judge from the spontaneous applause of an audience, it was a success."

"Not only an audience," he put in eagerly, "but the spontaneous expression of the press this morning. The critics for once are unanimous."

"Then," she laughed lightly, "I am sure you cannot have read them all. I have been an actress sufficiently long to know one barbed thorn ever lurks among the roses. But, what matter to me; the sweetest, proudest praise I can have is the voice of the people."

"And that is yours—even as their hearts," he exclaimed, earnestly bending slightly nearer.

"Their hearts?" she laughed. "Oh, that would be far too heavy a load to be desirable."

"Would that you would consider one not so?" he proceeded in lower, more fervent accents.

She glanced at him a second, then broke into a soft musical laugh.

"And that one of course must be Captain Melton's and no other."

What was the singular fascination in her eyes, her voice, that thrilled every nerve as the one gazed steadily into his, or the other fell on his ear?

It made his head swim at times like the sudden recurrence of a dream, confusing waking thoughts, yet which drew him more to her.

Was it her Mexican blood? Did the wondrous power of the rattlesnake lurk in the eyes shadowed by the jet-black brows?

"Others might be more worthy. I own that," he said; "but for them to be more sincere, more faithful, would be impossible."

"My dear Captain Melton," was the light response, "I would give much to know to how many others you have declared that before we two met. Recollect, the rarer an article is, the more a woman values it."

A faint colour passed over the officer's face as he remembered Catherine, but he answered promptly:

"A man in society may frequently make such avowals, but he can mean them only once. The steel may strike from the flint many a spark before that one which kindles the flame. Marinja," and abruptly he took her hand, "will you believe this? Will you believe me when I declare that no flame has ever been kindled in this breast save that which you have created?"

A peculiar light shone in Marinja's eyes as the captain spoke, as if she detected the falsehood in his heart.

But he observed it not.

Steadily she looked into his eyes and then rejoined:

"Why should I not believe it? Why should I imagine you speak falsely? No; if you desire it I will so believe, only, with that you must be content."

"Content! To be consumed by a devouring flame without hope," he rejoined. "Oh, that is cruel!"

"Did I bid you die of despair?" she smiled winningly.

"Oh, Marinja——"

"Neither," she laughed, checking him, "did I say hope. The fact is, I am very sorry; but they who would win must be patient. At present I enjoy my freedom too much to think of fettering it with that plain slender hoop of gold, more difficult to break than the chain of the galley-slave."

"Fetter, Marinja! call it rather a fairy rose-garland, twined by love."

"Yes; that I believe is what it is called before marriage. It is only after, when the leaves fall and leave nothing but the thorns, that the fetter is visible."

There was a slight pathos in the sweet voice as she said this, with difficulty repressing a sigh.

"Then you forswear marriage?" exclaimed the captain, disappointed.

"No, indeed; but I forswear its contemplation at present," she smiled. "So please," extending her hand, "let us change it. I give a supper to-night, after the theatre. Will you come? That is well. Now be good and tell me what the papers have said, for as yet I have not read one."

He talked for some while longer. Then gracefully Genevieve Marinja dismissed him from her presence.

When she was alone, covering her face with her hands, she fell into deep musing.

"He loves me. He would wed me did I consent. But no," she murmured, half aloud, "his is not the heart I would win."

Rising, she began slowly walking the elegant boudoir to and fro.

"Strange," she murmured after awhile, "how one particular face will haunt the eyes that have once rested on it. From the first time I saw his it has haunted me. No, not for a day has it seemed away. Yet how pale and haggard it was."

She paused a moment, an expression of sadness crossing her features, then continued:

"The heart beneath that countenance must have suffered much. Still, how full of fire were his eyes— how my very soul thrilled and quivered with a sensation of joy, akin to fear, as they rested on me! But there, why think of it? I shall see him again to-night, for not once has he missed since Launce Linden introduced him. Each night I look and see him in his stall. Can it be, is it possible, that he loves?"

A smile, so full of joy that it was radiant, passed over her countenance. Then she laughed a strange little laugh.

"All London at my feet, why not he? I will learn to-night, for I am determined that he shall be one of my guests. Launce Linden shall bring him. That's why I half invited him to visit me this afternoon. Surely he will come. Brandon!"

As she called her maid by name, she raised the *portière* and stepped into the ante-room.

She recoiled with an exclamation of alarm, for the woman, her face as pale as death, lay senseless on the floor.

The first impulse of the actress was to run to the bell to summon assistance.

Before, however, she had half traversed the apartment she paused in reflection.

This indisposition of her maid had been very sudden.

After a brief space, taking a *flacon* of perfume from the table, she returned to the ante-room, and kneeling, began gently bathing the woman's temples.

In a few moments the restorative had effect. She opened her eyes, then covered them with her hand, uttering a bitter moan, also, the actress fancied, accompanied by a word.

"Are you better?" she enquired gently.

The lady's-maid starting, gazed wildly, half in terror, at the speaker, then, evidently recollecting where she was, ejaculated, as she strove to rise to her feet:

"Oh, madame, pardon me; I am very sorry——"

"Sorry! pardon!" said the actress pleasantly. "Why, there is no occasion for either. I told you you should not have gone on with the work, but a wilfu' woman maun ha' her way, and you see the consequences. It has made your head worse, and you fainted. There, you will soon be better, only I insist on your going at once to lie down. Margaret can help me dress for dinner."

"Thank you, madame ; you are very kind," murmured the lady's-maid, adding with grateful fervour, as she moved slowly from the room, "God bless you."

Genevieve Marinja watched until the door closed on her, then, taking out her tablets, wrote in them the word she thought she had heard just then.

The servant, entering the boudoir, announced Launce Linden.

An expression of pleasure came to the actress's face as she said :

"Admit him at once."

When the guest, half an hour later, took his leave, pleased at and praising himself for the skilful fashion in which he had procured his friend Maurice Burgoyne an invitation for that night's supper, the actress herself, clasping her hands together, murmured :

"I have succeeded. He is coming to-night. I shall see him—sit by his side—look into his eyes—talk to him. How my heart beats, and my thoughts run wild at even the contemplation. Oh, Maurice Burgoyne ! Maurice Burgoyne ! shall I succeed in bringing you like the rest —the rest I do not care for—to my feet ? I will try, and then——"

She concluded the sentence with a rippling musical laugh.

CHAPTER XXXIV.

THE ACTRESS'S LOVER.

AURICE BURGOYNE'S pleasure was great when Launce Linden gave him the invitation to the actress's supper.

The whirl in his brain when first introduced to her never seemed to have quitted it.

Her face haunted him waking and sleeping. Her glance pierced to his very soul, and he caught himself wondering that he had ever preferred blondes to brunettes.

As Genevieve Marinja had stated, every evening saw him in the stalls, watching her every movement, absorbed, lost in her.

In what consisted this wonderful attraction?

Was it her beauty, her talent?

Maurice did not ask himself the question. He was only conscious that her tones thrilled him, that his blood turned hot and surged up to his brain angrily as he watched her stage-lover—as he saw her rest upon his bosom, saw her bend her eyes with fondness upon him, receive his kiss on her brow.

Maurice knew that it was all acting, that when the curtain was rung down each would go their separate ways, indifferent to each other's separate saying and doings; but he was madly jealous of the stage-lover for all that.

"What infatuation is this upon me?" he cried mentally one night, as he hastened from the stalls. "Is it infatuation? Is it love? Can I indeed have so soon forgotten Catherine?"

Was it infatuation? Was it love?

In its feverish possession of him it might have been judged the former.

When the little house in Kensington was parted with, it was done through an agent. Maurice Burgoyne felt the memories attached to it to be too painful to go near it. He told himself he could not, he would not look upon it again.

And lo, here was he haunting it night and day, to win a glimpse of the actress.

On the evening of the supper he dressed with scrupulous care and almost the nervousness of a woman. Then drove to Kensington.

A pang shot through him as he passed in at the familiar green door, and when his eyes wandered to the lawn lighted by moonlight.

How often had the graceful form of Catherine, her eyes aglow with love, come across it to meet him.

And now, that love he had believed in had been given to another—had proved itself a font, like the rose-cup, from which any bee might sip.

The remembrance brought a cloud to his face, but banishing it he entered the house and was soon in the intoxicating presence of Genevieve Marinja.

This was not the first time Maurice Burgoyne had visited actresses' boudoirs, nor accepted invitations to their suppers; but those others in no way resembled Genevieve Marinja's receptions.

Over the pretty drawing-room he so well remembered reigned an air of high refinement. Laughter, as conversation, was subdued, as if it had been rather a royal reception.

The lovely hostess sat attired in a rich, tasteful, but quiet toilette. Her glances were soft and feminine, and her manner full of graceful cultivated ease, as she conversed with the few standing near her.

Maurice felt his heart beat in his throat as he bowed before her, then, after a brief exchange of words, would have retired, but she indicated with a slight wave of her fan a seat near.

"NO THANKS ARE REQUIRED," SHE LAUGHED, EXTENDING HER HAND.

No. 11.

Maurice took it in a whirl of delight. So absorbed **was** he by the lovely woman before him, that he had never perceived Captain Melton, whose dark eyes clouded with jealous annoyance as he had to make room for his former friend.

That half-hour before supper numbered but five minutes to Maurice's thinking.

Then one who on State occasions wore a star upon his breast, advanced to the actress, who, rising, took his arm, and Maurice Burgoyne was alone.

During supper they were too far parted to converse, but yet he could look on her, watch how dazzling were her shoulders in the soft light of the waxen tapers; how her eyes shone, and the parting blossom of her lips disclosed the perfect rows of small dazzling teeth.

Actress! she might have been an empress!

What respectful deference each paid her. How refined was the tone of the conversation.

A pure, high-souled woman, she tacitly exacted pure and high-souled thoughts from those about her.

The supper over, the company once more repaired to the drawing-room.

The night was warm, and the French windows were thrown wide, permitting the sweet night perfume of the flowers in the vases on the verandah to float in.

Genevieve Marinja was talking earnestly to him who had taken her into supper. Maurice felt he had no right to force himself upon her, though he longed to, so having no interest in others there, he stepped out into the verandah.

His brain was heated; he was not yet strong, and this new excitement told upon him. Abruptly a flood of music came to him from the room. It was the actress singing.

He started, turning quickly, then resumed his former position in the shade.

"This place is full of memories to me," he muttered, his face bowed on his hands, "sad ones enough now. How could it be otherwise?"

And his thoughts went drifting back to the time when of an evening he would stand where he now stood, smoking and listening to Catherine singing, and deeming they two among the happiest of God's creatures.

The actress's voice somewhat reminded him of Catherine's, only Genevieve Marinja's was fuller, grander, more cultivated, and replete with that graceful flowing accuracy which arises from conscious power.

The song ceased. Maurice heard a guest or two taking leave. He must do so soon. There would be no hope of his speaking to her again that evening, save when he made his adieu.

Almost as the idea passed through his mind, a fan lightly touched his arm.

He turned, and found Genevieve Marinja by his side.

"Are you dreaming over the past, Mr. Burgoyne?" she said lightly. "Pardon me. I hope it was breaking no confidence, but Mr. Linden told me you once lived here."

"No confidence," he rejoined, yet secretly a little piqued. "I did reside here a while."

His breast heaved.

"Ah," said the actress quietly, "if you are like me, then there must be some sadness in returning, even though the memories be happy ones. I have an idea that our spirits haunt the houses where we have lived."

"It never occurred to me before, but to-night would make me a believer almost in your theory," he smiled wanly, "and my memories here had not one to sadden them."

The actress regarded him quickly.

His eyes were fixed as those are who see the past and are oblivious to the future. For the moment he was thinking alone of Catherine.

His companion, lowering her glance, pressed her pearly teeth on her lip, and tapped her dress softly but quickly with her fan.

"In that case," she remarked, after a brief pause, "I fear, Mr. Burgoyne, my invitation must have given you greater pain than pleasure."

"Pain !"

He said no more for the moment, but, as he turned and looked upon her, the monosyllable was more eloquent than speech.

A delicate flush rose to the actress's cheek, a smile to her lip.

"Ah," he added earnestly, "I am sure you could not think that—not for a moment. The memories here are dead and gone. Why should I not people the place with others as happy, if you will permit me ?"

"Why should I refuse that ?" she smiled. "Nay, if it be not pain for you to visit here, I shall reckon you among my favoured guests. You must come," she continued gaily, "and see the garden by day. I think it charming. There is a seat at the back of the house, under some trees, where I pass hours."

"I remember," he rejoined, a tremor in his voice, for had not that been Catherine's favourite seat ? He could imagine he saw her now as she used to sit reading there, with a pencil of golden light falling on her sunny hair. "I should much like to see it—indeed, very much."

"Then come to-morrow," smiled Genevieve Marinja.

"Since I have learned once you lived here, and were happy here, the place seems by right partly yours. Between twelve and one I shall be visible. Will you come ?"

"Gladly, delightedly !" he answered fervently. "How shall I thank you for this favour ?"

"No thanks are required," she laughed, extending her hand. "Now I must return to my other guests, or they will deem themselves neglected."

Stooping, he pressed her fingers to his lips.

As he rose their eyes met. Hers fell before the ardent glance of his, but not with displeasure, for the delicate muscles of her mouth quivered with a pleased smile.

Maurice saw it, and his heart beat wildly with hope as he followed her back into the room.

Hope ?

Hope for what ?

The interview, however, had not been wholly unnoticed.

From where he stood Captain Melton had been able to see those two figures in the verandah, and, himself a lover of the fair actress, had been racked by jealousy.

"Is this woman but of her class ?" he muttered. "A flirt, a coquette ?"

Maurice and the officer had met and exchanged greetings, civilly, not warmly, for the old friendship that had existed could never be renewed.

At the present moment Everitt Melton hated Maurice Burgoyne more bitterly than any man living.

Therefore they did not walk home together, and Launce Linden having long before taken his departure to meet Lady Gertrude Culverton at a State ball, Maurice proceeded to town alone, very glad of his solitude.

"This is no fascination, no fluttering of the moth around the deadly, hollow flame that burns and brightens but to slay," he reflected. "This is love. Such a love as I have felt before, and then believed man could never feel twice. Love her ? I ? Am I not sworn to Stephanie ? Oh, heaven ! is a curse set upon me, that torture in the sweetest sensation granted to mankind, not happiness, is to be my lot ? My love first betrayed, and now with this one a barrier, made by my own lips, is raised up between it and me ! "

There was one thing, he had no need to hasten his marriage with his cousin.

There was another which he did not at all like to contemplate.

Genevieve Marinja might not reciprocate his passion.

At that moment the actress was pacing her room in her soft dressing-gown that fell in classic folds around her figure, her hands clasped, her eyes sightless with thought, her face radiant.

"It is strange—very," she murmured, "yet I would vow I am not deceived. I could not mistake the deep, tender glances of those eyes. No, no, he loves me!" rapturously lifting her white arms aloft, her eyes raised, as in thanksgiving, to heaven, her dark hair falling loose over her robe, and reaching nearly to her slippered feet.

"Maurice Burgoyne loves me! I feel it. I know it. He holds me dearer than all women. How jealous you looked, *mon brave Capitaine Melton*. And how jealous you will be. Ha, ha!"

And she laughed again and again as she thought of the captain's disappointment when he learned of his rival's success.

When the actress laid her round, soft cheek on the pillow, the smile was yet in her eyes, while her beautiful lips murmured, as she fell asleep :

"He loves me. Maurice Burgoyne loves me beyond all women. I have succeeded. To-morrow—to-morrow I again shall see him. Yes, he loves me—he loves me !"

CHAPTER XXXV.

THE WOMAN IN THE HAYMARKET.

EEKS had passed, and Maurice Burgoyne's visits to the Kensington villa were frequent; far too frequent to please Captain Melton. Nevertheless, he believed he held two cards in his hand that utterly negatived any chance of his rival becoming the husband of Genevieve Marinja.

One was his engagement to Stephanie, of which he had learned.

The second was his doubtful union to Catherine. The flaw the husband might seize to free himself, the wife might use to prevent him wedding another. It was, indeed, a flaw, without a certainty: a delicate point of issue which a law-suit might be required to decide.

The captain, therefore, knew he had but to make this known to the actress for her at once to dismiss his rival from any danger-place in her heart.

The time had passed to Maurice in an atmosphere of exquisite happiness indescribable.

A feeling of blissful rest came over him in Marinja's presence. His troubles fell from him as though they had not been.

She had a charm, a fascination for him that no longer heated his blood to fever heat. All was calm, peace, joy.

He felt no fate he could wish better than to sit ever by her until the end; then, his head pillowed on her bosom, her beautiful eyes fixed tenderly on his, breathe out his final breath in a last kiss.

Was this love?

Ah, the truest, purest, most unswerving love.

Maurice Burgoyne saw no obstacle, save one, **why this** fate for which he craved should not be his. Earnestly, eagerly he had marked every look, every word of the actress, and he felt it was not vanity that made him believe she favoured him with a regard exceeding all his rivals.

More than once Maurice's love confession had hovered on his lips, but he had paused to utter it. First there lingered yet about him a loyal fidelity to the memory of her who had deceived him; secondly, he felt in honour he had no right to ask Genevieve Marinja to be his before he had acquainted her with that portion of his life in reference to Catherine.

Singular as it may appear, his engagement to Stephanie caused him the least uneasiness.

Had he not told her the love he could give was not worthy her acceptance?

Would not her noble, high-souled, yet gentle nature feel it quite so when she learned, as it was his duty to let her, whether the actress loved him or not, that, despite himself, his affection was another's?

Stephanie's manner had led Maurice to believe that she loved him—lately, at anyrate—and had consented to wed him as much out of pity as strong affection. His father's words had pointed that way. That she was ready to overlook much for his happiness.

Then surely she would release him of her own accord out of respect to her own self esteem?

And if not? If Sir Jaffery again disinherited him?

What matter if Genevieve Marinja was his.

One afternoon, Maurice, calling on the actress, found her alone on the garden seat, reading.

"You are welcome, Mr. Burgoyne," she smiled, "for you act the Samaritan in saving me from death, not from thieves, but ennui. This novel is of the stupidest. A man loves and loses, and lo, before long, he is head over ears in love again. Folly! I do not believe in second love do you? I think if a man truly loves a woman, he could never love another after."

A flush rose to Maurice's cheek, his eyes were troubled.

"I believed like you once," he replied gravely.

"But have changed your opinion," she smiled. "You have loved?"

"Deeply, passionately. With my whole soul."

"Why not have continued to do so?" she asked.

"Because my love was abused, betrayed," he rejoined in a low tone.

Only from the swelling of the veins on the temples, the spasmodic grip of the hands, did the actress perceive how intense was his emotion.

Her voice was low and sympathetic as she said:

"She must be a bad woman who could betray such an affection. I cannot conceive such, though it may be possible. And you, you have loved again?"

"Yes, Mademoiselle Marinja, as deeply, passionately— with my whole soul have I loved again, though I once deemed it impossible. But then the temptation has proved so great. The being is so beautiful, so good, so pure."

He raised his eyes, hers met them, and quickly ell, for she knew what he meant; she made as though she would rise.

"Mademoiselle Genevieve," he exclaimed imploringly, laying his hand on her arm, "have I been presumptuous, reckless, in revealing the passion with which you have inspired me? If so, as you are good and gentle, pardon, and—and—do not deprive me of all hope."

"Mr. Burgoyne," she replied in a low tone, "what I said about second love is more than a theory with me. I believe it, and I have often vowed never to give myself to—to one who has loved before, who grants me but a repeated affection."

"But may there not be one exception to a rule?" he pleaded eagerly. "May not in one case that second love prove as strong, as powerful, as the first?"

"Not more powerful?" questioned the actress, quickly.

"No," he rejoined with almost sadness : "else would that first have been love at all ?"

"You are right," she remarked. There was a quiver of her lip, she appeared suppressing some violent emotion.

Maurice proceeded with renewed fervour.

"Grant me one favour at least. Hear my history, the history of my first love."

"What good could that serve, Mr. Burgoyne ?" she remarked, adding with a faint smile, "without you would make me jealous of its object."

"Would that I could, Genevieve, for then I should know your love was mine. Love without jealousy does not exist," he answered. "But such was not my motive. I would win your pity if I could not aught else. I would wish you to see that I was not to blame, when—ah ! with what difficulty and pain—I tore that first love from my heart."

The actress, for a space, was silent, as if undergoing some mental struggle. Her eyes were lowered, her foot tapped the grass.

His gaze bent on her breathlessly, Maurice waited. Finally she spoke.

"Mr. Burgoyne," she said, "I do not wish to disguise that I feel a strong interest in you. Besides, it is the right of every one to be heard. If you wish it, I will listen to this history of your first affection, only not here. Let us go into the house."

She spoke calmly, but Maurice, as he followed her into the drawing-room, drew hope from the concession.

If she loved him, was it likely she would refuse because of that prior bestowal of his heart? No, or she would not be woman.

Seated in a low chair, her hand shading her face, Genevieve Marinja listened to Maurice's recital.

He told it with a simplicity more impressive than eloquence, while frequently he had to pause to suppress his emotion when he spoke of those days when he believed in his wife.

He told the history of their two lives. He made no mention of Captain Melton. He hardly referred to Stephanie.

"And you sacrificed wealth, position, for her sake?" questioned the actress.

"As I would as readily the faded flower I had worn in my button-hole," he rejoined. "I held it no sacrifice loving her, believing her love mine."

"And her infidelity made you suffer?"

"Suffer!" he ejaculated. "I would not wish my enemy such agony. Oh, my God!"

He seemed, in recalling that first passion, to forget that he was seeking hers before him. With a groan he buried his face in his hands, while his frame shook with agitation. Tears of pity rose to the actress's eyes. Brushing them away she said:

"And you were convinced of her guilt?"

"The proofs were only too strong. I would have given my life could one doubt have been left me."

"Well, you are free from her, and easily. Surely that is matter for rejoicing. Your marriage was no marriage, you say:"

"As Heaven hears me, I was unaware of it," cried Maurice. "Had I known it I should have been a villain every honourable man would have been just to spurn. I believed her truly and firmly my wife until—until that morning when I left her; then—then I was told that there had been an informality in the ceremony, the clergyman was not qualified for performing it, and I was free."

"And naturally you were glad," remarked the actress.

"No. I ought to have been, perhaps. I was not. I felt humiliated that I had done Catherine unintentionally a cruel wrong. But she was glad; she accepted her freedom at once, and went from me."

Rising, resting one hand on a chair, Maurice Burgoyne continued, in tones of intense feeling :

"Genevieve, you now know all—why I have ceased to love. Whether I am capable and justified in loving again, I believe, as I stand here, no woman could have made me do so save you. I await your decision—not blaming you though it be adverse to me. Only—only if I am given no hope, I must leave you now and for ever. It is more than I have strength for to see you and not love. Say, Genevieve, do you bid me go, or remain ? "

Again there was silence. Then Genevieve Marinja arose, and with half-averted face, held out her hand, answering softly :

"Maurice Burgoyne, remain. I have not strength to bid you go."

"Genevieve, my darling ! "

Delirious with his great joy, he sprang forward, and caught her in his arms.

She made slight resistance, then laid upon his bosom.

"Maurice," she whispered, "you will always love me ? "

Love you ! Beyond all women, my dearest," he answered, pressing his lips to her forehead.

Then she darted quickly from him, for a hand was upon the door-handle.

A second later the servant announced Captain Melton.

The two stood apart as the officer entered, but, his quick glance passing rapidly from one to the other, divined much, if not all, the truth. He saw it was time to play one, if not both his cards.

That evening it was generally remarked that the brilliant actress excelled herself. Maurice, seated in his stall, thought so, yet rejoiced that Genevieve had promised him, that, of her own inclination, she should renounce the stage directly she was his wife.

Also she had advised that for the present their love should not be made known. Maurice was not adverse to this, for had he not to see Stephanie ?

His conscience stung him when he thought of her; but in Genevieve he forgot everything.

At the stage door they exchanged one glance, one pressure of the hand, as she moved to her brougham. He whispered:

"To-morrow, dearest."

And the carriage rolled off.

Suddenly, as the brougham whirled round a corner into the bright lights of the Haymarket, she was aroused by a cry, a shout, and the abrupt reining in of the horse.

The actress, glancing through the window, saw a crowd collecting about it, and her coachman descending.

"What is the matter," she asked, lowering the glass.

"Only you've run over a woman, that's all," called a gaily-attired creature, the paint on whose cheek made more ghastly the hollow wasted face beneath. "'Tisn't much, is it, to you?"

Genevieve had already opened the door, and descending made her way to the injured woman. As she did so a murmur ran through the crowd.

"It is Marinja, the actress!"

"Tell me, is she hurt?" exclaimed Genevieve, then with a cry she fell on her knees by the unfortunate woman, who lay motionless on the pavement to which two policeman had borne her.

What a lovely face it was. The features so refined, with the golden hair escaped from the bonnet falling about her. Yet how wan and wasted the countenance.

Had Maurice accompanied the actress home, as he would have liked, he would have recognised that face among a thousand.

"No, ma'am," replied one of the policemen, stooping down. "I 'spect she's only fainted, stunned a bit. The horse caught her on the shoulder, and she reeled and fell."

"She ain't hurt," said the other. "I don't fancy we'd need even take her to a chemist's."

"Put her in the brougham," said Genevieve, rising.

"In the brome!" ejaculated the men in surprise."

"Put her into the brougham," repeated the actress authoritatively. "It was my horse that threw her down. It is I who must be assured she is not hurt, and compensate her for her injuries. Please do as I desire."

So, to the coachman's disgust, the woman, her dress stained with road dust and mud, was put in the actress's elegant brougham.

Genevieve followed, saying to the coachman ;

"Home, and drive as fast as you can."

The carriage rolled off, followed by a ringing cheer of applause.

Marinja hardly heard it. She was looking into the white sweet face, upon which the brougham lamps fell with a ghastly gleam.

CHAPTER XXXVI.

MAURICE ASKS FOR RELEASE.

AURICE BURGOYNE'S position was certainly in one light not to be envied, while it in no way made it better that his own conscience blamed him.

Engaged to Stephanie, he had no right to have proposed to Genevieve Marinja.

In justice to both he should have been free from the one before he confessed his love for the other.

But, seated under those trees, surrounded by the intoxicating influence of the actress's presence, that confession had escaped from his eyes and lips before he had been aware.

At the moment he had forgotten everything but his past love for Catherine, his present, equally as fervent, for Marinja.

He had never thought of Stephanie ; now he was compelled to.

That very morning following his acceptance by the actress, a letter had come from Mereton Travers, full of fond sentences and tender solicitude.

It was no longer as a cousin she addressed him, but as his future wife.

Maurice, leaving his breakfast untasted, paced the room, trying to grasp his position.

Love Stephanie as a wife he would never have been able. Now, he felt the tie even would madden him past bearing.

From the very altar he should be unfaithful to her. When his lips touched hers he should think of the actress's. As she lay on his breast, he should remember Marinja as she had lain there when he had learned he was loved.

Maurice's meditations came to one conclusion. He must own the truth to Stephanie without delay.

How?

He had turned coward, and recoiled from the thought of going to Mereton Travers.

Should he write?

That would be the best, only he could scarcely put all that he desired to say on paper ; for, whether right or wrong, he had an idea that Stephanie, for his happiness, might be won to release him.

It would be a difficult letter to write, requiring much time and consideration.

Looking at the clock, he saw he could not then give the latter, for he had promised to be at the actress's by eleven, an hour before she received other guests.

With that relief we all feel when compelled to defer a disagreeable subject, Maurice made a hasty breakfast, dressed preparatory to the arrival of his horse, and rode to Kensington.

He had now entered the house which had once been his so often, that he had ceased in doing so to recall Catherine.

But, on this particular morning—why, he knew not— her memory came back to him forcibly.

Her wan sad face, when he had followed her from the *bal de l'opera*, seemed more than once to rise before him in melancholy accusation. Never had her influence so hung about every spot and corner of the place. But suddenly the door opened, the actress appeared, and he forgot all else.

Marinja was attired in a soft, flowing white cashmere morning dress, that displayed the undulating grace of her figure to perfection. Her dark hair, usually confined in classic braids about her shapely head, was left to fall over her dress, held off the round cheek and warm white throat by a knot of scarlet ribbons, that grew vivid in contrast with her raven tresses. She advanced, her long lashes half shyly lowered, but her beautiful features animated by fondest love.

She put her hands into his, and let him draw her un-resisting to his breast.

"Ah, my Maurice!" she whispered fondly, as she stole her arms about his neck, "you love me. You are sure, sure?"

"Genevieve, do you believe otherwise to be possible?" he said, smiling. "If so, look, darling into my eyes, and read the truth there! Nay," he laughed, gently forcing back her face; "you shall look up, and, if you yet doubt, I will kiss the bitterness from these red lips until they are all honey and belief."

Suiting the action to the word, he rained kisses on the rose-leaf mouth, while she, laughing, strove, but power-lessly, to push away his head.

But, as lip met lip, the very soul of each seemed to enter into the other; a pure delirious joy came upon them.

The actress's hands dropped slowly down, and she murmured:

"Oh, Maurice, Maurice, my happiness feels more than I can bear."

"My darling!" he whispered, bending over her, the quick beating of her heart imparting itself to his. "Genevieve, do you doubt longer?"

"Doubt!" and her beautiful eyes looked into his. "Oh, were I too, it would kill me!"

Then abruptly again putting her arms about him, and raising herself, her face nearer him she proceeded:

"Do you know, Maurice, when Launce Linden intro-duced you I loved you. There was something in your eyes, your appearance, that went directly to my heart and held it captive. I said to myself, 'That is the only man I can ever love—the only man I will ever marry.' Then —then—a great trouble came upon me, for I thought how my affection might meet no response, that—that you might hate me."

"Hate you! Ah, darling, had you but known," he answered, "how similar my case was to yours! When I entered the theatre I believed happiness was dead for ever to me. But you appeared, and suddenly, as if some electric fire had darted from you to me, my melancholy life seemed full of light."

"And you were very miserable before we met?"

"Existence was a burthen, the prospect of death a blessing, a relief."

"And this cruel shadow upon you was of her doing. Ah, my poor Maurice," and fondly she rested her head on his shoulder, "it is sad, but too often true, that those we trust most—confide in most—are in secret our enemies. But there," she added with a gay laugh, "let us select some pleasanter theme. By the way, I have something to tell you—an adventure that occurred to me last night while I was returning from the theatre."

"Indeed, darling?"

"Yes; come, sit down here, and I will tell you. I acted the part of good Samaritan—I, Marinja the actress," she laughed. "I am sure you of all men will not blame me."

"I blame you? As if I could!" he smiled.

They were seated side by side, his arm around her, she leaning on his shoulder, her face raised to his, as she proceeded, smiling:

"Oh, it is short enough, and will not tire you. As my brougham turned into the Haymarket last night, the horse ran against and knocked down a woman. Hearing this I sprang out to see whether she was hurt."

"My brave, kind-hearted Genevieve!"

"Two policemen had borne her to the pavement, poor thing! Her dress was soiled, her bonnet had fallen off, and oh, Maurice, she was so pretty! What her life was, meeting her at that place, at that hour, and alone, one can conceive; yet so pure an innocence rested on the worn refined features! Looking upon them, who would not have been moved to pity? Stay, there were two who were not," smiled Marinja; "the policemen."

"Be just, sweet. Recollect the nightly scenes of vice which they must witness,"

"True. Well, they said the woman had only fainted; that she was not even hurt sufficiently for a chemist's help, when, to their amazement, I ordered them to put her in the brougham."

"The brougham, Genevieve?"

"Yes; I said that as I had been the cause of her mishap, it was my duty to see to her, and make compensation; so, making them obey me, I brought her home here."

"A noble act, but hardly a wise one, Genevieve. The miserable class to which this woman, no doubt, belongs——"

"Any other of her sisters might have belonged to, with the same education, under the same circumstances, with the same temptations," put in the actress quickly. "Ah, Maurice, are we all so free of sin that we may constitute ourselves our brother's judges?"

"Genevieve, you are an angel!" he said fervently.

A shiver, or rather shudder, ran through the actress, who, however, proceeded quickly:

"Well, I brought the poor thing home and sent for a doctor. Ah, Maurice, I was right, and those policemen were wrong. No bones were broken truly, but the shock had been terrible to a delicate frame, weakened by want and suffering. Maurice, the woman is very ill. The doctor says it will be weeks before she recovers—if she ever does. Learning her story, he proposed getting her into a hospital, but I would not hear of it. She shall be nursed here, and last night I sat up with her."

"Heaven bless you, Genevieve; a good Samaritan truly," remarked Maurice, kissing her. "And is your charge better?"

"Better, yes. But she lies yet in a kind of half sleep, half stupor, like one who requires rest as her chief medicine. Save an occasional disconnected sentence, murmured unconsciously, she has not spoken. The doctor says, however, she no doubt will be fully conscious to-day. When she is strong you shall see her. Once," smiling, "you admired blondes. Her face is so fair and looks so delicate, lying on her pillow amid the rich masses of her golden hair. Hark! there is the bell; I have denied myself to all visitors."

Glancing towards the window, she awaited the opening of the green outer door.

"Ah, it is the doctor; then, Maurice dear, I must leave you."

"May I not wait?" he pleaded.

"No, I cannot permit it," she smiled. "Already for this interview I have stolen moments from graver business. I have a part to study and a rehearsal at three. You shall hear how my patient progresses when we meet to-night. *Au revoir.*"

She held out her hand, but Maurice exacted a warmer parting, which, indeed, he so lingered over that Marinja had to break away and run from the room, in time to meet the doctor.

Together they ascended to the sick woman's room, together they stood by her bedside regarding her.

It was indeed a beautiful face; that was still perceptible despite its worn haggardness, while it possessed one peculiarity making it yet more striking.

The brows and lashes, instead of being of the hue of the hair, were dark.

Maurice, left alone, was about to take his departure, when something on the carpet attracted his attention.

It was the knot of scarlet ribbons which, loosened, had fallen from Genevieve Marinja's hair.

He started, recalling that other knot of ribbons of a similar colour which had worked such misery in his life.

He stooped to raise it, but stopped.

"No," he reflected, "even the fact that Genevieve has worn it, that it is permeated with the perfume of her hair, cannot make a knot of ribbons of that colour other than revolting to me."

So he left it where it lay and quitted the house, unaware that within it the curtain was slowly rising upon a small drama that was seriously, deeply to affect him, as also the actress.

Away from Marinja his thoughts again reverted to Stephanie, and taking his courage in both hands, he rode at once home, and sat down to write the letter.

He wrote it in a penitent and earnest strain. He owned how deeply he had been to blame towards her in offering her a heart wherein he believed, as he had told her, all love was dead. When he had spoken to her, moved out of gratitude for her kindness to him, he had imagined he had given her all the love of which he was capable.

But it was not so. One had crossed his path, that despite him, had awakened in his breast a passion as if he had never previously loved.

He felt, as he knew she would feel, that he had no right to keep this intelligence a moment from her. They were engaged truly. But he was assured her noble generous spirit, her pride, would revolt from wedding one who not only had no heart to give, but had to confess it was given to another.

"As I would have died before—I would have died now sooner than this should have been, dear Stephanie—for dear you ever must be to me," he concluded. "But, save we be criminal, death is not in our own hands. Sister, best of—nay, better than one—how can I make compensation for the wrong I have done you. I see but one way.

"By your union with me you would have become the mistress of Mereton Travers. It is not entailed. If my father does not do it of his own will, I will beseech him to give all—everything to you."

The above he put in kindest, most delicate sentences, enveloped, directed, and posted it.

That night the mail-bags carried down this terrible blow to Stephanie Royle at Mereton Travers.

Yet it did not fall so heavily as might have been imagined. A hint had already reached her in a private letter, received that morning from Captain Everitt Melton, who, "in strict confidence," and "as a friend," informed her of his fear that Maurice was getting dangerously entangled with a certain actress.

CHAPTER XXXVII.

STEPHANIE REFUSES.

HE disappointment Stephanie Royle had felt in the fashion Maurice had asked her to be his wife had gradually worn off, absorbed by the thought that, as Lady Burgoyne, all the power and influence as Mereton Travers' mistress would be hers.

Not once did a feeling of remorse arise in her heart respecting Catherine, whose place she intended to usurp— whose ruin she had compassed.

What was Catherine to her?

A creature that had dared to across her (Stephanie's) path, and whom she had properly removed.

She had no pity for her. Pity never goes with jealousy and hate.

Occupied by her own happiness, there was room for nothing else. The days passed swiftly in a glow of delight. Stephanie, moving from apartment to apartment, mentally arranged the alterations she would make here and there, which suite of rooms should be hers, and what colour would be most suitable for her complexion.

Once Sir Jaffery had shown her the family jewels, and once, finding the key in the bureau when her guardian was absent, she had hurriedly clasped the gems about her neck, the bracelets on her arms, the band of flashing diamonds in her hair. Then swiftly gliding to a cheval glass, she had gazed at her loveliness with a heart full of vanity and pride.

Why did not Maurice return and give her the right to wear these?

But Maurice gave no hint of doing so. His letters, full of kindness but not love, never spoke of his return.

Still, he had not been absent many weeks yet, and come he would in time.

Such was Stephanie's frame of mind when she was aroused to possible danger by the receipt of Captain Melton's letter.

"Maurice was getting entangled with an actress." Stephanie regarded the letter with darkening, shadowy eyes, and pale set lips.

Those words had a more dreadful significance to her than they might have had to others. Maurice would not get into any entanglement with any woman without he loved her ; and if he loved her, then——

Stephanie did not finish the sentence, but, casting the letter on the ground, stamped upon it in her anger.

"It is false—all false ! This Captain Melton, jealous at losing Catherine, would mar, or seek to mar, my happiness. But I will write to Maurice ; I will let him know what is said, and ask him—*command* him—to deny it."

But that letter was as difficult for her to write as had been Maurice Burgoyne's.

Besides, the more she thought over the communication the more she disbelieved. She felt there was a barrier between Maurice and second love.

Not—with much bitterness—his engagement to her, but his memory of his affection for Catherine.

Yes ; Stephanie could not deny it to herself. Maurice's passion was crushed, but not dead.

Still she would not credit that another on earth could rouse it into life if she failed.

Thus hesitating, Stephanie deferred her letter, and the next morning Maurice's arrived.

Stephanie was alone when she read it, for Sir Jaffery never descended to breakfast. She sat a while stunned, staring at the letter, hardly believing it. Then abruptly starting up, she staggered to the couch, wildly flung herself among the cushions, and burst into passionate, tearless sobs, half the outcome of indignant fury, half in real heart-breaking misery.

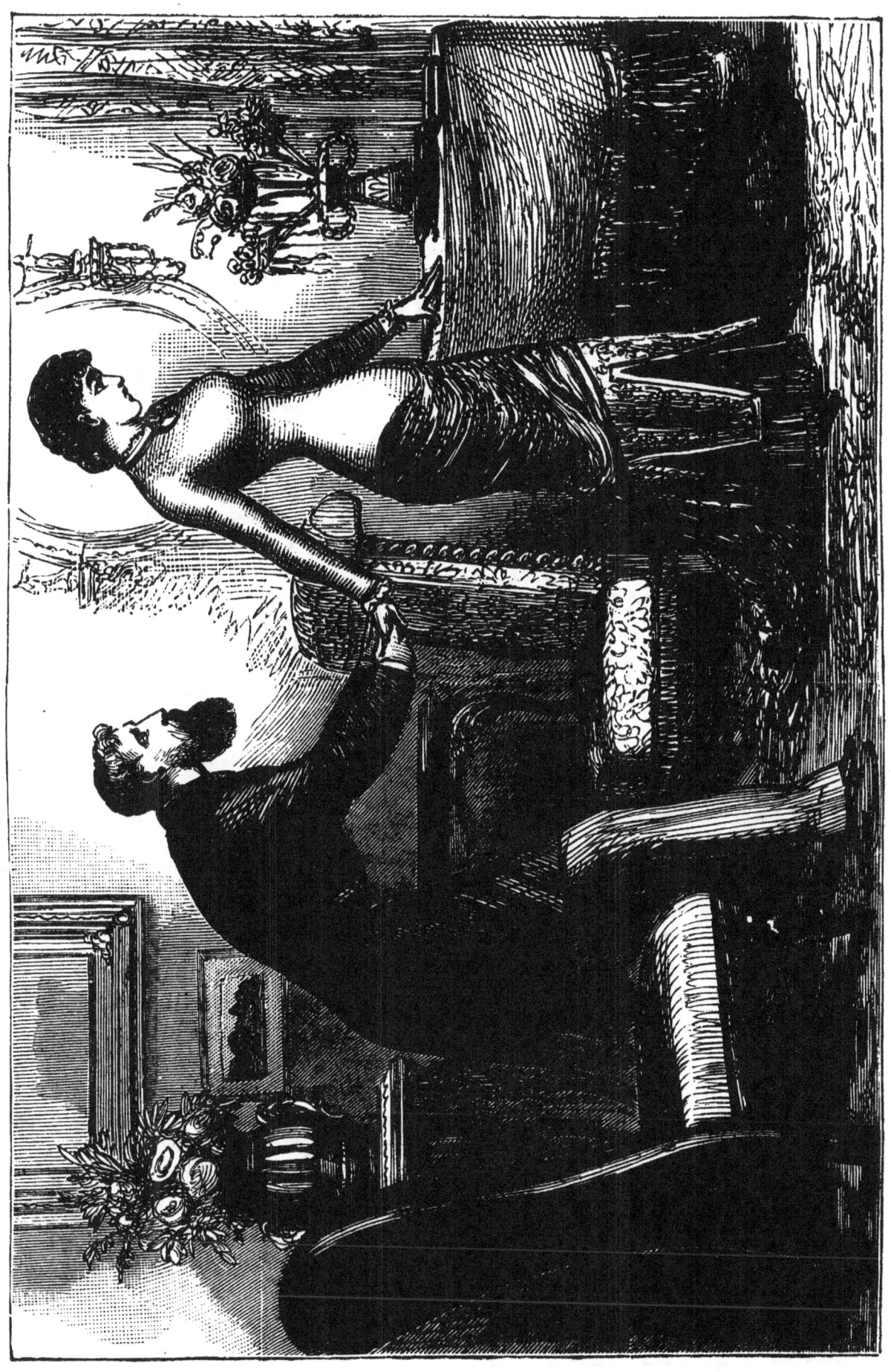

"MAURICE BURGOYNE, REMAIN. I HAVE NOT STRENGTH TO BID YOU GO."

No. 12.

Her small graceful figure writhed on the couch. Her slender fingers twined about her small head, and clutched and tore at the silken coverings; even her tiny pearl-like teeth fixed upon them in her furious agony.

Then she sprang up, sitting panting, flushed, her eyes dilated, her breath coming quick and short.

Maurice loved this actress then; it was true.

Maurice wished to be free. He wished—nay, he expected her to free him.

Could she? No.

What, give him up after all she had done?

Never. Impossible.

She would write and tell him so. What cared she for pride, honour? Maurice was hers—hers. Yes, she would write.

What would be the good?

He had done what he considered honourable, and if she refused to release him, why, he would release himself, even if honour kept him from wedding the actress.

Maurice would never marry one woman, loving another.

An actress! Why, Sir Jaffery would again disinherit him. He must know of this at once.

"Tush!" she interrupted herself bitterly. "What would Maurice care for disinheritance? Has he not proved it once? Does he not in this very letter quietly wish me to have Mereton Travers? If I inform guardie it may only hasten matters. No, no, no; that will not do," she added, pacing the room. "But what am I to do; what am I to do?"

An hour of fearful suffering, then Stephanie had determined upon what course she would pursue.

The only way, she was aware, to touch or move Maurice would be to appeal to his pity, his sympathy, to show to him her suffering. Honour, the sense of the wrong he was doing her, might cause him to sacrifice himself for her.

Ah, she would do anything, humble herself very low to hold him hers.

And if he still urged his release, still sought to win this woman, then, then she had another plan.

Her countenance was pale and composed as she arrived at that conclusion, but there was a very dangerous glitter in her eyes.

To carry out her plan she must see Maurice, and that necessitated a journey to London.

She must find an excuse for desiring to go.

That was easy.

Taking an old letter from her desk, she proceeded to Sir Jaffery's room.

"Guardie dear," she said, "I have just received a letter from my old schoolfellow, Juliet Brighouse. She wants me to come up to town for two or three days. Do you think you could spare me!"

"Spare you, my dear?" smiled the baronet. "Do you think I would keep you here a prisoner? I am only pleased you will have a change. Besides," patting her cheek, "you will be able to see Maurice, who will bring the roses back. They seem rather faded this morning. When do you start?"

"She asks me to-day, guardie, because they have a garden-party to-morrow.

"A garden-party? Go, by all means. Your maid will, of course, accompany you. And don't fear for my comfort. Sidford will see to that."

She stooped and kissed him without a blush at the deception she was practising, and hurried from the room.

Two hours after, she was speeding express to London to see Maurice.

That evening, Maurice Burgoyne was just preparing to start for the theatre, when his servant announced a lady desired to see him.

"A lady to see me!" he exclaimed, surprised, "and at this hour!"

Then the idea occurred to him it might be Brandon, Marinja's lady's-maid, and he added :

"Show her up."

Soon after, the visitor entered.

She was veiled, but as the door closed, and she threw the lace back, Maurice Burgoyne, uttering a low cry of surprise, almost consternation, ejaculated :

"Great Heaven ! Stephanie here."

Yes, it was indeed Stephanie, pale and agitated, that stood before him.

"Can you wonder ? " she said, in sad, sweetest tones. "Oh, Maurice, Maurice, my heart is breaking ! "

She extended her arms towards him, then dropping on her knees covered her face and sobbed aloud.

Pale with emotion, he stood awhile, then, advancing, tried to raise her.

"Stephanie, dear Stephanie," he murmured. "God pardon me the pain I have caused you ! You—you have had my letter ? "

"It is here—here—burning into my breast," she said, placing her hand on her bosom. "Maurice, tell me it is not true. If you would not see me perish here at your feet, say it is not ! "

She had resisted his attempt to raise her, and now she clung to his knees, her face lifted imploringly to his.

"Stephanie, dear Stephanie," he exclaimed, "I entreat you, rise, and we will speak of it. Such a position is derogatory to you—to me. Your self-respect——"

"Self-respect," she broke in passionately. "What is self-respect to me ? What is anything but my great love ! Maurice, that is my life, the very air I breathe. I move, speak, wake, sleep but with one feeling, one thought—you. You offer me wealth as a substitute. Oh, cruel, cruel insult ! Did you regard wealth when you loved ; and is my passion less than yours ? "

"Stephanie, rise—hear me," he exclaimed much agitated.

"Yes, if you will take me in your arms, Maurice, dear Maurice, as on that day you asked me to be your wife. If not I will remain here at your feet, humbly to sue for mercy at your hands, if you refuse me justice, your wife, your wife! Maurice, could you have felt the thrill that passed through me when you whispered that word, the wild, giddy beating of my pulses when your lips touched mine! No happiness promised in heaven could surpass it, my whole being was faint with joy, and now, now you bid me release you. Maurice, what have I done that you should treat me thus? Am I to perish by the will of him whom alone I have loved? No, no; my own, my darling, I cannot—cannot."

And dropping prone on the ground before him, she wept in her passionate sorrow.

Shocked, holding himself most bitterly to blame, yet with a sense of repugnance that the woman at his feet could show so little pride and self-respect, he again strove to raise her.

Stephanie no longer resisted, only clasping her arms about him, clinging to him, she cried:

"Oh, Maurice, love me, for I cannot give you up. It is impossible. Do not say another has won you from me! Her passion cannot equal mine;" and she sobbed against his bosom.

"Stephanie, listen to me," he pleaded. "Heaven alone is aware how bitter is my remorse at what has occurred. But you—who better must be aware how out of our control is our love. When grateful to you for all your goodness to me in my trouble, feeling the future a barren waste, I asked you to take pity on me and be mine—as my father's heir marriage was a compulsion— I told you the love a man should give her he makes his wife, the love of which you were so worthy, was not mine to bestow. I believed then it had gone out of my power to feel it for anyone."

"And," broke in the girl, "I said, with the affection you could give, Maurice, I could be content. For in my heart I knew that I would rather be your slave, Maurice, than another's queen. That a touch from your hand, oh, my love! would be better, sweeter, than another's caress. Maurice, there are men who are cruel to their wives, who scorn, mock, aye, even strike them. Were you of their nature, I would rather suffer your scorn, your mockery, your blows, than another's tenderness. Maurice, I cannot, so loving, release you. If you release yourself, then as an act of justice, of mercy, do so by depriving me of a life that will henceforth be misery. Strike! I will not flinch."

While speaking she had torn the soft muslins from about her throat, exposing its whiteness to him.

"Maurice," she said, "would she whom you prefer to me love you like this?"

He had averted his eyes from her. His feelings were difficult to explain, they were so blended—pity, remorse, self-blame, indecision; but over all, or meandering through all, a sensation of disgust of the woman who could so humiliate herself for his love.

To her interrogation almost involuntarily he answered:

"No, Stephanie. Her pride, her self-respect, would prevent her. She would be ashamed."

The words made the girl forget the part she was playing. Her anger took fire at the praise given to her rival.

"Shame! *She* ashamed! A woman, an actress, who nightly receives the caresses of men before the gaze of hundreds, until her cheek would not blush but for the rouge she wears! A woman at the public's beck and call, whom a smile can make or frown mar!" she cried with flashing eyes. "A woman who drapes her figure for the public's eyes, which criticise each action, limb, and feature as they would a hired model! A woman paid to be a people's amusement! And you will not speak of shame and her together! You stare,

Maurice Burgoyne.   Compare such a creature to me !"

The sentences had issued from the pretty blossom-lips in such a torrent of stormy anger that for a space Maurice was fairly overwhelmed.   But recovering, he felt he preferred his cousin's present temper to her previous one.

"Stephanie," he said quietly, "your reading of an actress of the class to which the one to whom you refer belongs—though how you knew she was an actress I am unaware—is utterly false, while all London would declare how you malign this one—a woman as pure, as noble, and full of sweet womanly self-respect and dignity as she is beautiful.   I have done you wrong it is true. I have made a base return for the loving devotion you have ever shown me.   Whatever you have to say, what blame to express, I will hear, as it is my right to ; but I will listen to no word against this lady who is worthy of the sincerest honour and respect."

Stephanie bit her lips with suppressed fury.

She perceived, too, she had lost ground, and tried at once to recover it.

"Forgive me, Maurice," she said humbly.   "Surely if I am angry I have cause.   Did I not love you, I should not feel thus.   Think of that love, and what you ask me to do."

"I asked, Stephanie !   I told you as in honour I was bound, that did I wed you I should be doing you a crueller wrong—one a woman would more deeply resent than a broken engagement, for my love would be another's.   I told you this.   You know it, and hold me to my word.   So be it.   I will keep to it, if it be your desire, only our union cannot be yet.   I for one could not support it ; neither I think could you."

"Maurice, I have been wrong ; I have said things I ought not to, but, tell me, are you so sure of this actress's love ?   If she refused you, would your engagement to me be no longer distasteful ?"

"Stephanie, I will not hide it from you, I was sure of her love before I wrote to you."

"Ah, yes; but woman's love at times changes. Should hers?"

"Then, Stephanie, I should hold her lowest among women."

"And our engagement?"

"Should rest in your hands to decide."

"Then we will arrive at no decision to-night. Maurice, I give you time. I desire it myself to accustom myself to—to the idea of our parting." Her voice faltered. "This change in you is not known to Sir Jaffery as yet; keep it from him. Will you agree to this?"

"Yes, Stephanie, and hold you generous," he rejoined.

She had not divined that he had proposed to Marinja. He could not tell her at that moment.

"If the expression of my regret——"

It was her turn to check him now. She did so with sad dignity.

"No. Expressions of regret would be useless, Maurice. We will wait the future. Should it be as you hope, I—I will try to forgive you. Now, farewell."

She did not quite know her cousin. Her present manner touched him more than the other. He felt the great cause she had to blame him.

"Stephanie," he cried, "what can I say?—what do——"

"Give up this woman."

He drew back silent.

"Then let matters stay as they are at present," she added. "My cab is waiting, will you see me to it?"

Opening the door herself, she passed out on to the landing as if—as was true—to prevent further conversation.

"Is my father also in town, Stephanie?" he asked, following her.

"No, I am staying with my schoolfellow, Juliet Brighouse."

He helped her into the cab, and gave the address to the cabman. But hardly had the vehicle got out of sight, than Stephanie, checking the man, gave him another direction. It was that of Captain Everitt Melton.

"I will not release him," thought Stephanie as she dropped back into her seat, "but if this actress be indeed honourable she shall refuse him. Ah, even if I had to work heaven and earth to prove Catherine properly married, I would to separate these two. I hate her more than Catherine?"

CHAPTER XXXVIII.

CAPTAIN MELTON PLAYS HIS SECOND CARD.

APTAIN EVERITT MELTON had played his first card—the informing Stephanie Royle—with what result has been seen; that done, he determined to lose no time in playing the second—the informing Genevieve Marinja.

It never occurred to him that Maurice would of his own accord tell the actress of his past life. But he told himself, that did that fail to move her when he related it, he would then declare that the flaw in the marriage was of such a nature that it left the tie in a state of exceeding uncertainty, and allowed not only room for contesting, but for many a lawyer's quibble.

An affair that might be moved from court to court for half a man's life-time, and go against him at last.

With this intent he had called at Marinja's residence an hour after Maurice had left but had found the actress not visible, nor would she be that day.

Annoyed, yet seeing no great need for haste, he took his departure, resolving to speak to the actress that night at the theatre.

He got no opportunity, however, until the play was over, for Genevieve came only in time to dress to go on, and when she came off, too many surrounded her.

When about to quit the theatre, the actress herself touched upon the subject.

" I regret, Captain Melton, that I was compelled to refuse myself to you this afternoon," she remarked with a sweet, sunny smile; " you must confess I do not often do so, but business before pleasure is, or should be, the motto of our profession. Rehearsals may not be put off, and managers, while very exacting, have not the most amiable tempers. I dare say, however, you were not very heart-broken."

"If I were to say how much I felt it, I might offend," he remarked in a low, earnest tone.

"Is a woman ever offended by a knowledge of her power?" smiled the actress.

"You judge your sex harshly; I would not, could not," he rejoined.

"No; I am aware that with the modern gentleman is blended in your nature the past knight of chivalry. A woman, in your eyes, is sacred; something above earth."

"In one case—yes," he rejoined.

"Thank you. I must reward so flattering a speech; I shall be disengaged and alone to-morrow between twelve and one. Will you come?"

"Will I? Gladly!"

"Now, please, see me to my brougham. By the way, you heard of my adventure?"

"Good deeds have angel wings, and fly over the world," he answered gallantly; "only evil ones, like curses, come home to roost."

"Really," she laughed musically, "do you believe that? I do. I believe in retribution. But I must show you my *protegee*, she is so pretty!"

They had reached the brougham, and he handed her in. As he did so, she asked:

"Have you seen Mr. Burgoyne? I do not think he is here to-night."

"No," he rejoined; "did you wish to see him?"

"I?" and the dark brows were raised in wonder. "I never wish to see those who do not wish to see me. Good-night; recollect to-morrow."

As the carriage rolled away she shot at him another sunny smile, and, waving her jewelled white hand in adieu, was gone.

A smile rose to Captain Melton's lips.

"She is a bit of a coquette, after all. Tush, all women are! She is hurt by that fellow's absence, so is kind to me. I need have no fear. My intelligence will have due effect."

Reaching home he discovered the cause of Maurice's absence in a hurriedly-pencilled note left by Stephanie Royle.

It asked for an interview, at a part of the park she mentioned, at eleven the next morning.

Captain Melton, smiling at the success of his first card, wrote and posted an answer in the affirmative.

Genevieve Marinja always received her favoured guests in her boudoir, where formality and the exigencies of society were not so strictly maintained.

Happy and honoured were the actress's admirers who were permitted to cross the threshold.

Captain Melton had done so frequently, yet he was none the less pleased to find that this morning the interview was to take place there.

Every favour shown him removed, in his mind, Maurice Burgoyne further off.

The actress was not present when he entered, but she speedily came in, more ravishingly beautiful, he thought, than ever in a fresh morning toilet, and a sunny, welcoming smile on her lips.

"Pardon me not being here to receive you," she said, as gracefully she sank back in her chair, "but you know lately I have added to my vocations that of nurse, and patients are exacting."

"And how is your most fortunate patient?" asked the captain.

"Fortunate!"

And Marinja raised her brows.

"Fortunate in having such a nurse," he retorted bowing.

"And unfortunate, Captain Melton," remarked the actress gravely, "in needing one. I forgot—you asked me how she was. Better, but very weak, yet able to tell me something of her history, which, as might have been imagined, is a sad one."

"The brightest spot in it, probably, will be similar to that of some others—her acquaintance with you," murmured Captain Melton.

The actress laughed lightly.

"I see," she said, "it is utterly impossible to be serious with you. You would discover a compliment in the gravest topic."

"Indeed, I am serious enough on one subject," he replied earnestly; "but it is upon that very one you will not be serious. Still you say you have not forsworn marriage."

"Far from it. I hold marriage the true and proper woman's right. Her only difficulty is—is——"

"Is what, may I ask?"

"Making her selection. It is a sad lottery, confess."

"At times; but there are some cases wherein a woman's influence, her beauty, makes her husband a slave."

"Oh, I should not like a slave for a husband," remarked the actress, with a musical laugh and lift of the shoulders. "Nay, I should not prove exacting. All that I would ask is that he should love me alone, and never really have loved any one else."

"Then," laughed the captain, a trifle nervously, yet seizing the opportunity with avidity, "Maurice Burgoyne is out of the running."

"Why?" asked the actress, so curtly, almost sharply, that the officer guessed how well his suspicions had been founded.

"Simply because he has loved, desperately, sincerely, too deeply ever to give such an affection a second time."

"Can this be really true," asked the actress in a lower tone."

"It certainly is. Why should I try to deceive you on such a matter," he smiled lightly, "which half-a-dozen inquiries about town can prove me right or wrong in ? Besides, I knew his wife."

"His wife," repeated the actress. "You knew her ?"

"Well ; frequently have I conversed with her in this very room."

The actress was silent awhile, her eyes on the single ring she wore. Abruptly looking up, she said :

"His wife—you knew her—then she is dead ? "

Captain Melton shrugged his shoulders before replying with a meaning smile :

"No, she is not dead—that is, as far as I know, or, I believe, Burgoyne himself knows."

"How do you mean ? " asked the actress. You excite my curiosity, and that is not the way to win a lady's favour, unless——"

"Unless ? "

"You gratify it by an explanation," she laughed ; but the visitor saw her colour had somewhat faded, while there was a slight spasmodic movement about the muscles of the delicate lips.

"I shall be most happy," answered the captain, sincerely speaking the truth. "I break no confidence. Only dared I, I would ask you not to mention to Burgoyne who was your informant."

"Nay, Mr. Burgoyne shall never hear it from me. So he is really a married man," proceeded Marinja, leaning forward, apparently deeply interested, "and his wife lives ? "

Captain Melton proceeded with his recital, delighted at having thus won Marinja's attention.

He told all, from the marriage to the separation.

"And this woman was guilty," said the actress.

"Who could doubt ? " was the response. "At least, her husband could not."

"Husband ! He is not her husband. I understood you," exclaimed Marinja, "the marriage was no marriage. You say Mr. Burgoyne devotedly loved her. No man deceives a woman, Captain Melton, whom he devotedly loves."

"You are correct. Mr. Maurice Burgoyne, who was ready to sacrifice wealth, position, for her, fully believed the marriage a correct one. It was only Miss Royle who discovered the flaw in it."

"Miss Royle?" interrogated the actress.

"A ward of his father's and his cousin, I believe."

"What interest had she to seek to discover this?"

"Two powerful incentives," laughed the officer. "Love and revenge."

"Love!"

"Yes, she had long loved Maurice Burgoyne, and, with an energy of character peculiar to her, resolved to be his wife. Baulked by his secret marriage—this is in confidence," he added.

Marinja inclined her head.

"She resolved upon revenge. Many a jealous disappointed woman does that, but never finds the means of gratifying it. It was otherwise in this case. By chance she learned who had performed the ceremony. The doubts that possessed her whether he was competent to do so she followed up. She discovered the flaw, and when Maurice Burgoyne quitted his wife, told him he was free."

"And he is so, is he not?"

Again the captain raised his shoulders.

"If I were a woman, and asked to wed him, I should not risk it," he answered. "The flaw is of that nature which might be a fortune for the lawyers, did either Maurice Burgoyne or his discarded wife care to go to law. And I see no reason why the woman should not, if she heard he would raise another to her place."

"She would be a brave woman indeed."

"Yet such a one exists. Miss Stephanie Royle has succeeded," laughed the officer; "she is engaged to Burgoyne, and shortly they will be married."

"Engaged! Mr. Maurice Burgoyne engaged to Miss Royle!" cried the actress.

"No less. I had it from her own lips—as I am sure, if you would desire, you might ; for she is in town. The truth is, that a report of his marked attentions to a certain lady——"

"Myself," put in the actress.

"Has reached her and excited her jealousy."

"No wonder," said Marinja. "But do you think Miss Royle would really come here ? I do not doubt your word, Captain Melton, yet there are reasons why there must be no mistake. I must be quite sure."

"Name the hour best to receive her, and I will be myself answerable for her coming."

"To-morrow, at this hour."

"She shall be here."

"And if all you have stated be true——"

"Well, dearest Marinja ?" he asked eagerly.

"I shall know how to unmask a villain and reward a friend. Now, farewell."

With a light rejoicing heart the captain took his leave.

"I have put a spoke into Master Maurice's wheel, I reckon," he reflected. "She likes him, that is certain. I am half disposed to think he has proposed and she has accepted him ; else why talk of unmasking a villain ? I must see Stephanie Royle at once. She will be delighted at the turn matters have taken."

Directly the officer had left, Marinja, advanced to the silken *portière*, raised it.

"Come," she said in low tones.

And Maurice Burgoyne entered the room.

"You have heard all ? He is a villain, not only to me, but worse to a woman—Stephanie."

"Everything. But why, Marinja, did you wish me to overhear this conversation ?"

"I had reasons. One to prove to you your friend ——"

"My friend ! He has been none since I and Catherine parted," answered the young man bitterly.

"And this flaw in your marriage, Maurice. He makes it doubtful ? "

"I cannot think that. Yet be assured, Genevieve, I will be certain before I ask you to stand with me at the altar."

"You must, Maurice, before I could be your wife. I am glad," she smiled, "that you prepared me for the intelligence of your engagement to Miss Royle. She is a woman undeserving pity or regard. She, Maurice, shall not stand between you and me. Did you hear, but of course you did, what Captain Melton said about her love—and revenge. How she had sought out this flaw in hatred to the woman who had won your love. Maurice, I could almost believe her capable of working your supposed wife's ruin. Certainly she selected a fitting confidant," laughing shortly. "She seems to have told the captain everything."

"Indeed, yes ; that struck me, Genevieve. She did not know him until they met beneath this roof. I cannot make it out."

"No," laughed the actress, "it is a mystery ; and, dearest, I'll tell you something else. Captain Melton loved your wife."

"Impossible ! "

"It is true. I read it in his voice, his eyes, as he spoke of your love for her. He was relating his own. Then the bitterness with which he related her disappearance. But there, enough of this. I told you to-day you should see my patient, and here she comes."

The *portiere* was raised, and the woman, wan and pale, stood before them.

Maurice Burgoyne uttered a great cry, as he reeled back.

"Catherine ! " he exclaimed. "My wife ! "

Then he would have sprung forward, as tottering back into the ante-room she fell on a couch, her face buried in her hands, but Genevieve Marinja barred the way.

"Not a step nearer, Maurice Burgoyne," she said. "I am answerable for her life. If it indeed be Catherine—she from whom you are separated—you are nothing now to each other."

She looked fixedly at him. He stepped back confused, pale, his eyes drooped, then .he lifted his hands to his face and shivering convulsively, murmured in inaudible accents :

"Oh, Catherine ! Poor—poor girl ! "

CHAPTER XXXIX.

THE ACTRESS'S PATIENT.

ESPITE the actress's protest Maurice might yet have gone to thát wan sad face ; but on looking up, he found the *portiere* dropped, and Genevieve Marinja standing yet before him.

There was an earnest, strange scrutiny in the eyes with which the actress regarded him.

"Maurice," she said softly, "you loved this woman very dearly ?"

"Forgive me, Genevieve," he remarked, his voice tremulous while he averted his gaze. "I mean no disrespect to you, but I knew not how much I loved her until this moment. Oh, Heaven, how altered, how terribly altered ! "

Again his emotion was too great for him to conceal.

"Yes," said Marinja seriously, "she has been on the verge of the grave. It will only be with care if she even now escape it."

"Oh, and to think, only to think of what she was, and now this shadow of herself," groaned Maurice, and, dropping on a couch, his features hidden, his frame quivered with emotion.

Genevieve Marinja regarded him quietly, then, gently resting her hand on his shoulder, murmured :

"Poor Maurice, you love her still ! "

"Not love ; it—it cannot be that after—after the past," he rejoined. "Genevieve, you will not be offended—ah no, I see tears of sympathy in your eyes. You feel for that unhappy girl, and for me. God bless you ! "

He took her hand and kissed it reverently.

"Feel, Maurice! I should not be a woman did I not," she said softly. "She has suffered much."

"Suffered! Heaven, how greatly to have changed like this!" ejaculated Maurice. "Believe me, Genevieve, this never should have been could I have helped her. It shall no longer continue; though she may be nothing to me, I nothing to her, yet no comfort shall she need that she shall not have."

"Nay, not yet," said Marinja. "At present she is my patient, my guest, and as such shall want for nothing."

"You are an angel, Genevieve. But to think of what she has become, that you should have found her; that beneath your roof I should discover Catherine after my long fruitless search."

"You did seek for her?"

"On learning she had left almost penniless, I used every means I could to discover her retreat, but without success. What she had done with herself, where gone, I could not divine. But, Genevieve," he added, turning excitedly to her, "you will let me see her?"

"Of course. She is not my prisoner—she is her own mistress," the actress replied. "But why should you? What good could it do?"

"Nothing truly," he answered sadly, "yet I should like to. I must make some provision for her. If I have yet any influence, I will entreat her out of the love I believe she once bore towards me to abandon the wretched life she has been leading. Oh," he added, with almost a cry, so great was his suffering, "not two years ago I would have given Heaven itself the lie rather than have believed Catherine could have stooped to such infamy."

Again emotion checked his utterance. He moved to the window to conceal it.

The actress had watched him keenly. Not an expression of voice or feature had escaped her.

More than once, pale with agitation, her lips had moved as if about to speak, but she had hesitated. Now advancing nearer, she said in a low, broken voice :

"Maurice, I feel it, I am sure of it, for I can read it in every accent, in every expression, you will never love another as you did—as you do Catherine."

"No, no," he broke in entreatingly. "Bear with me. You are to generous, Genevieve—too just not to understand, not to excuse what I feel. Oh, my dearest, in this emotion read the power I have to love. If that first affection has been abused, should it debar me from loving—ah, from more highly venerating that purity in woman, the lacking of which in one case has been my bitterest misery?"

He took her hand and looked down fondly upon her. Wistfully she gazed into his eyes.

"Yes, Maurice," she remarked, "you are capable of giving a second affection, but in every respect it would be secondary. My first opinion is confirmed. Man or woman can really love but once."

"Genevieve!" he implored, "do not judge me at such a moment as this. Think of how taken by surprise I have been."

"No," she smiled softly, "I will not judge yet; and when I do, it shall be leniently. But of this I am certain, deny though you may, could Catherine be proved to have been faithful and pure, you would still hold her dearer than all woman."

"And should it not be so?" he answered frankly. "Were she pure, though it is impossible, what right should I have to take my affection from her?"

"That is true; I should be the last to blame you. Now, please, I must bid you go. The morning has been full of excitement, and I must rest for to-night. Return to-morrow at about the same hour that you came to-day, and you shall see Catherine. More than this, should anything occur to cause you to regret our engagement, you are free."

"Regret, Genevieve! That is impossiple."

"I believe nothing is that is in this world," she smiled. "Now go."

"One instant. At the hour you appoint Stephanie will be here?"

"The woman who has angled for you?"

"But whom," with darkening features, "I swear now never shall be mine. Genevieve, why have you wished to see her? All she can tell you have heard from my lips."

"True. Still I have my reason—a woman's one, perhaps," laughed the actress, "and one Stephanie Royle can appreciate—to gratify the pleasure of triumphing over her rival. But go, go; indeed I must be alone."

To confess it, Maurice Burgoyne was by no means loth to accept his dismissal.

The sight of Catherine, her face haggard with suffering, had affected him deeply. As he had said, until that moment he had never known how much he had loved her.

He longed for solitude, when he could more composedly recall the events of that morning.

The dastardly conduct of Everitt Melton, the knowledge that Stephanie's behaviour had not been actuated by a generous disposition, but hatred of Catherine; that under the smiling mask of a friend she had, with diabolical patience, waited the opportunity to strike; and, Heaven help him, the opportunity had come!

Hence Maurice took leave of the actress, raising her hand to her lips. He felt she would have hardly granted him a warmer mode of parting.

When alone, Genevieve Marinja, throwing herself on a couch, broke into a passion of wild weeping.

"I was right," she ejaculated, "man can really love but once, and Maurice Burgoyne is faithful to his first passion. He could never give his heart to another."

Meanwhile Captain Melton had driven to the park. Here, consulting his watch, he found he had nearly three quarters of an hour to wait before the time he had proposed for Stephanie to meet him should arrive.

He was hardly sorry, he had so much to think about, and the subjects of thought were by no means unpleasant ones.

He was as assured as man could be that his only rival in the actress's affection was Maurice, and, to use his own phraseology in expressing his own belief, he had put a spoke into his wheel.

He could not be deceived in the emotion, the agitation Marinja had displayed while listening to his recital. She was certainly indignant with Maurice.

Perhaps he had already proposed, never of course mentioning that little affair about Catherine. Indeed, he would have been a fool if he had.

In that case the actress must be grateful to him, her informant, for saving her from so compromising a position.

Hence, to the captain, the future was clear.

"And well it is," he reflected, "for I am confoundedly hard up. My hand"—extending it in its exquisitely-fitting glove—"has hardly been as steady with the cards nor the dice as I could wish lately. Besides, a man cannot live with his wits always on the stretch. He needs repose. And with Marinja I can get it. She acts too well to care to give up the stage. And, let me see, how much can she be making a week at the present moment?"

He was in the midst of his calculations when he perceived Stephanie Royle advance.

Rising, he went to meet her.

"Well," she asked before any other salutation, "how have you succeeded?"

"Admirably. I have told her everything in my way, and from her manner, do you know, Miss Royle, I believe Burgoyne has already proposed to her."

"Infamous!" ejaculated Stephanie through her teeth, and her small hands clenching.

"So Marinja thinks, from her expression. I pity Maurice in his next interview with her," laughed the captain, "for I deemed it best to acquaint her with his engagement to you, who had been his best friend."

"Was that best?"

"Had you seen her face when she heard, you could not have doubted. It had more weight, I fancy, than any other part of my communication. As proof, she refused to believe me. Indeed, that she would believe it from no one save from you or Burgoyne himself."

For an instant Stephanie paused, then almost immediately replied :

"Did she say that ?"

"No less. Which confirmed me in my suspicion that he had already proposed, and she had accepted. Therefore, as we may be sure Burgoyne will not confess the engagement, I ventured to promise, Miss Royle, that she should hear my assertion confirmed from your mouth."

"Mine ! How !"

"I said you would visit her."

"I visit an actress !" cried Stephanie, in a tone of contempt.

"And your successful rival, if you refuse," quietly interrupted the captain.

"Why ?"

"Because, finding I fail in my promise, Marinja will attribute it to my want of power to perform. In plain words, she will believe I have tried to deceive her."

"No ; I will write, I cannot see her," said Stephanie.

"Useless trouble. Never having seen your handwriting, how is she to know the letter really comes from you ? She will refer to Burgoyne, who will deny everything, for I must confess he is over head and ears in love with her."

Stephanie bit her lip with fury, and her eyes sparkled with rage.

"Listen to me, Miss Royle," proceeded the captain more gravely. "You sought me to ask my assistance in this matter. Now, be wise, and take my advice. Put pride aside, and go. If not, shall I tell you what will be the result."

"Yes."

"MAURICE," SHE CRIED, WRITHING WHERE SHE KNELT, "PEACE, OH, PEACE!"

"Maurice Burgoyne and Genevieve Marinja—as Maurice Burgoyne and Catherine Crawford—will be married before you are aware of it, and this time he'll take care there is no flaw in the marriage chain."

"Did he," ejaculated Stephanie, with deep concentrated passion, "so deceive me, I would move Heaven and earth to prove his marriage true, that this actress might be disappointed and cast off, and her cup of happiness dashed to the ground."

"A long and difficult task. An easier means to prevent the union is in your hands."

"Well, I accept it. I will see this woman. When ?"

Captain Melton told her, and shortly after they separated.

Stephanie did not alter her mind.

The next day at the appointed time she entered a cab and drove to the residence of Marinja. Mentally calculating the result of the coming interview, her bosom panting with the suppressed excitement of love and hate, and the hope of triumph.

She arrived at her destination at the same moment as the captain, and they entered the garden together.

"What is it ?" asked the officer, perceiving her start.

"Nothing," she laughed lightly. "But recent anxiety has made me foolishly nervous. You are aware this place has many old associations to me, and as I lifted my eyes, for the moment I could have declared I saw Catherine at yonder window."

"Not much likelihood of that."

"No."

"I wonder what has become of her ? "

"I do not wonder, for I do not care. What is she to me ?" said Stephanie in a low tone, contemptuously raising her shoulders.

Then she became silent, the maid having arrived to conduct them to the actress's presence.

To the captain's surprise, Marinja intended to receive her guests in her private sanctum—the boudoir.

CHAPTER XL.

REVENGED.

THE actress rose when the two were ushered into her presence, and greeted Stephanie as haughtily and as distantly as she greeted her.

"Miss Royle," she remarked coldly, yet half cynically. "I have to thank you for the honour you do me by this visit; it is more than I had a right to expect."

"I came, madam," rejoined Stephanie, whose countenance for a moment had borne a strange expression, "because Captain Melton informed me you would receive confirmation of a statement that he had made from no other lips than mine."

"Confirmation concerning——" put in the actress.

"Mr. Maurice Burgoyne."

"And yourself, Miss Royle?"

"And myself."

"You are engaged to Mr. Burgoyne?"

"I have said that Captain Melton's statement is true, madam."

And a look of triumph and scorn flashed from her eyes.

"Again I thank you, Miss Royle, for your condescension"; and Genevieve Marinja gracefully inclined her head. "Captain Melton, of course I have your pardon; I did not, you know, really mistrust you, only on the point I desired no mistake, and people are deceived sometimes."

"Being now assured, madam," rejoined Stephanie, whose eyes had never quitted the actress's face, and speaking before the officer could reply, "our interview need not be prolonged. I came here in justice to you—in justice to myself, for it appears Mr. Burgoyne would have deceived us both. My mission being ended, I will say good-morning."

She rose as she spoke, but Genevieve Marinja remaining seated, said :

"Excuse me, Miss Royle, I must entreat you yet further to add to the honour you have done me, by favouring me with a few moments longer of your time. You have told me you are engaged to Mr. Maurice Burgoyne. I, too, am engaged to him, You love him. I love him."

"Madam !" ejaculated Stephanie, flushing haughtily.

"Pardon me, Miss Royle, surely I state facts ?"

"Such facts, madam, that if you hold them, there was no necessity for my condescending to come here."

"I repeat, Miss Royle, I am grateful for your condescension," with covert sarcasm, "but the facts are as I have stated. The question remains thus : which shall give place to the other—Genevieve Marinja or Miss Stephanie Royle ?"

Stephanie, enraged, for a moment remained speechless.

"Captain Melton !" at last she gasped. "See to what I am exposed by following your advice? I owe this to you."

"Miss Royle, I think you owe me more than this," he rejoined pointedly. Then addressing the actress : "I am surprised at this reception, I confess, Mademoiselle Marinja. You did not lead me to expect it."

"Pray, Captain Melton, do not be alarmed ; neither let Miss Royle be so," was the cool response. "There is no need. I put the question. I answer it. Genevieve Marinja, of her own accord, surrenders Mr. Maurice Burgoyne. Only, for her condescension, she requests Miss Royle to hear her."

"You surrender Mr. Burgoyne ?" involuntarily exclaimed Stephanie.

"The actress waives her claim to the prior one. But, before closing the interview, I have something to say, which I desire—nay, which I demand—both you, Captain Melton and Miss Royle, to hear.   Refuse, and neither are of any account to me."

Everitt Melton made a quick meaning sign, and, biting her lip, Stephanie resumed her seat.

What had this woman to say ?

What that she could care to hear ?

Still, had she not promised to release Maurice ?

Conquering her indignant fury, in silence she prepared to listen.

Captain Melton, wondering, surprised himself at what the actress could have to say, waited too.

Genevieve Marinja paused a while. Her delicate fingers played with the lace of her handkerchief. Her eyes were fixed thoughtfully on them.   Then, lifting her face, she spoke.

"This strange and peculiar history of Mr. Burgoyne's curiously reminds me of another (save, in mine, the wife was innocent), that I cannot refrain from giving you a recapitulation of it."

The actress addressed the captain, but her eyes never lost sight of Stephanie.

The latter made a haughty movement of impatience.

"Really, madam, my time is too valuable to waste in listening to the useless recital of stories."

"I did not say it was useless," remarked the actress, sweetly.   "Pardon me, but as it is I who am to make the sacrifice by which you are to profit, Miss Royle, pray be lenient.   Indeed, these stories are so similar that I can almost promise mine shall win your interest.   Then," proceeded Marinja, after a brief pause for further protest, "the gentleman in my recital, who, to speak theatrically, fills the *role* of Mr. Burgoyne, like him loved and wedded a lady far beneath him in position.   Despite this, their affection was so mutual, true, and pure, that their days passed in a round of happiness, and might have continued to do so but for three disturbing elements —love, jealousy, revenge ; a terrible trio."

Captain Melton looked sharply at Stephanie, whose brows were contracted angrily, then at the actress.

Was she going to reveal all and betray his confidence?

Marinja, apparently not perceiving his glance, went on quietly:

"The trio were embodied in two people, a gentleman, the husband's friend, and a lady. The latter had ever entertained a secret passion for the husband, the former formed one for the wife. So these two people put their heads together to ruin the innocent, unsuspicious wife, in the eyes of the equally innocent and unsuspicious husband."

"Madam," ejaculated Stephanie, quivering with fury, as she half rose from her seat, while the captain, changing colour, exclaimed hoarsely:

"Genevieve Marinja, what is your meaning?"

"Meaning!" surprised. "I have none. What could I? Believe me, 'I tell the tale as 'twas told to me.' I thought, however, it would win your interest, but now you will perceive the stories differ.

"The question was how to ruin the wife? There was but one way: to sully her purity and make her husband believe her infidelity made her unworthy of his love. Chance aided them by throwing in their way a woman of bad character bearing a wondrous likeness to the young wife."

"How have you learned this, Marinja?" cried Captain Melton, springing up and grasping the back of his chair, while Stephanie sat as pale as death."

"I'll hear no more," she gasped.

"Yes, Miss Royle, you must and shall!" said the actress, a stern authority creeping into her silvery tones. "You must hear me to the end. Recollect, you—both of you—are in my hands. To continue: these two honourable and loving people paid this woman to aid them— caused her to drive about the city attired like the wife, and in the society of strange gentlemen, so that all Paris believed it was the fair Englishwoman. Then they wrote anonymous letters to the husband, charging his wife with infidelity ; and, in crafty terms, under the semblance of friendship, gave him advice, and bid him hold his secret, while he watched his guilty partner."

"How do you know this ? " again burst in Captain Melton, while a startled look, almost of fear, shone in his eyes.

"Ah, you doubt my authority, perhaps," said the actress. "You yourself shall judge in a moment whether it be worthy of credence. But may I not finish my story ?—how these people dropped gloves on the balcony, thrust them—for the husband to discover—in the wife's work-basket. How they lured the wife to a strange house, and detained her there, drugged, while the plotters showed her who so resembled her to the unhappy deceived husband mingling in the wild orgies of the *bal de l'opéra* ? No," rising with dignity and scorn, "there is no need, the recital is already familiar. Miss Stephanie Royle, you sought revenge, and lo ! I am the avenger ; for I am about to clear an innocent woman's name from the slander you cast upon it."

They stood before her pale, agitated, wondering, furious, but helpless. What had they to say ? How had Marinja learned all this ? Learned it, of course, to use against them.

With finger upraised, the beautiful actress stood, her face glowing with scorn and indignation, like an avenging angel, pointing to the two who had worked so much wrong and anguish.

Overwhelmed with the strange turn that later events had taken, Captain Melton and Stephanie looked from one to the other in bewildered dismay and alarm.

Did she not love Maurice Burgoyne ?

Then the thought flashed through Stephanie's mind, and brought a triumphant smile to her lip : "Catherine innocent, Maurice would never wed another."

"You ask me for my authority," resumed the actress. "It is here. Come."

She had extended her hand towards the *portiére*, and she whom she summoned came into the room.

"Catherine," burst simultaneously from Stephanie's and the captain's lips.

"No, my patient Josephine Herault. What wonder the husband was deceived, when you, her paymasters, are so."

"But, thanks to you, Genevieve, he is deceived no longer."

The words were Maurice Burgoyne's. His face dark and terrible, he had followed the Frenchwoman into the room.

Captain Melton stepped quickly back.

Stephanie, with a frightened scream, dropped on her knees, her face buried on her chair.

She cowered before him.

She collapsed, and shrunk beneath his words.

"Thanks to you, Genevieve," he proceeded, "the mask is rent from the woman, the Lamia he believed in, whom he once loved ; and he sees her in all her revolting hideousness—a creature to be loathed, avoided, scorned ; a creature sent upon the earth a curse, a blessing to none."

A groan of piercing anguish escaped Stephanie's lips.

"Maurice," she cried, writhing where she knelt, "peace, oh, peace ! It was for love of you, the love that consumes me now, and will not let me hate you for these words you utter."

"Hate !" he retorted ; "your hate. Oh, give me that, but spare me from your love. Never again will I look upon you, never again shall my hand touch yours, Stephanie Royle. I abhor you, for you are too low, too vile, for hate."

She uttered a quick sharp cry, and slipped insensible to the ground.

Not heeding her, Maurice Burgoyne advanced upon Captain Melton.

"As for you, scoundrel, villain," he cried, "between us there must be something more than words."

"Stay," and Marinja threw herself between them. "Maurice, you gave your word this man should go untouched beneath my roof. He is not worthy even of your revenge. A better than you contemplate shall be yours. By to-morrow all London, every club, shall ring with this man's name, with the knowledge of the means he employed to ruin a woman's fair fame, to obtain that woman's love. Every finger shall be pointed at the dastardly coward, the back of every honest man turned as he passes."

The white foam of rage rested on the officer's lips.

"How know you this?" he ejaculated. "How dare you assert that I have loved Catherine Burgoyne?"

"Because Catherine Burgoyne herself was my informant."

"Catherine!" cried Maurice.

"Catherine!" repeated Captain Melton; adding with a short, taunting laugh: "Then she lives; then——"

"Hush!" and the actress gravely raised her hand. "She is dead."

"Dead!" cried Maurice. "Dead! Oh, cruel, Heaven, am I then debarred seeking at her feet pardon for the bitter and cruel wrong I did her?"

"Marinja will console you," laughed the officer scoffingly as he moved towards the door. "She might have been your mistress; Catherine dead, you can marry her."

Maurice Burgoyne darted forward, but the actress checked him.

"Maurice, remember. Come, come, those laugh longest who laugh last. Besides, I have one service rendered me by this honourable gentlemen for which I ought to show some gratitude. He generously put me on my guard against wedding one who the law might prove was wedded already. I could have appreciated the act better had not he—who really possessed a wife—entreated the hand to be given to him which I refused you."

"I married! It is false!" cried Captain Melton fiercely.

"Your memory is short lived. Let me introduce you—or restore you to—your wife. This curtain," she laughed, "is like a conjuror's box; whatever I desire comes at my call."

Approaching the *portiere* she returned holding by the hand her pale, sad-faced lady's-maid, the woman whom Captain Melton had last looked upon, as he believed dead—drowned, on the bank of the Thames.

"The wife you wedded—deserted—left to starve," said the actress.

"No, madam," said Harriet Melton, "not starve. He gave me a wretched pittance, which I was too proud to accept."

But Captain Melton had not waited to hear. He had dashed open the door, and with a bitter curse had gone.

Maurice Burgoyne now moved forward to Stephanie and raised her.

That Everitt Melton was married was a surprise, but at the moment he had other matters to think of.

Consciousness seemed fluttering back to the wretched Stephanie.

The actress perceiving it, said:

"Maurice, bear her to the drawing-room. There Brandon shall attend to her. It will be kinder to let her recover with neither of us by. Then come back to me."

He obeyed her, then quickly returned, for he had a question he was all eagerness to put:

Where had Catherine died?

"Oh, Genevieve," he exclaimed with emotion, "praise Heaven we are at last alone! Tell me of Catherine. Poor suffering girl! Never, never can I forgive myself."

"Not," and smiling fondly up into his face, she placed her arms about his neck, "if Catherine pardon you, seeing how little to blame you were?"

"Catherine! You stated but now, Genevieve, she was dead," he exclaimed.

"As she is to those to whom I stated it, as she is to the world, but not to you, Maurice."

"Then she lives?"

"She lives. I can tell you her history as well as she could. Listen! When left penniless, her one purpose in life was to discover the cruel plot that had been laid for her ruin, and to unmask the plotters. For this money was needed. How could she make it? Her mind turned to a profession that had become almost a craving to her— the stage. Fortune favoured her. She got an engagement with a manager going to America. On the voyage she studied the chief parts of the pieces to be played, though she was intended for little more than chambermaids. Again luck attended her. The second actress eloped with a rich Mexican to Arkansas. It was not discovered until the curtain was about to rise. The manager was distracted, for no one had understudied the part, as he knew. But one had—Catherine. He hesitated about entrusting her with it; but the people were clamorous. The curtain must be rung up. 'Go, girl, and may you get well through it.' She did more than get through it. It was a brilliant success. The people applauded to the echo, and, as the manager said, her fortune was made from that moment."

"Well?" he asked hoarsely, a wild, strange feeling in his brain.

"Well," she laughed, "is there need for more, Maurice? Women are keener than men. When Stephanie Royle first heard me speak she started."

"Great Heaven, what do you mean?"

"Mean!" she laughed. "Ah, Maurice, I was right. You loved Catherine, and you can never love another. Have these stained olive cheeks, these dyed raven tresses, disguised me so well even from your eyes?"

"Catherine!" he cried in ecstasy, as he pressed her with rapture to his breast. "My wife!"

In the bliss of reunion all the bitter past was forgotten. Like a dream it seemed, so full of anguish and sorrow. And now came the awakening—joy unspeakable.

"Oh, Maurice, Maurice," murmured the happy wife, as she clung to the beloved form of her husband.

"My darling! Oh, I must have been blind indeed to doubt you," murmured Maurice.

"Ah, say no more," whispered Catherine. "It was not your fault."

And then these two fond ones, so cruelly wronged and so basely deceived, mutually enjoyed the happiness that falls to the lot of those loving and divided that meet again at last.

Presently they were interrupted by a tap at the door.

"Madame," said Harriet Melton, entering hurriedly, "the lady has gone. I could not stay her."

"It is better so," muttered Maurice between his teeth, as, with eyes full of passionate affection, he looked upon his maligned, brave, suffering wife.

"Yes, it were better so.

CHAPTER XLI.

CONCLUSION.

HE mad passion which possessed Captain Everitt Melton when he quitted the actress's house would be difficult to describe. Not only had he been again defeated, but irretrievably disgraced.

Genevieve Marinja would, he knew, be as good as her word. Before morning the base act he had committed would be the talk of every club.

At none—not even in London itself for some time—would he be able to show his face. And all this had been brought about for, and by, a woman.

He cursed them all, from Eve downward. Then he remembered his wife, the wife he had believed drowned.

He had a curse on his lip for her, but paused. No, she of all he had known had done him the least harm.

He had deserted her, and she had let him go. For the first time, he wondered if she had really ever loved him.

"Possibly not," he muttered cynically. "Most weddings are the result of two things; a man's fascination of a pretty face, and a girl's longing to get married."

His horse had been waiting for him outside the actress's, and while these ideas swept through his brain, he was riding at a reckless pace towards Hammersmith.

He hardly knew where or how long he rode.

His chief thought was to get from London, to somewhere where there would be no chance of disturbance, and he could think his future out.

When it was night, he could get back to his apartments, pack, and start for Dover by the earliest train in the morning.

Yes, after all, there was little need for reflection. He must go abroad.

Twilight had settled down when, exhausted, he pulled rein at an inn near Ealing.

Clouds had been piling up in the west, and had now swept over the sky, shutting out the few faintly twinkling stars.

As he alighted, heavy rain-drops began to fall. He asked for and was conducted to a private room.

Was this the handsome, well-got-up, well preserved Captain Melton, the lover of Genevieve Marinja?

His face was grey and haggard. There were wrinkles about the eyes, and the eyes themselves were dull, lustreless, and vague in expression, save when they flashed up with fury. He ordered brandy, and until near midnight sat with that as his companion.

Then the landlord, wanting to retire himself, for the third time hinted that the gentleman had better change his mind and have a bed.

Captain Melton got up, and with an unsteady step descended to the door where his horse waited.

He reeled as he got in his saddle, but settling himself shook the reins and was lost in the darkness.

"What a dare-devil pace he's going," said the ostler to the landlord, as both listened to the sharp beat of the horse's hoofs coming out of the blackness; I shouldn't wonder if there won't be something wrong afore morning."

The ostler was right.

The next morning some labourers found a man lying at the roadside by a ragged fence, half fence, half hawthorn, and a horse grazing some fifty yards away.

It was evident that the man had been thrown. He was badly hurt, and had undoubtedly been struck on the face by the fence, for it was terribly lacerated.

It was Captain Everitt Melton.

Lifting him up they carried him into Hammersmith—to the police-station. The district doctor pronounced the case serious, and he was conveyed at once with extreme care—for it was seen he was a gentleman—to the hospital.

Fever ensued, and nearly a month elapsed before Everitt Melton was conscious.

And to what a consciousness he awoke.

He was blind !

The crash upon the fence had ruined the sight beyond restoring.

The misery of that knowledge to Everitt Melton must be passed over.

Calm succeeded, for all have to bow to the inevitable, but the officer laid on his bed gaining strength with trembling, contemplating the wretched future to which he was destined.

Helplessly blind.

What use now was his skill at cards or the dice ? Friendless, alone, what prospect was before him but starvation.

He had truly lived in a house of cards, and now they had tumbled in upon him.

"Alone, without one to care for me," he muttered, unconsciously half aloud in his weakness. "A pauper's existence. Heaven, why was not my life taken ? "

A cool hand was placed tenderly upon his, a sweet though faded voice whispered in his ear :

"Not alone, Everitt. There is one who cares for you while you have need of her. I'll never leave you."

"Harriet," he cried—" you ! Oh, God ! "

He paused in amaze at this proof of a woman's love, then taking the thin hand, pressed it fervently to his lips. After, he averted his face to hide the tears of shame and remorse that flowed down his cheeks.

"Thank Heaven," whispered Harriet Melton, as with emotion she bent over him, "his love has come back. He will care for me now."

*   *   *   *   *   *   *

Maurice Burgoyne could not tear himself away from his restored wife, not even when her engagement compelled her to start for the theatre.

Love coined questions that love might answer, while matter of wonder to both was the startling likeness between Catherine and Josephine Herault.

"I can account for it only in one way," replied the wife ; "my father had a twin brother, a rather wild, dissipated man, who went to France, where for some years they heard nothing of him. At last they instituted inquiries, and found that one of his name had died—shot in a duel."

" Then——"

"Then," said Catherine, "Josephine, if his child, would have been my cousin. I shall not inform her of our possible relationship, yet I shall regard it as such, to make the few months she has to live—for she has no more, Maurice—comfortable and free from evil. Now, please let us change the subject."

He did willingly, to one that concerned him deeply— the validity of his marriage with her.

"I shall put the matter in a lawyer's hands to-morrow, before I start for Mereton Travers," he said, "and if there really exists this flaw, why we must be married again."

Catherine paused awhile, then added gravely :

"Maurice, I told those two Catherine was dead. Let it be so, dear, to the world. You have proved you can love me as I am, then let the past be buried. Believe me, it will be better."

After a space he agreed with her that it might be as well for the world to imagine he married Genevieve

Marinja rather than to have his history and hers made a nine days' gossip.

"But, dearest," he remarked, "I must tell my father all. He must decide."

"So be it. I leave it to him," said the actress, rising to prepare for the theatre.

The next morning, Maurice saw his lawyer, then called at Kensington, afterwards returning to his apartments preparatory to leaving for Mereton Travers.

He hoped Stephanie had not yet gone back.

How could he meet her?

Shield her he dared not.

Entering his sitting-room he found a telegram awaiting him.

To his amazement he saw it was from his father, the address Charing Cross Hotel.

Then he was in town.

Yes, and something terrible must have caused his coming, for the telegram ran:

"Come to me instantly. Is it possible you have not heard? I need you. Come."

Maurice dashed downstairs, sprang into a hansom, and was speedily at the hotel.

As he entered Sir Jaffery's room, the baronet, pale, agitated, and with signs of unmistakable grief on his features, hastened to meet him.

"Oh, Maurice; oh, my boy; how can I tell you?" he exclaimed.

"Father! Does what you have to say concern Stephanie?"

"Yes. Be prepared for a shock. Nerve yourself, Maurice.

"Father," he answered seriously, "if anything has happened to Stephanie I shall be sorry, but not with that kind of sorrow you imagine."

"Maurice! How you speak. She whom you regarded as your future wife——"

"She will never be that to me, sir."

"No," put in the baronet gravely, "you are right, the poor girl is dead."

"Dead!" cried Maurice, springing back in his surprise and horror.

"Dead.   She returned home to the Brighouses, saying she was not well, and looking very ill.   She stated she would lie down awhile, and prayed not to be disturbed. When the dinner-hour arrived, her friend Juliet went to inquire how she was, and—and," the baronet's voice trembled "found her dead on her bed."

"Great Heaven!" gasped Maurice; of what, sir, did she die?"

"It is believed she died by her own will, for her hand grasped an empty phial bearing the label 'poison,' and the address of the chemist.   The Brighouses wired for me, and I came this morning.   Maurice," and his features flushed with angry reproach, "you are, I feel, in some way to blame for this—you two have quarrelled. Poor Stephanie was highly sensitive, you drove her to this."

"As Heaven hears me, sir, I did not," cried the son, "I am innocent of all blame.   She is guilty, father, of the cause as well as the act of taking her life.   Oh, sir, though it is hard to speak ill of the dead, and I must tell my tale with different feelings than I imagined this morning, yet it must be told."

"What do you mean?"

"Listen and you shall know."

And clearly, but as briefly as he could, Maurice related everything.

Sir Jaffery heard with deep sincere emotion.   Gladly would he have doubted, but it was impossible.

"Can it be?   Oh, can it be true?" he could only moan, and all the while he knew that it was.

An inquest of necessity had to be held, but it was conducted in the "most private and respectable manner," and the verdict was "Death from misadventure."

The evidence of the West End chemist, who recollected selling the poison to a lady of Miss Royle's description, went to show the nature of the drug.

In small quantities it produced rest and a general soothing of the nerves. Slightly increased doses produced a species of stupor, which, though not hurtful to the general health—nay, the contrary, acted upon the brain so as to render the owner bowed down by so oppressive a languor as not to be capable of controlling his thoughts nor actions.

As the valet Sidford heard that part of the evidence, and saw the phial, he started violently, and resolved to make a certain communication to Maurice on the first opportunity, respecting certain suspicions he had had during Sir Jaffery's illness.

The chemist concluded his evidence by stating that if inadvertently taken in too large a dose, the result would be an instant but easy death.

There were many witnesses to speak to the excitable temperament Stephanie Royle possessed, and excitement that verged, it almost would seem, on madness.

What more possible than to obtain rest, to soothe this nervous excitement, the girl should have had recourse to this effective but most dangerous drug?

What more probable that, owing to that very excitement, by accident she had taken too large a dose?

So said the twelve jurymen, and the foreman announced the verdict accordingly.

The death and the disclosure of the real nature of Stephanie Royle had a great effect upon Sir Jaffery's health. He seemed suddenly to age and grow helpless, unmindful of worldly concerns. Only he clung to Maurice.

Almost piteously he entreated him not to leave him.

"Bring your wife home if she's a good woman," he said once, "but don't you leave me, though how could she hurt me now?"

That last sentence surprised Maurice, but one day Sir Jaffery, when stronger, explained it.

The chemist's evidence had opened his eyes as well as his valet's. It made suddenly clear many circumstances, and the baronet knew how much he did owe to the girl he had fostered and cherished, and who, for her own ends, had caused him to pass months in a dreary stupor.

The lawyers having proved that, Catherine and Maurice both being consenting parties, the marriage was valid—indeed, that it would need a straining of the law to make it otherwise, Maurice brought Catherine, or Genevieve Marinja as the world knew her, to Mereton Travers, where her sweetness and gentle womanly solicitude speedily won the baronet's trust and affection. For Sir Jaffery's sake, the doctors recommending change, they took a villa in the south of France, the young husband and wife rejoicing, in fact, at the idea of a seclusion, where uninterrupted they might enjoy their rapturous reunion.

It chanced one evening that they had walked to a distant pretty fishing village. As they returned along the moon-lighted bank, they became aware of a man and woman slowly approaching them.

They were attracted by noticing that the man leaned on the woman as if feeble from ill-health.

As they drew nearer, Catherine uttered a low cry of surprise.

It caught the woman's ear. She looked up, made a quick imperative motion for silence, went a little further on, spoke to her companion, then, leaving him standing, came swiftly towards them.

It was Mrs. Melton and her husband.

"I recognised you, madam," she said, as Catherine pressed her hand, "but, if you please, do not let him know you are here. It would pain him."

"You are right, dear Mrs. Melton. And you—are you happy?"

"Very—oh, very, indeed."

"And he ?   Is there no hope of his ever recovering his sight ? "

"I don't know, a doctor here has said there is," and Maurice wondered at the sadness of the tone.

"I hope he is correct," said Catherine kindly.

"I do not," answered Harriet Melton, evidently off her guard, for blushing, confused, she added, "I didn't mean that ; yet it is so sweet to know I am of use to him. Pray excuse me now.   He will be wondering what detains me."

"Can it be possible ? " remarked Maurice, as Harriet hurried to her husband, "that she fears did he get back his sight, he would be villain enough to forget her noble great love, and again neglect her ? "

That, indeed, was what Harriet Melton dreaded, but Heaven rewarded her by letting her, before the year was out, learn, to the contrary, that her devotion had won the grateful affection of him she loved best on earth.

A year or nearly so had passed.   The rose-garden at Mereton Travers is in a rich glow of blossom as Catherine and Maurice pace the path Stephanie used so frequently to traverse.

Their talk is of her, and Catherine says :

"Maurice, I have often wanted to ask you, but did not like, what that unhappy girl said in the letter addressed to you, which they found in her desk."

"Did I never tell you, darling ?   Then it was driven out of my head by the joy of bringing you to Mereton. The letter was destroyed.   But I remember its brief contents.

The words ran thus :

"MAURICE,—There was a flaw in your marriage chain that you can rectify.   There has been a flaw in my life nothing can alter—my love for you.   Farewell.   STEPHANIE."

THE END.